CW00705768

TEXAS HERO

Susan's shoulders shook and great sobs escaped her as she climbed over the seat into the back of the wagon. Ryan pulled her down beside him with his good arm, holding her to him as she cried.

"Susie, what's wrong?"

"I almost got you killed!" she wailed.

"You didn't know we were riding into an Indian raid. And my wound isn't that bad. Really."

Susan sniffed. "That Indian was far enough ahead of you that he might have gotten away if he'd kept going. Why would he stop just to kill me?"

A lump rose in Ryan's throat, and a chill ran down his spine. "I suspect to take you captive."

Her voice was barely a whisper at the implication of Ryan's speculation. "A captive?"

Ryan held her securely to him. "I'm so glad I was riding Pegasus. He's probably the only horse in the whole state of Texas that would have got me to you in time."

Other *Leisure Books* by Connie Harwell:

TEXAS WOMAN

Ryan's Enchantress

Connie Harwell

LEISURE BOOKS NEW YORK CITY

For my daughter, Gina.
God blessed you with intelligence, beauty, a sweet
disposition, and a loving and gentle heart. He
blessed me with you. I love you.
Mom

A LEISURE BOOK®

April 1993

Published by

Dorchester Publishing Co., Inc.
276 Fifth Avenue
New York, NY 10001

If you purchased this book without a cover you should be aware that this book is stolen property. It was reported as "unsold and destroyed" to the publisher and neither the author nor the publisher has received any payment for this "stripped book."

Copyright © 1993 by Connie Harwell

All rights reserved. No part of this book may be reproduced or transmitted in any form or by any electronic or mechanical means, including photocopying, recording or by any information storage and retrieval system, without the written permission of the Publisher, except where permitted by law.

The name "Leisure Books" and the stylized "L" with design are trademarks of Dorchester Publishing Co., Inc.

Printed in the United States of America.

Ryan's Enchantress

Chapter One

1874, Comanche County, Texas

The midday sun beat down unmercifully on the tired man as he rode slowly along the tree line and underbrush bordering the creek. Removing his hat, he wiped the sweat beading his forehead with his sleeve.

Ryan Sommerall could have cut across the Adams place to his house that sat on a rise about a mile from the creek, but decided that a refreshing dip in his swimming hole justified riding the extra distance.

He, along with eight other ranchers and farmers in the area, had just spent the past five days on the trail of a band of marauding Comanches who had stolen horses and cattle from two of the ranches. It had taken them two days with the aid of Ryan's best trailing dog to catch up with the Indians. After a brief battle, the Comanches scattered and fled, leaving five of their dead behind. The ranchers had suffered only a couple of minor wounds and they had recovered most of the horses and cattle. The return trip herding the livestock had been slow going.

Ryan wiped his brow again, muttering out loud, "Damn, not even the end of May yet, and the sun's hot enough to scald a man's brain." Uncorking his canteen, he took a long drink of the tepid water before splashing the rest on his face and neck. "That cool creek water sure is going to feel good, ain't it, Dog." The mixed breed dog, white with black-and-brown blotches, sitting on its bed-like perch atop the pack horse, looked silently at his master.

His swimming hole was a deep stretch of water in the creek bed, formed by two outcroppings of hard limestone. Over the years, especially in times of flooding, the water had cut out the softer, decayed rock and clay between the two formations, creating a pool about a hundred yards long that sloped from either end to a depth of ten or twelve feet in the middle and thirty feet wide.

The creek was fed by several springs along its length that kept it running a few inches deep even between rains, so the hole was always full. It was shaded by tall, ancient pecan trees on both sides of the pool. The beauty of the still, clear pool, hidden from the view of the rest of the world, always gave Ryan such a feeling of peaceful tranquillity that he felt the place must surely be enchanted.

Actually, the pool was on the Adams place, a few hundred yards up the creek from Ryan's property line. But he had always thought of it as his own since he'd been going swimming and fishing there for the past four years. He had come to feel that he had it all to himself as he had never seen anyone else there.

When he arrived, he was surprised to find a beautifully dappled gray mare tethered to a small bush in the shade of the same pecan tree where he always tied his own horse.

Taking a long, careful look around, but seeing no one, he concluded that the rider must be down in the creek bed or somewhere in the underbrush along the creek. He tethered his horse and lifted Dog from the pack horse to the ground. Wondering who the owner of the gray mare could be, he made his way along his well-beaten footpath, knowing that if there was someone nearby in the brush, Dog would scent him.

When he reached the edge of the creek, his wonder turned to total shock. There, just below him, a young woman walked gingerly over the rocks through the ankle-deep water at the end of the pool—as naked as the moment she was born!

Her slow progress across the slippery rocks gave him ample time to take in every detail of the beautiful creature as he stood in a spell-bound trance.

The sun caused her auburn hair to flash patches of dusky red as it brushed against her waist. A gentle breeze lifted it slightly, exposing creamy white shoulders. His eyes caressed her smooth back, stopping at her slender waist, before gliding over gently rounded hips and down long, perfectly shaped legs. His eyes journeyed back to her hips. Even in his most pleasant fantasizing, he had never conjured up such a beautifully formed bottom.

Suddenly he had an overwhelming feeling that he was gazing upon an ethereal scene not meant for human eyes to behold. His sense of decency shook him from his trance.

Damn, he thought, *I've got to get away from here before she sees me standing here, gawking at her.* He took hold of the dog's collar and started to step back into the brush to make his retreat just as she turned to enter the deep water.

She caught his movement in her peripheral vision and turned toward him, giving him a full frontal view of her naked beauty.

Ryan slipped back into his spellbound trance. His eyes feasted on her full high rose-nippled breasts, her smooth flat belly, the patch of curly auburn fluff between her thighs. Burning the image of this lovely nymph into his mind, he realized that his fantasies had fallen far short of matching what he was now seeing.

Ryan stared at her softly sculptured heart-shaped face, her perfect slightly upturned nose and generous, full lips.

Her sky-blue eyes shaded by long sooty lashes widened first in shock and then in fear. She froze for several seconds before letting out a screech, and then began backing away from him.

Her scream jolted Ryan back to life. He whirled away from her, holding his palm upward. "I'm sorry. I didn't mean to frighten you. I'm not going to hurt you," he managed to choke out as he started moving away from her.

But before he reached the place where he would no longer be able to see her, he couldn't resist one last glance over his shoulder.

This time her outcry was more of protest than of fear.

"I'm leaving," he said in as convincing a voice as he could muster.

He quickly went to his horse, swung into the saddle, and spurred the big, black stallion into a gallop. The pack horse and dog ran along beside him. He knew the girl would hear the sound of hoofbeats and be assured that he had left. He didn't want to cause her any more distress than he already had.

Who was she and where had she come from? He'd started his horse ranch here over four years ago, and that along with his duties as a volunteer Texas Ranger, had taken him to every nook and cranny in the county and to most of the surrounding counties. If she lived anywhere in this part of the country, surely he would have met her before now.

And one thing he knew for certain. If he'd ever seen her before, he would have not forgoten! Indeed, the memory of her would forever be etched on his brain.

But could it be, he fantasized, that she had always been in this place? After all, he'd always felt a certain aura of enchantment when he was at the swimming hole. Could she be the enchantress of that beautiful spot? He shook his head as though to dispel the thought. *You've been in the sun too long, Sommerall,* he scolded.

He slowed his horse to a trot after a short distance, not wanting to overheat him. He kept glancing back from time to time to see if the girl would come fro her horse. She hadn't emerged from the bush by the time he'd let himself through the gate in the rail fence that separated the Adams ranch from his.

He rode on a short distance to a clump of scrub oak and dismounted. Sitting in the shade of the trees, he rolled himself a smoke. Before he'd finished his cigarette, the girl came out of the tree line, mounted the gray mare, and rode away at a brisk trot in the direction of the Adams ranch house.

"Well, I'll be damned!" Ryan exclaimed out loud. "So that's who she is." It should have dawned on him before. The Adams ranch wasn't the "Adams" anymore. Lowell Adams' wife had died a few months back. Since he was getting up in years, he'd decided to sell out and move to Austin to be near his son who had a law practice there.

Ryan and his foreman, Kyle, had met Seth Bradford, the new owner of the ranch, about two months before. Ryan'd stopped by a couple of times to visit, while Seth was seeing to the building of his new house. He remembered Seth telling him about selling his holdings down along the Brazos River. And that his wife and daughter were living with his wife's brother in Waco until he could get the house ready for them to move into.

While he'd been out chasing Comanches, they must have moved in. At least he hoped his reckoning was correct, because the thought of not seeing that gorgeous lady again was mighty depressing. But, if he was right, she was going to be living just a couple of miles across the way.

He whistled a peppy little tune the rest of the way home. He forgot he was hot and tired and dirty. In fact, the only thing he was aware of was how alive and energized he felt all of a sudden.

Disjointed thoughts flashed through Susan Bradford's mind as she stood in a state of shock in the water. Somehow she managed to comprehend that the tall, broad-shouldered, lean-waisted, long-muscled, handsome man, wearing a white Stetson and a Texas Ranger's badge pinned to his shirt, who had stood there gawking at her nakedness had to be Ryan Sommerall.

She had met Ryan's foreman, Kyle Weston, shortly after she and her mother arrived from Waco. She'd been admiring the fine horses in the pasture that adjoined her father's and Kyle had ridden over to greet her. He had told her that his boss was a Texas Ranger and was off chasing Indians. Remembering that had eased her fear of him somewhat. But when she had tried to scream at him to get the hell out of there, the words hadn't come out.

Wading out of the water, she went to her clothes and took her pistol out of its holster. She laid it on a rock and quickly dressed. Then, gun in hand, she climbed out of the creek bed. Looking carefully into the nearby underbrush on both sides of the path, she made her way to her horse. She stopped behind a bush at the edge of the tree line. From there, she could see the horse and rider just as he was approaching the fence.

She watched as he let himself through the gate. This confirmed that he was Ryan Sommerall, the owner of the neighboring horse ranch. She remained behind the bush a couple of minutes after he entered the grove of small oak trees before walking quickly to her horse, mounting, and heading home.

She was fuming as she rode but admitted to herself that it was more from embarrassment than anger. The audacity of him, just walking right up to her private swimming hole—uninvited and unannounced—and then standing there ogling her like that!

As her thoughts continued to flash, she remembered noting that the path through the brush to the pool had been well used and therefore easy to follow. Naturally, she'd assumed the people her father had bought the ranch from, or maybe some of their employees, had fished or swum there. But since none of them were around any longer, she had just figured she had the pool all to herself.

She moaned, wondering how she'd ever face him again and knowing she'd have to, sooner or later. Her cheeks burned when she remembered how she hadn't made any effort at all to conceal herself or even to utter a single word of protest other than a couple of silly little screeches. Instead, she'd just stood there like she was posing for him, which was probably exactly what he thought she was doing!

"Honestly, Susan Marie," she castigated herself. "How in the world do you manage to get yourself in such predicaments?" It had seemed like such a simple thing to do. Just to go for a swim on a hot day. Nothing complicated about that. Right? But, nooo, she had wound up acting like Lady Godiva! She sighed a long, resigned sigh, shaking her head slowly from side to side.

*   *   *

Kyle Weston was just stepping out of the tack room when Ryan led his horses through the gate into the corral.

"Well, I see ya made it back all in one piece. And looking mighty pleased with yourself at that. Ya must've caught up with them Indians."

"Yep. We caught them all right. Had to trail them all the way up into Palo Pinto County to do it, though."

"Well, tell me 'bout it," Kyle prompted as Ryan began to unsaddle his horse.

· "Now you know the rest of the boys will want to hear about it, too. It's just about time to eat so let's wait till then."

"Sure, I guess I can hold out till then," Kyle replied. "Besides, I got some news fer ya I think you're gonna like. Our new neighbor's family arrived the same day you took off after them Indians."

"That is good news, but we've been looking for them to show up most any day for some time now." Ryan was trying his darnedest to sound casual. Not an easy thing to do when his mind was sending out shock waves to the rest of his body with its memory of the water nymph.

"It's not them arriving that I figured you'd get excited about. It's their daughter, Susan. Prettiest little gal I ever saw. If I wasn't nearly old enough to be her grandpa, and didn't already have my Hazel, why, I'd sure set my sights on her."

"Hmmm. Well, what does she look like?"

"What do ya mean what does she look like? I just told ya she was real pretty, didn't I? You'll see fer yourself. She's been comin' to the fence to look at the horses every mornin' since they been here. She even came through the gate and rode in amongst them a couple of times after I told her it'd be all right if she wanted to.

"She took a real likin' to that little paint filly. Patted and talked to her awhile both times she's been over in the pasture." Kyle nodded his head. "You'll be seein' her in a day or so."

Ryan chuckled. "I think I might have already gotten a real good glimpse of her." He quickly changed the subject before Kyle could question his remark. "How did the horse races go?"

"Well, that there's another story that's gonna knock your socks off. I didn't go, what with the Indian trouble, and all. And I kept Bill and Nolan here, too, but I let Ray King go ahead and run Wildfire. He won his race, of course, but that ain't the big news." Kyle paused to be sure he had Ryan's full attention. "John Wesley Hardin came ridin' in with three horses like he wasn't worried about a thing in the world."

"John Wesley Hardin! He came to the race meet?"

"Yep. Big as life. Had him some fine horses, too. He raced all three of 'em. And they all three won their races. I'm told he bet heavy on 'em and won over *three thousand dollars cash*, and 'bout fifteen saddle broncs and fifty head of cattle."

"Well, I'll be damned."

"You'll be more than that when I git through telling ya what happened *after* the races." Kyle pulled his tobacco sack and a paper out of his shirt pocket. "Ya know Charlie Webb, the deputy sheriff from over in Brown County?"

Ryan nodded his head. "Yeah, I've met him."

"Well, he was there, and he bragged off and on all day that he was gonna kill Hardin. Didn't have no particular reason fer doin' so. Just said he figured most of the men that Hardin had killed was closer to murder than self-defense, and he was gonna do Texas a favor and kill him. Well, after the races Hardin was a celebratin' at Jack Wright's Saloon when Webb walked in.

"Hardin politely invited him to have a drink and Webb accepted. Hardin turned back to the bar and Webb drew his pistol, intending to shoot Hardin in the back. Somebody yelled a warnin' and Hardin whirled, drawin' his pistol and steppin' back just in time to cause Webb's bullet to mostly miss him. It did slightly graze him. But Hardin didn't miss. Shot Charlie in the face, killin' him on the spot." Kyle paused to catch his breath and light the smoke he'd finished rolling.

"Then what happened?" Ryan prompted.

"Nothing. The same day you took off after them Indians, Sheriff Thomas left fer Hamilton to pick up a prisoner wanted fer horse stealing here in Comanche County. There weren't a lawman in the whole damn town! I don't know if Hardin managed to sell the cattle and horses he won, and really don't care, but not long after the gunfight, Hardin just rode out of town with his race horses, casual as ya please. An' nobody gave him any trouble 'bout it neither."

Ryan shook his head. "I sure can't say that I blame them. From what I've heard of John Wesley Hardin, he's not a man you'd want to tangle with unless you're pressed to. In fact, as weary as I am right now, I think I'm kind of relieved that he's more than four days removed from here so that I don't feel obliged to go after him. All I want is some food, a bath, and some sleep. Let's go eat before Hazel gets her dander up for letting dinner get cold."

Rising to his feet, Ryan stretched and yawned. "Well, boys, you're gonna have to get along without me for a couple of hours. I'm going to take a bath and catch a little shut eye. I haven't had much sleep the past few days and I'm just plumb beat."

He had told them all about the Indian chase and battle while they ate their noon meal, and for a short time after they had finished eating, they had discussed whether or not that would put an end to the Indian problems. He and Kyle had decided that for the time being, it might be a good idea to keep the night watch, just in case.

"I'll help you get your bathwater and then I'll get out of the house for a while," Hazel said as Kyle and the three young horse trainers Ryan employed rose to leave.

"You won't bother me none if you have things to do here in the kitchen," Ryan told her. "No amount of noise you could make would keep me from sleeping now."

"That's okay. I need to do a little cleaning in my own house, anyway, so I'll just clear out until it's time to start cooking supper."

Ryan closed the bedroom door, shucked his dirty clothes, and stepped into the large oval-shaped galvanized tub. As he began to scrub himself, his thoughts turned to Clara Beeman, the lady whom he planned to visit after supper.

Clara was a childless widow about the same age as the twenty-seven-year-old Ryan. She and her husband had opened a small mercantile store in Comanche six years earlier, but her husband became ill and died of pneumonia that first winter.

Since she had no other family, Clara decided to stay in Comanche and continue to operate the store after his death. She and Ryan struck up a relationship almost immediately after becoming acquainted four years ago when he'd bought his ranch.

After finishing his bath, Ryan stretched out on his bed waiting for sleep to claim his tired body. Now, however, Ryan's thoughts were having trouble dwelling on Clara as he lay on his back in the soft comfort of his bed. His mind's eye kept overshadowing Clara with an image of a naked enchantress as sleep engulfed him.

Sleep did not clear the vision of the beautiful Susan Bradford from his mind. In a short time he dreamed of standing on the creek bank, gazing at the lovely nymph below him, just as he had earlier in the day. In his dream, however, her face did not reflect the wild-eyed expression of fear.

Instead, her wide-set blue eyes were soft and inviting. Her baby soft face was faintly smiling as the tip of her tongue moved slowly over her full, sensuous lips. Her right hand was stretched out to him and her forefinger was opening and closing in the universally understood come-hither motion.

She was moving toward him with slow, short steps. Ryan's heart was pounding. He was stiff and throbbing with anticipation as he eased his body down the bank and into the creek bed. By the time he met her at the water's edge, he was as naked as she.

The beautiful nymph wrapped her arms around his neck, lifting her body until her face was even with his. Ryan's breathing was heavy and labored as she wrapped her legs around his waist. His hands rested under her thighs and her soft heat radiated through his palms, sending waves of passion throughout his body.

Raising her hips, she shifted tantalizingly and slowly lowered herself on him, taking in his full length.

Ryan's orgasm was instant and complete, and his breath became ragged. As consciousness invaded his dream, he tried to fight it off, hoping to remain asleep and resume his dream.

But it didn't work. Suddenly he was wide awake, unmoving for a minute or two, reliving the erotic experience he had just had.

Finally he raised his head and looked on either side of him to see if any of his release had stained the bed sheets. He didn't want Hazel to see it when she changed them on wash day. There was nothing. It was all on his belly and chest.

Scooting out of bed, he crossed to the tub of now cold bathwater. Wetting the cloth draped over the side of the tub and washing himself, he decided that maybe he wouldn't go visit Clara later tonight after all.

Chapter Two

Susan puttered around the house until mid-morning pretending she had things to do, when in actuality she was chilly-dipping. And she knew it.

The incident at the swimming hole the day before continued to occupy her thoughts. She was still embarrassed and yet curious.

No man had ever seen her unclothed before. How could she meet him face to face—she knew she'd have to sooner or later since they were neighbors—knowing that he had seen her naked? How would he act? What would he say? What should she do or say?

She sighed. Since she'd already ruled out the possibility of avoiding him for the rest of her life, she decided she'd just have to hope she didn't run into him for a long time. At least long enough for her to figure some plausible rationale for why she'd done such a dangerous thing, although her actions hadn't seemed dangerous at the time. Reflecting, she realized that she'd been lucky an honorable man had stumbled upon her. What if it had been an outlaw or even some of the renegade Indians who had been causing havoc recently?

She shuddered at that last thought which sent chills down her spine.

"Why aren't you going for your ride this morning, Susan? Aren't you feeling well?"

"I'm feeling fine, Mama. I guess I'm just getting tired of having nothing to do but go for a ride," she hedged, not wanting to reveal the real reason for her procrastination. "I'll be glad when we get acquainted here so we'll have someone to visit with once in a while."

"Yes, I know, dear, but that takes time. I'm sure we'll be finding plenty to do before long."

"I hope so." She sighed. "But since there's nothing else to do now, I guess I will go for a ride."

As Susan saddled the gray mare, she decided to explore the ranch on the other side of their house. Even though she would miss not petting his horses, she certainly didn't want to run into Ryan Sommerall accidentally, especially this soon after their encounter.

But she couldn't keep her eyes and thoughts from straying in that direction as she walked her horse out of the barn. She stopped and stroked the mare's soft nose as she pondered her decision.

She really enjoyed watching the neighbor's horses romp around the pasture. Some of them would even hold still for her to pet them. Besides, as late in the morning as it was, Ryan might not be in that pasture anyway. Surely he had a great deal of work to do running such a large ranch, didn't he? She chewed on her bottom lip as she tried to justify changing her mind.

She finally decided that she was not going to let Ryan Sommerall disrupt her life. She mounted and rode away in the direction of the fence.

"If I do run into him today or whenever, and he pokes fun at me, I'll just tell him off good. That's what I'll do," she proclaimed, her chin raised in stubborn determination.

But, for some reason, she really didn't think he'd do anything like that. After all, he had been gentlemanly enough to leave her at the swimming hole as soon as he'd been able to compose himself.

And, now that she thought about it, seeing her must have been as much of a shock to him as it had been to her. After all, it probably wasn't everyday that a man happened upon a naked woman in a swimming hole in broad open daylight. Besides, Kyle had spoken very fondly of him, both as a friend and an employer.

Her skin tingled as she thought about the tall cowboy. She wondered what color his eyes were. With the brim of his hat shading his eyes and several days' stubble, she had only a vague idea of what his face might look like clean-shaven.

But something inside her told her that his face would be as handsome as the rest of his body. And the rest of his body was certainly well-formed. She remembered the way his black pants hugged his lean hips, and his shirt molded itself to his broad shoulders. She wasn't sure she'd ever seen a man that looked quite so ... so ... blatantly masculine in real life. Brown. She'd bet his eyes were brown.

A distressing thought suddenly occurred to her. Kyle hadn't said, and she hadn't thought to ask, but she wondered if he was married.

"Oh, mercy," she thought out loud. "I sure hope he isn't."

She blushed vividly at her errant thoughts. What in the world was the matter with her?

Her wayward musings were interrupted by a bawling cow as she neared the stock tank which was about four hundred yards from the fence and almost in line with the gate.

The cow was walking back and forth at the shallow intake end of the tank, and seemed to be in distress. The cause was easy to spot as she rode up to the bank. A newborn calf of four or five days was bogged down in the mud.

Damn it, Susan Marie, she admonished herself. *You've thought about your rope three or four times in the past few days and it's still not on your saddle. Now you'll pay the price.*

Dismounting, she pulled off her boots, hat, and gun belt, rolled up her breeches' legs to mid-thigh and started sloshing through the mud to the calf, rolling up her shirt sleeves as she went.

Sitting in the shade of the scrub oak grove, Ryan had watched as Susan rode toward him but knew she couldn't see him. He had ridden out to the big pasture to check on his horses and then had walked his horse slowly along the fence line, glancing in the direction of Susan's house, until he'd reached the oak grove.

He was more than a little disappointed that she hadn't come to admire and pet the horses today. His disappointment was so keen that he had decided to sit in the shade of the trees and have a smoke or two in hopes that she would still show up.

He had taken note of the cow at the tank but hadn't attached any importance to it until he saw Susan walk to the end of the tank and disappear behind the dam from his view. He decided then he'd better see what was happening.

When he reached the tank, he was surprised to see her in mud above her knees, trying to pull a calf free. She had managed to free the calf just enough so that it lunged forward and splattered her with mud.

"Why you goddang little son of a bitch! I ought to just leave you here," she fumed loudly.

Ryan's mouth fell open. He could hardly believe his ears. How could such a string of cuss words come from such a delicate, refined lady?

Susan grabbed the calf by the tail and one of its ears and, with a strength that was reinforced by anger, she lifted it forward a couple of times to where it was able to move on its own. "Now get your butt out of here," she ordered at the same time slapping it on the rump.

The calf bounded out of the mud and ran to its fretting mother.

"What the hell do you think you're doing?" Ryan asked.

"Ahhh!" Susan screeched at the sound of his voice. When she recognized him, her fear from being startled turned to anger mixed with exasperation.

"What do I think I'm doing?" she retorted with exaggerated amazement at his question. "It should be plain to see that I was dragging that stupid calf out of this mud hole."

"Well, a delicate, fragile lady like you shouldn't be doing a thing like that," Ryan admonished her. "You could hurt yourself."

"Delicate? Fragile? Do I *look* like I'm delicate and fragile?" she flung at him acrimoniously as she twisted her body first to one side and then the other to display the muck she was splattered with.

Her twisting and turning became a little too vigorous for her slippery footing to support and, with an audible splat, she sat down in the mud. "Now look what you've done!" she shouted, glaring at him accusingly.

Ryan could not utter a word of defense. He was too busy trying to hide his muted laughter behind his hat brim. His shaking shoulders gave him away, however.

"I'm glad somebody is getting some pleasure from this," Susan railed at him as she regained her footing and sloshed out of the mud to dry ground. "What are you doing here anyway?" she demanded.

"I saw the commotion from over yonder." Ryan jerked his thumb in the direction of the fence. "And I just rode over here to see what was going on."

"Well, the show is over so get out of here," Susan ordered as she started walking around the tank. "Oh, never mind. Just bring my boots and gun belt to the other end of the tank."

"What are you going to do now?" Ryan asked as he dismounted to do as he had been told.

"Well, I was seriously considering washing off some of this muck. Ouch!" Susan exclaimed as she stopped to balance herself on one foot, lifting the other foot to remove a grass burr from her heel.

"What's the matter now?" Ryan asked.

Susan was amused and puzzled at the genuine concern she heard in Ryan's voice. "I just got bit by a rattlesnake."

"You what!" Ryan exclaimed as he rushed to her, dropping her things along the way.

Susan cupped her hands over her mouth as though to muffle the sounds of her giggling. Her eyes were sparkling with impish delight.

"Why you little minx," Ryan scolded. "You shouldn't scare me half to death like that just because you're mad at me."

"Well, you've scared me enough, and it's high time I got even."

Ryan ran his fingers through his thick dark brown hair and squirmed under her accusation.

Susan began to feel a little compassion for him. "I'm not mad at you anymore, though. I'm just a bit peeved at everything in general. I haven't had a very pleasant morning, you know. Now if you'll excuse me, I'd like to clean myself up a little. Bring my stuff on around to the dam."

Choosing a spot where the ground at the water's edge was clean and sandy, she pulled her belt from her jeans, rinsed the mud off it, and tossed it up on the dam. Then, wading into the tank until the water reached her hips, she took her bandanna from around her neck, and using it as a washcloth, began scrubbing the mud from her clothes.

Ryan placed her boots and stockings near the water then moved up the slope of the dam to a small willow tree and sat in its shade.

Watching her wash the mud from her clothes, his mind kept returning to the events of the day before. Her hand scrubbed a muddy spot on her shirt; he saw her firm, creamy breasts. She wiped the side of her pants; he caressed her gently rounded hips. Reality mingled with fantasy. He shook his head and took long, ragged breaths, trying to dispel his mind's treacherous wanderings. But his body betrayed his heightened awareness of the woman wading out of the water onto the sandy bank. Wringing the water from her bandanna, she wiped her feet and legs and, sitting on a clump of grass, pulled on her stockings and boots. Then, much to Ryan's surprise, she walked up the bank and sat no more than a foot from him.

Her nearness made Ryan nervous. He pulled a Bull Durham sack from his shirt pocket and began to roll a smoke. After spilling more tobacco on the ground than he got in the cigarette paper, his trembling fingers began to twist the paper around the tobacco, but he only managed to tear the paper.

"Would you like for me to do that?" Susan offered, taking the tobacco sack and pack of papers from his clammy hands. The thought that she was making this big handsome man nervous was giving her a pleasant, heady feeling.

"Do you smoke?" Ryan asked with amazement.

"Of course not, silly. I just learned to roll them because I like to do little things like that for Papa. Give me a match." She lit the cigarette and handed it to him, noticing his eyes.

31

She would have lost her bet. They were blue-gray.

"You must be real close with your father. He talked about you quite a bit when I visited with him while he was working on your house."

"Yes, we are real close. I'm an only child, you know, so I guess he just decided to enjoy me as much as he would have a son. He taught me to ride and fish and hunt and all kind of things like that. We fished and hunted on the Brazos River a whole lot."

Ryan shook his head in amazement. "I can't understand why a father would make a tomboy out of a girl like you."

"I am not a tomboy!" she shouted at him. "Why does everybody think a girl is a tomboy just because she likes to fish and hunt? Lots of girls and women would like to fish and hunt—well, fish at least—if their fathers or husbands would just take them once in a while. But that does *not* make me a tomboy!" she emphasized, looking him straight in the eyes and just daring him to contradict her.

"No, ma'am. It sure don't. You've made your case. That's why I was so surprised to see you wrestling that calf."

"Well, neither am I such a delicate, fragile piece of fluff that I can't help a calf out of a mud hole, either." She sniffed indignantly.

"Well, that brings up another question. Why didn't you snake it out with your rope?"

"I don't have a rope. At least I don't have it with me," she admitted, chagrined.

Ryan gave her a puzzled look. "How in the world can you work cattle without a rope?"

"I don't work with the cattle very much. I just don't like the dumb, ornery critters. We don't have many cows anyway, only forty or so. Mister Adams sold most of the cows, thinking he could more readily sell the land without someone having to buy a large herd of cattle, too. That suited Papa fine. He wants to choose his brood cows carefully, and he's going to get some European bulls. His main interest is breeding a better quality of beef cattle. So it will be several months yet before we have much of a herd."

"Well, you must like horses. Kyle tells me you've been over most every day petting and pampering mine, and just generally spoiling them," he teased.

"Oh, Kyle's just putting you on. I pet some of the gentle ones and the little colts that will hold still long enough. But, yes, I do love horses. I wish Papa would have chosen to raise them rather than cattle when he retired from the cotton business."

They fell silent for a while.

Ryan glanced at Susan and grinned mischievously. "I sure don't know how I could have suggested that you were a tomboy. There ain't nothing about you that even resembles a boy. Those clothes you're wearing don't hide that none." His eyes focused on her breast. "Why, that shirt's just busting out with girlish pride."

33

Susan snapped her head around toward him at the same time impulsively lifting her hands as though to cover her breasts. She stopped her movement and instead whacked him over the head with her wet bandanna.

"Now what did you do that for?" he exclaimed in mock anger. "Dang it, woman, I thought I was complimenting you."

"That's not what I whacked you for. You've been sitting here all this time and haven't uttered one word of apology for slipping up on me and gawking at me at the creek yesterday. You've just been sitting there chitchatting and acting like it never happened."

"Now gall danged it, Susie, that ain't fair. I didn't slip up on you. I've been going to that hole fishing and swimming for more than four years now and there ain't never been any naked . . . I mean there's never been anybody there before. I didn't have any reason to suspect that I'd find a naked woman in my fishing hole."

"It's not *your* fishing hole and you didn't have to stand there gawking at me."

"Well, damnation, woman! What would you expect me to do? Shut my eyes?"

"That would have been the gentlemanly thing to do. Or, better still a gentleman would have left immediately."

"I did leave as soon as I was able." He grabbed his hat and started to rise to his feet.

"Wait a minute." Susan grabbed his shirt sleeve. "Maybe . . . maybe I was a little too hard on you. I know you really didn't intend to slip up on me. I guess it was partly my fault for being careless. It was plain to see that there had been others there, but I thought it was the people who had owned the ranch before us. It is on *my* land, you know."

Ryan studied her intently for a moment. "I guess I should have apologized but I didn't exactly know how to do it without embarrassing you again." He looked at her pleadingly. "Does this mean I can't use my fishing hole anymore?" he asked.

Susan chuckled. "I'll make a deal with you. I'll let you fish in my swimming hole if you won't object to my petting my horses whenever I want to. Agreed?"

"Agreed. But they are *my* horses. They're on *my* land, you know." He grinned as he tossed her own words back at her.

Susan laughed. "I'm glad we got that settled." She made a face as she pulled at the dirty shirt clinging to her. "I've got to get out of these yucky clothes."

Ryan couldn't resist. "Well, wait till I'm gone from here before you do that. I sure don't want to stir you up again and maybe lose my fishing privileges," he teased.

"Oh, you. You know what I meant." She laughed. "Are there really some fish in there?"

"Yep. I've caught some pretty good-sized ones over the years."

"Hmmm, well, I'll have to check that out some other day. Right now, I gotta get home. This mud is starting to get stiff." She started to leave then turned back to Ryan. "Are you married?" she blurted.

"No."

"Oh."

Molly Bradford glanced out the back window at the sound of a horse entering the yard.

At forty-three, Molly was still considered pretty even though a little on the plump side. Her husband, Seth, often told her she was like a rose in full bloom. Prettier than the new bud not yet blossomed and just as soft and sweet.

She smiled thinking about Seth. She had fallen in love with him when she was only nine years old. He had come with his father to buy a breeding bull from her father. At fourteen, Seth had already begun to plan his future as a cattle rancher, even though his father firmly believed that cotton was where the real money was to be made.

Molly hadn't cared about the differences between cattle breeds but she had eagerly hung on Seth's every word about his future as a cattle rancher. And she had made up her mind that very day that she was going to be a part of Seth's future.

As cute little Molly grew into a pretty young lady, Seth's visits became more frequent. On her sixteenth birthday, Seth asked for her hand in marriage.

Seth and his father built a thriving cotton exporting business. Seth seemed to have a knack for knowing just when to put their cotton on the market to get the highest bid or hold it off and wait for the price to go higher. Even so, he'd never completely given up his dream of raising a quality breed of beef cattle.

After eight years of marriage, Molly had given up all hope of having any children when she became pregnant with Susan. All during her pregnancy, Seth had teased her that the reason it had taken so long for the good Lord to bless them with a child was because He wanted them to be old enough and wise enough to raise it properly.

There were days when Molly had wondered if there was more truth to Seth's teasing than they'd realized. Today looked like it might be one of those days. She could tell by her daughter's muddy clothes that something had happened. She shook her head in consternation, wondering what misadventure had befallen Susan who seemed to have a proclivity for the unexpected.

Her daughter stomped into the kitchen and plopped down into a chair. "Why does everything happen to me?"

"I don't know, dear. What 'thing' are we talking about this time?" Molly was almost afraid to ask.

She shook her head from side to side with

unbelieving dismay as she got a better look at Susan. "On second thought, I don't think I even want to hear about it."

"Oh, Mother. Must you always practice your dramatics?"

"Well, you certainly give me plenty of opportunities, young lady," Molly admonished. "You're not hurt, are you?"

"No, I'm not hurt. I just had to drag a stupid calf out of the mud at the stock tank over there."

Molly shook her head again. "Well, I'd like to hear the calf's side of it as to which one of you did the dragging."

Susan smiled, reliving the incident in her mind. "Well, I'm sure glad the calf can't talk. It could make a pretty good case for itself."

Molly could no longer restrain a little laughter.

"Oh, Mother. You're as bad as that Ryan Sommerall. He laughed at me, too."

"Oh?" Molly raised an eyebrow.

"He owns the land that joins ours. I met him over at the tank."

Molly stared at her daughter. "You mean he was there and he let *you* get the calf out of the mud?"

"No, Mama, I mean he got there right after I got the calf out of the mud. He's very nice and handsome, too. I think I'm going to like him."

"Well, I doubt you made a very favorable

impression on him looking like that. But you can tell me about him later. Right now we'd better get you cleaned up before your father sees you."

Susan smiled impishly. "I don't think Mister Sommerall will soon forget his first impression of me."

Chapter Three

Susan was feeling twinges of guilt as she stood at the kitchen window watching her father hitch the team to the wagon load of fence posts and barbed wire. She hadn't decided *not* to tell him that she was going fishing at the creek, she just hadn't decided *to* tell him. She knew he couldn't go with her since he and Jim Morgan, the neighboring rancher, were busy building fences and she knew there would be a debate about the safety of her going alone. She also knew that she was going fishing. So she had simply decided to eliminate all the hassle and just not tell him or her mother where she was going.

With the table cleared and the breakfast dishes washed, the last of her morning chores

41

were finished. When her father was far enough from the barn that he wouldn't notice her leaving with her fishing pole, Susan turned from the window and went to her room.

Buckling on her gun belt and taking her rifle from its usual place in the corner, she headed out the front door. Her mother was puttering in the flower bed as Susan knew she would be.

"I'm going for a ride, Mama."

Molly turned to her with her usual expression of concern. "Be careful and don't be gone too long."

"Oh, Mama, will you never quit fretting over me like I was a child? I turned eighteen last month, you know."

"I didn't fret about you like this when you were a child. I knew where you were and what you were doing then. Now, you just go prowling all over the countryside and I never know what you're doing." Molly shook her head in resignation. "Oh, never mind. I know my talking isn't going to change anything now."

Susan went to her mother and gave her a hug with her free arm. "Please don't worry about me, Mama. You know Papa taught me how to take care of myself in the outdoors."

Molly returned her daughter's show of affection. "I know, dear, but please do be careful and don't be gone too long."

"Yes, Mama, I'll be careful and I'll be back before noon."

Susan walked around the house to the barn, saddled her horse, got her fishing pole from the tack room, and headed in the direction of the creek.

She couldn't see the big buckskin gelding that was tied under the pecan tree until she was almost to the tree herself. She reined up sharply and recognized the horse immediately. It was the same one Ryan had been riding yesterday.

"Oh, hell," she muttered in frustration, thinking the situation over for a minute. She decided she probably should just forget about fishing and go back home, but she really didn't want to. Besides, she asked herself, wasn't she secretly hoping to see Ryan again soon? She had to admit the answer was yes. Well, here was her chance. She had come to fish, so she would fish.

She rode under the tree, dismounted, and tied her horse. Then, fishing pole in hand, she walked along the path about halfway to the creek before she stopped and called to him. "Ryan, are you down there?"

There was a momentary silence.

"Is that you, Susie?" His surprise was evident in the tone of his voice.

"Yes, it's me. Are you decent?"

"Well, I think most people would consider me to be a pretty decent sort of fella."

"Oh, smart aleck! You know what I mean. You're not swimming or anything like that, are you?"

"Nope. I'm fishing. What were you figuring to do?"

"I was going to fish, too."

"Well, come on down. There's plenty of room for both of us."

Susan walked on down to the creek. Ryan had moved from where he was fishing to stand just below where she would slide down the bank.

Susan started to step down but then stopped. Ryan sensed that she was hesitant about whether she should be there with him.

"I'll leave if you'd rather be by yourself."

She hesitated for another moment before sliding down the embankment. "Oh, don't be silly. I'm not afraid of you."

"Well, I sure wouldn't want you to be," he said as he caught her at the bottom. "Where's your rifle?"

"It's on my saddle. Why?"

"You should always take it with you when you're leaving your horse for a while like this. I'll go get it."

Susan spotted the grasshoppers in the jar near Ryan's fishing pole and was threading one on her hook when he returned carrying her rifle.

"Have you caught any fish yet?" she asked.

"Only one small one, but I haven't been here very long. They're just not biting very good today."

"Nonsense. This is the prettiest fishing hole I've ever seen. There's nothing even on the

Brazos River to match the beauty of this place. I'll show you how to catch 'em. Anybody that can't catch a fish here, just doesn't know how to fish," she boasted as she swung her bait into the water. She stood watching her cork as though she expected it to be pulled instantly beneath the surface by a fish.

Ryan chuckled as he placed a flat smooth limestone rock behind her. "Well, while you're giving me fishing lessons you might as well be comfortable." He returned to his own rock seat a few feet from her.

After a minute or two, Susan concluded that the fish weren't biting and sat on the rock.

"It's the Indian trouble that caused your concern about my rifle, isn't it?"

"That's mostly it. There's been two bands of them in this area in the past month. They haven't killed anyone yet. It seems like they're mostly after horses."

"That's strange. Papa was told there hadn't been any Indians around here for two or three years. What do you suppose has got them stirred up again?"

"I think it's those damn buffalo hunters. They've killed almost all of the buffalo in Kansas and Nebraska. Now they're working the plains country of northwest Texas. They're killing hundreds of them every day just for their hides and the Comanche and Kiowas are not taking it very kindly. Trouble is, the settlers are catching the brunt of their anger. The folks west and north of here are having a lot worse time of it than we are."

"I hope it ends soon. I love to ride around this beautiful country. And I would like to do so without my parents worrying about me."

"It's mighty pretty country all right. I came through here on my way back from one of our cattle drives. As soon as I laid eyes on it, I knew this is where my horse ranch would be."

"Why did you decide to raise horses?"

He shrugged his shoulders. "I don't like cows, either. Racehorses are my real passion."

"But Kyle told me you grew up on your father and grandfather's cattle ranch down in south Texas."

"Yeah. That's right. But things changed. My father went off to the war, of course. But my grandfather was too old and I was too young. My grandfather was designated a cattle supplier by the Confederate government. And they paid a premium price for the beeves with Confederate money, of course. But my grandfather didn't figure from the start that the Confederacy was going to win the war so he didn't keep the money. For every cow he sold, he took the money and bought four or five more calves. When the war ended and my father came home, we had our brand on more than twenty thousand head. They were worth two dollars in Texas and twenty dollars, sometimes more at the railheads in Kansas. So we drove them to Kansas."

"All at one time?" Susie asked in amazement.

"No." Ryan chuckled. "It took three years to get them all there. Unfortunately, my father didn't live to enjoy the fruits of his labor. He was killed on our last drive by some horse-thieving Osage Indians. My grandfather died of sickness in sixty-seven while we were away on a drive. I never did like that country much anyway and there was no one left to keep me there but Kyle and Hazel. They were delighted to come along with me. So, here I am."

"What about your mother?"

"I never knew her. She died shortly after I was born. The only thing I have to remember her by is her name. Ryan was my mother's maiden name."

"Why did you decide to be a Texas Ranger?"

He pondered her question a moment. "Didn't exactly decide to." He shrugged his shoulders. "I just do what I have to do. Besides, I'm not a full-time Texas Ranger. I'm an unpaid volunteer given authority by the governor to enforce the law whenever I see a need to."

They fell silent for a while, each enjoying the sunny morning and the peaceful solitude of the creek.

"I think we're using the wrong bait," Susan suddenly decided, getting to her feet. "I'm going to try to catch some minnows. Sure wish I had my net."

"I've got a net right back there."

"Well, why didn't you say so in the first place?" she scolded as she picked up the small homemade dip net. She eyed the jar containing the grasshoppers.

"Yes, you can use it. The fish aren't biting anyway."

Susan shook the grasshoppers from the jar as she walked along the water's edge to the end of the pool.

"I would have used minnows to start with," she continued to grumble. "Honestly. I would have thought you knew how to fish."

Ryan's mind was not on fishing as he watched her walk along the creek bed. The vision he was seeing was not wearing breeches and shirt. He felt himself growing hard. He shook his head and tightly closed his eyes as though to make the vision leave. *Quit tormenting yourself*, he scolded himself silently. *You know you can't be fooling with young innocents like her.* His self-admonishments did not lessen his longing for her, however.

Susan quickly located a school of minnows in the shallow water at the end of the pool. With a few dips of the net, she had twenty-five or thirty of them in the jar.

"Now, I'll show you how to catch some fish," she boasted as she stuck the hook through a minnow's tail.

Ryan gave her a patronizing smile.

She dropped the minnow in the water, and in less than a minute the cork went under. "I've got one!" she squealed. After a short struggle she lifted a good-sized, about a pound and a half, catfish onto the bank.

"Well, I'll be damned," Ryan muttered as he moved quickly to her fish to take the hook from its mouth.

"I know how to do that," she informed him.

"I'm sure you do. But can't you let me play the gentleman and do it for you?" Dadburn independent woman. Every time he tried to impress her with his chivalry, she was quick to let him know that she was as competent as he was. She sure was hard on a man's ego, as well as some other parts of his anatomy.

Susan was secretly pleased and flattered by his pampering. "Thank you, sir. But hurry up and put another minnow on my hook."

Ryan had hardly gotten the fish in the tow sack he had tied to a stob and laid in the water when Susan squealed again.

"I've got another one."

This time the struggle was a little longer and the fish a little bigger.

Ryan removed the fish from the hook and hung on another minnow.

"Now you're on your own, lady. I'm going to start fishing." Chivalry be damned.

"What happened to the gallant gentleman?" she queried saucily.

"The gallant gentleman turns into a fisherman when the fish start biting."

"I told you I'd show you how to fish," Susan gloated.

Ryan smiled, marveling at the lovely girl deriving so much pleasure from such an earthy sport as fishing. They each caught several fish in a relatively short time, then there was a lull for several minutes.

"Looks like they've stopped biting again, Susie. Must be because the wind is getting up."

"No, they haven't. You just have to move around some," she informed him as she lifted her line and moved down the creek a few feet. She dropped her bait in the water and within seconds, her cork went under.

"See, I've already got one," she exclaimed as she gave a hard yank on her pole. "It's a big one," she squealed as her pole bent from the fish's struggle.

Ryan watched with delight as Susan lifted with all her might but couldn't get the fish to the surface. She began backing up lifting and dragging at the same time until she finally got the fish out and pulled it back three or four feet from the water.

"I told you it was a big one," she boasted as she dropped her pole and rushed toward the catfish that looked like it would probably weigh about three pounds.

The fish began to flop toward the water.

Susan, fearing it would shake the hook loose, went into a wild scramble trying to grab it. She was on her knees at the water's edge when she finally caught it.

"Now there's a nice channel cat," she boasted, holding it up for Ryan's inspection. The fish made a final effort and managed to free itself from Susan's grasp and landed in the water.

Susan grabbed for the fish but lost her balance and fell face down into the creek. Flailing the water with her hands, half in the water and half on the bank, she was helpless to get out of the water, or to get all the way in where she could swim out.

Ryan rushed to her. Sticking one hand under the waistband of her breeches and belt, he lifted her out of the water. Then he grabbed her fishing line in his other hand and gave it a pull. The fish was still hooked. He began wrapping the string around his hand and backing away from the water at the same time, carrying Susan in one hand and pulling the fish out with the other.

"Put me down, you big ape!" she sputtered.

"Not until I get this fish corralled I ain't. You'd probably just chase it into the creek again. You dadburn crazy woman."

Susan was flailing her arms, kicking her feet and yelling some emphatically unladylike phrases.

When he got the fish out far enough that he was sure it would not get away again, he reached under her bosom to set her on her feet. His hand inadvertently cupped a breast as he did so.

"Well, I'm glad you finally decided to give me some attention. You'd think that dang fish was more important than me!" she fumed.

Ryan laughed. "Lady, after all you went through to try to save that fish I sure didn't have the kind of courage it took to let it get away."

51

Susan, suddenly aware that Ryan's arm still encircled her waist, backed away from him, pulling at her wet shirt and trying to brush her tangled wet hair away from her face.

Embarrassment flushed her cheeks as she visualized what a sight she must look—again. Finally, throwing her hands in the air, she whirled and stomped a few feet away before turning on Ryan.

"Why is it, *Mister* Sommerall, that something humiliating always happens to me when you're around? What are you, my bad luck charm or something?" Her sapphire-blue eyes shimmered with unshed tears of embarrassment.

Ryan closed the distance between them in two long steps. Pulling her into his arms, he tipped her face up to look at him and, gently brushing her wet hair out of the way, he kissed her on the forehead.

"You shouldn't get so upset. Really, it's not that bad. You only got your shirt a little wet," he consoled. His eyes roamed over the soaked garment plastered to her, clearly displaying the gentle mounds and taut nipples beneath it.

"Besides," he murmured hoarsely, "if a wet shirt made me look that good, I'd go around with a wet shirt all the time." He slowly lowered his head, letting his lips caress hers.

Susan pulled her head back and looked up at him in wide-eyed bewilderment.

Ryan took her lack of resistance as acceptance and pulled her tight against his chest and kissed her firmly.

Susan pulled away from him, her hand trembling as she touched her slightly parted, quivering lips.

Ryan immediately stepped back from her. "I'm sorry, I shouldn't have done that."

Susan turned away, unable to meet his eyes, as she started to take the fish off her line.

Ryan beat her to it. "I'll take care of that."

"Thank you," Susan murmured as she picked up her pole and began wrapping the line around it.

"You're quitting, aren't you?"

"I think I'd better go." She turned to pick up her rifle.

Ryan pulled in his line and wrapped it around his pole.

"You don't have to quit just because I am." Did her voice sound as breathless to him as it did to her? she wondered.

"I'm not in the mood anymore. If you'll wait a minute, I'll walk you to your horse." He desperately wanted to make amends for the liberties he had taken.

Susan nodded mutely and waited until Ryan finished gathering up his fishing equipment before turning back to continue along the path to their horses.

"I leave my pole in that brush over there. Saves from having to pack it back and forth. I'll put yours there, too, if you'd like." He was half-afraid that she'd tell him she never intended to come here again. If only she'd say or do something to give him a hint as to what she was thinking or feeling. He almost melted into a puddle of happiness when she smiled at him and handed him her pole.

"That would make it more expedient when I want to fish again."

After Susan placed her rifle in the saddle boot, Ryan took her by her shoulders and turned her to him.

"Susan, please don't hold what happened down there against me. I know I shouldn't have kissed you like that, but . . ."

"Yes, you should've. I mean . . . I'm not upset that you kissed me. I just didn't know what to do. I didn't know how to handle it. I mean . . . Oh, I don't know what I mean." She pivoted away from him and cupped her face in her hands.

Ryan momentarily panicked, thinking she was going to cry and was relieved when she didn't. He wondered what the real cause of her frustration was; then suddenly it dawned on him.

"You haven't had a man kiss you before." It was a statement, not a question.

She whirled back to him. "And just what's wrong with that?"

"Not a thing, Susie." He smiled. "Not a thing."

"Just don't think there hasn't been plenty who wanted to. They just didn't have a chance to. I haven't known a man before whom I wanted to kiss me."

"Well, I sure feel mighty honored to be the first, and I guess I ought to warn you that I'll do it again if you give me half a chance." He was smiling devilishly and with great relief.

As Susan gazed up at him, the tenseness in her face gave way to a soft smile. Her lips quivered ever so slightly as she waited expectantly.

Then her eyes began to express impatience. Suddenly, she placed her hands behind his head and rose to her toes as she pulled him to her. Her firm, passionate kiss lingered until she felt his hands at her waist. She then released him and, turning abruptly, moved to her horse, and swung into the saddle.

Ryan stood staring up at her as though in a trance.

"You're as slow about taking your kissing chances as you are about changing your fish bait," she saucily reproached him from her position of safety.

"Why, you little . . ." He raised his hands and stepped toward her as if he meant to drag her from her saddle.

She nudged her horse from him, giggling with delight. A gust of wind swept the pecan tree above her, dislodging a small dead branch.

The limb landed on her mare's rump and raked on down its legs. The mare jumped, tucking her hoofs under her, then took off at a dead run. Had Susan not grabbed the saddle horn, the mare would have left her behind.

"Whoa!" Susan yelled. "Whoa!" She reared back on the reins, but the mare didn't break her stride. "Damn it, Spooky, whoa!"

Ryan sprang on his horse and set off in pursuit. He had hardly gotten started before Susan's mare stopped as suddenly as she had bolted.

Ryan reined in next to Susan. "That horse needs some training. She spooks too easy. That's kind of dangerous, you know."

"Yeah, I know. That's why I named her Spooky. But she doesn't do it very often and she usually doesn't run very far. Seems like it's just when something scares her from behind that she takes off like that. She's such a sweet thing, though, and rides so smooth that I put up with that one little fault. Well, I gotta get on home."

"Don't you want some of the fish?"

"I'd sure like to have some, but I was a bit sneaky and didn't tell my folks I was going fishing alone, so I can't very well go home with fish, now can I?"

"Wouldn't it make it all right with them if you told them I was here to protect you?"

"Are you crazy or something! That would only verify what Mother's always telling me about Indians and evil men lurking around the countryside just waiting for little girls like me to come along."

"Ouch." He grimaced. "Reckon I had that coming. Well, guess I'll have to throw some back. We can't eat them all."

Susan and her mother had just finished washing the dishes from the noon meal when they heard a horse trotting up to the back of the house. Susan looked out the window and was very much surprised to see Ryan Sommerall.

She stepped out on the porch just as he was swinging down from the saddle.

"What are you doing here?"

"Now is that any way to greet a neighbor?"

"Well, I'm just surprised to see you again so . . . I mean . . ." She glanced behind her to see if her mother had heard her slip. "I'm just surprised to see you."

Molly joined her daughter on the porch and nudged Susan with her elbow.

"Oh, excuse me. This is Mister Ryan Sommerall. Mister Sommerall, this is Mama. I mean, this is my mother, Mrs. Molly Bradford." Susan's embarrassed blush warmed her face.

Molly patted her daughter reassuringly on the back. "I'm very pleased to meet you, Mister Sommerall. Susan told me about meeting you at her calf-wrestling match." Her eyes glistened in amusement.

"Pleased to meet you, too, Mrs. Bradford. I hope Susan explained that I arrived at the scene too late to be of any help with the calf." He glanced at Susan, a mischievous smile beginning to form.

The fire in her eyes told him he'd better drop the subject of the calf fast.

"Please, come in," Molly invited.

"Thank you, ma'am, but I didn't come to visit. I came to invite you and your family to have supper with us this evening. I know it's sort

57

of short notice but, you see, I caught a bunch of catfish this morning, far more than we can eat, and Hazel suggested that I invite ya'll over. She's anxious to meet you and Susan, so she figured what better time than a fish fry."

Molly glanced at her daughter, not missing the hopeful look in her eyes. "Thank you, Mister Sommerall, for the invitation. I think we'd all enjoy that. Don't you agree, Susan?"

"Of course, and I'm sure Papa would enjoy it, too." She smiled sweetly at Ryan. "It's very nice of you to invite us, Mister Sommerall."

"Good, then it's settled. And, please, call me Ryan. We'll eat about six-thirty or so, but Hazel said to come early if you can. She wants to give you some vegetables from the garden. She has more than we can use and since ya'll arrived too late to plant a garden, she wants to share hers with you."

"Well, we certainly can use some fresh vegetables," Molly assured him. "Suppose we arrive about five. It'll still be light enough to pick the vegetables, and it'll give us time to help Hazel with the cooking."

"Sounds fine to me. I'll tell Hazel." He mounted his horse and tipped his hat to Molly. "Nice to have met you, ma'am. See you tonight, Susan."

Susan watched Ryan ride away. Her fingers moved to touch her lips, and her heart beat faster remembering the warm feeling of his lips moving against hers. The special scent that was uniquely his, a pleasant mixture of tobacco, leather, and maleness, lingered in her mind.

"Susan. Susan?" Molly stepped back on the porch.

Susan jumped guiltily at the sound of her mother's voice.

"I called you twice. Didn't you hear me?" Molly smiled when she looked off in the distance and saw what held her daughter's rapt attention. "He is a handsome man, isn't he?" Her eyes glittered as Susan's face turned a darker pink.

Susan wouldn't meet her mother's glance. "What did you want?"

"You'd better go tell your father to come home in time to get cleaned up so we can go visiting."

Chapter Four

A mixture of excitement and nervousness assailed Susan as her father pulled the wagon to a stop in front of the Sommerall house.

She had chosen a gown of soft mint-green with darker green trim, which she knew flattered her small waist and brought out the red highlights in her hair, and had fashioned her auburn hair in curls on top of her head with a few wispy tendrils framing her face. She knew it made her look more mature and feminine. Then she had positioned herself on the bed, not daring to move one inch, until it was time to leave, determined that this time, Ryan Sommerall was going to see her looking like a graceful lady instead of some hoyden fresh from the backwoods covered in muck.

"Howdy, folks." Kyle ambled around from the side of the house to greet them.

"Come on in. Hazel oughta be here in a minute. You know how it is with womenfolk," he said, shaking hands with Seth. "They always want to look their best when meeting new neighbors. You certainly look lovely, Miss Susan," he complimented, helping her down from the wagon.

His eyes glittered with amusement. He might be old, but he wasn't too old to notice Susan's extra care to look her best. And he didn't have to think twice to know who *she* wanted to impress. *And*, when he'd passed Ryan's room a few minutes ago, his nose had caught the distinct aroma of that fancy toilet water that Ryan used when he went acourtin'. Yep, he thought to himself,'bout time somebody roped his boss, and he'd bet his next month's pay that this little lady was just the one to do it.

"Hmmm, I do believe that catfish was as good as even Molly has ever cooked," Seth complimented.

"There's plenty more, and there's apple cobbler for dessert when anyone's ready," Hazel said.

"Thank you, ma'am, but I think I'll have to let my supper settle some before I could eat another bite."

A chorus of "me too's" went around the table.

"Ryan, my boy, that was mighty good eating," Kyle said, patting his full belly. "I'm sure glad you went fishing today."

"You say you caught these in the creek?" Seth asked Ryan.

"Yes, sir, sure did. There's some mighty big fish in that hole." He glanced across at Susan. "Course you have to know how to catch them. I'd say knowing which bait to use is the secret. This morning, for instance, I started with grasshoppers but it didn't take me long to see the fish weren't going to eat them, so I switched to minnows and right away I started snatching them out. Moving around is important, too. Yep." He smiled, taking delight in galling Susan. "There's a definite art to catching the big ones."

Why that no-account scoundrel! He's taking credit for my fish, Susan silently fumed. She smiled sweetly at Ryan and, carefully steadying herself in her chair so others would not detect her movement, placed a sharp kick to his shin.

Ryan grunted, caught completely off guard by Susan's action.

"Did you say something?" She smiled innocently at Ryan.

"I was just going to caution your father to keep an eye on you if he took you fishing at that hole. The bank sometimes gets very slippery and if you caught a really big fish and it started flopping toward the water, and you started grabbing for it, you might fall into the water and have to be pulled out by the seat of your breeches."

"Oh, is that a fact?" Susan gasped as the color began to sneak up her neck.

Another kick found its mark on Ryan's shin.

"Well, I'll keep your advice in mind if Papa should take me fishing with him."

Hazel and Seth looked puzzled at the exchange between Susan and Ryan. Molly raised an eyebrow at her daughter, and Kyle quickly took a drink from his glass to hide his snicker.

Seth shrugged his shoulders wondering why Susan didn't own up to the fact that she was a good fisherman. Hell, he'd taught her himself and she usually managed to out-fish him.

"Well, if no one wants dessert right now, I'll clean the table off; then we can have some coffee and visit," Hazel said as she began gathering up the dirty dishes.

"Susan and I'll help you," Molly volunteered. "It's so good to have another woman to talk with."

After finishing the dishes, the women joined the men in the parlor.

"Molly, Kyle is taking me into town tomorrow for supplies. Would you and Susan care to come along? I could introduce you to some of the womenfolk."

"Could we, Mama?" Susan implored.

"I don't see any reason why not. Thank you, Hazel. Do you need anything, Seth?"

"Nah, but I think I'll go along anyhow."

"Well," Ryan chimed in. "I think I'll just go, too. We men can play some billiards while the women shop and then all get together for lunch at the cafe."

Hazel began telling Molly who they'd likely meet in town. Kyle and Seth started talking about the advantage of using "that newfangled barbed wire" instead of rail fencing.

"Ah, Susan, I need to go check on some new colts. Would you like to go with me?" Ryan asked, not quite sure if she'd forgiven him for taking credit for her fish.

"New colts? I'd love to."

As they walked toward the barn, Ryan decided he'd better make amends. "You sure look pretty tonight."

"Thank you."

"I . . . ah . . . I'm sorry about taking all the credit for the fish."

"Well, you certainly should be. That wasn't a very gentlemanly thing to do." Truth was, she'd forgotten she was supposed to be mad at him for his bragging.

"And I suppose the two kicks you landed on me were ladylike?" he countered. "You damn near cracked my leg."

"You deserved it," she sniffed, tilting her chin up.

"Yeah. I guess I did." He glanced sideways at her like a little boy in trouble. "Am I forgiven?"

"I don't know. I'll think about it." She wasn't going to let him off the hook that easy.

Ryan got a lantern from the tack room to light their way to the stalls.

"How many newborn colts do you have?"

"There's five here at the barn. Three that I've been holding in the lot for a couple of days and one born yesterday. The one in there arrived about four hours ago," he said, motioning toward a chestnut mare and baby as he hung the lantern on a nail by the stall door. "I'm going to go check on the mare in the stall down at the end. I expect her to foal any time now."

Ryan came back to find Susan on her knees beside the hours-old colt. She looked up at him expectantly. He shook his head. "She should foal soon, probably before morning. How's that little fella doing?"

Susan grinned up at him. "This little 'fella' is a little filly, for your information, and she's still trying to figure out how to make all those spindly little legs go in the same direction at the same time." Susan giggled as the gangly colt fell on its nose—again—and toppled against its mother. The mare gently licked and nuzzled her new baby.

Ryan hunkered down beside Susan, delighting in watching her watch the colt's antics.

What was it about this woman, he wondered, that made him want to forget all the reasons why he shouldn't pull her into his arms and make love to her until they were both limp with sated passion? *She's cast a spell on me. That's what it is*, he thought.

Suddenly aware of the charged atmosphere, Susan looked at Ryan. She could see the desire in his eyes. They held hers as he slowly caressed the side of her face with his callused palm.

"So pretty." His whisper was barely audible. She rubbed her face against his palm, mesmerized by his touch, his scent, his voice. She saw, as if in slow motion, his face moving closer to hers. She felt his breath brush her lashes as she raised her lips to his. His kiss was a warm, cherishing embrace fanning out from her lips to touch her innermost essence, filling her with an odd, almost expectant sensation.

She eagerly returned his kiss, wanting to savor more of this new, exciting feeling. She could feel his heart pulsing strong and rapid under her hand against his chest, echoing her own racing heartbeat.

He slowly lay her back against the clean-smelling hay, cradling her head on his arm as his lips moved over hers again. His other hand glided up her slender neck, pausing to rub the back of his knuckles gently against the side of his face as he drew back to look into her flushed features.

"You are so beautiful."

"Thank you," she replied shyly.

He had never been very good when it came to putting his feelings into words. How could he tell her that her auburn hair, glistening in the lamplight, reminded him of the last rays of sun setting behind the hillside? Or how her eyes, now a midnight-blue with desire, looked like the early morning just as the first fingers of light pushed the night aside?

He couldn't.

He wished he were glib, but he knew he'd only embarrass himself if he tried to voice his true feelings.

With his face only scant inches above hers, she reached up and brushed back an unruly lock of hair that had fallen across his forehead.

He caught her hand and kissed her fingertips, never taking his eyes off hers. He knew exactly what his actions were doing to her. Her face clearly mirrored her newfound passion. He traced her lips with his finger before replacing it with his lips. His hand fell to her slender waist as he pulled her tight against him, deepening his kiss.

She shuddered when his hand moved up her side to cup the swell of her breast. Her heart skipped a beat when his thumb moved seductively back and forth across her taut nipple, sending electric sensations skittering down her spine. Oh, the things he was doing felt so good. She wanted to let go and flow with the feelings, letting them take her where they would. She desperately wanted to but she couldn't.

"Ryan." Her voice was husky with emotion. She covered his hand to stop the wonderful torment. "Please . . ."

Ryan dropped his forehead to touch hers, trying to regain control over his rioting emotions. "Susie, I . . ." He was breathing heavily.

Susan looked up at him with trust and innocence, waiting for him to complete his sentence.

"You shouldn't look at me that way, little girl, you have no idea what it does to a man."

Tilting her head sideways in puzzlement, she said, "I don't—"

"Never mind," Ryan interrupted, standing up and pulling her to her feet. He was thankful that the dusty lantern globe hid the price his body was paying for her innocence. "We'd better get back."

Susan, confused by her conflicting emotions, nodded her agreement and turned to leave.

Grabbing her arm to forestall her departure, Ryan said, "Wait a minute. We'd better leave some of that hay you're wearing here." He began to pick the straw from her hair before turning her around to brush the back of her dress. "This don't want to come off," he murmured, as his gently stroking hand lingered at her hips.

Susan twisted her head, while at the same time pulling her dress around to see what the problem was. "Oh, you. There's no hay there."

Ryan chuckled. Making her face him, he surveyed her closely. "Hmmm, I guess you look decent enough to go back now," he teased, pulling her into his arms for a quick peck on the lips.

"Oh, Ryan," she admonished lightly, again turning to leave the barn. "You act like they'd think you were trying to seduce me."

Ryan feigned a hurt look. "You mean, I wasn't?"

Susan whirled to stare at him in surprise.

He shrugged his shoulders. "I must be losing my touch. Maybe I need a little more practice. Come here."

"Ryan!" she exclaimed.

Ryan laughed, propelling her toward the door. "Go, woman, before I change my mind."

Susan settled herself on the wagon bench between her mother and father. She was excited about finally getting to go to town.

"I hope you and your mother aren't going to be disappointed when you see Comanche, Susan. Remember, I told you it's not a big city like Waco."

"But it does have some stores that Mother and I will like, doesn't it, Papa?"

Seth chuckled. "Yes, Susan. There's a sufficient number of stores to supply the needs of the ranchers and farmers in the area. In fact, a hotel just opened for business a couple of weeks ago and there's a small furniture factory that's almost completed. Comanche even has a weekly newspaper."

"The people who first settled here must have been very adventurous and hardy," Molly mused.

"Yes, they were," Seth agreed. "The original settlers were mostly from Tennessee and were encouraged by Stephen F. Austin to come to what he called his 'upper colony.' He felt like they would be strong enough to wrest the land away from the Indians and keep it, and he was right. They managed to fight off the

Indians who repeatedly tried to steal their cattle and horses, as well as destroy their crops and burn their homes to the ground. It was the settlers' relentless pursuit of the Indian raiders, with the help of the fine trailing hounds they had brought with them from Tennessee, that was the key to the community's survival in this untamed frontier.

"Others just happened on the area like I did. The main road into Comanche connects Fort Gates which is east of here, with Fort Phantom Hill to the west," he explained. "Families passing through this area fell in love with the beautiful, rolling terrain. They looked around them and saw the place on which to build their dreams, just as I did."

As they reached the outskirts of Comanche, Susan looked around her and felt a sense of pride and fulfillment at being a part of something so new and vibrant.

"Well, ladies," Seth said, pulling the wagon to a halt in front of Beeman's Mercantile. "Since I know you're gonna want to visit every store in town, how about I drop you off here?"

"Oh, Papa." Susan grinned. "You know we won't have time to see everything today."

Molly laughed. "This doesn't seem to be all that big of a town, dear. I believe we'll be able to visit all the stores and shops we'll be interested in. This is fine, Seth. We'll meet you at noon at the cafe."

Atop his horse, Ryan patiently waited for Seth and Kyle to get the women settled before they took the wagons and his horse to the watering trough. Smiling at Susan's impatience to get started shopping, he didn't notice the woman until she spoke.

"Hello, Ryan. I didn't know you were back in town."

Caught off guard, Ryan shifted uneasily in his saddle. He'd forgotten about Clara. "Hello, Clara. I got back a day or so ago," he hedged.

"Oh, I see. Well, I'm glad to see that you made it back safely. Can you come in for a while? I have some coffee on the stove."

"I . . . ah . . . can't right now. Maybe later. I have some things I need to take care of." Turning his horse in the direction of the nearest saloon, he tipped his hat in parting to the women. "I'll meet ya'll later at Jack Wright's saloon, gentlemen."

Susan looked from the comely woman to Ryan, who suddenly acted very uncomfortable and eager to leave. She thought she saw a glance pass between Hazel and Kyle before Hazel quickly spoke up.

"Clara, I want you to meet my new neighbors. They bought the Adams place. This is Seth and Molly Bradford and their daughter, Susan."

Clara watched as Ryan rode away, puzzled by his behavior. She'd known he was back because the men who had ridden with him had regaled everyone with the details of their success. Each night she had anxiously waited for him to visit her, but he hadn't come. As Hazel's words, "new neighbors," began to register, she looked at Susan. Was this woman the reason?

"This is Clara Beeman. She owns the mercantile store," Hazel hurriedly continued the introductions. "Molly and Susan haven't had a chance to meet any of the townsfolk yet."

Clara quickly recovered herself. "Please come in, I'm glad to meet you. A new shipment of fabric and notions arrived today. In fact, I was in the process of unpacking the crates when I saw . . . when I saw you."

"It's nice to meet you, Miss Beeman," Molly said, as Clara led the way into her store.

"Actually it's Mrs., but, please, call me Clara. I'm a widow. My husband died six years ago."

Covertly, Clara took inventory of her competitor, and she was sure in her own mind that Susan was the reason Ryan hadn't come to her. Young and shapely in an immature way, Susan didn't look like the sort of woman who would hold Ryan's attention very long. At least she hoped not.

Although Ryan had made no promises and Clara had not pressed for any, she knew Ryan cared as much about her as he could about any woman. When they'd first met four years before, she had sensed that he was a man tormented by something in his past. On the occasion or two that she had tried to draw him out about what was troubling him, he had deftly sidestepped the issue.

Time had passed, and they had settled into a comfortable relationship. At first she had worried that their closeness would cause the upstanding citizens of Comanche to ostracize her. Even though they were very careful to be discreet, Comanche, like any small town, had its share of busybodies, but if anyone privately thought that the Widow Beeman was a fallen woman for keeping company with the handsome Ranger, no one made a public issue of it.

Susan wasn't sure why, but she got the notion that Clara Beeman didn't like her. Oh, she was friendly enough with Hazel and her mother, but Susan sensed a distinct coolness in Clara's attitude when she'd tried to strike up a conversation with her. Susan had never been disliked before and, considering that they had just met, she couldn't imagine what she had said to antagonize the woman.

Well, she wasn't going to worry about it. It was probably just her imagination that Clara felt some animosity toward her. After all, what could she have possibly done to cause it?

After having finished lunch, Seth was struggling to get out the door of the restaurant without dropping the many brown paper-wrapped packages. "Tarnation, woman, were you trying to spend all my money in one trip?" he grumbled good-naturedly.

Molly patted him patronizingly on the arm. "Now, Seth, dear. You know we wouldn't buy one single thing that wasn't a necessity."

Seth dubiously eyed his wife over the top of the packages.

Susan chuckled.

"Well," Molly amended, "maybe just a couple of things."

"Humph," Seth snorted.

Kyle, who had his own armload of packages to wrestle with, laughed. "Hazel always feels it's her civic duty to help the merchants show a good profit when she comes to town."

"Oh, Kyle, you might as well quit your grumbling 'cause it won't do you a lick of good, and you know it."

Ryan chuckled at his friends' good-natured teasing as he stood patiently holding the cafe door open for the ladies before stepping out behind them onto the sidewalk.

"Ryan!" A sharp voice rang out.

Ryan turned toward the voice.

The man was standing in a slight crouch about ten paces from him, glaring intently, his right hand hovering over his gun butt.

"It is you, ain't it?"

Ryan began moving sideways into the street.

"Ryan, what's the matter?" Susan asked anxiously. "What's happening?"

"Susan, move away from me, go inside. Kyle, get the women back in there."

Ryan continued moving into the street, still facing the man who had accosted him. His arms were hanging loosely at his sides. His right hand was just below the butt of his low-slung gun.

The other man was compelled to move with him. "I told you I'd see you face a firing squad. Well, I'm it."

"It's been a long time, Mister. Why don't you just drop it?"

"I ain't dropping it. And that tin badge you're wearing ain't gonna stop me."

They were now facing each other in the middle of the street.

"Then take it before a court of law."

"I make my own laws."

"Yeah, I saw you make your own laws once before. I should have killed you then. Now the choice is yours. Why don't you decide to live?"

The man continued to glare coldly at Ryan for a moment, then he relaxed his stance. "Yeah, I guess I will."

He made a half turn as though to walk away from Ryan. When his hand was hidden from Ryan's view, it closed around his gun butt. He whirled back, drawing his gun at the same time.

Ryan wasn't fooled. Just as the man started to pivot, Ryan swept his gun from its holster in a smooth, lightning-fast motion, bringing it in line with the man's chest, and fired.

His opponent's bullet dug into the ground four feet in front of Ryan. The man had fired his gun in a death reflex as Ryan's bullet plowed through his heart.

Ryan stood for a moment looking at the man as the hot blue-white smoke rose and drifted in the slight breeze. Then, lowering his gun, he walked to the body. Sheriff Ed Thomas arrived at about the same time.

"What in the hell was that all about, Ryan? Who is he?"

"I don't know his name, Ed. Never did. But I'd know his face anywhere. It stems from a personal matter of some ten years ago when I was a boy of sixteen. Have you seen him around here lately?"

"Nope. Never saw him before." The sheriff motioned to the small crowd who had begun to gather to stay back. "He holds a long grudge. Must be something mighty serious between you two for him to want to just shoot ya on sight. What do ya suppose took him so long to find you?"

"I don't know that he's been looking for me. He was probably just passing through and happened to see me. Would you do me the favor of going through his pockets and saddlebags, if you can find his horse, and see what you can learn about him? I'll be nearby for a while."

Ryan walked to the hitching rail in front of Maggie's Place. Grasping the rail and staring straight ahead, he saw nothing. He only heard ghosts from his past.

Having never left the sidewalk, Susan had witnessed the entire episode. Now she could see the muscles of Ryan's jaw knotting, relaxing, and knotting again. His blue-gray eyes seemed more steel-gray than blue. She moved toward him, but stopped as Kyle stepped past her.

"Is that the sergeant?" he asked Ryan.

"That's him, Kyle. Damn, you figure he's been looking for me all this time?"

"Naw, I don't think so. Just pure happenstance. Like you said, he was probably drifting through and happened to see you."

"I wonder how many more will do the same." Ryan clenched his fists in frustration.

"Probably none. I doubt that any of the others felt about it the way he did. It's been ten or eleven years now, and you haven't run into anybody else who saw what took place that day."

"Yeah. Trouble is, I recognized the sergeant but I don't know if I would recognize them all. And there might be some who saw what happened who I don't even know about." He paused a moment, taking a deep breath. "Aw, hell." He sighed in resignation. "I'll cross that creek if I ever get to it."

"Now you're thinking straight again," Kyle agreed as they fell silent, each hoping that this was just a coincidence.

Susan was near enough to them to overhear the conversation. Stepping up to him and placing her hand on his arm, she asked, "Are you going to be all right, Ryan?"

"Yeah, I'm okay, Susie." He glanced toward the man still lying in the street. "He's not the first man I've had to kill, but you just never feel too good about a thing like this. Let's have a cup of coffee while I wait for Ed to find out what he can about the man." Taking her arm, he moved her toward the cafe they had left only a short time before.

Sheriff Thomas caught up with them before they could enter the cafe.

"Ryan, I found his horse right away. Some of the folks saw him ride in. But we didn't find anything that shed any light on him at all. Not a single thing."

"Well, see that he gets properly buried and tell the undertaker I'll pay for it next time I'm in town. But, unless you have something to charge me with, I'm gonna be heading for home now."

"Oh, hell, Ryan. You know I ain't got no charges to make against you. I was right over there in front of the barbershop and saw the whole thing. I heard you try to talk him out of it. It was a plain case of self-defense. The man challenged a Texas Ranger and got himself killed. Far as I'm concerned, the matter's closed."

"Thanks." Ryan turned to Kyle. "I'm going home. You and Hazel come on when you get ready." He turned toward the saloon where his horse was tied.

Susan started to follow him, but Kyle caught her arm.

"Let him go, Susan."

She looked from Kyle to Ryan's retreating back. "But, Kyle, he's hurting. He needs—"

"No, Susan," he interrupted, watching his friend walk away. "You can't help him. This is something he's got to work through by himself."

Susan knew Ryan was hurting. She had seen it in his eyes, heard it in his voice. "But . . . I don't understand. Why would that man, a man whose name Ryan didn't even know, want to kill him on sight? Why?"

Kyle watched Ryan ride slowly out of town. "I can't answer that, Susan."

"Can't, or won't, Kyle?" Susan pressed.

Kyle looked into Susan's troubled face—and she knew the answer to her question.

Chapter Five

"Why do you think that man wanted to kill Ryan?" Susan voiced the question that Seth and Molly were silently pondering.

What started out as such a joyful occasion only hours before, turned into a solemn, almost oppressive ride home.

"Papa?"

Seth shook his head. "I don't know, Susan. I keep turning it over in my mind, but it doesn't make any sense. Ryan is such a likable person it's hard to imagine him having any enemies. Although, I suppose, as a Texas Ranger he might have made a few along the way."

"But I heard him tell Sheriff Thomas that it had something to do with something that happened ten years ago."

"Ten years ago!" Molly exclaimed. "How

could that be? He'd have been only a boy then."

"Hmmm, ten years ago? That would have made him fifteen, maybe sixteen years old. That makes even less sense." Seth rubbed his chin as he continued to reflect on why a man from that long ago in Ryan's past would still want revenge. And for what?

Susan shivered. That was the first time she had seen two men stand face to face in a kill-or-be-killed situation. She hoped she never saw it again. She could still feel the way her heart had seemed to stop beating as she watched the man draw his gun and fire at Ryan.

She shivered again, even though the day was sunny and warm. She didn't in any way understand the why of what had happened, but she intended to find out. First thing tomorrow morning.

As soon as breakfast was over, Susan headed for Ryan's pasture. She had spent the night tossing and turning in fitful nightmares, awakening several times drenched in a cold sweat as the sound of gunshots shattered the still night air. Each time she awoke, she was grateful to discover it was just another bad dream.

Somewhere between the dark and the dawn, Susan realized that she cared very much for Ryan. She had been having one of her distorted dreams when her subconscious brain had insisted on being heard. In her dream, Ryan was walking away from her. Repeatedly, she called out to him that she loved him, but he didn't seem to hear her. The sound of her own voice crying out had awakened her.

She had huddled in her bed until dawn, wondering if it were true. She had never been in love before, so she didn't know how love was supposed to feel. But if it meant having a sick feeling in the pit of her stomach at just the thought of something bad happening to him, and feeling an overwhelming need to see him to reassure herself that he was okay, then she was most definitely afflicted with love.

As Susan approached the gate, she saw the paint mare leave the group of horses she had been grazing with and come trotting to meet her. After securing the gate, Susan rubbed the horse's nose and patted her neck a couple of times.

"I don't have time for you this morning, Patches. I've got to find your owner."

She mounted Spooky and headed for the nearest high ground. Patches followed her. Reaching the high point, she carefully surveyed the part of the pasture she could see from there. Not seeing Ryan, she set out for another high point several hundred yards away.

Although the pasture was several hundred acres in area, she had learned from her previous rides that from three places on the highest ground she could get a pretty good overview of the entire pasture.

She was so disappointed at not being able

to spot him from the third and last vantage point, she momentarily thought about riding to his house, but decided that would seem too bold. Instead, she rode down into the glade where Patches had tired of following her and was grazing on the succulent grass.

"I'll just spend a little time with you and then take another look around for your owner," she mused out loud. "Better still, I'll see if you ride as smoothly as I suspect you do."

She transferred the bridle and saddle from Spooky to Patches. As she began putting the horse through its gait, she was not at all surprised that it was perfectly trained for riding. She became so engrossed in her pleasure that she forgot all about finding Ryan. So much so that when she saw him she was so startled that she reined Patches in sharply.

Ryan was in the shade of a big pecan tree, sitting on a large dead limb that had fallen from the tree, probably the victim of a windstorm. His ground-reined horse was leisurely munching grass nearby as he casually smoked a cigarette.

Susan composed herself and rode toward him. Ryan remained silent, smiling softly as he watched her.

"Where did you come from?" Susan demanded tartly.

"No place in particular. I just saw you here and stopped to watch."

"Well, don't you have something to do besides slipping around and spying on me all the time?

Shouldn't you be out chasing outlaws or something?"

"Ain't no outlaws in particular to chase right now. Besides, it looks like I caught me a horse thief right here. Seems like I've seen that paint filly someplace before."

"You don't have a case. I haven't stolen her yet. I was just trying her out to see if she was worth stealing."

"Well, get down and come sit here in the shade while you make up your mind. I'd sure hate to have to do some horse trading with you." He chuckled. "That's a new one on me. A horsenapper who wants to look in the horse's mouth before she steals it."

Susan tried to think up a lighthearted response as she sat down beside him but nothing surfaced. She sensed he was as nervous as she.

"You're wanting to talk about what happened in town yesterday, aren't you?"

"Not unless you would like to."

Ryan smiled faintly. He knew that meant "please tell me all about it." Taking one last draw, he blew the smoke on the tip of the cigarette, watching as it flared. Then he ground the butt into the dirt with his boot heel.

"Susie, I wish I could explain the whole thing to you, but right now I just can't. I will one day. I hope it will be soon. I think the whole matter probably died with that man."

"But I heard you tell Kyle there were others."

"Yes, there were others, but I doubt any of them felt about it the way he did. It's such a thing that some would feel, even till this day, that I should be hanged. But some would feel that my actions were just and honorable."

"Then why can't it be settled? Surely those other men could find you if they wanted to. Couldn't you find them? They know your name, don't they? That man knew your name."

"Yes, he called me Ryan. That's the only name he or the others knew. And I suspect they took it to be my surname. As for being able to find me, some of them knew that I was from someplace in Texas, but Texas is a big place, you know. As to my finding them, even though I might remember a name or two, I wouldn't know where to begin to look. This didn't happen at home where we were all well known by one another. It happened in Tennessee."

"Tennessee? What were you doing in Tennessee?"

Ryan's tight-lipped expression told Susan she had gone one question too far.

"Can you at least tell me I can quit worrying about you being in imminent danger?"

"Yes, Susie, you can quit worrying about me."

"Just one more little bitty question," she pleaded, measuring a tiny distance between thumb and forefinger. "If you told me what it was you did, would it change the way I feel about you?"

"Gosh, I would hope so. I'd settle for most

anything that would change the rogue image you have of me."

"Oh, you. I don't think you're a rogue. Well, a rogue, yes, but a nice rogue. Now be serious."

"No, Susie, I don't think it would change the way you feel about me. But then I wonder how your father would feel about it. Now that's it," he stated emphatically. "I'm not going to talk about it anymore. I'm going to ride around the pasture to check on the horses. Would you like to tag along?"

"Sure, I'd love to. It'll just take a minute to saddle Spooky." She went to Patches to remove her saddle and bridle.

"Why don't you just ride the paint?"

"Her name is not 'the paint.' It's Patches. But, no, I think I'd better ride Spooky. She's already getting jealous."

Ryan approached Susie and placed his hand over hers as she grasped the saddle horn, about to pull the saddle from Patches' back.

"Well, Spooky will just have to learn to accept Patches. I decided while watching you ride her that I was going to give her to you."

"Give her to me? You want to give Patches to me?" Susan asked incredulously.

"Sure I do. I can't use her for a brood mare. She's too much of a throwback to the wild mustang. And I wouldn't want to sell her as a workhorse. It's plain to see that the two of you are fond of each other. So why shouldn't I give her to you?"

"But I can't accept such an expensive gift."

Ryan looked at her in puzzlement. "Why not? I want you to have her."

Susan patted the mare's soft muzzle, trying to figure out how to explain her predicament to Ryan. She certainly wanted the horse and she knew Ryan meant well, but what would her mother say about such a gift?

Ryan watched the conflicting emotions chase each other across Susan's face and he didn't understand any of them. "You do like the horse, don't you?"

"Of course I do. But . . ."

"And you want her, don't you?"

"Well, yes, but . . ."

"But nothing. She's yours. End of debate." Ryan started to refasten Patches' cinch.

Susan stilled his hand. "Ryan, you don't understand. Of course I want Patches but it's not . . . proper for a single man to give a single woman an expensive gift. People would think . . ." Susan's face flushed a deep red, and she turned her back to Ryan as she mumbled, "Well, you know what people would think."

"Damn it! I couldn't care less what people think," he stormed. "If I want to give a lady a gift, I'll damn well do it! And to hell with what people think. And if some busybody wants to make something out of it, they'll have me to deal with."

Susan turned to face Ryan. She had hurt his feelings and she hadn't meant to. She knew there were no strings attached to his gift, but he just didn't understand how people loved to gossip.

Placing one hand against the side of his face, she said, "I'm sorry, I didn't intend to hurt your feelings."

"You didn't," he replied gruffly, pulling away from her to yank the saddle off Patches and swing it onto Spooky's back.

As he reached under Spooky for the saddle cinch, Susan interrupted him. "Wait a minute." An idea had begun to form in her mind. She really did want Patches and the hurt look in Ryan's eyes when she'd turned down his gift made her heart twist with pain knowing she was the cause for his distress.

Ryan dropped the cinch, straightening to look at Susan. "What?"

"I changed my mind. I accept your gift, but with one small request."

Ryan raised an eyebrow at her sudden capitulation. "And that is?"

"That you'll let me keep Patches in your pasture. Just for a little while," she hastily added. "I'll groom her and take care of her, but just not take her home with me yet. After we've known each other longer, I don't think Mama or Papa would object to my accepting her as a gift." She looked up at him expectantly. "Is that okay?"

He smiled at the almost childlike look on her face. "I think I like that idea even better. If Patches stays here, I'll get to see you more often," he agreed, planting a playful kiss on her upturned lips. "Now why didn't I think of that?"

His question gave Susan an opening for a little mischievous needling that she couldn't resist. "I guess you're just a little slow at some things."

She stood with her hands on her hips, head tilted cockily to one side, her eyes gleaming in enjoyment of her dry humor at his expense. Her lips parted in a patronizing smile.

"Is that so?" he said, pulling her into his arms. "I believe you once accused me of even being slow to take my kissing chances."

"You're not getting any 'kissing chances' now. I've got to . . ."

Her words were muffled and trailed off as Ryan's lips closed over hers. He pressed her close to him. Her hands ceased pushing against his chest, moved to the back of his head, and she timidly kissed him back.

With his arms locked around her waist, he leaned back to look into her eyes before his lips closed over hers again, this time with a fierce longing. His heart thundered against his rib cage as his lips savored her sweetness. He felt her startled movement as his gentle kiss turned more aggressive.

Susan wrapped her arms around Ryan's neck as she leaned into his kiss. His persuasive gentleness sent an inner warmth flooding through her. The sensations assaulting her senses started in the vicinity of her womanhood, vibrated down to her toes and back to the top of her head. Breathless and lightheaded, she clung to him.

Ryan pulled her tight against him, deepening his kiss until he felt like he was drowning in her taste and scent. He cupped her breast with one hand as his other hand roamed across her back and down her behind, pulling her against him. He was a man tortured past human endurance with the image of the first time he had seen her. His mind wouldn't—couldn't—let go of it. It had returned nightly to torture and torment him.

Slowly, he backed her up against the pecan tree, effectively trapping her body between him and the tree. He straddled her legs with his, bringing her body into intimate contact with his. His mouth moved from her lips to nibble at her ear before trailing kisses down her neck. His hands went on a journey of their own, tracing each curve of her body. Pausing to free the top buttons of her shirt, he released the creamy mounds straining against the material to his hungry eyes and mouth.

Susan groaned as his tongue and teeth on her sensitive earlobe sent shivers of pleasure skittering down her spine. She sucked her breath in, then gasped for air when Ryan's warm mouth closed over one hardened nipple. She clutched his shoulders in a desperate attempt to keep her feet beneath her, her legs suddenly too weak to support her. Never had she felt such unbridled passion before. She squirmed as her body heated, twisting her head from side to side, alternately trying to push him away, while at the same time pulling him closer.

"Ryan . . . Ryan," she moaned as pleasure swept through her. "Oh, Ryan . . ."

The sound of her voice, which didn't sound like her voice at all, startled her back to reality. She pushed Ryan's mouth away from her breasts.

"Ryan . . . don't . . . Please, stop," she pleaded raggedly, trying to push away from him.

Ryan groaned and took a step back from her when he realized she was pushing him away. What was it about Susan that made him forget himself? He couldn't believe he had her half undressed in broad open daylight where any of the ranch hands could have happened by and seen them. Damn, was he just plumb crazy!

His body ached for her. She'd been constantly on his mind since the first time he'd seen her. He shook his head in puzzlement. This woman did strange things to him. And he didn't understand it at all. All he knew was that he wanted her like he'd never wanted another woman in his entire life. What was wrong with him?

He drew a long, ragged breath into his lungs, exhaling slowly. "Susie, sweet, beautiful Susie. It's all right, baby," he crooned, smoothing her hair away from her face.

Ryan pulled her to him, holding her tight against him, waiting for his heart to settle down to a somewhat normal pace. He could feel Susan's heart thudding hard against his chest as she, too, struggled to regain control of her emotions.

"It's all right, baby, I understand," he assured her. He kissed the top of her head as she buried her face against his neck.

"I think I'd better go now," she said shakily, pulling away from him.

Ryan took her by the arm. "Hey, wait a minute. I thought we were going for a ride."

"We were, but it seems that something distracted us."

Ryan's shoulders slumped. "You're not going to let me off easy, are you? You're mad at me."

"Oh, quit fishing for sympathy. You know I'm not mad at you."

He stepped closer to her and placed his hands on her shoulders. "Then why won't you go with me?" He leaned down and placed a light kiss on her forehead. "Don't you trust my powers of restraint anymore?"

She smiled faintly as she gazed up at him. "I'm not worried about *your* restraint. I can handle you." She pulled his head down and kissed him softly on the mouth. "It's *my* resistance I've lost faith in."

She whirled and ran to Spooky. Placing her left foot in the stirrup, she took hold of the saddle horn and swung her right leg up and. . . .

"Susie, wait! Your cinch isn't . . . fastened." Ryan's well-meant warning came too late. She had already started to swing onto the saddle.

"Oh, no," she cried out as she fell. She landed on her back with the saddle on top of her,

her hand still clutching the pommel. She lay there a moment, trying to comprehend what had happened.

Ryan, seeing that she wasn't hurt, started laughing as he came to help her up.

Pushing the heavy saddle off her, she jumped to her feet, glaring at Ryan and madder than hell.

"What in the hell do you mean putting a saddle on a horse and not fastening the cinch!" she yelled.

"Ahha, the little girl who likes to taunt a man and then run away got caught in her own trick. Didn't she? That'll teach you not to do that again." He laughed, rocking back on his heels.

"Well, I don't know about that, but it'll sure teach me to see that my saddle cinch is fastened before I do," she grumbled, grabbing the blanket off the ground and tossing it on Spooky's back.

When she turned to pick up the saddle, still mumbling under her breath, she caught a glimpse of Ryan's smirking face.

"Need some help?" he asked, not even trying to conceal his amusement.

She straightened up and, looking into his laughing eyes, replied haughtily, "I don't think so, Mister Sommerall. I've had enough surprises for one day, thank you very much."

Just as Susan hefted the saddle to place it on her back, Spooky chose that moment to shy away, causing Susan to lose her balance and lunge forward.

Ryan grabbed her around the waist, preventing her and the offending saddle from once more tumbling to the ground.

"You certainly are having a hard time with that saddle today, Susie." He tried to keep from laughing out loud but not hard enough. Laughter bubbled up from deep within his chest.

As Ryan held her suspended in air, saddle in hand, it suddenly occurred to her what a comical sight she must look. Dropping the saddle and regaining her footing, she turned, arms akimbo, lips twitching, to face Ryan. She grinned, trying to look contrite. But, before she could stop it, a chuckle escaped and then she was laughing at herself as hard as he was.

Susan wiped at the tears running down her face. "It wasn't that funny," she protested, even though she couldn't stop laughing.

"You should have seen it from my angle," Ryan assured her, drying his own eyes. "Would you *please* let me put that damn saddle on Spooky before you hurt yourself?" he begged.

Susan rubbed her bottom, and muttered, "I already did."

"I'll be glad to do that for you," he volunteered, moving toward her.

Susan retreated a step. "Never mind. If you'll just saddle my horse, I'll tend to my own wounds, Mister Sommerall."

Grinning, he shrugged his shoulders and turned to pick up the saddle.

After saddling Spooky, Ryan gave Susan a courtly bow. "Your steed awaits you, my lady."

Stepping to the horse, she raised the stirrup and peeked under it.

"What are you doing?"

Susan gave him an impish grin. "Just making sure you remembered to buckle the cinch this time."

"Why you little—"

Susan all but jumped into the saddle to make her escape.

But this time Ryan was prepared for her action. He grabbed her and hauled her off the saddle and into his arms. "I thought you'd learned your lesson about kissing and running," he warned.

"I didn't 'kiss and run,' " she admonished him. "I just ran this time." She giggled.

"Well, I'm kissing."

He laid a kiss on her that made her tingle from the top of her head to the bottom of her feet. When he raised his lips from hers, they were both breathing as if they'd just made a run for their lives.

He put her back in the saddle.

"Now you'd better run," he warned huskily, slapping her horse on the rump.

Ryan watched Susan ride away. The realization that his feelings for her ran deeper than he'd thought possible made his chest tighten with pain. Mounting his horse, he sat watching until he could no longer see her in the distance.

Why, after all these years, had the sergeant shown up? Just when he'd begun to believe that his past was truly behind him, and he might be able to live a normal life. Why did the man have to show up in Comanche now? Now that he'd found Susie?

Never had he felt so frustrated in his life. He wanted to lash out at something, anything to relieve his tension. Spurring his horse, he raced across the pasture as if he was trying to outrun his past, stopping only when he and his horse were both sweating and exhausted.

"Sorry, boy." He patted the blowing horse's neck, ashamed of himself for setting such a punishing pace.

He walked the winded horse back to the barn. His wild ride had eased his tension some but had not solved his problem. There had to be a way, if only he could think of it.

All these years he'd accepted the fact that because of his impulsive action, he'd never be able to marry and settle down with a family. At first it had bothered him greatly. But then he'd met Clara, and it hadn't seemed to matter as much.

But that was before he'd found Susie. Now it mattered more than anything else in the world. He wanted Susie.

"Ryan? Did you hear me?"

Ryan looked around him in a daze. He'd been so deep in thought about his problem, he hadn't paid any attention to his surroundings.

"What?" He shook his head. "Sorry, Kyle. I was thinking. What did you say?"

Kyle smiled knowingly. "Saw Susan in the

pasture, didn't ya? That pretty little gal's got you tied in knots, ain't she? You've been as moody as a gimp-legged mule. Why don't you do all of us a favor and court her?"

Ryan slammed his hand against the wall, venting his frustration. "Damn it, Kyle. You, of all people, should know why I can't do that. Do you think I don't want to? Don't you understand? What woman would want to marry a man who stands the risk of being hanged or hauled off to spend the rest of his life in some damn stinking prison for murder!"

Kyle felt his friend's anguish as strong as if it were his own. He'd known Ryan since the day he was born, and he knew him to be an honorable man. Even though they'd never talked about it before, Kyle had long suspected the reason why Ryan shied away from marriageable women.

"Ryan, I don't think there's much chance of that happening now, with the sergeant's being dead. From what you told me, I just have to believe the past died with him yesterday."

Ryan's pain was reflected in his eyes. "But what if you're wrong, Kyle? What if I court Susie and fall in love with her? If you're wrong and they do come after me, what do I do then? And what would it do to Susie?"

Kyle looked Ryan straight in the eyes. "I think it's too late for you to worry about falling in love with Susan."

Kyle's statement chilled Ryan all the way to his heart.

Chapter Six

"Papa, why don't you take off from fence building today and let's go fishing?" Susan asked, pushing the eggs around on her plate.

She was restless from spending the night in disturbing dreams rather than peaceful sleep. Come to think of it, she wasn't sure she'd had a peaceful night's sleep since she'd first met Ryan.

Having acknowledged to herself that she was in love with Ryan, and remembering the intensity of their embrace in the pasture, she was left with an unsettling feeling of anticipation.

"I sure would like to do that, Susan. But we're just about finished with the fence. Billy and Jimmy Don Morgan were going to work on it for a while last night, digging the last of the post holes. I think we might finish that fence today. And I promise you in the next day or so we'll go try out that fishing hole." Seth drained the last of his coffee and pecked Molly on the cheek before heading out to the barn to saddle his horse.

Bored and with nothing to keep her occupied, Susan walked with her father to the barn and helped him saddle his horse.

"You certainly made an impression on Billy the other day when you came to tell me to come home early for the fish fry at Ryan's place. That boy asked more questions than a schoolmarm after you left. I suppose, if you're too bored, you could always ride over and visit with him while we work."

"Oh, Papa." Susan blushed at her father's teasing. "He's sweet and nice-looking, too, but he's just a boy."

"Ha. He's about eighteen, same age as you."

"Well, I'm just not interested in him."

"Yeah, I know. I was just teasing." Seth put his arm around his daughter's shoulders as they walked his horse out of the barn. "I knew the minute you heard Ryan say there were fish in that pool, you'd be hankering to go. I promise we'll go fishing tomorrow or the next day for sure. Okay?"

Susan nodded her head as her father mounted the gelding. The sound of hoofbeats caught her attention and she turned in that direction.

"Wait up, Papa. Here comes Ryan and Kyle."

"Hmmm, wonder what they're in such a hurry about?"

As they reined in their galloping horses, Ryan pointed in the direction of the Morgan ranch. "Have you seen that smoke, Seth? Looks like it's coming from Jim Morgan's place."

"Sure looks like smoke all right," Seth agreed after a moment's study. "But it doesn't seem like it could be that far away. It's more than three miles from here to Jim's place."

"Well, distance can be deceiving on a clear morning like this. Kyle and I are going to ride on to get a better look. You might come along. Just in case."

"Of course I will. Let's get going."

Even though they felt a sense of urgency, the men held their horses to a moderate gallop in order to keep from winding them, as they left Seth's ranch.

Susan worked feverishly to saddle her horse. She knew her father and Ryan, too, for that matter would object to her following them. But there was excitement in the air, and she wasn't going to miss it.

"What in the world is going on?" her mother called after her as she ran through the house to her bedroom to get her rifle.

"There's a fire across the way," she answered, her voice loud with excitement. "They think it might be the Morgan place," she added as she dashed out the kitchen door.

"Susan, come back here!" Molly yelled from the back porch.

"Don't worry, Mother. I'll be back in a little while," Susan shouted as she sprang on

Spooky's back and galloped away.

"Susan Marie! Oh, what's the use," Molly mumbled to herself. "All I ever get is 'don't worry.' She's running wilder here than she did back home."

After about two miles, the men topped out on a low ridge. There was no longer any doubt where the smoke was coming from. The Morgan barn was in full blaze, and they could hear the faint sounds of gunshots.

They didn't break their horses' pace as they descended the slope of the ridge. Reaching the bottom of the slope, they were hidden from view from the Morgan house by a cluster of scrub oak and hackberry trees.

The trees were about three-quarters of a mile from them and a quarter of a mile from the ranch buildings. They kept the trees between themselves and the house as they closed in.

Ryan pulled his pistol and twirled the cylinder to be sure it was fully loaded. He knew it was; he was only acting out a compulsive habit. Kyle and Seth performed the same ritual. Then, drawing their rifles from their saddle scabbards, they checked to see that they were ready for use, too.

They rode through the cluster of trees, stopping when they reached the edge. From there they had a clear view. The Morgans were under attack by a band of Comanche Indians.

The men cleared the trees just in time to see the Indians charge out of a dry wash about two hundred yards from the Morgan house. Within a hundred yards of the house, the Indians fired a volley and then retreated quickly to the wash again which was high enough to give the Indians cover from the Morgans' return gunfire.

"I count fourteen Indians and two riderless horses," Kyle observed. "The Morgans must have already got a couple of 'em."

"What are we gonna do, Ryan?" Seth prompted.

"This is a tough one to figure, Seth, seeing as it's more than three hundred yards to cross with no cover."

Ryan had hardly finished talking when they saw the Indians leave the gully and charge the house again. Whooping and screeching, the Comanches fired and retreated to the gully again.

Ryan made his decision. "Looks like that's what they've been doing right along. We're gonna wait a couple of minutes and see if they do it again. If they do, then the instant they leave the gully, we're going to charge in. We should reach the gully by the time they retreat from the house. We'll have the advantage of surprise. But what will happen after we engage them is anybody's guess. We'll just have to do the best we can as things develop."

"I suggest you do what you think is best and me and Seth will just follow your lead," Kyle said.

The Indians made their charge just as Ryan had anticipated they would.

"Let's go!" he yelled.

The men sprinted their horses full speed for the gully and were in easy range by the time the Indians began their retreat from the house. When they opened up with deadly volleys from their lever-action Winchesters, the Indians in startled confusion continued their retreat to the gully.

Ryan was a couple of lengths out front. Just before he got to the gully, he swerved the big black stallion sharply to the left and brought him around in a wide loop, stuffing bullets into the magazine of his rifle as he went. Kyle and Seth did the same.

They left two Indians dead on the ground and three more wounded but able to sit their horses. One of them fled down the gully.

Ryan led off another charge directly at the Indians. As the men closed in on them, the rest of the Indians fled.

Ryan had reined his horse to follow them when he saw the first Indian who had escaped leave the gully and charge up the slope toward some large oak trees.

"Good God Almighty!" he exclaimed as he saw what had distracted the Indian from his flight.

He spurred his horse into full speed toward the trees, at the same time yelling to Seth and Kyle to follow the rest of the Indians.

When Susan reached the top of the ridge, she saw the men about halfway between her and the trees they were apparently heading for. Hearing the gunfire, she decided not to follow directly behind them. She set out at a fast gallop toward two large oak trees that were about four hundred yards below the burning barn.

She reached the trees just as the men made their first charge. She was awestruck as she reined in her heavily breathing horse and watched the battle unfold.

When one of the Indians fled down the gully toward her, she suddenly realized that he would pass no more than a hundred yards below her.

She pulled her rifle from the scabbard and tucked the stock between her arm and body, wondering frantically whether she should try to shoot him.

Suddenly the Indian left the gully and came straight toward her, yelling and whooping. He was a terrifying sight in only a breechcloth and moccasins. Most of his face was painted black, and his body was decorated with small yellow and white circles.

He was almost upon her before she was finally able to move. She didn't have time to shoulder the rifle. She simply pointed it and pulled the trigger.

The bullet gashed the left side of his rib cage, and he lost whatever control he might have had of his horse.

Spooky reared and began to spin away from the oncoming horse. The Indian's horse plunged into the side of Spooky's hindquarters, knocking her off her feet and partially from under Susan.

This made it easier for Susan to fall in the opposite direction from which Spooky was falling, thus preventing her leg from being caught under the horse. She had to scramble fast to get away from Spooky's thrashing hoofs as the horse struggled to regain its feet.

The other horse had gone down from its impact with Spooky, causing the Comanche to take a hard fall.

Susan was on her feet before the Indian was, looking frantically around her for her rifle. By the time she'd spotted where it had landed several feet down the slope, it was too late. The Indian was on his feet. With a savage yell and his knife held high, he charged her.

She had to try to make it to her rifle. Whirling to run, she saw nothing but blackness which was moving and making noise. She slowly took in that it was a great black stallion thundering past her.

Ryan leaned far away from his horse and fell. His outstretched arm knocked the running Indian down with him to the ground. The blade of a large knife sunk deep into the muscle of Ryan's left shoulder, stopping only as the point grated against the bone.

The savage sounds coming from the men snapped Susan's addled mind to attention, and she ran to her rifle.

Ryan rolled on his back as the Indian sprang to his feet and charged Ryan. He caught the

Indian in the midriff with his feet and threw him back and sprawling on the ground.

Ryan rolled quickly to where his pistol had fallen to the ground. As the Indian reached his feet, Ryan's bullet and the bullet from Susan's rifle struck him in the chest at the same time, rocking him backwards. His knees buckling, the Indian fell to the ground, shuddered and died.

Ryan had moved no further than a sitting position when Susan reached him. She laid her rifle aside as she dropped to her knees between his outstretched legs.

"Ryan, I . . ."

Ryan gathered her into his arms and pulled her close against him, burying his face in her breasts.

Susan was shocked. She was expecting a tongue-lashing, but his embrace was telling her of his relief that she was unhurt. She encircled his head with her arms and clasped him closer to her chest.

Ryan pressed her tighter against him. The exchange of warm strange energy flowing between them conveyed their deep caring in a way that words could not.

"I thought for a moment I wasn't going to make it to you in time." Ryan's strangled words were muffled against her breast as he held her to him. "Oh, God, Susie, I was so afraid I would be too late!"

Susan turned toward her father, already dismounting as his horse slid to a stop, spraying them with dirt. "Papa, Ryan's hurt. The Indian stabbed him in the shoulder."

Seth opened his pocketknife as he dropped to his knees beside Ryan. He immediately began to cut the younger man's shirt away from the wound.

"Why didn't you just shoot the Indian instead of taking him on hand to hand?"

"I couldn't shoot him. By the time I got close enough, Susan was between me and him."

Seth paused from his destruction of Ryan's shirt and glared at Susan.

"Please, Papa. I know I'm in for a bawling out but not now. We've got to help Ryan, he's bleeding badly."

Seth snapped his pocketknife shut. "We can't do it here. That's a nasty stab wound. We'll have to get him to the house to clean and bandage it properly. Get his horse."

Ryan started to get to his feet but fell back down as a grunt of pain escaped him.

"Papa, we'll have to make a sling for his arm."

"It's not my arm, Susie. It's my leg." Ryan pulled his breeches' leg up, exposing his already swelling right knee.

"You think you can ride?" Seth asked.

"Yeah. I'll make it all right. Might need a little help getting mounted."

They'd just gotten Ryan settled on his horse when Kyle rode up to them. "You hurt bad, Ryan?"

"Naw, just a knife wound in my shoulder and

my right knee is banged up some. Why didn't ya'll keep after those Indians?"

"Them Indians ain't gonna give us no more trouble. Six of 'em are dead, and at least half of the rest of 'em are wounded. We're gonna be sure they git on out of here, though. Slim Wilson and his two sons just rode in. They're waiting for me down there now," Kyle said.

Ryan glanced in the direction of the Morgan house. "I see there's already seven or eight men around the Morgans' house." Ryan click-clicked his horse into motion, grimacing as pain shot through his arm.

"There's probably some more on their way, too," Kyle observed. "I'll get a couple more of 'em to go along with me and Slim and his boys. We probably won't try to catch up to the Indians. We'll just follow them a few miles to be sure they move on out of here."

Kyle shook his head as he rode alongside Ryan. "Them Comanches sure were a determined bunch. Slim said they tried to steal his horses about midnight last night, but he heard 'em in time to run 'em off. Well, I'd better git going. I'll probably be back before dark," he added as he rode off down the slope.

Ryan raised his good arm in acknowledgment.

"Jim," Seth called as they approached the group of men and boys standing around the barn, watching as it burned to the ground, helpless to do anything about it.

Jim Morgan walked quickly to them. "Sure do appreciate you folks coming to help us. Don't know when I was so glad to see anybody before," he declared. "Damn, Ryan, you're wounded!"

Ryan shrugged his shoulders. "Nothing much. Just a knife stab."

"It's a pretty bad wound, Jim," Seth corrected. "And his knee is hurt, too. We'll clean and bandage his shoulder here and then get him home. Will you send somebody to town to tell Doc Thornton to get out to Ryan's house to sew up his shoulder and take a look at his knee?"

"Sure will, Seth. Lynn is in the house. She'll help you take care of the shoulder, Ryan."

"Hi, Susan." The cheerful greeting came from Billy Morgan who was striding toward them.

"Hello, Billy."

"What are you doing here?"

"Same as everybody else. I saw the smoke and came to see what was causing it."

"Damn, Ryan. When did you start taking women with you to do your Indian fighting?" Billy goaded.

"Watch your tongue, boy!" Jim's voice was sharp with anger. "You were taught better manners than that."

"Aw, I was just joshing, Pa."

"Well, this isn't the time for it."

Ryan wasn't paying any attention to Billy. He was watching Susan. To his way of thinking, Billy seemed a little too friendly to suit him.

"Ryan didn't *take* me with him, Billy. I came by myself. Now, if you'll excuse me, I need to tend to Ryan's wounds." Susan was worried about Ryan and in no mood for Billy's unwanted attention.

It galled Ryan that Jim and Seth had to help him dismount and into the house. His knee was swollen so badly that just the pressure from the fabric of his breeches was excruciatingly painful. He exhaled raggedly as they eased him into a chair. For a moment, he'd been afraid he was going to black out from the pain.

Lynn Morgan could tell from the sweat beading his forehead and his pallid complexion that Ryan was in great pain. She set a pan of warm water on the table.

"Susan, help Ryan ease his shirt off while I get the coal oil and my scissors. Be very careful not to pull the wound," she cautioned. "The bleeding seems to be slowing. If the shirt is stuck to the blood, we'll have to soak it off with warm water."

Susan nodded her head and carefully began easing Ryan's shirt away from the puncture. From the way his jaw was clenched, she could tell he was in more pain than he'd admit to.

When Lynn returned with the coal oil and scissors, Ryan said, "Lynn, cut up the side of my breeches. I've got to release the pressure on my knee. It hurts worse than the stab." Hurt, hell! That was a major understatement. His knee was throbbing in time to his rapid heartbeat.

"Oh, my goodness!" Lynn exclaimed, after revealing his swollen knee. It had already started turning purple. She pulled a chair around to face Ryan and gingerly helped him prop his leg on it. "Are you sure it's not broken?"

Ryan shook his head. "I don't think so. That relieved the pain considerably."

Susan felt helpless. "What do we do now?" She looked at Lynn, twisting her hands together.

Ryan heard the quiver in her voice. "It's all right, Susie. It's not near as bad as it looks," he assured her, taking one of her trembling hands in his. "It helped a whole lot just releasing the pressure on it."

Knowing Susan needed to keep busy in order to defuse the tension after her ordeal, Lynn handed her a wet rag.

"First, we're going to cleanse the dried blood from around the wound. Next, we're going to disinfect the wound with coal oil and bind it until Doc Thornton can take a look at it." Her voice was firm and calm as she inspected the slash in Ryan's shoulder. "Hmmm, I think it's going to need a couple of stitches, Ryan. But we'll let Doc decide that, if it's okay with you."

"Yeah, that's fine, Lynn." He watched Susan as she carefully did as Lynn instructed her. When she finished, their eyes met. "You okay?"

Susan nodded her head before looking away. She didn't want Ryan to see the tears welling in her eyes. She felt so guilty. If it hadn't been for her impulsiveness, Ryan wouldn't have gotten hurt. In fact, he could have been killed and it would have been all her fault. That thought made her sick to her stomach.

"The fire's out," Jim stated, walking into the kitchen. "We managed to keep it from spreading to the other outbuildings."

Seth leaned over and peered at Ryan's purple knee. "Hmmm, doesn't look too good."

"Doesn't feel too good," Ryan quipped.

Lynn handed Jim a cup of coffee. "Anyone else hurt?"

Jim shook his head and took the cup Lynn offered him. "No."

"Ryan, maybe we ought to borrow Jim's wagon to get you home. Seems to me that knee needs to be kept as still as possible. Is that all right with you, Jim? I'll bring it back in the morning when I come over to help clean that mess up out there," Seth said.

Susan spoke up before Ryan had a chance to refuse the loan of the wagon. "I can drive Ryan home, Papa."

"Well, that would help. Is that all right with you, Ryan?"

Ryan looked at Susan, trying to get her to meet his eyes. But she wouldn't. "Yeah, that's fine. I'll have my men bring the wagon back this afternoon. They can help ya'll clean up."

"Susan, tell your mother that I won't be home for lunch, but I'll be there in time for supper."

Susan mutely nodded her head and walked outside.

*   *   *

Ryan waited until they were on the road and out of sight of the others before questioning Susan. He could tell she was very troubled and upset. She hadn't spoken more than ten words the whole time she and Lynn were tending his wound and she hadn't spoken a single word since they'd left the Morgans'.

"Want to tell me what's wrong, Susie?"

She shook her head, afraid to speak, knowing the tears were just below the surface, waiting to spill forth.

"Stop the wagon."

Ryan was riding in the back of the wagon with his leg propped up with a quilt to cushion it from the jolts, and couldn't see her face.

Susan ignored the request.

"I said stop the damn wagon, Susan," he ordered.

Susan reluctantly pulled the horses to a halt, but she didn't say anything or look around at Ryan. The tears had started.

"Are you crying?"

She shook her head.

"Damn it, Susie, look at me."

Again she shook her head.

"Susan Bradford!" he bellowed. "Get down off that seat and come back here where I can see you. I'm not talking to the back of your head. And we *are* going to talk about this *right now*."

Susan's shoulders shook and great sobs escaped her.

Ryan's heart twisted. "Baby, don't do this to yourself. Please, don't do this," he pleaded. "Come here."

Susan climbed over the seat into the back of the wagon. Ryan pulled her down beside him with his good arm, holding her to him as she cried.

"Susie, tell me what's wrong. Please."

"I almost got you killed!" she wailed, sobbing harder. "If I hadn't followed you, that Indian wouldn't have come after me and you wouldn't have had to fight him and—and gotten hurt."

"Susie, look at me. You didn't know we were riding into an Indian raid. It's not your fault. And my wound isn't that bad. Really. I'll be good as new in a day or so." Using his chin, he brushed the hair away from her forehead and replaced it with a kiss. "Please don't cry."

Susan sniffed. Why did her nose have to run every time she cried?

"Why did that Indian stop? He was far enough ahead of you that he might have gotten away if he'd kept going. Why would he stop just to kill me?"

A lump rose in his throat, and a chill ran down his spine. "I suspect his intent was to take you captive. But after you shot him and Spooky collided with him, knocking him off his horse, I think that's when he decided to . . . kill you."

All the horror stories she had ever heard about white women being taken captive by the Indians rushed to her mind. Her voice was barely a whisper at the implication of Ryan's speculation. "A captive?"

Ryan held her securely to him. "I'm so glad I was riding Pegasus. He's probably the only horse in the whole state of Texas that would have got me to you in time."

Chapter Seven

Doc Thornton removed his spectacles, tucking them into his shirt pocket. "Keep those stitches dry. I'll stop by in a week or so and take 'em out. If you'll stay off that leg four or five days, and I mean completely off it, and then favor it a few days, it'll heal. But if you go hobbling around on it now, you'll still be hobbling a month from now."

Ryan scowled. The idea of being cooped up in the house for almost a week didn't appeal to him in the least. Especially if it meant he wouldn't get to see Susan for that long.

"I'll do the best I can to see that he follows your orders, Doctor," Hazel said, giving Ryan a stern look. "I've tanned his breeches before and I can do it again, if I have to."

The doctor nodded his head sagely. "Doesn't

surprise me in the least." He picked up his black bag. "See ya in about a week, Ryan."

"Thanks for coming out, Doc." Ryan was in a foul mood, but it wasn't the doctor's fault. "I'll stop by your office next week. No need for you to make another trip all the way out here."

"I'll bring you something to eat after I show the doctor out."

Ryan nodded his acknowledgment before turning his gaze to the world outside his bedroom window. His mind replayed every horrifying second of the morning's events. It made him shudder even now to think how close the Indian had come to killing Susan.

Closing his eyes, he pinched the bridge of his nose with his thumb and forefinger, trying to ward off the threatening headache. He knew without a doubt that he'd relive those tense moments for a long time to come.

Susan stood silently in the doorway. Ryan was propped up on pillows with his eyes closed. His upper body was naked; a sheet covered his lower half. The white bandages around his shoulder and under his arm stood out in stark contrast with his tanned chest and dark curly chest hairs.

Even though he was frowning, he was handsome. Her heartbeat quickened. Her love for Ryan was all-consuming. She had considered waiting until tomorrow to come back, but she just couldn't stand it another minute. She had to see him today.

Twice now she had witnessed his staring into the face of death and winning. This time, as before, she was overwhelmed with the need to see for herself that he was all right.

She didn't want to disturb his sleep because he needed the rest. She knew he must be totally exhausted from the morning's turmoil. Now that she'd seen him, she could wait until tomorrow to talk with him.

Ryan opened his eyes just as Susan turned to leave. He thought for a moment that his intense yearning to see her had conjured up her image. The rustle of her skirt assured him, however, that she was real.

"Susie, don't go." He held out his hand to her.

"Ryan," she whispered, rushing into his outstretched arms.

They held on to each other as if it would be the last time, each filling the emptiness inside them with the other's touch.

Sitting on the side of the bed, Susan smoothed the frown lines from his forehead, savoring the look and feel of him. "I was worried about you," she stated simply.

"I thought you had gone home."

"I did. I had to let Mama know what happened. Papa didn't want her to worry when he didn't come home for lunch."

"I'm glad you came back."

"What did the doctor say?"

"He told me to stay off my leg for a few days. I'll probably die from boredom. Nothing to do but sit in this bed and stare out the window." He sighed melodramatically.

Susan giggled. "You're fishing for sympathy, Ryan Sommerall," she accused.

"Did it work?" he questioned.

"Did you doubt it for a minute?"

Hazel smiled as she heard the laughter coming from Ryan's room. Susan was good for Ryan. She had done what no other woman had been able to accomplish, and several had tried. She had broken through Ryan's shell of resistance. And there wasn't a doubt in Hazel's mind that Susan, if she hadn't already, would easily conquer his heart.

"I'm glad to see that you were able to get the grouch to smile," Hazel said, entering the room and setting the tray of food on the nightstand. "I fixed you a sandwich, too, Susan. Figured you might be hungry by now."

"Thank you, Hazel."

"I am not a grouch," he grumbled, as Hazel smiled and left the room.

Hazel sat at the kitchen table doing some mending and nervously waiting for Kyle to return. The sun had settled in the west nearly an hour earlier. She'd expected him home before now.

She lay her mending aside when she heard the men returning from the Morgan ranch. Hurrying to the back door, she was relieved to see that Kyle was with them.

She immediately started putting the food she'd kept warm on the table. They'd stopped at the pump to wash up a bit, but Hazel knew they were more interested in filling their empty stomachs than getting clean.

Kyle was the first one through the door. He hugged Hazel, knowing without her saying so that she had worried until she'd seen him ride up. "I hope you didn't fret too much. I surely intended to be back before now, but we wanted to be sure those renegades were long gone from here. What did Doc say about Ryan's wounds?"

"He put a couple of stitches in his shoulder and told him to stay off his leg for several days."

"Hmmm. Knowing Ryan as we do, did you tell the doctor it'd be easier to stop the wind from blowing than to keep Ryan in bed even for one day?"

"Oh, I think he'll follow the doctor's orders this time. Susan told him what would happen if he didn't." Hazel laughed at the skeptical looks Kyle and the other men were giving her. "She told him she'd come visit him if he did, but she wouldn't come if he didn't."

"Bribery will do a man in every time," Kyle quipped as he and the rest of the men laughed.

The men wolfed down their supper as if they were afraid someone was going to take it away from them.

Kyle pushed back his chair. "Guess I'd better tell Ryan how things went. Reckon he's still awake?"

"If he's not, he said for you to wake him when you got back," Hazel said.

Kyle knocked at Ryan's door before entering. "Hear tell you gonna be laid up a spell," he said, straddling a chair by the bed.

Ryan laid aside the book he'd been reading. "Yeah, for a few days anyway. How'd it go? Did any other Indians join up with them?"

"Not that we saw. They tried to circle back around west but when they saw we weren't gonna let 'em, they headed north toward Erath County. Sure got a bad feeling 'bout all this, though." Kyle shook his head.

Ryan frowned. "Me, too. It's those damn buffalo hunters who's got them all stirred up. I need you to go into town and take care of some things for me tomorrow. Stop by the hardware store first and send a wagonload of lumber out to the Morgans. And then post a letter to the Rangers at Fort Fisher and another one to Governor Coke. Better let them know what's happening up here just in case we need some help."

Kyle nodded his head, rising from the chair. "Will do. What about the men? The Morgans sure have a mess over there and could certainly use the help. You want a couple of them to go back tomorrow?"

"Yeah."

"If you don't need anything else tonight, Ryan, I'm going on home," Hazel said from the doorway.

"Thank you, Hazel. I'm fine. See you both tomorrow."

* * *

Ryan glanced out the window. It looked like it might rain. He frowned. If it rained, Susan wouldn't be able to come see him today as she had for the past two days.

The swelling in his knee was beginning to go down, but it still pained him when he attempted to put weight on it. He hobbled to the table and two chairs set in front of the window. Picking up the deck of cards, he decided to play solitaire to pass the time and hoped it didn't rain.

"Frowning will give you wrinkles," Susan said cheerfully as she walked into Ryan's room. "Where's Hazel? I knocked but she wasn't in the kitchen."

"She probably had to go do something at her house. And I had good reason to frown. I didn't think you'd be able to come today."

"Why not?"

"Because it looks like it's gonna rain."

She shook her head. "Nah, it's not going to—"

Thunder drowned out the rest of her sentence.

She looked sheepishly at Ryan. "Of course I could be wrong."

Ryan threw back his head and laughed. Her ignoring the approaching storm just to spend a few hours with him pleased him immensely. He'd worry about getting her home later. Right now, all he wanted was to be with her, to hear her laughter, and to see her sparkling eyes.

Without him even being aware of when or how it had happened, Susan had invaded his very soul, and he didn't care. He didn't want to understand it; he just wanted to experience it. When she was with him, all of his senses were as alive and intense as the lightning flashing outside the window. She had become as vital to him as the very air he breathed.

She smiled impishly when she noticed the cards he held in his hand. "What's the matter, Ryan? Did you decide to practice some before I got here?"

"Practice?" He followed her gaze. "Why, you little imp. I think I created a monster. I should never have taught you how to play poker. And I'm still not convinced that you didn't already know how to play."

She giggled. "Why? Just because I won all your toothpicks? You said yourself it was beginner's luck."

"Hmmm, we'll see. Today I'd better teach you the etiquette of poker playing. First, it's not polite to gloat when you win and, second, come here."

She walked to his side of the table. She knew he was up to something; mischief was written all over his face.

"And, third," he continued, "the winner is supposed to give the loser a kiss or else it'll jinx the winner's good luck."

He pulled her down on his lap and, holding her face between his hands, he took his kiss. He'd intended for it to be a short, playful kiss, but when their lips met, a fire ignited between them.

Susan felt the passion leap between them. She wrapped her arms around his neck and kissed him back with urgency. She loved the feel of Ryan's arms around her.

"Hmmm," she moaned. "Papa forgot to tell me about this particular rule of the game. Oops." She clapped her hand over her mouth, her eyes sparkling.

"Aha! I knew it. I should have known the way your papa spoils you rotten that he would have taught you how to play poker. I *knew* you were conning me somehow. I oughta turn you over my knee and give you the spanking your papa should have given you years ago."

Susan jumped to her feet. "You'd have to catch me first, and I can run faster than you since your knee is hurt," she teased mischievously.

Ryan rose to his feet. "Oh, you think so, Miss Smarty."

He grabbed her arm as she tried to jump out of reach. But the backs of her legs bumped against the side of his bed, throwing her off balance. She grabbed at Ryan to keep from falling, but he was already teetering himself, trying not to put pressure on his bad leg. They both tumbled onto the bed.

The fire simmering just beneath the surface burst into flames. Bracing his weight on his elbows, Ryan captured Susan's hands above her head. The expectant look in her eyes made his skin sizzle. His mouth closed over hers in a kiss that sent sparks streaking from low in her abdomen to the rest of her body.

Until Ryan had kissed her that first time, she had not known that a kiss could reach other parts of her body far removed from her lips. But now she did. And she eagerly embraced the multitude of feelings that his kisses and caresses ignited in her. Each time their emotions flared, her feelings made her a little more tense and restless.

Ryan released her hands as his lips nibbled her throat. He could feel her heart beating rapidly as he gently nipped her neck with his teeth. He slipped the buttons on her blouse open and placed a kiss where each one had been. He raised his head slightly to gaze at the delicate white skin hidden from him until now. Slowly, his mouth lowered toward her dusky nipples.

Susan sucked in her breath. Her nipples hardened in expectation of Ryan's warm mouth. Her stomach tightened, her womanhood flooded with heat and moisture as his mouth suckled the taut pebbles. Gasping, she was unable to breathe naturally. Twisting her head from side to side, she arched her back, pulling at Ryan's shoulders. She felt the evidence of his arousal hard against her thigh as it throbbed and pulsed against the material restraining it.

Ryan was losing control. Another moment and he wouldn't be able to stop. He swallowed hard, trying to restrain his wanton desire before it was too late. Susan, in her innocence, didn't understand that a man could only hold back just so long before he reached the point of no return.

He pulled back, breaking the contact between their bodies. Looking into her desire-flushed face, he knew she wanted him as much as he wanted her. But he knew that even though she was willing, it would be wrong to take her.

"Susie," he murmured hoarsely. "Susie."

Reality returned to her with a jolt. Her face flooded with embarrassment. She was lying on Ryan's bed, with him on top of her, letting him take liberties with her that no proper woman would have ever dreamed of doing. And worse than that, she loved every single liberty he'd taken! And still worse, her body craved more. She buried her face against his chest, mortified.

"Susie, look at me." Ryan had seen the shocked look cross her face before she'd tried to crawl inside him.

"I know what you're feeling and there's nothing wrong with having those feelings. It's not your fault. It's mine. I shouldn't have let things get out of hand."

Tipping her face up, he gently brushed a strand of silky hair back behind her ear. "I don't understand why, but every time we touch, it's like flint hitting stone. I think you've cast some kind of spell on me. I can't seem to keep my good sense about me."

Susan smiled. She knew why they struck sparks off each other. She loved Ryan. It was that simple. And surely he must feel the same way about her. His actions said he did.

Laying the palm of her hand against his cheek, she smiled timidly at him, ready to admit her love to him. "Ryan, I . . ."

The sudden slamming of the back door sounded as loud as a gunshot. They jumped up guiltily, hurrying to button buttons and straighten clothes. They had been so absorbed in each other they'd forgotten there was anyone else in the world.

"Goodness gracious, it's raining," Hazel exclaimed as she shook raindrops from her umbrella before standing it in the corner of the kitchen. She walked to the open door of Ryan's room. "Susan, I didn't know you were here."

"Good morning, Hazel. I got here just before it started raining." Susan hoped she didn't look or sound as guilty as she felt.

Hazel pretended not to notice Susan's flushed features and kiss-swollen lips. But when her eyes met Ryan's, he knew that she knew.

Well, Hazel thought to herself, *at least he has the decency to look guilty. I'm going to have to have a talk with that young man.* She knew how easy it was for young men to get carried away. The only reason Susan's parents weren't concerned about their young unmarried daughter coming to Ryan's house was because they knew she was there to chaperone.

By mid-afternoon the rain had stopped. Susan decided she'd better head for home before the next line of clouds already building on the horizon moved in.

"I wish you'd let me have one of the men saddle one of my horses for you. I don't like the idea of you riding Spooky home. If it starts lightning and thundering before you get there, there's no telling what that crazy horse of yours might do."

"Will you quit worrying? I'll be fine. Spooky is a good horse, most of the time. I told you she only spooks when something startles her from the rear."

"Hmmm, so you say, but I still don't trust her."

Susan stood on tiptoe and gave Ryan a long, slow kiss. "I'll come back tomorrow if the weather's not bad," she promised.

Ryan closed his arms around her. He was a glutton for punishment. His body was still paying the price of their earlier lovemaking, but he couldn't help himself. He returned her kiss with ardor. "Be careful, baby. I don't want anything to happen to you."

She nodded her head and left Ryan's room, bidding Hazel good-bye when she went through the kitchen.

Ryan, being careful not to put any weight on his injured leg, leaned against the windowsill, watching as Susan mounted her horse, waved at him, and rode away.

He didn't turn around when he heard Hazel enter his room. He knew she was upset with him and rightly so. What could he say in his defense? Nothing. He didn't understand himself how one auburn-haired, blue-eyed woman could cause him to forget all his good intentions with just a simple smile.

Hazel stood silently for a moment, hesitant to scold him, but she knew the time had come. She had been there to wipe his runny nose, kiss his hurts, and when he'd needed it, which wasn't often, tan his breeches.

"Hazel, I know what you're thinking."

"I'm going to say it anyway. You're a grown man, and I understand how it is with single men. Susan doesn't. She's too young and innocent. I taught you better than that."

"I know you did, Hazel."

"Well, that's all I have to say on the matter."

After Hazel went back to the kitchen, Ryan continued to stare out the window. He deserved the dressing down she'd given him. He had castigated himself a lot worse than she had, and his body fairly screamed its frustration at his behavior.

His thoughts turned to Clara. There was no way to avoid it, he'd have to go see Clara.

The bell jingled as Ryan closed the door behind him.

"I'll be with you in just a moment," Clara called from the back room of the mercantile. "Go ahead and look around."

Ryan walked through the door to the storage room, closing it behind him.

Clara straightened from the box she'd been

unpacking, and started turning toward her customer as she dusted off her hands. "What can I help you . . . Ryan!" She rushed to him, threw her arms around his neck, and kissed him passionately. He hadn't come to her in such a long time, and she had missed him terribly, but now he was here.

Ryan placed his hands on her waist and eased her slightly away from him. "Clara, I . . ." Damn, this was going to be more difficult than he'd thought.

Something inside her told her that Ryan wasn't back. Not in the way she wanted him. She had kissed him, but he hadn't returned her kiss. She moved hesitantly away from him.

"Is something wrong, Ryan?" She feared she already knew the answer.

The bell over the door jingled, announcing a customer. Clara glanced toward the front of the store, then back at Ryan.

"Wait for me upstairs. I'll close for the day after I help this customer."

Clara waited until Ryan climbed the stairs leading to her living quarters before leaving the storage room.

"Oh, there you are, Clara."

Clara smiled at the rotund little woman. "Hello, Mrs. Campbell. What can I get for you today?"

"I need some dried apples, if you have them, and this yarn. Goodness, I was beginning to think the rain was never going to let up. But I'm not complaining, mind you. Come August, we'll be wishing we had these three days and nights of rain."

Clara smiled, only half listening to the woman's chatter as she wrapped her purchases.

"Oh, my, I'd better hurry," she said, glancing out the window at the growing darkness. "I didn't realize it was getting so late." She patted the package and smiled cheerfully. "My Henry always gets a sweet tooth when the weather turns bad. Thought I'd surprise him with an apple pie for supper tonight. Well, you take care, Clara." Mrs. Campbell sailed out the door like a misdirected whirlwind.

Clara locked the door, pulled the shades down, and hung the Closed sign in the window. She slowly climbed the steps to her apartment, stopping to take a deep breath before opening the door and facing the man inside.

Ryan stopped his pacing when he heard the door open.

"Sorry to be so long," she apologized, not looking directly at Ryan. "Have you eaten yet? I can whip us up a quick supper. Would you like a drink? It won't take me but a few minutes . . ." She suddenly stopped talking. She was nervous, and when she was nervous, she chattered like a magpie. Twisting her hands in her skirt, she turned to face Ryan.

"You didn't come to have supper, did you?"

"No, Clara, I didn't."

Steeling herself against his answer, she looked him straight in the eyes. "Why did you come, Ryan?" She was surprised at how calm her voice sounded. It belied her inner turmoil.

Why indeed had he come? He raked his hand through his dark hair in agitation and turned away from the hurt he saw in her eyes. Damn, he didn't want to hurt Clara. That was the last thing in the world he wanted. But when they had kissed earlier, it was further evidence that he was doing the right thing.

"Clara, I . . . I came because . . ." He clenched his jaw trying to think of the right words to use to ease the hurt.

He turned back to Clara and held his hand, palm up, to her. "Will you come sit with me on the sofa? We . . . I need to talk to you."

Clara nodded her head and lay her trembling hand in his as he led her to the sofa.

Taking a deep breath and slowly letting it out, he tried again to find the right words to explain to Clara why he'd come.

"Clara, you know that I care about you and I wouldn't intentionally hurt you, don't you?"

"Yes, I know that," she said quietly, but her mind was screaming, *Please don't say what I think you're going to.*

"In the four years we've been together, I never made any promises or tried to lead you on."

"No, you never put any promises in words, but I always felt the promise was there," she admitted.

"Please believe me when I say that I've felt more for you than any woman I've ever known."

"I believe you."

"Even so, I know—maybe think is a better word—you hoped that someday I'd ask you to marry me. And, if things had been different at the beginning, maybe I would have. But there were things my past that prevented me from settling down with a wife and raising a family."

"And now, Ryan? Have you killed the ghosts from your past?"

"I hope, pray, that I have."

"And now you don't need me anymore. Is that it, Ryan?" She couldn't keep the hurt and anger from her voice, even though she knew her accusation was false.

His jaw hard, he growled and answered, "That's not the way it is and you know it! Don't try to turn what we shared into something cheap and shabby."

She lowered her eyes, willing herself not to cry. "I'm sorry, Ryan. That was a bitchy thing to say. We shared something very special. At least to me, it was."

Ryan lifted her chin to look into her face. "It was to me, too. That's why it might seem like I'm dropping this on you abruptly, but it's because I do care about you that I couldn't let it go on any longer. It wouldn't be fair to you or me." He sighed, glancing at the ceiling, wishing for guidance. "I know I'm making a mess of this. I wish I knew the right words to make it easier for you, but you know what I'm trying to say, don't you?"

She mutely nodded her head. Ryan was telling her that it was over between them. There were no words to make it hurt less.

"And you're not going to make it easy for me, are you?"

"No." She shook her head. "I'm not. I won't willingly give you up to another woman. I can't. Because . . ." She squared her shoulders and took a deep breath. "Because even if you don't, or can't, love me, I still love you. I think I have since we first met, and I can't pretend otherwise."

The anguish in her eyes tore at his heart. He pulled her to him, holding her tight. "I'm sorry, Clara," he whispered. "I tried. I honestly tried, but it's just not there. I'm so sorry."

She pushed him away and stood up. "I think you'd better leave now." Her voice was completely devoid of emotion, even though her heart was breaking into little pieces.

He got to his feet and reached for her.

She inched away and turned her back to him, wrapping her arms tightly around herself, biting her trembling lips to keep from screaming. She refused to let him see the tears flooding unchecked down her cheeks.

Sadly, he dropped his arm to his side and walked to the door. "Good-bye, Clara."

Chapter Eight

Ryan leaned against the bar, absently swirling the amber liquid around the sides of the glass.

The laughter of men and women having a good time, the clickity-click of the roulette wheel, all the usual sounds of gaiety in a busy saloon on a Saturday were an oblivious blur in the background to him.

He tossed back his drink and motioned to the bartender for another one. He was miserable as hell and he didn't know why. Well, that wasn't exactly correct. He did know. He hadn't seen Susan in four days and he felt like he had been deprived of one of life's necessities.

"What's the matter, Ryan?" Kyle asked, walking up to the bar and ordering a whiskey.

"Nothing," Ryan growled, taking a swallow of his drink.

"Hmmm, glad to hear that." Kyle nodded his head knowingly. "Saw Susan and her parents a few minutes ago," he said casually.

"Oh?" Ryan tried to sound just as casual, but Kyle definitely had his attention now.

"Uh-huh." Kyle took a sip of his drink before continuing. "They'd just finished loading some supplies in the buckboard and were getting ready to go home."

Ryan hastily tossed some coins on the counter. "Well, guess I'll head home, too." He went toward the swinging doors, leaving the rest of his drink untouched.

Kyle chuckled. "Thought you might," he mumbled, smiling at his friend's retreating back.

Susan looked behind her at the sound of a rider approaching.

"That looks like Ryan," she said eagerly.

Seth glanced back. "Wonder what he's in such a hurry about?"

Ryan reined his mount alongside the Bradford wagon. "Evening, folks." He touched his hat to Molly. "Hello, Susan," he said, maneuvering his horse to the side where she sat.

"What's your hurry, Ryan?" Seth asked.

"Hurry? Ah, well . . . I . . ." Ryan didn't have a good answer for Seth's question. "Actually, Kyle told me he saw ya'll leaving and, since I was fixin' to leave, too, I decided to catch up

138

and ride along with you," he admitted.

"Good. Glad to have the company." Seth grinned. He knew Ryan's real purpose was to talk with Susan.

"Is your shoulder doing okay?" Molly asked.

"Yes, ma'am. Doc took the stitches out today. Said it was healing just fine."

He spoke to Molly, but he couldn't keep his eyes off Susan. Just looking at her soothed some of his frustration. The blue of her dress matched the blue in her eyes. She looked so soft and feminine with her hair loose and flowing about her shoulders. He wanted to run his hands through it, to feel its silkiness sliding off his fingertips. His body ached to hold her in his arms.

"Ryan, are you going to help with the barn raising at the Morgans'?" Susan was looking forward to the dance that would follow the barnraising. She had bought material to make a dress especially for the occasion. She felt sure Ryan would ask to take her to the dance.

"Yep."

"I'm so excited I can hardly wait," she admitted.

Ryan looked puzzled. "Why? It's just gonna be a lot of hot, hard work."

Susan shook her head, exasperated. "I'm not excited about the barn *raising*, silly. I'm excited about the barn *dance*." Susan looked expectantly at Ryan. She was sure there wasn't a more handsome man around.

She waited anxiously for him to ask her to the

dance. But he didn't. Instead, much to her consternation, Ryan and her father started talking about ranching.

Susan was really miffed when they were almost to the lane where they'd turn off to go to their house and Ryan still hadn't mentioned the dance.

"Ya'll take care. See you later, Susan," he said as they took the turn.

As she helped her parents unload the wagon, it occurred to her that the reason Ryan hadn't asked her to the dance was because he didn't want to ask her in front of them, but there was plenty of time. The barn raising wasn't for two weeks yet. She was confident that he'd ask her the next time they were alone.

Reverend Meadows, the circuit preacher, had finally come to Comanche. With such a large area to cover, it was usually six or seven weeks between his visits to the one-room school that doubled as the community's church. And today would be a busy day for the reverend. He had two couples to marry, four young people to baptize, and two babies to christen.

The churchgoers milled around the school yard, visiting, until it was time for the sermon to begin. Susan kept one eye on the road, while trying to keep up with the women's conversation around her.

Her heart fell when she saw Kyle and Hazel's wagon come into view. Ryan wasn't with them. She'd thought for sure he'd come to the services today. Disappointed, she turned her attention back to her friends.

"You are so lucky," Becky whispered to her. Becky, a cute little blonde the same age as Susan, was watching a group of men riding into the school yard. "I wish I lived practically next door to him like you do," she said wistfully.

"Lucky?" Susan followed Becky's admiring gaze.

Ryan had come to Sunday service after all. He was riding with a couple of his ranch hands, Nolan and Ray, and also Billy and Jimmy Don Morgan. Susan's earlier disappointment vanished immediately.

She watched the men dismount and tie their horses to one of the ropes strung between the trees serving as makeshift hitching rails. They were laughing and ribbing one of the younger men about something.

Susan couldn't take her eyes off Ryan. This was the first time she'd seen him in a suit. He was so handsome it took her breath away.

Becky tugged at her arm excitedly. "They're coming this way. Oh, Susan, I hope he asks me to the dance at the Morgans'."

Susan only vaguely heard her friend, and she didn't notice that the other women had started going into the school. She watched Ryan as he walked toward her in his slow-walking, long-legged stride.

Their eyes met the instant he'd turned around and started toward her. Blue-gray eyes locked with sapphire-blue ones, communicating in an unspoken language as he drew nearer.

He held his hand out and she lay hers in it.

"Hello, Susan." His fingers closed around hers.

Susan was the first to lower her eyes. "When I saw Kyle and Hazel arrive and you weren't with them, I thought you weren't coming," she admitted softly.

He smiled, pleased that she was looking for him. "I wasn't going to, but Hazel insisted."

"Hi, Susan, Becky." The rest of the men had reached them.

Susan blushed. Ryan dropped her hand. They'd been so lost in each other that they'd forgotten other people were around.

Susan quickly glanced around and saw that their group was the only one not already inside.

"I . . . I guess we'd better go in. It's time for church to start," she said.

Susan and Becky took their seats beside Becky's family just as the preacher announced the first hymn. Ryan and his friends sat in the last row of chairs.

"He asked me," Becky whispered happily as the singing started.

"Who asked you what?" Susan whispered back.

"Nolan. He asked me to the barn raising Saturday."

Susan couldn't resist sneaking a peek at Ryan. She quickly turned around when she heard

Becky's father pointedly clear his throat.

She tried to pay attention to the preaching, but her thoughts kept straying to the man sitting at the back of the room. Several times in the past week she'd ridden Patches around in his pasture, hoping to see him, but he hadn't been there. She was relieved that he was here today.

After the preaching was over, everyone would have a picnic and then they'd adjourn to Indian Creek for the baptizing ceremony.

It suddenly occurred to Susan that she'd been so happy to see him after thinking he wasn't coming, that she'd plumb forgot to ask him to share the picnic lunch she and her mother had fixed.

Susan was beginning to fidget before the long-winded reverend finally said his last amen and dismissed them. She was eager to catch Ryan so she could ask him to eat with her and her family.

After giving the two newly married couples her best wishes, she hurried outside to find Ryan. She glanced around the groups of people but didn't see him. She went back in the schoolroom, thinking she might have missed him, but he wasn't there, either. Going back outside, she looked to where the horses were tied.

Ryan's horse was gone.

A gentle breeze stirred the early-morning air, sending the fragrance of wildflowers wafting about. The sky was a clear blue, and the sun was shining brightly. Birds flitted from tree to tree, filling the morning with their melody. And Susan was miserable.

The day of the barn raising for the Morgan family had arrived.

For two weeks Susan had looked forward to this day. She'd carefully planned exactly how she'd style her hair and what jewelry she'd wear to compliment the dress she'd made. She wanted to look her absolute best for Ryan. She couldn't understand why he hadn't asked to escort her to the dance. But, not only had he not asked, it seemed as if he'd tried to avoid her. Still, she hoped he would ask her today.

"We'll probably be the last ones there," Seth grumbled when they were finally on their way to the Morgans'.

Susan knew his exasperation was aimed at her. First she had decided she'd wear her new dress; then she'd changed her mind and her dress. Then, at the last minute, she decided she wasn't going to let Ryan's strange behavior spoil the day for her so she changed back into her new dress.

There were several wagons already at the Morgans' when they arrived, but there would be more. Children were running around in the yard, squealing and hollering as they played ball.

Seth assisted Molly from the wagon before he unhitched the team and led them away to be tethered.

Susan remained in the wagon, absentmindedly handing her mother the cakes, pies, and bread they had baked the evening before.

Even though she tried to refrain from taking notice of whether Ryan had come, she had spotted Ryan the minute they'd arrived. He was with a group of men making the final preparations to raise the assembled framework into place. The sight of him made her reflect on the events of the past two weeks.

Each time she had been with him, she'd pointedly mentioned the barn dance, but he had not asked to escort her. Her emotions had run the gamut from frustration to distress to downright depression. What had come over him? Had she done something to offend him? Her thoughts were interrupted by her mother's voice.

"The rest of the stuff can stay in the wagon for now. Hand me one of the chairs, Susan, and let's visit awhile."

The women had little to do during the morning hours and that suited them just fine. They hadn't come to work; they had come for the festivities. The morning would be spent sitting in the shade of the large knotty oaks, visiting and chitchatting until time for lunch.

The noon meal would be kept simple, consisting of cold fried chicken and sandwiches. The real work for the women would begin after the noon meal when they'd start cooking the food for the party.

Molly and Susan spent the morning undergoing the tactful, yet sometimes rather probing, interrogation that was customarily imposed upon newcomers to the community.

Susan noticed that the young single men were spending about as much time watching the young single women as they were working. All except Ryan.

Only once, when he'd stopped to get a dipper of water, did she see him looking her way. And then only briefly before he dropped the dipper back in the bucket and climbed the ladder to the roof.

Jim Morgan finished hammering a nail. Straightening up, he glanced at the sun hanging low in the sky. The barn was essentially finished. The floor was down, the walls were up, and the roof was on. The heavy joists that would support the loft floor were in place. The framework for the attached tack room and the stable shed were complete.

"That's enough, boys. It's time to quit," he announced.

"There's still time to put down the loft floor," Seth offered.

"Thanks, Seth, but that's not necessary. Me and the boys can handle the work that's left at our leisure. Everyone has worked hard today and now it's time for some fun. The womenfolk have been cooking up a feast all afternoon. So I say let's get washed up and get on with the eating and dancing."

"Yahoo!" the younger men shouted in unison. They quickly dropped their tools and headed for the stock tank, eager to wash off the sweat and dirt, change clothes, and get ready to party.

After everyone had finished eating, the women hurriedly gathered up their dirty dishes and put the baskets in their wagons. They'd worry about washing them tomorrow. They were just as ready as the men for the dancing to start.

The musicians plucked strings and twisted keys until fiddles, guitar, mandolin, and banjo were all in harmony. Some of the men moved the chairs back against the walls. One table, covered with a white cloth, was set against the far wall. It was covered with cakes and pies and two large punch bowls.

Susan had put their baskets in the wagon and entered the barn. She inhaled the smell of new lumber. It was a pleasant smell. She glanced around the large structure, searching for one face in particular. When her search had come full circle, she felt a terrible disappointment. Had Ryan left? She walked to where her mother and father were sitting and dejectedly sat down beside them.

Jim Morgan, holding Lynn's hand, stood near the musicians. "Folks." He waited until the talking quieted and he had everyone's attention. "Before we get started, Lynn and I want to thank each of you for all the help you've given us—the wagonloads of lumber, the food, the supplies, and other stuff, and for all the hard work getting this building raised today. I don't know any eloquent words to express myself, so all I can say is a heartfelt thank you." He cleared his throat self-consciously.

"I know ya'll noticed that Sheriff Thomas here showed up after the work ended but before the eating began." He paused until the laughter subsided. In a more somber tone, he continued, "Ed has something to tell us that some of you might have already heard, but it's serious, folks, and I suggest you listen carefully."

"Yes, it is serious," the sheriff agreed. "A few days ago, June the twenty-sixth to be exact, several hundred Comanche and Kiowa Indians attacked buffalo hunters up at Adobe Walls. Them buffalo hunters shot the Indians up pretty good and, needless to say, the Indians are mighty riled up. I got word from the Rangers that they have split up into small bands and are raising hell all over the place up north of here. There's little doubt that they'll give us plenty of trouble around here, too, so I just wanted to warn you to stay alert. Now I'll get out of the way and let these guys behind me get this party going."

The murmur that the sheriff's words caused among the people faded quickly as the band, after a couple of false starts, began to play a waltz.

Several couples quickly made their way to the dance floor. Susan watched as her father gracefully whirled her mother around the floor. She smiled when she saw her mother blush and lower her eyes at something her father said. It was obvious that, even after all these years, they were still deeply in love.

Susan sighed. She wanted Ryan to look at her that way, to whisper sweet things that would put a blush on her cheeks. She knew she loved Ryan and, maybe he didn't love her yet, but she certainly thought he cared deeply about her. What had gone wrong? Whoever had said love was the grandest thing in the world could never have felt as awful as she felt right this minute.

"Susan, may I have this dance?"

She was so lost in her misery that she hardly heard the young man speak to her.

"Oh, ah, thank you for asking me, Sid, but I'm not quite ready to dance yet. But please ask me again a little later."

When the music stopped, Susan heard a familiar laugh. She looked around at the group of men standing at the back of the room. Her heart skipped a beat. Ryan hadn't left.

Another dance started. She waited expectantly, confident that Ryan would be at her side any minute to ask for this dance.

Another young man asked her to dance. But she declined and requested that he ask her again later.

When the third dance started, Susan covertly glanced in Ryan's direction. What was wrong with him? He was casually leaning against the wall talking with Sheriff Thomas!

Now Susan was mad. Ryan was completely ignoring her. He acted like she wasn't even in the same county. *Well, damn it*, she thought, *I came to dance and I'm not going to sit here and turn down dances while everyone else is having fun.* Her chin jutted out in determination.

Billy Morgan was smiling as he walked toward her. "Susan, would you like to dance?"

Susan gave him her warmest smile. "Thank you, Billy, I'd love to."

Billy was quite a good dancer, and they moved smoothly around the room. As they neared where Ryan stood talking with the sheriff, she couldn't keep from glancing his way to see if he was watching. He still appeared to be oblivious to her.

They had just danced past Ryan a second time when the band went immediately from a two-step into a waltz. Sid and Jimmy Don almost ran over each other in their haste to ask Susan to dance.

"Oh, my goodness." She laughed, pleased at their eagerness. It was like a soothing balm to her bruised feelings at the way Ryan was pointedly ignoring her. "Well, I did promise Sid a dance," she replied tactfully, not wanting to offend anyone. "So will you ask me again later, Jimmy Don?"

When Sid pulled Susan into his arms and whirled her around, her eyes met Ryan's. Her body turned cold at the stricken look on his face.

His eyes followed her a few more moments, then he abruptly turned and walked out the door.

Chapter Nine

Susan thought the waltz would never end. She smiled and tried to pay attention to Sid, but her thoughts were on Ryan. Twice she'd missed a beat and stepped on his foot. By the time the dance finally came to an end, she was sure Sid probably thought she had two left feet.

But she couldn't help it. Her mind was on Ryan and the strange look he'd given her before he'd turned away.

He looked like someone had just kicked him in the gut. But why? What had she done to cause such pain? She had thought that he hadn't even been aware that she was around. Obviously, she'd been wrong.

She politely thanked Sid for the dance and headed for the door Ryan had gone through. She couldn't imagine what she'd done to hurt him, but she was determined to find out. He had been acting strange for two weeks, and she made up her mind that, even if she had to follow him all the way back to his ranch, she was going to get to the reason for his strange behavior.

She stood still for a moment in the horse lot, letting her eyes get adjusted to the darkness. She saw the glow of his cigarette before she could see him in the pale moonlight. He was leaning against the fence across the lot from her, his arms resting on the top rail of the fence.

Ryan glanced over his shoulder as he heard Susan approaching, then turned back, looking into the blackness, seeing nothing.

Susan stopped a few feet from him. "Ryan, what's the matter?"

"What do you mean, what's the matter?" he hedged.

"I think you know what I mean. Why have you been treating me the way you have?"

"Don't know what you're talking about. I haven't been treating you any way in particular," he disclaimed.

"Oh, yes, you have," she insisted. "You know I expected you to escort me to this dance. I have given you plenty of chances and outright hints, but you not only didn't ask me, you have actually been avoiding me. And now that we're here, you won't even dance with me. Please tell me what's wrong."

He took the last draw off his cigarette before

flipping the butt across the fence. "Damn it, Susie. Do you really think I didn't *want* to ask you?" Ryan's voice expressed both frustration and long suffering. "I just couldn't, that's all."

"Why couldn't you, Ryan?" she asked softly. "You know I would have accepted. Have I offended you or something?"

"No, Susie, you haven't done anything."

"Then tell me," she insisted again. It was obvious that he was trying to avoid the issue, but she wasn't going to let him. She wanted a straight answer. "Why didn't you ask me to the dance?"

Ryan turned to face her. His shoulders sagged. He flopped his hands at his sides as though he was resigned to confessing some great humiliation.

"Susie, I don't know how to dance."

It took a few seconds for his words to settle in on her.

"You don't know how to dance! That's it? That's the only reason?" she sputtered in disbelief.

"Well, damnation! Ain't it enough? How could I ask to take you to a dance and then not dance with you?" He shrugged his shoulders, waiting for her reaction to his revelation. "Well, go ahead and laugh at me," he said when she continued to stare at him.

"No, I'm not going to laugh at you." She stepped closer to him and, doubling her hand into a fist, she punched him square in the stomach. "That's for all the torment you caused me over the past several days."

"Damn, that hurt!" he exclaimed, rubbing his stomach, completely surprised by her reaction.

"It did? Well, let me give you a little better sample of what I'll do if you ever do that to me again." She doubled her fist and again aimed for his midsection.

This time he caught her hand before it made contact with his body. "I think I'd rather you laughed at me instead of beating me up."

"I'm not going to beat you anymore." She smiled sweetly at him. "You deserve worse punishment than that."

Ryan eyed her suspiciously, wondering what was going on in that pretty little head of hers. Her too-innocent smile convinced him that whatever it was, it didn't bode well for him.

"I'm going to teach you how to dance," she stated.

"I think I'd rather you beat up on me," he grumbled, but her tone of voice told him that he didn't have any choice in the matter. He was about to take dancing lessons, like it or not.

"Nonsense. It's not that hard to learn a few simple steps." After placing his hands in the dancing position, she said, "Now, you . . ." Her voice trailed off as Ryan pulled her tight against him, covered her mouth with his, and kissed her until she was panting for air.

"Hmmm, I think I'm going to like learning to dance after all," he said before hugging her and kissing her breathless again. As he held her to him, his hand stroked her back, drifting a little lower with each stroke.

"Am I doing this right?" he questioned, barely raising his lips from hers.

Susan moaned. His touch, as usual, had set her body aflame with love and desire. "Yes," she mumbled mindlessly. "No!" she quickly amended, pushing Ryan backwards a respectable distance and repositioning his hands. "Ryan Sommerall, be serious," she admonished.

He grinned broadly. "I was serious."

She raised an eyebrow at him and ignored his innuendo. "We can hear the music plainly out here. That's a waltz they're playing now, so that's the dance you'll learn first. Watch my feet. The tempo is one, two, three, one, two, three."

He followed her lead, quickly catching on to the rhythm. "This isn't so hard," he said just before they bumped against the fence.

"You're doing great." Susan was quick to assure him.

"Yeah, great," he mumbled dejectedly, dropping her hands and stepping away. "How do I keep from knocking everybody down or dancing us right into a corner?"

She pulled him back into dancing position. "When we're dancing, you guide me with the pressure of your hand on my waist. Like this." She demonstrated. "Now let's try it again and you do the leading."

This time Ryan, albeit a bit stiffly at first,

maneuvered them around the horse lot without mishap.

She knew the minute he became confident of his ability. His hand at her waist relaxed its tight grip.

As they continued to sway gracefully to the music, she couldn't help thinking what a paradox this big, handsome man was. He could face down a gunfighter without flinching, and fight Indians without fear, and then be terrified of dancing with a woman.

She smiled to herself. He had been embarrassed at his inability to dance, but his vulnerability only made her love him more, if that were possible.

By the time the waltz ended, Ryan was doing quite well. When he'd also mastered the two-step with perfection, Susan announced that it was time to go inside.

"Can't we just stay here in the horse lot and dance by ourselves?" he protested.

"No, we cannot. I didn't spend hours making this dress and fixing my hair just to stay out here in the dark and dance with you," she insisted lovingly but firmly.

"You do look beautiful in that dress. Did you know that blue is my favorite color? And I love your hair down like that, all soft and curly."

Susan gave him a stern look. "Compliments will get you nowhere, Mister Sommerall," she informed him, pointing in the direction of the door. "Go."

"Won't do nothing but make a spectacle

of myself," he grumbled, reluctantly moving toward the sound of the music.

"Nonsense. No one will be watching you—except every female between the ages of six and sixty," she teased.

Ryan groaned, not in the least amused at her humor.

"Now, remember, you have to dance with some of the other women, too, like Lynn, Mama, and Hazel. That is one of the rules of etiquette."

"Well, if I have to dance with all the women here, how will I ever get to dance with you?" he bemoaned.

"Oh, you don't have to dance with *all* the women, dear. You're not expected to dance with the single women at all," she fibbed.

"Why can't I dance with the single women? Whose rules are those?"

"Mine," she informed him, smiling impishly, her blue eyes twinkling.

"Oh, I see." Ryan chuckled, pleased at her possessiveness. "Well, I sure wouldn't want to break any 'Susie' rules."

The band was in the middle of a square dance when they entered the barn.

"Let's get some punch and join my parents until the next dance starts." She grinned mischievously. "Unless you'd like to learn to square dance."

"No. No, I definitely do not want to do that."

After getting a cup of punch, they sat down beside her parents.

Seth eyed Ryan. Except for the fact that he looked about as happy as a man going to his own hanging, he seemed to have survived his dancing lessons. When Seth had missed Susan a little earlier, Molly informed him she was in the horse lot teaching Ryan to dance.

Thinking back to a special day on the banks of the Brazos River, he remembered when Molly insisted that he was going to learn to dance. He'd protested, but it hadn't done him a lick of good. By the end of their picnic, he knew how to dance.

He smiled to himself. "Wondered where you two got off to," he commented dryly.

Ryan squirmed in his chair, certain that everyone knew what he and Susan had been doing in the horse lot.

Susan gave her father a don't-you-dare-tease-Ryan look. "It was a little warm in here so I stepped out to get some fresh air."

"Oh. That's what I figured," Seth replied blandly.

Molly jabbed her elbow in his ribs, giving him a warning look of her own.

Ryan listened as the band began playing another tune. Taking a deep breath, he decided to get his punishment over with. "Ah, Susie, may I have this dance?"

Susan beamed with pride. "I'd be honored, Ryan."

At first Ryan felt like everyone in the room was watching him, but Susan's gentle squeeze of his hand quickly put him at ease.

As they danced past Nolan and Becky, Nolan couldn't help ribbing his boss a bit. "Well, golly, Ryan. Ain't never seen you dance before."

Ryan smiled at Susan. "Never been anyone I wanted to dance with before."

Susan blushed slightly and lowered her eyes. *Sometimes wishes do come true,* she thought.

Susan knew she was the envy of most of the single women in the room. Ryan didn't seem to notice the wistful look on their faces, but she did. She couldn't help but smile. After days of worrying over why he had been avoiding her, Susan was sure she was the happiest woman at the dance.

For an inexperienced dancer, she thought Ryan was surprisingly graceful. Or could it be that her love for the handsome man made her feel like she was floating on air? Whatever it was, she felt good all over.

Ryan looked at Susan's glowing face. She felt so good in his arms he pulled her closer.

"No, dear, you can't do that," she reprimanded, pushing gently away from him. "Not unless you want to cause raised eyebrows and wagging tongues. It's not considered proper behavior to hold a lady too close."

Susan chuckled at his disgusted look about all the rules he'd been blissfully unaware of until he'd learned to dance.

"Well, I just don't like people telling me what I can and can't do. Especially when there isn't any good reason not to, except that some old biddy might get the vapors. Besides . . ."

Susan tilted her head sideways, waiting for Ryan to finish his sentence. "Besides what?"

"Darn it, Susie. I want to take you home from the dance and I'm afraid you're gonna tell me I can't do that, either." He raked his hands through his hair in exasperation. "And there ain't no good reason why I shouldn't. After all, I would have asked you to the dance in the first place if I'd known how to dance. So now that I've learned to dance and I'm dancing with you I oughta get to take you home."

"Ryan," she said patiently, "the only reason you can't take me home is that you haven't asked me."

Ryan ducked his head and smiled a bit sheepishly. Susan would almost swear he'd momentarily blushed.

"Oh. Well, in that case, will you let me take you home from the dance?"

"Yes, Ryan. I'd like that very much."

To his surprise, he discovered he was really enjoying himself. He'd even gotten brave enough to try a square dance. After he'd watched a couple of them and learned that the "caller" told everyone what to do next, it was easy.

Ryan obediently danced with Lynn, Hazel, and Molly. When he returned Molly to her seat, Seth yawned and glanced at his watch.

"Molly, it's past my bedtime. Are you ready to head home?"

"Yes, dear. Let me say good-bye to a couple of people and then we'll go."

"Mama, I'm going to stay awhile longer." She smiled at Ryan standing beside her. "Ryan asked to escort me home."

Molly looked from one smiling face to the other. Love was definitely blooming between the two young people.

"All right, dear, but don't be too late."

"No, Mama, I won't be."

A couple of hours later, Susan reluctantly decided it was time to leave. The party would probably go on until the wee hours of the morning, but she knew her parents expected her home at a reasonable time.

After saying good-bye to the Morgans, she and Ryan left.

"I'll wait here while you hitch up the horses and bring the wagon around," Susan said, standing in front of the barn doors.

Ryan got a strange look on his face. He shuffled from one foot to the other. "Ah, Susie. I . . . ah . . . Well, I don't hardly know how to tell you this, but . . . ah . . . Well, you see I didn't . . . ah . . ."

Susan looked at him expectantly. "You didn't what?" she prompted.

Ryan flopped his hands at his sides. "I . . . ah . . . don't have a wagon."

Susan stared blankly at him for a full fifteen seconds. "You didn't bring the wagon?" she asked incredulously.

He shook his head.

"You rode your horse?"

Connie Harwell

He nodded.

"You asked to take me home from the dance, and you didn't bring the wagon!"

"You don't . . . mind, do you?" he asked apprehensively.

"Mind! You ask to take me home from the dance, you don't have a wagon, and you ask me if I *mind*!" She couldn't believe what she was hearing.

"Well, I just didn't think about not having my wagon. I was thinking about you and wanting to spend more time with you and I just . . . forgot."

"Forgot?"

He nodded again.

"Well, this is a fine mess." She threw her hands in the air. "Just how do you propose to get me home, Ryan Sommerall?" she demanded.

"We'll figure out something."

Susan eyed him skeptically.

Taking her hand, he started walking to his horse. "We'll just have to ride double."

Susan dug her heels in. "Ryan, I can't straddle a horse. I'm wearing a dress," she reminded him.

Ryan tugged her along. He wasn't going to let a little thing like a dress stop him. "Then you'll just have to sit across the saddle." He tossed the blanket and saddle on his horse. "It's not that far to your house," he reasoned.

Ryan mounted and removed his foot from the stirrup. "Now put your right foot in the stirrup and swing up and turn around like you were riding sidesaddle."

Susan followed his instructions and found herself positioned between Ryan's body and the saddle horn. She swung one leg around the saddle horn and wrapped one arm around Ryan to brace herself, resting her other hand on his chest.

"Hmmm, this might not be so bad after all," she murmured, snuggling up to him and kissing him on the neck.

Ryan was immediately aware of his miscalculation. It was going to be a long, *long* way to Susan's house. The instant her warm desirable behind touched him, he became hard. And her playful kiss didn't help matters, either. He sucked in air and mentally tried to will his throbbing member to ignore the situation. Which was like asking the wind to blow in a different direction!

When Ryan didn't nudge the horse into motion, she looked sideways at him. "Is something wrong?"

"Ah, no. Nothing's wrong," he croaked hoarsely.

"Then would you mind getting us out of here before someone sees us? So help me, Ryan, if any of my friends see the ridiculous situation you've gotten me into, I'll—I'll . . ." She tried to think of some terrible torture she could threaten him with. "Well, I'll think of something awful to do to you."

Ryan didn't bother telling her that he was

suffering punishment enough for his lapse of memory.

He set his horse into a trot and quickly discovered that the motion caused Susan's thigh to bounce against his engorged manhood, and the side of her breast moving against his chest was almost like a gentle caress.

He slowed the horse to a walk, thinking the slower pace might alleviate the undulating motion of her supple body against his.

That didn't work worth a damn! The slower motion now made her thigh *and* her breast feel like a caress.

Susan squirmed to get a little more comfortable in her makeshift sidesaddle. Her motion sent Ryan's desire soaring. When his horse started sidestepping and snorting, he realized he'd been unconsciously gripping the animal tightly with his legs.

"Whoa, boy." He patted the horse's neck to calm its nervous prance.

Susan clung to Ryan, afraid she was about to lose her tenuous seat on the saddle. "What's wrong with him?"

Ryan cleared his throat. "He's . . . ah . . . not too comfortable having two riders on him. He'll be okay now."

"Well, I'm not real thrilled about the idea myself." She peeked behind them to see if anyone was on the road. "I'll never live it down if any of my friends see us. If you hear anyone coming, you get off this road and into the trees pronto. Understand?"

164

"Yes, ma'am."

As they continued their trek, Ryan tried to concentrate on anything but Susan's warm body pressed so close to his. But neither his mind nor his body would cooperate.

The warm night air blew a strand of her hair against his face and neck. He inhaled its fresh lavender scent. He felt its softness against his cheek. He saw moonbeams and starlight bounce off its red highlights.

His eyes accidentally drifted lower to settle on the gentle jiggling of her breasts. His breath seemed to stick somewhere between his throat and his lungs. He watched spellbound, as the soft mounds ever so slightly bounced in rhythm with the movement of the horse. He ached to close his mouth around one of the rosy nipples he knew was hidden beneath her bodice. He swallowed hard. Another five seconds and he'd be drooling! He closed his eyes hoping to block out the sensuous sight.

Susan glanced at Ryan. His eyes were closed. He'd been very quiet since they'd left the dance.

"Ryan, is something wrong?" she asked hesitantly.

He opened his eyes and groaned silently when they met her innocent look.

Wrong? Not unless one considered a severe case of aching in his groin as something wrong. "No, nothing's wrong. I was just . . . thinking. Did you enjoy the party?"

Since thinking didn't get his mind off her supple body caressing him until he felt like he might explode at any second, maybe talking would.

"Yes." She sighed dreamily. "I don't think I've ever enjoyed myself more." Susan hugged him, giving him the most devastatingly beautiful smile he'd ever seen in his life.

Well, so much for talking. He knew he was lost the minute he looked into her upturned face glowing with happiness. He might as well surrender gracefully and admit defeat. He could no longer fight the desire she had instilled in him from the first moment he'd seen her.

Slowly lowering his mouth, he caressed her lips before slipping his tongue inside to explore the delicate velvet within. His hand sought the softness his eyes had coveted only minutes before. His thumb moved restlessly against the pebble-hard nipple. His hand closed over her breast, gently kneading the warm flesh until it was taut and throbbing against his palm.

Releasing her mouth, he trailed kisses along her cheek, pausing to nibble her sensitive ear lobe before continuing his journey down her neck, alternately kissing and sucking.

Ryan guided the horse off the road, stopping only when they were far enough back in the trees that no one would disturb them.

Slipping his arm beneath Susan's legs, he agilely dismounted. Cradling her against his chest, he dropped the reins and carried her to a lush patch of grass. He released her, letting her body slide slowly down his, inflaming every inch of him, until her feet touched the ground.

Susan was only vaguely aware when they left the road. Reality ceased to exist for her when Ryan's tender ministrations pushed her into a world filled only with sensuous yearnings for pleasures yet to be. She loved Ryan with every fiber in her body. She trusted him completely.

Ryan's hands caressing her back left a pleasant heat where they touched her. Her passion which he could so easily stir mounted rapidly. His lips left hers to nibble her ear lobes before trailing kisses down her neck.

Her heart pounded wildly, her breathing coming in heaving gasps. She could feel the pounding of his heart against her breast and his hot breath on the soft skin of her neck. Her love for him, mingled with the passion he stirred in her, was building to a fierce craving. She knew he must surely feel her love for him.

His roving hand was moving ever lower. When it reached her bottom, he pressed her firmly against his crotch. She moved her hips slowly from side to side, savoring the ecstasy of the moment. A low moan escaped her as her tongue moistened her dry lips.

Ryan's hand moved to cup her full, firm breast. The nipple swelled as he gently squeezed, released, and squeezed again. Her breathing became more ragged. He released the first tiny buttons of her bodice and lowered his mouth to her swollen nipples. His flicking tongue and his nibbling lips were making a promise of a fulfillment yet to come, a quenching of the desire he inflamed in her.

Slowly, he lowered her to the ground, his mouth never leaving her taut nipples as he lay her gently on the soft grass. His lips and tongue at her breasts tantalized her as his hand slipped beneath her skirt and caressed her inner thighs. His hand sought and found the slit in her pantaloons. He covered her soft mound with his hand. His breathing was labored as he eased his finger inside the hot, moist canal. Feeling her tender flesh quiver and pulsate around his finger, he knew she was ready for him.

Removing his hand from her, he unbuckled his belt and began undoing the buttons on his breeches. He could hold back no longer. He wanted Susan with an urgency he'd never before felt.

Susan moaned when his fingers left her body. She was at first shocked and then amazed at how he could take control of her body with his hands and mouth, leaving her no choice but to follow where he led.

Ryan hurriedly tugged Susan's pantaloons down and positioned himself between her legs.

She hoped Ryan felt her love as she felt his. But suddenly she knew something was wrong. She wasn't feeling his love. She was only feeling his lust, his desire for her body.

"Ryan," she gasped as she began to twist away from him.

He took her gyrations and gasping his name as an expression of her wanting him. He held her hips firmly between his hands and kissed her belly.

"Ryan . . . please stop." Her voice was ragged, and she twisted violently away from him. She got to her knees and began buttoning her dress with trembling fingers.

"What's the matter?" Ryan asked in startled amazement. "Did I do something to displease you?" He rose to his knees and tried to take her in his arms.

She pushed him away.

He stopped and stared at her, trying to figure out what had come over her.

"Susan, what's wrong? I don't understand."

"I just don't want this, Ryan."

"You don't want it? Well, you damn sure fooled me!" Ryan's voice revealed a thread of anger.

Susan couldn't hold back any longer. Great tears welled in her eyes and flooded down her cheeks. She was unwittingly using the one feminine weapon a man could not cope with.

"Ah, come on, baby. Please don't cry." Ryan gathered her in his arms. His attempt to console her only brought on spasms of sobbing.

He rocked her gently back and forth on their knees, gently massaging her back until her crying subsided.

"I'm sorry. I thought you wanted me. I didn't realize I was forcing you."

Susan's body tensed. "You weren't forcing me. I wanted you. I just didn't want what you were giving. I wanted all of you." She pulled back and looked up at him. "Don't you understand?"

"It's all right." He wiped away a tear with the tip of his finger.

"You *don't* understand," she wailed. Tears were flowing from her eyes again as she cupped her face in her hands.

"Susie, please don't cry again. It's tearing my heart out to see you like this. You should know I wouldn't purposely do anything to cause you such hurt."

He took his bandanna from around his neck and, pulling her hands from her face, began to wipe away the tears.

"I'm not hurting the way you think. I'm mostly just frustrated with myself for leading you on like that only to—"

Ryan placed a finger on her lips. "Hush. Hush," he pleaded softly. "You weren't leading me on. It's my fault. I just wanted you so bad I lost control. I'm sorry."

Ryan knew by the sad look on Susan's face that he'd hurt her. And she was right: He didn't understand. He was positive that she had desired him as much as he had desired her. What had he done to cause her to change so suddenly?

Susan felt her heart flip. He wanted her, but he didn't love her. He cared about her; she had no doubt about that, either. But that wasn't enough. She wanted his love. She couldn't—wouldn't—accept less than his love.

She could feel that her nose was ready to dribble. It always did when she cried. She took the bandanna from Ryan and blew her nose vigorously into the expensive material.

"Oh, for heaven's sake. Now look what I've done."

"That's all right," he reassured her as he folded the material to a clean spot and tenderly wiped her cheeks again. "You could get away with most anything right now."

She smiled, knowing he was patronizing her. "I'm all right now."

She got to her feet and, turning from him, pulled her pantaloons back into place. She started walking to the horse.

"I want to go home now."

"Susie, I . . ." His voice hung in his throat. She had the most doleful look on her face he'd ever seen in his life. "Susie, wait," Ryan pleaded.

Catching her by the shoulders, he turned her toward him. She turned her face away, refusing to meet his eyes. Gently he tipped her face up, forcing her to look at him. Unshed tears shimmered in her eyes. Sadness replaced the trust that had been there before.

"Susie, I'm sorry. I don't . . . I mean I . . ." He turned and walked a couple of steps away before whirling to face her. "I know I shouldn't have tried to . . . ah . . . seduce you like that. And I didn't mean to," he hastened to assure her. "It's just that you felt so good and . . . and somehow everything seemed so right. I guess I just didn't think about the consequences of letting my body take control instead of my mind." He raked his hands through his hair in agitation.

"I can't even apologize coherently. Damn it, Susie, I've never felt this way before and it confuses the hell out of me!" he admitted in exasperation. "I would never intentionally hurt you, and I don't blame you for being angry with me."

"I'm not angry with you, Ryan. I, too, thought everything seemed so right tonight. I admit that I wanted you just as much as you wanted me. But I need more than just your body—or your mind. Have you stopped to think that maybe it's not your body or your mind that's to blame?"

"What are you talking about?"

"You'll have to figure it out for yourself, Ryan. If I have to tell you, it wouldn't mean a thing."

Ryan continued to stare at her for a couple of seconds, searching her face, trying to figure out what she was thinking.

Susan turned, mounted his horse, and removed her foot from the stirrup so he could swing up behind her.

"Susie?"

"Please take me home now," she requested, despondent and downhearted.

Ryan let out a long, dejected breath and swung into the saddle. He had never been more miserable in his life.

Neither of them broke the silence until they reached Susan's house.

Ryan stopped the horse a short distance away, not wanting to wake her parents. He hugged her against him, feeling the need to say something.

"Susie, I don't want us to part this way. It hurts me to know that you're angry with me."

"I told you I'm not angry, Ryan."

"But do you really mean it?"

She nodded.

Tucking a lock of hair behind her ear, he placed a kiss on her forehead. "I did enjoy the dance. You were the prettiest woman there, you know."

She smiled weakly. "Thank you." Swinging her leg over the saddle horn, she slid to the ground. "Good night, Ryan," she said, dispirited.

"Susie."

"Yes?"

When she turned and looked up at him, Ryan leaned over and gently kissed her lips. "Good night."

He waited until she shut the door behind her before he turned his horse and started home. Even though she said she wasn't angry with him, he felt like he'd lost something very precious. It made him feel empty and alone.

Susan watched through the curtains until Ryan was out of sight. Then, slipping quietly out the door, she walked over to the corral. Her heart and mind were in such a turmoil, she knew it'd be next to impossible for her to sleep.

173

Spooky, catching her mistress's scent, trotted to the fence, eager to be petted.

Susan absentmindedly rubbed the mare's velvet nose, as she tried to sort through her troubled thoughts. Hoping the cool air and tranquil, starlit night would ease her tension, she let her mind wander.

She thought back to when she was a little girl. Her favorite bedtime story was about how the beautiful princess met the handsome Prince Charming. They had fallen instantly in love, and he'd swept her up on his white stallion, and they rode away to live happily ever after.

Like all young girls, she'd fantasized about what her Prince Charming would look like and all the possible ways that she might meet him so they could fall blissfully in love.

She smiled whimsically at her immature fantasies. In all her imagined scenarios, not one of them had come anywhere close to reality.

She hadn't been wearing a beautiful gown; she'd been standing naked in ankle-deep water. Ryan hadn't swept her off her feet; he'd fled from her. And he didn't even *own* a white stallion!

The only part of her dream that had come true was that she'd fallen in love with Ryan. But instead of being blissful, she was miserable.

"Oh, Spooky, what do I do now? How do I make Ryan love me back?" She swiped at the tears running down her cheeks.

Chapter Ten

"Oh, I can't make up my mind," Becky moaned in indecision, flipping through the pages of the latest fashion catalogue for the umpteenth time. "Which style do you like best, Susan?"

"Hmmm, I think you ought to order this one." Susan grinned mischievously and pointed to a low-cut white bridal gown.

"Oh, my goodness!" Becky sucked her breath in, her face turning a bright red. "Susan Bradford! That's positively indecent!"

Susan giggled. "I know. Can you believe it? Clara, are women really wearing dresses like this back East?"

Clara Beeman turned from the glassware she was dusting to look at the picture Susan pointed to. "That's what I've been told." She lowered her voice to a whisper even though she and the girls were the only ones in her store at the moment. "If you think that's bad, you should see what they're touting as the latest fashion to wear *under* a dress."

"Can you just imagine the look on Reverend Meadows' face if you walked down the aisle wearing that?" Susan exclaimed.

All three women laughed at the scene Susan's remark conjured up.

"He'd probably fall over dead at the sinfulness of such action," Clara agreed.

"Ya'll are just terrible." Becky wiped her eyes, trying to control her laughter. "And you're not much help, either."

Becky finally decided on a demure white gown with a high neckline and tiny puffed sleeves. The full satin skirt was overlaid with lace and fit snugly about the waist.

"Are you sure it will get here in time?"

Clara smiled, understanding the young bride's jitteriness. "Don't worry, Becky. I promise it'll be here in plenty of time for your wedding. It'll be late August before the preacher comes back," she reminded the fidgety blonde.

"I know. I just want everything to be perfect." Becky looked at Susan in dismay.

"Oh, no." Susan had seen that look on her friend's face too many times lately not to know what it meant. "Now what have you thought of to worry about?"

"What if it rains? Oh, Susan, I don't want it to rain on my wedding day," she moaned.

Susan shook her head in dismay. "Becky, we should be so lucky. It hardly *ever* rains here in August, you know that. Will you quit thinking of things to worry about before you make a nervous wreck out of all of us?"

"Are you going to order your dress today, too?" Clara asked Susan.

"Yes." She pointed to a silk dress with a scooped neckline, elbow-length sleeves edged in lace, and a fitted bodice with tiny buttons down the front that flared into a full skirt. "I want this one in pink. Unlike my nervous friend here, I'm not a bundle of indecision."

The bell over the door jingled as Molly entered.

"Good morning, Molly."

"Hello, Clara. Decided I'd better come see what was keeping the girls. Haven't you decided on a dress yet? It's already past one o'clock and your father's ready to eat lunch."

"Sorry, Mrs. Bradford. It's my fault," Becky answered. "I couldn't make up my mind and these two"—she nodded toward Susan and Clara—"didn't help a bit. Come see what I picked out. I need a serious opinion."

Molly admired Becky's choice of a wedding gown. "It's a lovely dress, Becky. And I know you'll be a beautiful bride. Nolan is a very lucky man."

Becky blushed. "Thank you. I'm so excited I can hardly wait," she exclaimed. "Thank you for meeting me today, Susan, and helping pick out the dresses."

"Are you sure you don't want to have lunch with us and visit for a while?" Susan asked as they left the mercantile.

"I'd like to, but I promised Mama I'd help her this afternoon. I'll see you later in the week. Hello, Mister Bradford. I'm sorry to keep Susan so long but I just couldn't make up my mind about my wedding dress," she apologized.

"That's okay, Becky. I understand." Seth was leaning against the hitching rail, leisurely smoking a cigarette. "I fully expect the day to come when Molly and Susan will disappear into the mercantile never to be seen or heard from again," he teased.

"Oh, Papa. We weren't gone that long." Susan laughed.

Strolling toward the cafe, they stopped a couple of times to chat briefly with neighbors they saw only on Saturdays, or when the circuit preacher was in town.

Moving slightly ahead of her parents, Susan turned around to walk backwards so she could face them. "I sure am glad we moved here, Papa. Everyone's so friendly. I like Comanche."

Seth smiled at his daughter's exuberance. "I'm glad you like it here, but you better watch where you're going before you—"

Seth's warning came a fraction too late. Susan collided with a hard masculine chest.

"—back into Ryan."

"Hello, folks. Fancy running into you like this." He smiled at Susan.

"Sorry." She returned his smile. "I was just

178

telling Papa how glad I am that we moved here."
Especially because I met you, she thought.

Ryan looked into Susan's eyes, forgetting they were standing in the middle of the walkway. "I'm glad you moved here, too," he said huskily.

Seth and Molly glanced knowingly at each other and smiled.

"Ryan, we were just on our way to eat lunch. Can you join us?"

Seth's words reminded the young couple that they were not alone. They quickly broke eye contact, each glancing guiltily away.

"Sounds like a fine idea. I haven't had time to eat yet, either."

Ryan turned and matched his step with Susan's as the foursome made their way to the cafe.

Almost an hour later Seth pushed back from the table and patted his stomach. "That was good. But now, ladies, we need to get on home. I've got a couple of chores I need to do before dark." He turned to Ryan. "If you're fixin' to leave town now, you're welcome to ride along with us."

"I need to pick up a bridle I left to be repaired at the blacksmith's. I'll walk you to your wagon and catch up with you on the road."

Ryan hoisted Susan onto the seat of the buckboard. "I'll see you in fifteen or twenty minutes."

Seth snapped the reins over the team of horses, turning them toward the road home.

They had barely cleared town when Susan knew she would soon have to stop. Ten minutes later they were approaching a small stream with the usual growth of trees and thick underbrush along its banks. She knew the brush would be interlaced with briars. Not relishing the thought of trying to make her way into the likes of that in the dress she was wearing, she decided instead on the large pecan tree that was about fifty yards from the road. There were ample bushes and tall grass under it to conceal her.

"Papa, I've got to stop a minute."

Seth halted the team and held Susan's arm as she stepped down onto the wheel and hopped off to the ground. He shook his head in mild exasperation as he watched her lift her skirt and trot to the trees and hide herself from their view behind some bushes.

"Worse than when she was a little girl. Ain't been on the road more than ten minutes and already she's got to go to the bushes."

"Oh, be patient with her, dear," Molly consoled, patting him on the knee.

Seth took his tobacco sack and papers from his shirt pocket, rolled a cigarette, and lit it. After taking a couple of puffs, he glanced back toward the trees.

"Why didn't she go in town?"

"She couldn't use the facilities in town, dear. Ryan kept hanging around chatting with her right up till it was time to . . ." Molly's words trailed off as she saw the men ride out from behind the tree line and onto the road in front of them. There were six of them. Before she or Seth could speak a word, the men were charging and shooting at them.

"Molly! Jump! Run!" Seth shouted, at the same time reaching behind the seat for his rifle.

Molly was frozen with terror, unable to move.

Seth shoved her, sending her tumbling off the seat and onto the ground.

"Run!"

He rose to his feet and got off one quick shot before a bullet struck him. He fell over the back of the seat and onto the supplies piled in the bed of the buckboard. The frightened team retreated from the oncoming horses and men, unable to turn and run since both horses kept pulling in opposite directions.

Eager to catch up with Susan and her folks, Ryan quickly retrieved his repaired bridle from the blacksmith and headed out of town.

When he passed the last house, Ryan shaded his eyes with his hand and gazed down the road. Although they were a full mile from him, he could see the Bradford's buckboard and team.

Suddenly he heard the faint sound of gunshots, and shortly thereafter he was sure he could see several horses milling around the Bradford's rig.

"Good God Almighty! Something bad is happening there," he uttered out loud as he set spurs to his horse's flanks, urging it into a dead run.

"Jake, hold them horses. Red, go catch that gal that went to the bushes."

The burly man hauled his horse back on its haunches alongside the buckboard and swung down as he gave the orders. He spat a stream of tobacco juice, further staining his heavy black beard.

A quick glance at the blood-soaked head of the owner of the wagon assured the leader of the gang that he was no longer a threat to them. He pushed the body off the supplies.

Red headed straight for Susan the instant his feet hit the ground.

"The rest of you git ta loading this grub on your horses. And be quick about it," the leader ordered. "That marshal is still trailing us and he might've raised him a posse by now."

His loud, gruff voice sent the men scurrying to obey him. All but the small, skinny one who was standing by the woman, gulping the last swallows from a flat-shaped pint whiskey bottle. He watched the blood oozing from a wound on her right temple.

"Damn such luck," he muttered. "She'd a been a comfort under a man's blanket at night if'n she hadn't a caught a bullet in her head." He jabbed the toe of his boot sharply against her ribs.

"Damn you, Charlie. There's plenty of time ta look at that woman later. Now git ta loading this grub."

"Won't be lookin' at her none, Bart," the little man grumbled, turning to do his leader's bidding. "She's deader 'en hell."

Bart lifted a bag of sugar from the buckboard. A bullet shattered the bag before he heard the shot.

All the men dropped down low, facing the trees at the stream where the shot came from. A second shot rang out. They opened fire at the puff of smoke they could clearly see.

"There's another rider coming fast down the road!" one of them shouted.

"Get mounted and follow me!" Bart yelled. "It's that damn marshal. He's got a posse coming at us from every direction." He spurred his horse to full speed in the direction from which they had come.

Three men followed Bart. They crossed the stream, turned south, and disappeared from view behind the tree line.

One man was having trouble getting on his horse. He had a firm grip on the reins but every time he tried to mount, the horse shied away from him. Red was still chasing Susan.

Susan had just started back to her parents when the men charged the wagon. She stopped momentarily, frozen with terror. Her feet felt leaden as she started to run again to her mother, who had toppled off the seat and fallen to the ground. Why wasn't she moving? Was she hurt? Had a bullet struck her?

Suddenly a tall gangly figure blocked her view.

"Well, now. Look at this little pretty we got here."

The words came from a dirty, pockmarked face only partially concealed by a scraggly red beard.

Susan changed her course to go around him, but he moved with her. She turned and circled back in the opposite direction, trying again to get past him. She saw the little skinny man kick her mother, but now her tormentor was so close he was grabbing at her. She whirled and ran from him as fast as her feet could carry her.

His rancorous laughter mixed with a steady stream of vulgarity made it difficult for her addled mind to concentrate on a way to outwit him. Her flashing thoughts settled on a little trick she'd seen played out several times on the school playground. She dropped to her knees and elbows, twisting her body sideways at the same time. Her pursuer tripped over her and fell sprawling face-down.

She sprang on him, grabbed his gun, and wrested it from the holster. She aimed it between his shoulder blades and pulled the trigger. The gun didn't fire.

She squeezed the trigger harder, but still it wouldn't fire. She felt the man jerk his legs from under her. Her panic-stricken mind flashed with conflicting thoughts. Why wouldn't the gun shoot? Suddenly she realized that it was a single-action gun. The hammer had to be cocked back with the thumb. By the time she finally had the hammer cocked, her assailant was on his knees, facing her.

His pale blue eyes were glinting with violent anger that she had outsmarted him. His foul cursing had never ceased. He was reaching for her.

She had little time. Quickly, she swung the gun at his face and fired.

She missed him. The bullet only seared the side of his jaw and tore away the bottom of his ear lobe. But the muzzle blast from the big Colt .45, so close to his face, was more than sufficient to stop him momentarily.

He clutched his powder-burned face and cursed all the louder.

Susan had the hammer cocked and, holding the big gun tight in both hands, was taking careful aim at him by the time he recovered.

When he moved his hands from his face, she fired. The bullet hit him in the mouth and took away a portion of his skull as it exited the back of his head.

She had to move fast to keep the man from pitching forward onto her. She got to her feet and stood looking down at him a few seconds. For just those few fleeting moments her tortured mind was soothed by a gratifying sensation that she had destroyed evil.

But there were more.

She turned to go to her mother. She was surprised to see that the outlaws were gone, all but the one having trouble with his horse.

She need not worry about him. Ryan was closing in on him fast.

The man reached for his pistol as Ryan's bullet struck him down.

Susan started running to her parents.

Ryan reined his horse in, swinging his leg over the saddle horn at the same time. He slipped from the saddle and was running to Molly before his horse had stopped. He felt a need to get to her before Susan did.

He determined in a moment that the wound at her temple was not caused by a bullet, and she was moaning softly.

"She's all right, Susie," he assured her as Susan dropped to her knees beside him. "She just hit her head on a rock or something. She's already coming around. Stay with her. I'll see about Seth."

Susan gently brushed the hair back from Molly's ashen face. "Mama? Mama, can you hear me?"

Molly groaned and frantically clutched Susan's arm as she tried to raise her head. "Seth? Help Seth . . ."

"Lie still, Mama. We're safe now. Ryan's here. He's checking on Papa now."

"He's alive, and I think he's going to be okay. A bullet grazed the right side of his skull. He's unconscious, but his heartbeat is strong, and he's breathing easy. I need some cloth for a compress and bandage," he said as he neared Susan.

186

He cut through the hem of her petticoat with his pocket knife and ripped off what he needed. He saw that Molly's eyes were open, and she was muttering incoherently.

"Your mother will be throwing questions at you any moment now. Be prepared to calm and comfort her."

Ryan had the compress in place and began to wrap the bandage around Seth's head when a voice called out, "Hello the wagon."

Ryan tensed and picked up his rifle from where he had laid it beside Seth.

"Who are you?" he answered.

"My name is Heck Ballinger. I'm a Deputy U.S. Marshal. I've been trailing those men who attacked you. Now don't shoot, I'm coming out."

A horse and rider emerged from the trees about a hundred yards upstream from the road.

"Come on in, but keep your hands in plain sight. I'll be watching you."

Ryan felt that a heavy load had been heaped on him as he continued bandaging Seth. He was not at all sure that Seth would live and the thought of what it would do to Susan if he died tore at his heart. Molly sounded like she was about to become hysterical in spite of Susan's attempts to reassure and calm her. He had outlaws to run down and kill. He was pondering whether the man riding toward them could be trusted. He knew the marshal and the two deputy marshals who served in this federal judicial district. This man was not one of them.

He tied the last knot on the bandage then walked quickly to Susan and Molly. He abruptly picked up Molly, carried her to the wagon, lifted her over the sideboard, and lay her down.

"Molly, now get a hold of yourself!" he said firmly. "Seth is going to need you and don't get alarmed at the sight of him. He looks a mess. His head is all bloody, but he hasn't lost as much blood as it might seem. He's going to be all right. Susan, get in there with her."

He picked up his rifle and took a stance beside the wagon, facing the approaching rider.

"That's close enough," Ryan ordered. When the man was within a few yards of him, Ryan saw there was blood on his shirt at his left shoulder.

The man stopped his horse. "Mister, I understand your concern, but I'm not one of those outlaws. You can see my badge. I really am a deputy marshal, and I could use a little help. I caught a bullet in my shoulder."

"What district do you serve?" Ryan questioned, still keeping his rifle aimed at the man.

"The western district of Arkansas. I've been trailing those men all the way from Fort Smith."

Ryan was so astounded by the man's answer that he no longer felt any suspicion. No one would make the claim of having trailed a band of outlaws all the way from Fort Smith, Arkansas, to Comanche, Texas, and expect it to be believed if it were not true. He laid his rifle in the wagon, approached the marshal, and helped him from his horse.

"You think you can drive the team?" Ryan asked.

"Yeah, I can manage it. But I need a sling for my arm and I want to take a look at that man the young lady killed. I saw it all from where I was."

Ryan turned to Susan. She was already tearing another strip from her petticoat. Ryan and the marshal went to the outlaw, looked at him briefly, and returned to the wagon.

Ryan tied the reins of both horses to the back of the wagon. Then he climbed in and lifted Seth across his legs, cushioning his head in his arms.

Susan held Molly's head in her lap.

The marshal turned the team and put them into a brisk trot. "Little lady," Heck addressed Susan. "That man you killed was one of the meanest, most downright evil varmints that ever desecrated the face of God's green earth. It's right fittin' that he got it from a woman and with his own gun at that. I hope he seen it coming."

"He saw it coming, sir," Susan assured him. "He saw it coming twice."

"That's good." The marshal's voice conveyed a note of praise. "That's real good."

189

A boiling anger was building in Susan as her mind relived what had happened to her parents.

"Ryan, aren't you going after those men?" She was puzzled that he was not already in pursuit of them.

Ryan sensed her frustration. "Of course, I am, Susie. But to just go chasing wildly after them now is not the way to go about it. I'd probably just ride into an ambush and get myself killed. Besides, you need me here now."

"But they are getting farther away all the time."

"I know, but I'm not concerned about that. A couple of hours one way or the other won't make much difference. As soon as we have taken care of your parents and the marshal, I'll go home and get my trailing dog and rig a pack horse. I'll need a little food and water and my big rifle and a few other things. It might take two or three days before I catch up to them and get a good opportunity to move in on them. But I'll get them. Don't fret about it."

He was mostly running his plans through his own mind rather than feeling a need to explain to Susan.

"Won't you get up a posse?" Susan asked.

"Nope. That would only get some good men killed unnecessarily. I'll take care of them myself."

Molly interrupted them. "Susan, why did those men do that to us? They could have had the food. Seth wouldn't have risked getting us hurt, or even killed, by standing up to them over a little food. They didn't have to shoot us."

"They wanted more than the food, Mama. They wanted you and me. But they will pay. I will see them dead. I promise you those evil fiends will be destroyed."

Ryan studied Susan's face trying to understand the meaning of the promise she had made her mother. His thoughts were interrupted by the marshal.

"You're right, ma'am. They would have took you and your mother with them. They did need the food. That's why they were lurking there, waiting for someone to come along. They lost their pack horse yesterday and most of their food with it. But they most surely would have taken you and your mother if we hadn't driven them off. We're coming into town. What's the name of this place?"

"Comanche," Ryan informed him.

"Comanche?" After a moment's reflection he shook his head. "You folks sure got a strange sense of humor."

Chapter Eleven

Marshal Ballinger pulled the wagon to a stop in front of the doctor's office and set the brake.

Doc Thornton glanced up from his paperwork and looked out the window. He recognized Ryan but not the man with his arm in a sling and blood on his shirt. Removing his spectacles, he stepped to the door as the marshal was climbing down from the buckboard.

"Doc, we're gonna need some help. The man in the wagon is bad hurt." The marshal kept his voice low, not wanting to alarm Susan and her mother.

"There's a litter leaning against the wall in the corner of my office. Get it while I take a look."

The doctor stepped around to the back of the wagon and climbed in. "What happened,

Ryan?" He placed his hand on the side of Seth's neck, checking for a pulse.

"They were ambushed by a gang of outlaws about a mile out of town. Luckily, I wasn't too far behind them, and the marshal was chasing the outlaws from the opposite direction."

By the time Marshal Ballinger returned with the litter, a small crowd had gathered around the wagon.

"What happened?"

"Was it Indians?"

"No, it was a band of outlaws," Heck assured the nervous crowd.

"A couple of you men get up here and help us lift Seth onto the stretcher. Susan, help your mother down from the wagon and into the office. Now be careful. She might get a little dizzy when she starts walking," the doctor cautioned.

Molly scooted to the end of the wagon. "I don't want to leave Seth," she protested.

"Mama, you can't do anything to help Papa right now, and I don't want you fainting in the middle of the street. The men will get Papa in the doctor's office in just a few minutes."

Susan understood her mother's anxiety. She felt it, too. But for her mother's sake she knew she had to stay calm. She glanced at Ryan, needing his reassurance that her father was indeed going to be okay.

Ryan read the uncertainty in Susan's eyes. "Molly, go with Susan. We're fixing to bring Seth in right now."

Molly hesitated a few seconds more before she let Susan help her into the doctor's office.

"Ryan, hold Seth's head as still as you can. Homer, you lift him under his shoulders and I'll lift his hips. Doug, you slide this stretcher under him. Okay, everybody ready?" the doctor asked.

At Ryan's nod, the three of them eased Seth up and onto the cloth stretcher.

"Careful now, try not to jar him." The doctor led the way into a small room that was partitioned off from his main office.

Susan followed close behind the men carrying her father, watching as they gently lay him on the bed.

The doctor went to a basin of water and started washing his hands.

"Ryan, get everyone cleared out of here while I examine Seth's wounds. There's a cot and folding screen in the closet. I'd appreciate it if you would set them up in the outer office and help the marshal until I can take a look at his shoulder."

Ryan nodded his head and stepped into the crowded office. "Will one of you men go get Sheriff Thomas and the undertaker?" Ryan asked the group of men gathered around the door.

Ben Walker, the owner of the general store, stepped forward. "I saw the sheriff ride out early this morning. Don't think he's back yet, but I'll go get Oscar."

"Tell him there's two dead men about a mile

out of town, just before you get to that first small stream. One of them is right by the road, and the other is back toward a large pecan tree. He shouldn't have any trouble finding them. And bring the horses in if he can catch them. Tell him not to bury the men until the sheriff gets a look at them."

"Sure thing, Ryan."

"Thanks, Ben. The rest of you can go on about your work. We'll let you know something as soon as possible. And thanks for your help," Ryan said as he ushered the rest of the men out the door.

Susan stood at the doctor's side, waiting anxiously as he examined her father.

"The bullet creased his skull. He has a concussion and will probably be out for several hours, but he'll live. I'll have to keep him here for two or three days. Maybe longer. Stay with him a minute while I take a look at the marshal."

Molly was seated in an armchair holding her aching head in her hands. The doctor mixed some laudanum in a glass of water and held it out to her.

"This should make you feel better, Mrs. Bradford." The doctor's voice startled Molly.

"Seth? Is he . . ."

"He's doing fine. He's going to be like new in a few days. Now drink this and settle back and relax."

Ryan had helped the marshal get his shirt off by the time the doctor stepped behind the screen.

"Well, at least I won't have to dig for a bullet," the doctor observed, leaning close to peer at the wound.

"Nope. It went all the way through," the marshal stated.

"Looks like it might have passed through an area where it shouldn't have done much bone damage. Can you move it?" the doctor asked.

"Yeah. I've been testing it some. It moves pretty good, but it sure hurts like hell."

"Well, I'll get back to you as soon as I clean up and stitch Mister Bradford's head. Ryan, make him as comfortable as you can."

Susan left her father's side only when the doctor insisted that she could be of no help to him and that she needed to relax and rest herself.

She sat down in the doctor's chair and lay back in the comfortable leather-covered cushioning and closed her eyes. But she was keenly alert as Ryan began questioning the marshal.

"Tell me about those outlaws you were after. But make it as brief as you can. I'm a Ranger and I've got to be getting on their trail. What are they wanted for?"

"What they were wanted for to start with was to be brought back to Fort Smith and hanged. They had all been convicted of murder, bank robbery, rape, and some other things, and sentenced to hang. They managed somehow to escape. Me and two other deputies were assigned to bring 'em in or kill 'em. And told not to come back till we did. But they're wanted for a lot more than that now. There were five of them."

"Six," Ryan corrected.

"Nope. Just five. The one you killed joined up with them along the way. That's been our problem from the start, especially while they were passing through Indian territory. We moved in on them four times and killed two or three every time. Hell, Mister. We killed ten men, but they all turned out to be some other riffraff running from the law who had joined them along the way. The little lady killed the only one of the five we were after."

"How did you manage to stay on their trail so long?"

"That wasn't too hard to do. Partly just plain trackin', of course, but mostly just following their trail of depredations. They've killed two men and a young girl. One of the men was trying to protect his womenfolk. The girl wasn't more than fifteen. I was told they treated her so bad that she strangled to death on her own vomit. They raped and abused at least three other women I know about. The other man was a deputy sheriff at a little town north of here called Palo Pinto. He was trying to protect his town. They've been looting and raising hell in towns all along the way." He shook his head in resignation. "We ain't had no trouble following 'em. They have been heading steady south ever since they left Indian territory."

"What happened to your partners?"

"They both got killed late yesterday evening. Them varmints have been settin' ambush traps for us right along and yesterday evening, we finally rode into one. I just kept following 'em, hoping to get help at the next town I came to."

Ryan rose to his feet. "You found your help, and I've got to get going."

"Well, I gotta give you a little advice, even though I don't think you need it. Don't try to take those men alive. Don't give 'em any more chance at you then you absolutely have to. They know there's nothing waitin' for 'em but the hangman's noose. They won't be taken alive. Don't you think you ought to reconsider and take a posse with you?"

"Nope." Ryan shook his head. "I think you would agree that the only way a posse could get at those men is in a close quarters shootout and that would get some good men killed or wounded. I just don't think that's necessary. I intend to lay back and pick them off from long range, well out of sight of their Winchester carbines or any other rifle they're apt to be carrying."

"I heard you tell the young lady you was takin' a big gun with you. What kind is it?"

"A Sharps fifty-caliber buffalo rifle."

The marshal nodded his approval. "That oughta do it. I never owned one, but I've seen a couple. I'm told they'll kill a man at more than half a mile, if you can hit him that far away."

"You were told right." Ryan extended his

hand for a farewell handshake. "Well, I'd better get going. If you're gone by the time I get back, I'll make my report to the Federal District Court at Fort Smith."

Susan was already moving to Ryan as he turned toward her. Their bodies met in a warm embrace.

"Now don't you sit around and worry yourself sick about me. I can take care of myself."

"I know. I'm not going to sit around and worry about you at all."

"Good girl." He raised her face, kissed her gently, and abruptly left the office.

Susan moved to the screen where the marshal lay on the cot.

"May I come in, Marshal?"

"Why sure, miss. Come on in."

Susan stepped around the screen and knelt beside him. "Your name didn't register when you identified yourself back there."

"Heck Ballinger, ma'am."

"Thank you, Heck Ballinger, for risking your life to help us. I will be forever grateful."

"Just done what I had to do, ma'am."

Susan was astonished by the man's statement. That's the same thing Ryan had said. "Just did what he had to do." She wondered if they understood *why* they did what they had to do. Probably not, she reasoned. Such men didn't make a deliberate, thought-out decision to give of themselves, to risk their lives for others, expecting nothing in return. Their selfless nature simply forced them to do what they saw as their duty.

"You are quite a man, Mister Ballinger. This country could use more men like you."

"Thank you, ma'am. That's a real nice compliment, but I reckon I'll just go on back to Fort Smith soon as I'm able to. They need all the help they can get there, too."

Susan smiled. "I consider myself privileged to have met you, Heck Ballinger. You will be a special man in my memories."

Heck ducked his head and cleared his throat. He was pleased but embarrassed by Susan's compliments.

"You just see that that Ranger of yours looks out for himself. Those are mighty dangerous men he'll be after."

"I will, but what makes you think he's my Ranger?"

"First off, he told me he was, but even before he told me I thought so 'cause I ain't never seen a man in such a hurry to ride up against six gunmen before. He had that horse stretched out and bellied down like he couldn't get there fast enough. Soon as I seen you, I knew what his hurry was."

Susan smiled shyly. "I hope you're right about the way he feels about me. Now I'd better let you rest. I'm going to look in on my papa."

Doc Thornton was stitching her father's wound when she entered the room.

"Are you sure he's going to be all right, Doctor?"

"Sure as I can be right now. There's always the possibility of an infection, but, barring that, he'll be healed in a few days."

"He's not going to like the haircut you gave him."

The doctor chuckled. "They usually don't, but I just explain to them that I'm not a barber. I'm just an ole pill roller."

"Well, if you're sure he'll be all right, I'm going to leave now. I'll be gone for a while, but my mother will be here to help you take care of Papa. And Hazel will probably help some, too."

"Don't fret about it. Run along and do whatever it is you need to do. Your father will be well taken care of."

"Thank you, sir. And about the marshal. Put your fee for his care on Papa's bill."

She went to her mother and knelt down beside her. Molly seemed to be sleeping. Susan gently shook her shoulder.

"I'm sorry to wake you, Mother, but I have to talk to you."

"That's all right, dear. I really wasn't sleeping. I was just dozing. Is something wrong?"

"No. Papa is doing fine. Now listen closely. I'll be gone for a while. I've got to help Ryan get ready to go after those outlaws. I want you to take a room in the hotel so that you can be here close to Papa until he can go home. Hazel will come and help you. Do you understand what I'm telling you, Mother?"

"I think so, but why do you have to be

gone so long?" The laudanum the doctor had given her for her headache made her a bit woozy and sleepy. She was having difficulty comprehending exactly what Susan was trying to tell her.

"You don't have to understand right now, Mother. You just sit back and relax. I'll be back as soon as I can."

"All right, dear. But please do be careful and don't be gone too long."

"Yes, Mother. I'll be careful," Susan assured her. "I'm going to leave a note for the doctor to give to Papa when he wakes up."

Susan kissed her mother on the forehead and gave her a reassuring hug before she again sat in the doctor's chair to write a note for her father. When she finished, she carefully folded the note and slipped soundlessly into the room where her father lay.

"Susan, your father is going to be all right. Quit worrying."

Susan nodded her head. "Doctor Thornton, will you give this to my father when he is fully conscious? Or if Kyle Weston comes in before Papa wakes up, you can give the note to him."

"Aren't you going to stay with your mother?" the kindly doctor questioned.

"I'll be back. Right now I need to help Ryan. I want to be sure he knows what those murdering outlaws look like," she hedged.

Susan pushed the team hard as she headed home. She had lingered at the doctor's office in order to let Ryan get far enough ahead of her so he wouldn't see her leaving town. Now she had to make up for lost time. She knew Ryan would be in a hurry to get home and gather the things he needed to start tracking the outlaws. She couldn't afford to let him gain any more time on her.

Pulling into the yard, she jumped out of the wagon, unhitched the team, and hurriedly yanked the harness off them before turning them into the corral.

She saddled Spooky as fast as she could. Grabbing her saddlebags and a canteen out of the tack room, she ran to the house, unbuttoning her dress as she went. After changing into her pants and shirt and pulling her boots on, she stuffed some clothes and a few other necessities in one of the bags. She put extra ammunition for her pistol and rifle in the other bag.

Strapping her gun belt on and grabbing her rifle from its place in the corner of her bedroom, she plopped her hat on her head and headed to the kitchen. After filling her canteen with water, she wrapped what was left of a chocolate cake in a dishcloth and did the same with a loaf of light bread. She looked quickly around for what else she might take, but decided that Ryan would have all they would need. Quickly adding these to her saddlebags, she ran out the back door to the barn. She hurriedly tied her bedroll behind her saddle, tossed her saddlebags across Spooky's back, and hung her canteen of water on the saddle horn.

Swinging into the saddle, she set Spooky into a gallop and headed to the spot where the outlaws had attacked them. She knew that Ryan would start trailing them from that point.

When Susan reached the place where the outlaws had left the road, she could plainly see the hoofprints left in the soft, sandy loam. She dismounted and walked along the tracks for a short distance, being careful not to step directly on the trail.

Even though some of the tracks overlapped, she felt sure there were no more than four horses. Seeing no sign of a dog or bootprints, she was satisfied that she had beat Ryan there.

She led Spooky into the shade of the trees to wait for him. She would be able to see him a quarter of a mile from her where the road made a bend around a grove of large knotty oaks.

Twenty minutes later she was beginning to wonder if she really had arrived ahead of him when suddenly he came around the bend. He was riding Pegasus, the big black stallion he'd ridden at the Indian fight at the Morgan place. The pack horse galloping along beside him was a beautiful roan.

She stepped onto the road leading Spooky with her.

Ryan reined up a few paces from her and looked at her. Then he looked away as though he was studying something off in the distance.

"Why am I not surprised to see you here?" His question was more of a statement of exasperation.

"I guess it's because you expected to."

"Well, you guessed wrong. Now get on that horse and get on back to town."

"You know I'm not going to do that, Ryan. I can't let you go after those men alone. I'm going with you."

"No, you're not going with me. I could have raised a posse of twenty men or more if I thought I needed any help."

"Yes, you could have. Why didn't you?"

"Because I never had any intent of charging in and shooting it out with those men. I'm going to shoot them from long range."

"I know, but I also know you won't do that unless you're positive who you're shooting at. I can identify them with your field glasses."

"Well, I must say that would be of some help. But that's still not a good enough reason to take the risk of letting you go with me."

Looking him square in the eyes, her hands firmly planted on her hips, she stated in a tone of voice that she thought left no room for argument, "Ryan, I am going with you."

Ryan took off his hat and ran his fingers through his hair. "Susie, please don't give me any more trouble. I don't have time for it."

"You're right," Susan agreed. "Every second we spend talking those men are getting farther away. So let's get started after them."

"Damn it, Susan!" Ryan exploded. "You know

damn well you can't go with me. I know how you feel but—"

"No! You don't know how I feel, Ryan. You just know how *you* feel. Sure you feel anger and a desire to kill those evil monsters for what they've done. But you see, Ryan, I feel more than that. I feel a sickening revulsion at what my mother would have suffered had she fallen victim to those creatures. You heard what Heck said about how they had treated other women. I don't think it's possible for a man to fully understand the horror that a woman like my mother—"

"Susan, please stop," Ryan interrupted. "Don't say any more. I think I do understand what you're telling me. You must know that it chills me to the very depth of my soul to think that you would have suffered the same fate."

"No, Ryan. I wouldn't have. That's what makes it even worse. I would have simply fought them until they killed me. But my mother . . ." Susan's voice cracked. She turned from Ryan to hide her emotions.

Ryan swung down and went to her, taking her in his arms. "Please hush and quit thinking about it. I do understand how you feel."

Susan took a deep breath and composed herself. She looked up at him through tear-blurred eyes. "Then you understand that I must see those creatures dead. One of those bastards even kicked Mama because he thought she was dead and he wasn't going to have his fun with her!"

Susan's emotion-choked words tore at Ryan's heart.

"Yes, Susie. I understand that you must be assured that they will be killed. I do assure you that whatever it takes, or however long it takes, they will be killed."

"How long will it take, Ryan? How long do I wait before I start looking for you?"

Ryan held her at arm's length, studying her. "What do you mean? Damnation, Susie. You don't start looking for me. You just wait till I get back."

"Oh, I see. And if you're not back in a month, do I just wait another month? Surely, at some point, I have to decide that you didn't make it and that you're not coming back. Then I would have to forget you and get on with my life. Right? No, Ryan." She shook her head. "I can't do that. I just can't handle it. I'm going with you. Wouldn't you rather have me with you than out wandering around looking for you?"

Ryan pulled her to him and held her close. "You're making this mighty difficult for me."

Susan pulled away so that she could look into his eyes. "I'm just doing what I have to do."

Ryan's eyes met hers, pleading for understanding. He saw only determination, and his shoulders sagged in resignation.

"I hope you told someone what you were going to do."

"Yes. I left a note with the doctor to give to Papa or Kyle."

Ryan nodded his approval. "Kyle will be there before dark. He'll be able to reassure your parents somewhat. He's the sort that if you get one leg broke, he'll soon have you assured that you're lucky you didn't get them both broke. Well, let's get started."

Ryan walked to his horse and, taking a paper pad and pencil from his saddlebag, went to the tracks left by the outlaws' horses. He squatted and began writing and making sketches.

"What are you doing?" Susan asked.

"I'm making notes of identifying markings of the hoofprints."

"I thought the dog would do the trailing."

"He will. But if a heavy rain comes and washes out the tracks and scent, I'll need this to get us back on their trail again."

Susan looked at the dog laying on the mat on top of the pack horse, wondering just how much help it really would be.

"Come here, Dog," Ryan commanded.

Dog leaped from the horse and ran to its master.

Ryan put the dog on the trail, got on his horse, and they moved out behind the dog.

"What's the matter with that horse?" Susan asked when the pack horse forced its way between her and Ryan.

"You're riding on her side. You'll have to ride on my right side or behind me except when Bluebell has to get behind me, too. If she has to get behind me, then you will have to get behind her."

Susan gave Ryan a skeptical look. "You're joking, of course."

"Nope. That horse is trained to stay right with me on my left side. Makes no difference whether we're walking or running. If conditions are such that she can't stay beside me, she will drop in behind me. In either case, she will not tolerate another horse being between me and her."

"Well, I never!" Susan exclaimed.

Ryan chuckled. "You will now. I trained her that way so I wouldn't have to drag her around on a lead rope."

Susan dropped back and moved to Ryan's right side. "I don't see how you can train horses so well," she grumbled. "You don't even know enough about horses to know that the mythical Pegasus is a white horse."

Ryan chuckled. "Don't blame that on me. Hazel thought this black stallion was the prettiest horse she'd ever seen. She just had to give him a poetic name."

"I suppose then it was Hazel who named the mare Bluebell."

"Yep. I would have just called her Blue."

"Does the dog have any peculiar temperaments I need to know about?"

"Nope. He's content just to follow whatever trail I put him on."

"Why don't you use a pure-blooded trailing hound?"

"They make too much noise. I wanted a dog that didn't give voice at all. A bird dog never barks when it's hunting or pointing. So I crossed a trailing hound with an English Setter bird dog. I was lucky to get a pup with the trailing instincts of the hound and the silence of the bird dog."

Susan watched the dog moving steadily along in front of their trotting horses, its nose a few inches above the grass-covered ground. She looked for hoofprints ahead of them but could only occasionally make out what she thought might be one.

"Are you sure that dog knows what it's doing?"

"Yep. I'm sure. As long as he's moving steady and acting like he knows what he's doing, everything's fine. It's only when he acts like he don't know what he's doing that you have to be concerned that he might have lost the scent."

They kept moving at a steady pace. Sometimes side by side and sometimes through the wooded areas, Susan was forced to drop back behind Ryan only to be displaced by the pack horse.

The four outlaws arrived at the stream just before sundown.

"This is good clean water. We'll camp here," Bart stated with authority.

Jake looked nervously back over their trail. "Seems to me like we oughta keep movin', Bart. We could go a good piece yet before it gets plumb dark."

"Aw, hell, Jake, you worry too much. We ain't seen hide nor hair of anybody following us. I think we might have killed that damn marshal. He didn't shoot no more after we shot at him."

"Maybe so," Jake agreed. "But somebody done some shootin'. I heard three shots after we lit out, and Red and Link ain't showed up yet. Makes me suspect they got killed by that fella that was acomin' hell bent for leather down the road at us."

"Serves 'em right if they did. That stupid Link never did have the sense of a pissant," Bart retorted. "Anybody that don't have sense enough to git on his horse is bound ta git it sooner or later. That damn Red was so intent on catchin' that gal he didn't know what the hell was goin' on."

"Yeah," the little man called Spike chimed in. "You shoulda let me git that gal. She'd be here now if'n you'd a left her ta me. What really galls my ass though is that that other woman got killed. Damn, she was fine lookin'. If'n I knowed who shot her, I'd shoot his balls off."

"Aw, hell, Spike. You wouldn't have lasted two minutes with either of 'em nohow," Bart goaded. "Now that's enough gripin' from the both of you. We're campin' here."

The sun was touching the horizon when Ryan stopped and dismounted.

"We'll eat supper here and feed the horses a little grain."

"You want me to start a fire?" Susan asked.

"Nope. Supper's already cooked. We're having fried chicken and corn bread."

"Fried chicken and corn bread?"

"Yep. Hazel was cutting up chickens for supper when I got home. She fried me some while I readied my pack horse. The corn bread was left over from their dinner."

Susan shook her head in disbelief. "I hope you pay Hazel well."

"Don't exactly pay her anything. She just helps herself to whatever money she needs. She knows she can have anything she wants, and that everything I own will be hers in the event of my death. Hasn't it occurred to you yet that Hazel is the only mother I've ever known?"

"Of course it has, silly. My reference to paying her was just my way of saying I hope you appreciate her as fully as you should. Now where's the food? I'm starved."

"It's in my left saddlebag. I'll feed the horses while you get it out."

Susan opened the bulging bag and removed two napkin-wrapped bundles. Then, sitting down cross-legged on the ground, she unfolded them.

"There's more than enough food here for three people!" she exclaimed. "How did Hazel know there would be someone else with you?"

Ryan laughed. "She didn't. She cooked for me and Dog. Any time Hazel cooks for two, there will be enough for three."

Ryan sat beside Susan and picked up a piece of chicken for himself and tossed a piece to Dog.

"They'll be making camp about now. Wonder why they're heading west?"

"Do you think we have gained on them?" Susan asked before taking the last bite of her piece of chicken. She tossed the bone to Dog and licked the grease from her fingers.

"No, not much anyway, but we will before we stop for the night," Ryan said, amused at Susan's unladylike action.

"It is night. I thought we were going to spend the night here. How can we keep following their trail in the dark?"

"That's where Dog comes in. He don't need to see to follow their trail. There will be enough moonlight for us to follow Dog."

Susan looked at Dog who was waiting expectantly for more of his share of the food. The mixed breed, white with black-and-brown blotches, flicked his ears back and forth. He knew they were talking about him.

"Seems to me you could have come up with a more appropriate name for such a marvelous dog than just Dog," Susan said.

Ryan shrugged his shoulders. "Seems to suit him." He gave the dog another piece of chicken and a square of corn bread.

They finished their meal in silence. Ryan wrapped what food remained along with the bones in the napkins and put it in his saddlebag.

"You're gonna have a good breakfast, Dog, but you'll earn it before this night is over," Ryan said.

Ryan put Dog back on the trail. The pack horse and Susan fell in behind him.

When the last vestiges of sunlight faded away, leaving only the faint light of the half-moon, Susan could barely see Dog from her rear position. She knew Ryan was having to give his total attention to the dog as they wound their way through the woods.

"Aren't you concerned that we might ride into an ambush?" she asked.

"Nah. Dog will scent them if they try that. We can't talk much, though, except when you're beside me. Our voices carry a long way in the night air. They would hear us before Dog could scent them."

"Well, I hope there is a lot of clear country ahead of us so I can ride beside you. I'm getting a bit weary of looking at your pack horse's behind."

Susan was enjoying one of her few opportunities to ride beside Ryan when he ordered Dog to stop. He shielded the light of a match carefully in his hands and read his watch.

"Quarter to eleven. If they camped at sundown, we've been moving nearly as long as they have. We'll stop here."

He took Susan's bedroll from her saddle and spread it in the best place he could find.

"I'll take care of the horses. There's good grass here for them to eat. I'll stake them out on ropes."

"I can help you," Susan offered.

"Nope. I want you to get all the rest you can.

215

It's gonna be daylight again long before you'd like for it to be." He dropped his own bedroll near Susan's before leaving to take care of the horses.

Susan pulled her boots off and rolled her head from side to side, trying to ease the tight muscles in her neck before stretching out on her blanket. She hadn't realized just how tense and tired she was. The day's events had just about drained all of her energy. She tried in vain to stay awake until Ryan finished with the horses.

Ryan stood silently looking down at the sleeping woman. Susan lay curled up in a ball on her side, one hand beside her head, the other under her chin. She didn't even stir when he tucked the blanket around her to ward off the chill of the night air.

He smiled thinking how innocent she looked in sleep, almost like a child. Looking at her now, no one would believe that only a few hours earlier, she had stood her ground against a gang of ruthless outlaws.

He had been there, yet it was still hard for him to believe that she had shot one of the killers in the face—twice.

Spreading his blanket close enough that he could reach out and touch her, he leaned over and lightly kissed her lips before lying on his side facing her.

Even though his body was weary, his troubled thoughts wouldn't let him find sleep as easily as Susan had. He hoped—prayed—that

Kyle was right about the sergeant being the only man who cared enough about what had happened that fateful day ten years ago that he would want to send him to prison or kill him.

But what if Kyle was wrong?

Chapter Twelve

Susan awoke to the sound of snapping sticks and crunching bones.

Ryan was breaking the sticks and adding them to the fire he had started. A coffeepot was next to the fire, and Dog was crunching the bones.

"Couldn't you have waited for second light to do that?" she quipped, yawning.

Ryan chuckled. "I was sorely tempted to. Have never been too fond of first light myself. But I had to figure they would be up early, too. We can't let them get any further ahead of us."

His reference to the outlaws brought Susan to her feet and moving to the fire.

"I was going to let you sleep as long as

I could," Ryan continued. "But since you're up, you can cook breakfast while I ready the horses."

Susan stared down at the half-dozen eggs and salt bacon beside the frying pan.

"How did Hazel get those eggs here? Hand deliver them while we slept?"

Ryan chuckled. "She packed them in lint cotton. Sometimes they make it, sometimes they don't. But I don't ever tell her when they don't."

Susan put the bacon in the frying pan and walked to her saddlebag to get the loaf of light bread she had packed.

"Seems like you don't suffer too much when you're out on the trail. Chicken and corn bread for supper. Bacon, eggs, and toast for breakfast. I can hardly wait for lunch," Susan teased.

"Lunch will be jerky and hardtack," Ryan informed her.

"I was afraid of that," she muttered.

They were about a hundred yards from a major creek when they came upon the remains of the outlaws' campfire.

"Kind of figured they would stop here," Ryan said.

He watched as Dog sniffed out the area where the horses had been staked for the night, trying to sort out what had taken place. Dog circled the area until he picked up the trail where the horses left the campsite.

"Let's go," Ryan said when Dog hesitated only momentarily before splashing into the water.

"Looks like they went straight on across the creek."

There was abundant evidence on either bank to verify that Dog was right.

Ryan filled their canteens from the crystal-clear water that bubbled over the limestone bedrock and let the horses drink their fill.

When they left the thick growth of the creek valley behind, Susan moved up beside Ryan. They traveled about five miles, holding their horses to a steady trot, when suddenly the trail turned south.

"I suspect one or more of those men knows a good bit about Texas," Ryan observed.

"What makes you think so?"

"I figured they knew if they headed south from Comanche, it would take them through the more populated areas. Instead, they rode west until they got past Brownwood, and now they've turned south here. They know they'll be traveling through a much more sparsely populated part of the state—all the way to Mexico."

"Do you think we'll overtake them soon?"

"Yeah. They don't seem to be in any big hurry. Mostly just walking and sometimes trotting their horses. If they keep on that way, we should be within a mile or so of them in a few hours."

"What do you mean by a mile or so? What will we do then?"

Ryan shrugged his shoulders. "Just follow along behind them and wait for an opportunity. Just wait for them to make a mistake."

"That could take a long time."

"Maybe so, but that's the way it's got to be. I'm not going to give them a shot at us. But don't fret about it. We'll get them. We'll camp on their trail until we do," Ryan assured Susan. "Hold up a minute."

Ryan got off his horse and called Dog to him. "You're gonna ride awhile," he said as he lifted the dog to the pad atop the pack horse.

"You think you can follow the trail without him?" Susan asked.

"Yeah. It has rained recently, making the ground soft. They left tracks easy to follow. Besides, it's plain to see they're headed for that gap in the ridge there." He pointed to a split in the ridge ahead of them. "Ain't no use for Dog to run that three or four miles."

"Well, Dog certainly deserves a rest. He's been working hard. I don't see how he does it."

"Oh, he can run all day if he has to. Gets kind of rough on his feet, though. I let him ride whenever I can."

When they reached the ridge, Ryan stopped and scanned the area around the gap through his field glasses.

"Don't see nothing, but it's a good place for an ambush. Keep your eyes peeled."

Halfway through the gap, a band of Comanche warriors dashed from behind a cedar-covered landslide mound and spread out in a line effectively blocking Ryan and Susan's path. There were eight of them. Shots sounded behind them. There were five more Indians galloping toward them, firing as they came, even though they were out of range.

"What'll we do?" Susan's voice was shrill with excitement.

Ryan's mind was quickly assessing the situation. "They're not looking for a close-quarters fight. They're trying to make us take cover, hoping to pin us down and finish us off at their leisure. They're after these three fine horses."

A bullet struck the ground close behind Spooky, spraying her hind legs with the caliche soil. Spooky spooked and lunged into a full run—straight at the eight warriors.

"Whoa!" Susan screamed. "Whoa, Spooky! Whoa!" She aimed her rifle and fired. "Whoa, damn it! Whoa!" She screamed and fired and screamed and fired.

Her unexpected action took Ryan by surprise. She was a hundred yards ahead of him before his mind had registered the fact that Spooky was out of control. He set the heel of his boot into Pegasus' flanks and opened fire with his Winchester when he was in range. He saw an Indian fall from his horse. Another one fell whom he was not shooting at.

Susan was screaming and shooting ahead of him. Indians were whooping and shooting behind him. A bullet tore at his hat brim. Another burned his side.

The Indian line broke and parted, half going one way and half the other. Spooky sprinted between them, carrying Susan rapidly away.

The Indians behind Ryan were closing in.

He would have to stop them or they would continue to pursue them. He hauled Pegasus back on his rump and spun him around. A bullet clipped the side of his boot top. He shot two Comanches from their mounts. The other three peeled off and headed up the slope. His rifle hammer clicked on empty. He slipped bullets from his gun belt as he whirled his horse around. He would stand his ground, holding the Indians' attention until Susan was far away.

But Susan was not going far away.

"Good God Almighty! She's coming back!"

Susan was holding her empty rifle in one hand and shooting her pistol with the other.

Ryan switched his own empty rifle to his left hand as he urged Pegasus into a full sprint and drew his pistol. Bluebell was running beside him. Dog was barking at the Indians from his perch on top of Bluebell.

Ryan motioned wildly at Susan with his rifle, yelling at her to turn back, while at the same time firing at the Indians to his right.

A warrior slumped and grabbed his horse's mane as Ryan swept by him.

By this time Susan had Spooky turned around and was riding abreast of Ryan, as though she had rehearsed it.

Ryan pressed Pegasus for full speed, glancing behind them every few seconds, but also watching closely ahead for the outlaws. He had no way of knowing for sure just how close they were to them.

Spooky was running beside Pegasus. Bluebell was close behind. The Indians were not pursuing them. After a half-mile he called to Susan to pull up. They held their pace at a gallop for a little while, then slowed to a trot, letting the horses catch their wind.

"Shouldn't we be pressing on?" Susan asked. "Aren't you afraid the Indians will come after us?"

"No, I don't think so. They've got four dead or badly wounded and two or three others wounded to some degree. I suspect all the fight has gone out of them for a while. They won't follow us."

Ryan slowed the heavily breathing horses to a walk and ordered Dog off the pack horse. They zigzagged until Dog picked up the outlaws' trail again. Then Ryan stopped, dismounted, and started unbuttoning his shirt.

"Susie, I got shot back there. I reckon we'd better clean the wound and put some coal oil on it."

Susan's heart was pounding in alarm and she was off Spooky and to him in an instant. "Why didn't you tell me you were hurt?" she demanded.

"Take it easy. It's just a little nick on my left side here."

Susan breathed a sigh of relief when she saw that it truly was just "a little nick." It had hardly even bled. Actually, it was more of a burn than a wound. She went to her saddlebags and pulled out a cotton shirt. "Give me your knife." She cut the seam and tore a three-inch wide strip from the bottom of the shirt to use as a bandage. Then she ripped off another piece to use as a cleansing cloth.

"The frontier is hell on a woman's wardrobe, too," she muttered as she destroyed the shirt.

Ryan chuckled at her quip. He took a small metal flask of coal oil from his saddlebag and handed it to her.

"Those Indians didn't seem to be shooting at me," Susan stated as she cleansed the wound. "I wonder why?"

"I noticed that myself. Could be that you scared the hell out of them. Don't reckon they've had too many women come charging at them, screaming and hollering like you did." He chuckled. "But I more nearly suspect they figured you must be touched in the head by the Great Spirit."

"That makes me feel a little sorry for them," Susan said.

"Don't feel sorry for them, Susie. Don't *ever* do that. You give a Comanche warrior the advantage of sympathy and he'll hang your scalp from his lodge pole. Except in your case, he'd make you his squaw. And then his Comanche squaws would make you their slave. They'd have great fun waking you up in the morning by sticking firebrands to the bottom of your feet. That serves two purposes: They get to hear you scream and it keeps you from running away. Then when they had sufficiently burned your feet they'd take great delight in sticking the firebrands to your nose."

"All right, all right. That's enough. I'm not sorry for them anymore."

"Well, see that you remember it. The reason we beat them so bad and escaped as easy as we did is because that spooky mare of yours surprised them with her sudden charge. They were not quick-witted enough to cope with such an unexpected event. That crazy mare is going to get you killed yet."

Ryan flinched as Susan applied the coal oil directly on his wound.

"Now don't you start picking on Spooky. She got us out of there, didn't she?"

"She gave you a break all right. Why in the hell didn't you keep going?"

Susan looked up at him, puzzled by his question. "Keep going? You mean just run off and leave you there by yourself against all those Indians?"

"Yes, that's what I mean. That's what you should have done," he insisted.

"No. That's not what I should have done. I couldn't do that. I will never run away and leave you to fight alone."

She wrapped the bandage around Ryan's waist. There was barely enough to tie it.

Ryan walked around Pegasus, examining him closely as he buttoned his shirt. "Look Spooky over good to be sure she didn't get hit."

"Oh, my gosh," she exclaimed, darting to Spooky.

"Find anything?" Ryan asked as he examined Bluebell for wounds.

Susan breathed a sigh of relief. "No, thank God. She seems to be fine." She patted Spooky's neck affectionately.

"Looks like the only hit we took is this bag of oats." Ryan determined that the bullet had not penetrated through the leather pack pad. "Bluebell would have gotten gut-shot but for the pack she's carrying. Well, let's get going."

He mounted and took a long, searching look behind them before moving out on the trail.

"I'll say one thing for Spooky. She sure can run. I had Pegasus stretched out and bellied down for all he's worth, but Spooky stayed right with him."

Susan patted Spooky's neck. "She can run when she wants to," she acknowledged proudly. "Outrun anything you've got," she boasted.

"Is that so? Well, maybe we'll just see about that when we get back home. Pegasus is not the fastest horse I've got. He's fast all right, but I look on him mostly as my war horse. We might just get up a race between Spooky and Wildfire," Ryan challenged.

"Is Wildfire that magnificent sorrel stallion I've seen?"

"Yep. That's him," he said proudly.

"That still wouldn't prove anything. I said she could run when she wanted to. But she wouldn't want to run off and leave Wildfire any more than she did Pegasus. She'd just run along beside him and it'd be a tie match." She grinned impishly.

He smiled at her and shook his head. "You're priceless."

Ryan stopped at noon to get some jerky, hardtack, and Susan's chocolate cake from the pack.

Susan dismounted, looking around for the best place to empty her bladder.

"We'll have to eat on the move. They haven't stopped so we can't either."

"Okay, I'll only be a couple of minutes. You said awhile back there that we would be catching up to them in a few hours. Why haven't we?"

"We have. They're only a mile or so ahead of us."

"How can you tell? I haven't seen them. Have you?"

"Nope. Dog tells me. He gets eager when the scent is hot. He's been wanting to move faster for some time now. We'll stay close and watch for a chance to get a shot at them."

Five hours later when they topped out on a ridge, the chance still had not come, but Ryan felt it would soon. He had been through this country before and knew that Brady Creek ran through the wide valley they were overlooking. He figured the outlaws would camp at the creek. They descended the ridge, and he located a campsite.

"We're probably going to camp here, Susie. I'm going to scout on ahead a piece to be sure. You can rest but don't unsaddle until I get back." He tethered the pack horse before mounting Pegasus again. "I should be back in thirty or forty minutes."

Susan offered no objection. Since he was leaving his big rifle behind, she knew he wouldn't attack the outlaws until he came back for it. She sat down on the soft grass to wait for him.

Ryan stopped about six hundred yards from the outlaws' camp. From there, he had a good overview of their campsite. They were near the creek in a cluster of live oak trees. Not much chance of getting a shot at them there, he thought. But their horses were staked in a grass-covered clearing adjoining the trees. When they went to their horses in the morning, they would be in the clear—and he would be waiting for them.

"I'd say this creek dumps into the San Saba river not far from here," Jake mused as he sipped his coffee.

"What about it?" Clem asked.

"Nothing special except the town of San Saba sets about a mile off the river. I used ta hang out there some about four or five years ago. I got friends there."

"What the hell interest is that suppose ta be to us?" Spike asked as he lit his cigarette from the glowing end of a small stick.

"None, I reckon. But I bet the women at the saloon there wouldn't have any trouble gittin' your interest. Kept the prettiest bunch I ever seen. Had one plumb little Mexican gal that

230

was my favorite. She really knew how ta give a man a ride," Jake said.

"How you know they'd still be there?"

"Well, hell, Spike. I don't know. No saloon keeps the same women forever. What I was atellin' ya is that ya could always count on some pretty ones bein' there."

"How far is it ta this San Saba?"

"Don't rightly know since I ain't never gone there from this direction before. I bet it's less than a day's ride, though."

"Ya hear that, Bart? Jake says there's a saloon a little ways from here that keeps a bunch of hot-assed women."

"Yeah. I heard all that bullshit, but ya might as well forget it. We're gonna keep on aheadin' straight fer Mexico. There'll be plenty women there ta take care of that little pistol barrel pecker of yours."

Ryan stood looking down at Susan lying on the soft grass, sleeping soundly. He took her bedroll from behind her saddle and spread it beside her. He carefully worked his arms under her thighs and shoulders.

She awoke with a start the instant he lifted her from the ground. "Wha–what's happening? What are you doing?"

Ryan lay her back down. "I was lifting you to your bedroll. Seemed like a good idea at the time. Didn't know you were such a light sleeper."

Susan sat up. "Well, I hope I don't get to be

such a heavy sleeper that someone could just pick me up and carry me away. Why were you putting me on my bedroll anyway? We've got to pitch camp and cook supper if we're going to stay here tonight."

"That was the whole idea. I figured you must be exhausted to fall asleep so quick. I was going to let you sleep while I pitched camp and cooked supper."

"Oh, nonsense." She got to her feet. "Actually, I feel refreshed from my little nap. I'll cook, unless you think the outlaws will see the fire."

"Naw. Too many trees between them and us and there's enough wind to dissipate the smoke before it even reaches the top of the trees. You don't have to cook, though, if you'd rather not. We can have cold beans, jerky, and hardtack. Or I'll build a fire and you can cook potatoes and heat the beans." He grinned, knowing without a doubt which option she'd choose.

Susan laughed. "I don't even have to consider your bribe. Build me a fire."

Ryan started the fire and got some potatoes and a tin of beans from the pack. "Cook enough potatoes so that we can have some for breakfast."

Susan had the potatoes fried and the beans ready by the time Ryan had taken care of the horses. He spread his bedroll beside hers and sat down on it. He unbuckled his gun belt and laid it close by. She handed him a tin plate of food and sat down beside him. Setting her plate aside, she removed her boots and twinkled her toes in the cool night air.

"Feels like releasing them from prison."

"Does feel good," Ryan agreed after taking off his own boots.

They ate their meal in silence. Susan pitched her empty plate beside Ryan's at the end of the blanket. She lay back and placed her hands under her head, looking up at the sky.

"We'll have a full moon soon," she observed. "It's getting bigger every night."

"Uh-huh," Ryan agreed, not even bothering to look up at the sky. He was more interested in looking at Susan.

As Susan scanned the sky for familiar star formations, Ryan's eyes scanned her beautiful, heart-shaped face with its slightly upturned— and slightly sunburned—nose and full lips that were just begging to be kissed.

"There's the little dipper," she said, removing one arm from beneath her head to point at it.

"Ummm-hmmm." Ryan's stomach and groin tightened in response to her arm movement as it pulled her shirt snug across her high, full breasts. "Is that so," he murmured. *Damn, doesn't she know what's she's doing to me?* he thought.

She turned her head slightly in Ryan's direction and pointed to a spot just over his shoulder. "And over there is the big . . . dipper . . ." Her voice trailed off as her eyes made contact with his. His blue-gray eyes had turned a deep steel-gray.

Susan looked into the face of the man she loved and saw the love he felt for her.

Ryan lowered his head and kissed her gently as if she were a fragile piece of crystal that might shatter. His lips left her mouth to place feather-kisses on both eyelids before slowly moving down to nip at her slender neck.

He pulled back from their kiss to look at Susan. Her face was flushed and her breathing was as labored as his. Even through her clothes, he could feel the heat of her body matching his. He knew she was feeling unbridled desire at its hottest. But, in her innocence, did she understand that she was pushing him to the outer limits of his control?

When they touched, they ignited the ember that had laid dormant since their first encounter at the fishing hole. Each time they'd met, it moved a little closer to the surface, burned a little hotter, yet still it waited for just the right moment to spring to life. But tonight it would no longer be denied. Under a clear night sky with a brilliant blanket of stars, it burst into full flame.

His hand closed around her breast as his lips returned to hers. He kneaded the soft mound until he could feel her nipple harden in response. He gently nipped at her ear lobe before moving lower to her neck. He kissed the pulse point at the vee of her collarbone as he opened the top buttons of her shirt.

His lips sent shock waves surging throughout her body when his warm mouth closed over her hardened nipple and he began to suckle it. His hand closed over her other breast and he caressed it until it too was rigid before he covered it with his mouth. Each time his rough tongue laved her sensitive nipple he could feel Susan's body quiver.

As his fingers released the buttons of her shirt, he replaced each one with a kiss until he'd worked his way down to the waistband of her breeches. He unbuckled her belt and undid the buttons on her pants and the rest of her shirt.

Slowly, he fondled her soft stomach with his warm hand before leaning down and claiming it with a kiss. He lifted her slightly, removed her shirt, and tugged her breeches past her hips. Nuzzling and kissing her soft inner thighs, he moved the breeches down her slender legs and tossed them aside. He paused to look at Susan. The moonlight glistened against her nakedness. With her kiss-swollen lips, her passion-filled eyes, and her long auburn hair fanning out about her face, she looked almost ethereal.

Susan sucked her breath in at the touch of his mouth on her stomach. Her heart was pounding so hard she could barely catch her breath. Her whole body was pulsating as an exciting, yet at the same time frightening, pressure was building within her. With each caress of his hand, each touch of his mouth on her body it grew stronger, threatening to erupt at any moment. When he took her breast in his mouth, she thought she would surely die from the exquisite pleasure. Her body jolted with each flick of his tongue on her tender nipple.

She could see the desire in his eyes. Her body responded with a flood of hot moistness in answer to his undisguised desire for her.

Ryan rolled away from her, quickly pulling his shirt and breeches off and tossing them aside. He moved back to cover Susan's body with his. He settled himself between her legs. He braced his weight on his elbows with one hand on either side of her face. Slowly, he entered her, then paused, allowing her body to adjust to his invasion.

Susan moaned and twisted beneath him. Her whole body was on fire and pulsating from the top of her head to the tips of her toes. The pressure, now centered at the core of her femininity, was throbbing almost painfully, each throb releasing a hot, creamy liquid. She pulled at him, silently begging him to quench the fires burning within her.

He had wanted Susan for so long and now she was his. He knew he wouldn't last long. Lowering his mouth to hers, he gently kissed her as he pushed past her restraint and buried himself deep inside her.

Susan cried out as she felt a sharp, burning sting. She pushed at Ryan trying to move away from the pain, but he held her tightly to him and slowly started moving within her until he felt her relax.

When he quickened his thrusting, Susan felt the wonderful sensations return even stronger than before. She moved against him, matching his rhythm until suddenly her body began to quiver uncontrollably. She cried out and instinctively arched against Ryan.

Ryan felt the pulsating of Susan's climax. Her body closed tightly around him, pulling at him until he spewed his seed deep within her.

He collapsed on top of her momentarily as he tried to gasp enough air into his lungs to move away. Her breathing was as ragged as his. He could feel her heart pounding as rapidly as his.

As his breathing and heart rate returned to normal, so did reality. He started to pull away from her, appalled at what he'd done.

"Susan . . . I . . . I'm . . ." He looked remorsefully at her and shifted to move off her.

Susan wrapped one leg over his to keep him from leaving her. "Shush." She placed her finger against his lips. "Please don't spoil this for me."

He let out a long, slow breath as relief swept over him. Now that the heat of the moment had passed, he'd been afraid that she would feel regret—or even anger—because of what they'd done. But she didn't.

Bracing his weight on his elbows, he cuddled her to him, enjoying the afterglow of their lovemaking. He nuzzled, then gently nipped the sensitive spot he'd discovered just below her ear.

A slight breeze blew across them, cooling their passion-warmed bodies and tousling

Susan's long hair. Brushing it away from her face, Ryan kissed her lovingly.

Susan wiggled slightly when his lips touched her neck. Before when his lips had touched that same place, it had sent erotic shivers of excitement through her body. Now it tickled. She cupped his face in both her hands and returned his kiss.

"I didn't expect anything so grand as that." She placed her hand at the back of his head, entwining her fingers in his hair, and pulled him down to her and whispered in his ear. "Can we do it again?"

He moaned. Her words sent waves of passion surging through him, and once again they were swept away in a maelstrom of sensual feelings until at last they slumped to the blanket in complete exhaustion.

Ryan carefully eased himself away from her and rolled to his back. Pulling Susan to him, he wrapped his arm around her, drawing her close to his side.

Susan turned her face up to him for another kiss before laying her head on his shoulder and snuggling closer to him. She could feel his heart thumping strongly under her hand on his chest. The rhythmic beat was about to lull her to sleep.

Ryan rested his cheek against the top of her head, both arms wrapped around her. He could feel Susan's body relaxing as she drifted toward sleep. He would have liked to spend the night just as they were, but they had things to do.

He kissed the top of her head. "Susie?"

"Hmmm?" she said sleepily, wrapping her arm around his waist and trying to wiggle closer.

"We need to get up and get dressed before we fall asleep. Might be a little embarrassing if we had to defend ourselves in the middle of the night naked as jaybirds."

With only the moon's light to aid them, they gathered up their hastily discarded clothes. Ryan sensed that Susan was feeling a little shy and uncomfortable about dressing in front of him.

He pulled on his breeches and boots. "I'll go check on the horses and give you some privacy."

Susan smiled at his thoughtfulness. "Thank you," she said shyly. She was holding her wadded up clothes in front of her, looking at the ground. No man had seen her naked before. Well, not until Ryan had happened upon her at the swimming hole, but this was different. Maybe she shouldn't feel so timid after what they had just shared, but she did.

Ryan guessed what she was thinking. He walked to her, tipped her chin up, forcing her to meet his eyes. "I think you are very, very lovely. There is nothing for you to be ashamed of," he stated simply. He placed a chaste kiss on her forehead. "I'll be back in ten minutes or so."

She nodded as he turned and walked away. When he was out of sight, she quickly washed herself and pulled on her underclothes, shirt, and breeches. Then she set about straightening their bedrolls. She shook the grass and small pebbles out of the tangled blankets before spreading them on the ground.

When Ryan returned a few minutes later, Susan was sitting on her blanket. He smiled when he saw that she had straightened their bedrolls and placed them side by side, touching.

Ryan sat down beside her and pulled off his boots. "We better get some sleep."

Susan nodded her head, trying to stifle a yawn. "I didn't realize I was so tired. I didn't feel tired before." Susan blushed at her unintended innuendo. "I mean . . ."

Ryan chuckled knowingly and patted the spot beside him, indicating that she was to sleep on his blanket with him. "Come here."

Susan smiled shyly but quickly moved to him, snuggling close when he wrapped his arm around her.

He kissed the top of her head. "Now, go to sleep." She nodded her head and Ryan felt her body relax in sleep almost immediately.

As he held Susan to him, waiting for sleep to come, he thought about his plans for the next morning. If he was lucky, he'd be able to shoot all four of them and be done with it.

Susan turned on her side and wiggled back against him.

Ryan groaned and turned on his side. He knew he wouldn't get a wink of sleep with her firm little butt snuggled up to his front.

Admitting to himself that he was a glutton for punishment, he wrapped his arm around her and snuggled closer. He closed his eyes. He knew it was going to be a long, sleepless night for him, but she felt too good to resist.

Chapter Thirteen

When his eyes opened again, it was still dark. Susan's head rested on his shoulder. Her leg lay across his belly. Except for the fact that he felt rested and refreshed, he would not have realized that he had slept. He looked at his watch. Four o'clock. Earlier than they needed to get started but he dared not go back to sleep again. They'd have time for coffee.

He eased from under Susan's head and leg. Her steady breathing was broken only by one deep breath as she rolled to her back.

He started a small fire, just enough to brew the coffee, then turned his attention to the horses. Fifteen minutes later he set a pan of water by the blanket and placed a bar of soap and a small towel beside the pan.

Kneeling beside Susan, he kissed her gently on the lips.

She stirred, wiped her hand across her face, and rolled to her side, turning her back to him.

He kissed her neck and gently massaged her breasts.

Her hand moved to his hand. She opened her eyes. She rolled to her back and stared wide-eyed at him a moment before pulling his lips to hers.

· He kissed her firmly then raised his head. "Are you awake, sleeping beauty?" he asked quietly.

"I am now," she answered softly, smiling at him.

"Then get your butt off that blanket and wash the sleep out of your eyes," he said in a normal tone of voice. He motioned to the pan and towel before getting abruptly to his feet. "Coffee's ready."

"Why you—" She was speaking to his back. "I'll get even with you for that," she assured him as she walked on her knees to the pan of water. She heard him chuckling to himself as she washed her face and hands.

"Why are we up so early?" she asked as she walked to him.

He handed her a cup of coffee. "They made their first mistake, Susie. I think we're about to get a shot at them."

Susan's hand shook slightly as she accepted the tin cup of hot liquid. She met Ryan's eyes in determination. The time had come.

*   *   *

Dawn was just breaking when Ryan stopped a hundred yards short of where he would take his stand. He securely tethered the horses and lifted Dog to his pad on top of Bluebell. "Dog, stay." Dog obediently lay down on his stomach and stretched his paws out in front of him. Ryan took the buffalo rifle from the pack and pulled his Winchester from the scabbard. "Bring your rifle with you, just in case."

They made their way to the large tree on the ground, obviously the victim of a recent storm. Ryan placed Susan behind the cottonwood log. They would wait here for the outlaws camped in the trees six hundred yards from them.

Ryan handed Susan his field glasses before moving a few feet down the log from her.

"When they leave the trees to go to their horses, look them over good, but quick, and tell me if you recognize them."

They waited thirty minutes and still the men had not emerged from the trees. That suited Ryan fine. It was good light now. He could see clearly through his telescopic sight.

Suddenly four men stepped from the trees, carrying their saddles slung over their shoulders.

Susan spoke quickly. "The big one with the black beard was the one shouting orders. The little weasel kicked my mother," she said vehemently.

The thunderclap of the big Sharp's rifle shattered the silence of the valley.

The chest of the little weasel seemed to explode with the impact of the fifty-caliber bullet. His companions froze in their tracks.

Echoes rumbled through the valley as Ryan jerked the breechblock open and stuffed in another shell.

The big man had taken two running steps toward his horse when the valley shuddered again. The burly man collapsed in a heap, then pitched forward on his face. The other two men were running to the woods, leading their horses.

The buffalo rifle roared, once again sending echoes thundering through the valley, mingling with the fainter ones that had not yet faded away.

"God damn it!" Ryan cursed, jerking the breechblock open. "I missed him."

He reloaded the rifle, but the men had reached the shelter of the trees.

"You got two of them!" Susan said with excitement. "What will we do now?"

"We'll wait a minute or so and see what happens. They'll probably go straight on across the creek."

The two remaining outlaws began frantically saddling their horses as soon as they were behind the safety of the trees.

"Damn, Jake, we're in a hell of a fix. Somebody up there's got a damn cannon and he knows how to use it!"

"Yeah, I know, Clem. It's a damn sure cinch

we ain't gonna make it ta Mexico with him tracking us with that damn thing."

"Hell, that's what I just said. What the hell we gonna do?"

"I'm headin' down the river to San Saba. You can come along, if'n ya want to. Maybe somebody is still there that'll help us. If not, at least we can shake that son of a bitch off our trail."

"How do ya figure that?"

"Damn it, Clem! Ain't you got a lick of sense? He won't be able to trail us in a town, what with all the other hoofprints there. We'll just head out of town in a different direction. He won't know which way we went."

"Sounds good ta me. Let's get the hell outta here afore he comes in after us."

They swung on their horses and headed down the creek.

Ryan was surprised when he saw the men dash from the woods and head down the creek through a sparse growth of willow saplings instead of crossing the creek as he had expected them to do. He quickly shouldered the big rifle.

Susan clamped her hands to her ears, protecting them from further assault.

Shock waves swept through the valley for the last time. The horses and riders disappeared behind some large trees and undergrowth. Neither of the riders seemed to have been hit.

Ryan grabbed his Winchester. "Let's go!"

They were running to their horses before the

echoes from his last shot had completely faded.

They rode to the clearing and Ryan dismounted. He looked briefly at the dead men then went quickly to their horses and set them free.

"I hate not to bury them, but we can't take the time," Ryan said as they rode to the trail left by the fleeing men.

Susan looked back over her shoulder. "Doesn't bother me any. They don't deserve to be buried. Let the buzzards have them."

Ryan placed Dog's nose to the tracks he now wanted him to follow. He took jerky and hardtack from the pack and handed Susan a portion.

"That's breakfast. The potatoes and beans were still in the frying pan this morning."

"Your fault," Susan accused. "I'd have put the food away if I hadn't been distracted."

Ryan chuckled as he swung into his saddle. He put the horses to a trot behind the dog. But they were soon slowed to a walk as they made their way through the thick undergrowth. He searched ahead of them every few minutes with his field glasses.

"Shouldn't we be moving faster?" Susan complained an hour later.

"Nope. They can't move any faster than we can. They're about half a mile ahead of us. I spotted them twice through my glasses. I'm puzzled, though, why they've turned east and are sticking to the creek."

By noon they had passed the point where

the creek emptied into the San Saba River and had been following the river for four or five miles when Ryan stopped for more jerky and hardtack.

"Susie, I'm becoming a bit troubled. Seems like they intend to follow the river to San Saba."

Susan reflected on his statement a moment. "We can't let them reach a town. That could cause all kinds of complications."

"Yeah. I know," Ryan agreed as he got on his horse.

"Well, what will we do to stop them?"

Ryan shook his head. "Don't know yet. But we'll find a way. I rode this river before, when I was looking for a place for my horse ranch. I'll know when our chance comes."

Three hours later the river turned south. The outlaws' trail continued along the river.

Ryan stopped. "They're riding into a horse-shoe bend, and I suspect they don't know that. It's four miles or more around that bend, but only a couple of miles straight across there to where the river completes the bend and turns east again. Come on. We're cutting across."

Ryan scanned the area, searching for a likely place to set up an ambush as they approached the river again. He guided the horses toward a stand of tall ancient pecan trees that stretched about three hundred yards along the riverbank. The shady ground beneath the giant trees was virtually devoid of undergrowth, just as he had suspected it would be.

"This is about as likely a place as we'll find. I'll be able to get one of them here. Maybe both, if I'm lucky. Come on. We'll circle around to the other end so we don't leave any tracks in the clearing."

"Why do you think you'll have to get lucky in order to kill both of them?"

"Because the clearing is so narrow. I figure as soon as I shoot one, the other will bolt for cover. I might be able to snap off another shot, but it would be pure luck if I hit him."

They tethered their horses in the thick trees and undergrowth far enough back that they couldn't be seen by the outlaws. Ryan took his Winchester from his saddle scabbard.

"If anything goes wrong, I'll yell instructions to you as to what to do."

Susan already had her rifle in her hands. "You won't have to yell very loud. I'll be right beside you."

"You're staying right here," Ryan stated, dismissing Susan's assertion as though it had little meaning.

"I'll do no such thing."

"Don't give me any trouble, Susan. I don't have time for it."

"I don't intend to give you any trouble. I'm going to help you."

"Now listen, Susan—"

"No, Ryan," Susan interrupted, "you listen. You have pampered me long enough. I was content to lay back and let you shoot them with your buffalo gun. Well, you've done that.

But now that they know you have it, you're not apt to get a chance to use it again. We've trailed these men all day, waiting for them to make a mistake so we could get a shot at them. You just said that we won't find a better place than this, but you'd probably only get one of them. Why should we let the other one get away?"

"Susan, I have told you repeatedly. I'm not going to let them get a shot at you."

"They're not going to get a shot at me or you, either, and you know it. You know that I'm fully capable of shooting one of them at the same time you shoot the other." She turned and started walking to the clearing. "Now come on and let's kill the bastards and be done with it."

Ryan started after her. "Damn it, Susan!"

Susan cut him off again. "You best quit talking. They might hear us."

Ryan considered her reasoning. He had to admit that she was capable. After all, she had defended herself from a vicious criminal with nothing but her wits for a weapon. Yet she had killed him with his own gun. She had handled herself well in two Indian fights. He also knew she had her neck bowed and that any further argument would be of no avail.

Ryan sighed. He knew when he was beat. "All right. Get behind that hackberry tree with the forked trunk over there."

Susan rested her rifle in the fork of the trunk and sighted down the barrel to be sure she'd have a clear shot when the outlaws came in view.

Ryan removed his hat and knelt on one knee behind a stump a few feet from her.

"Aren't you concerned that they might see us?"

"Naw, the sun will be partly in their eyes. They won't see us in the shade of the trees here. See that tree with the broken limb hanging from it?"

Susan nodded her head.

"When they get even with that tree, start aiming at the one on your side. I'll give you about five seconds for you to hold your aim. Then I'll say 'now.' Don't jerk the trigger, squeeze it easy."

"I know how to do that," Susan assured him.

Ten minutes later the two men came into view at the far end of the pecan grove. They were riding side by side, heading straight toward them. They were glancing over their shoulders every few seconds.

"Get ready," Ryan whispered.

As the men rode past the designated tree, Susan held her aim.

"Now."

She squeezed the trigger. The Winchester bucked against her shoulder. The outlaw fell from his horse. She worked the lever to reload the rifle. But it wasn't necessary. Ryan's man was down, too.

"Stay where you are," Ryan ordered.

He went to the outlaws in long quick strides and examined each briefly.

Susan stepped from behind the tree and

waited for Ryan to return to her.

He took her in his arms and held her close. "It's over, Susie. God, I'm so relieved we've gotten through this without you being harmed in any way."

"I'm just glad the horrible monsters are dead," she said vehemently. "Not only for what they have done but to stop them from perpetrating their evil deeds on others."

"Well, it's done. Wait here, I'll bring the horses on in."

They led the horses to the outlaws, and Ryan took a small sharp-shooter shovel from the pack.

"I don't believe what I'm seeing. You brought a shovel with you?"

"What's so surprising about that? I took up their trail with the intent of killing them. If I kill 'em, I've got to bury 'em. I learned sometime back it's a lot easier to dig with a shovel than with a stick or your bare hands."

Susan sat on a fallen limb and watched him dig for a while. "I don't know why you bother to bury them. I would leave these evil creatures for the buzzards to eat, like we left the other two," she said.

Ryan paused momentarily from his digging and looked searchingly at Susan. "Yeah, well, we had no choice with them. But if we left these men, my conscience would begin to tell me that I heaped punishment on the evil after I destroyed it. And if I'm going to continue to punish the evil, I've got to carry it around with me. And I can't do that, Susie. You've got to bury the evil and forget it."

Susan pondered his philosophy a moment then went to him and tapped him on the shoulder. "Looks like you could use a break. Let me dig for a little while."

A faint smile conveyed his understanding of her gesture. "Yeah. I could use a sip of water."

They had traveled only a short distance when they reached the bend where the river turned east again.

Ryan reined up. "Susie, we've got a decision to make. It's about two hours on down the river to San Saba. There we can get a hot bath, delicious Mexican food, or most any other kind you prefer, and a soft bed with clean sheets in a hotel. Won't be any further from home, but won't be any closer, either. Or we can head straight home. We can have jerky and hardtack for supper, and sleep on the ground two hours closer to home."

Susan turned Spooky and headed down the river. "If you decide to head straight home, I'll ride hard tomorrow morning and try to catch up with you. Right now, I'm going to San Saba."

Ryan chuckled. "Kind of figured you would. I reckon I'll just go along with you."

Two hours later they crossed the river at the low water crossing and followed the wagon road on in to the town that was about a mile from the river. The wagon road became the main street as they entered the city of San Saba.

"No use toting our rifles, saddlebags, and stuff," Ryan said, tying the horses to the hitching rail in front of the hotel in the center of the city. "I'll just drop them and you off here and then take the horses on down to the livery."

The young Mexican desk clerk eyed Dog as they walked across the lobby.

"I am very sorry, *Señor*, but you cannot take the dog—"

"Stop! Don't say that, *hombre*." Ryan held up his hand to silence the clerk. He looked anxiously at Dog.

"But, *Señor* . . ."

"Let me explain." He took his badge from his shirt pocket and held it up for the clerk to see. "I'm a Texas Ranger and Dog thinks he is, too. He's killed three Comanche warriors, two *gringo* outlaws, and one bandido. He rides a pack horse when he's not trailing.

"One time, a grizzly bear scared that horse causing it to rear up and throw Dog off." Ryan paused and sadly shook his head. "What Dog done to that grizzly bear was a terrible sight to behold. Why, I was so mortified, I sat down right there on the spot and wrote sympathy letters to that poor, unfortunate bear's relatives."

Ryan nodded his head in proud acknowledgment. "Yep. He's some Ranger, all right. He's got one bad trait, though."

The desk clerk eyed Dog nervously. "And what is that, *Señor?*"

"He turns mean when told he can't stay in my room with me."

Susan had turned her back to them and was attempting to hide her laughter behind a faked cough.

The clerk looked from Dog to Ryan, then to Susan and back to Dog. He decided discretion was truly the better part of valor. Taking a deep breath, he pulled himself to his full height and squared his shoulders. "*Señor*, it is the policy of this hotel to ignore such minor rules when honored by such distinguished guests as Texas Rangers. I am surprised that you would not know that."

"Aw, of course, I should have known that. Please forgive me. I didn't mean to insult you."

"Your apology is accepted, *Señor*. Think no more about it. Now to take care of business. How many rooms will you require?"

"One." Mischief was evident in Ryan's voice. He waited for Susan's outburst which didn't come.

"One room," the clerk quoted. He placed the register in front of Ryan and turned to the key rack.

Ryan glanced sidelong at Susan. "One room?" His arched eyebrow emphasized his question.

Susan's blush and demure smile set his heart to thumping.

"One room," he repeated. His hand shook as he signed the register.

The desk clerk turned back to Ryan, key in hand. "This is our very best room, *Señor*," he said proudly.

Ryan nodded his head and began gathering up the rifles, saddlebags, and other stuff he'd set on the floor beside the desk.

The clerk hurried around the corner, keeping a nervous eye on Dog. "Here, let me help you carry some of this." He led the way up the stairs and to a room at the end of the hall. Unlocking the door, he motioned for Ryan and Susan to enter the room.

Susan glanced around the large room. It smelled clean and was tastefully decorated. The walls were papered with scenes of roses climbing a white trellis under which sat three ladies sipping from blue teacups. Thick velvet drapes decorated the two windows, one facing east, the other south.

"Where is the best place to buy a good hat? I seem to have been a little careless with mine." Ryan grinned and stuck his finger through the bullet hole in the brim of his hat.

"The mercantile is four buildings down and across the street." The clerk motioned in the store's direction. "They have fine Stetson hats a great deal like what you are wearing. And next door there is a man that makes beautiful boots and belts." The clerk smiled and shrugged his shoulders. "He is a cousin of mine. You tell him I send you and he will give you a very good price on the most comfortable boots in all of Texas," he said proudly.

"Thanks, I'll stop in and see what he has. I'll be a little while, Susan. I'm going to try to find a new shirt and pants, too. Come on, Dog." Dog obediently followed Ryan out the door, his toenails clicking on the highly polished hardwood floor.

"Is there anything I can get for you, *Señora?*"

Susan smiled but did not correct the man's error about her marital status.

"Yes, there is." She went to her saddlebags and, removing a small leather pouch, she dropped a gold coin in the man's hand.

"Would you have someone bring a tub and lots of hot water up just as soon as you can? I want to take a long, hot bath."

The clerk's eyes grew large and round as he stared at the five-dollar gold piece in his palm. A big grin slowly stretched from ear to ear.

"*Señora*, you will have water here before you hardly know it. I have water already hot that I was about to send up to a man that I don't like very well. I'll just send you his water and make him wait awhile longer."

Susan laughed at the man's conspiratorial look.

He started out the door, stopped, and turned back to face Susan. "Ah, *señora*, the Ranger, about the dog, he was pulling my leg, no?"

Susan laughed and nodded her head. "The Ranger, about the dog, he was pulling your leg, yes. But please go ahead and let him keep the dog in our room because he is a very valuable

258

dog and the *señor* is very fond of him."

The clerk nodded his head and smiled. "I understand."

The hot bathwater felt like heaven to her after the long days on the trail. She quickly washed and rinsed her hair and then leaned back against the oval tub, letting the heat penetrate her sore muscles. While she was soaking, she decided that she wanted to buy a dress to wear when she and Ryan went to supper later.

All she had stuffed into her saddlebags were breeches and cotton shirts. And she only had one shirt left anyway. She had torn the other one into strips to bandage Ryan's wounds.

After brushing her hair almost dry, she left the room and stopped at the desk to ask directions to a store that might have ready-made clothing for women.

The desk clerk was most happy to help her. He pointed to a building across the street and catty-corner from the hotel. "Right across the street there is a lady that sews beautiful things. Maria's clothes are the finest made in all of Texas," he proclaimed proudly.

Susan laughed at the man's enthusiasm. "Let me guess. She's your cousin. Right?"

"Oh, no, *señora*," he said solemnly. Then he grinned broadly, showing even, white teeth. "She is my sister."

Susan laughed again at the man's sense of humor. "Does your family own all the stores in town?"

He shrugged his shoulders apologetically. "I have a very big family, *señora*."

"Please tell the *señor* where I've gone when he returns. I wouldn't want him to worry."

She smiled in amusement and left the hotel.

Chapter Fourteen

"I dunno, Mister." The livery man rubbed the back of his neck as he eyed Pegasus with apprehension. "I don't much like the idey of keepin' a stallion in my stables. Them's mean critters mostly."

"Pegasus won't make any trouble if you'll put him in a stall between the two mares. Dog will stay in his stall to keep him company. That horse has followed the dog on the trail many hundreds of miles. I guarantee you he'll be all right."

The livery man was not convinced. "Well, I guess I'll have ta take yore word fer it, Mister. But, if'n he goes ta actin' up, I'm turnin' him loose an' yore a payin' for any damages he done."

"That's fair enough," Ryan agreed. He

reached in his pocket and handed the man some coins. "Give all three of them an extra ration of feed. They've worked hard."

Taking the reins of Spooky and Bluebell, the livery man started walking toward the back stalls. "I'll take care of the mares, Mister, but I'm gonna let you unsaddle him," he said over his shoulder as he eyed the stallion again.

Ryan unsaddled Pegasus and rubbed him down. When the livery man returned with a bucket of water and some grain, Ryan secured the gate.

The big stallion stuck his head over the top of the gate. Ryan patted him on his neck. "Pegasus, you behave yourself. Dog, I'll be back with some food for you in a little while." Dog lay down on his stomach, resting his head on his outstretched paws, and closed his eyes.

Ryan walked into the restaurant and sat down at the nearest table. The place looked clean and the food smelled good. He decided he'd bring Susie here for supper.

"What can I get for you?" The pretty waitress looked him up and down approvingly.

Ryan smiled at the woman's blatant appraisal. "I'll have a cup of coffee here and wrap up a thick steak to take with me."

"One coffee and one steak. How do you want it cooked?"

"Just wrap it up raw."

The waitress looked at him skeptically. "Raw?" When Ryan nodded his head, the waitress shrugged her shoulders, turned, and walked back to the kitchen mumbling something about *"loco gringo"* to the cook.

After taking Dog his supper, Ryan went to the mercantile and purchased a hat, some breeches, and a couple of shirts. As he passed the leather shop, he glanced down at his comfortable old boots. He decided they did look like they had seen better days, but he sure hated the thought of breaking in a new pair of boots.

The smell of dye and newly tanned leather momentarily stung his eyes when he entered the shop. The desk clerk hadn't exaggerated. His cousin had everything from belts to saddles and each was intricately hand-tooled with careful attention to detail.

Thirty minutes later, Ryan left the shop wearing a new pair of black boots. He'd also bought two belts, one for himself and one for Kyle, and a pair of butter-soft leather gloves for Hazel.

When the desk clerk saw Ryan enter the lobby wearing his new boots, he flashed him a broad grin. "Did I not tell you my cousin makes beautiful things?"

"Yes, you did. And they are very comfortable just like you said."

The man nodded his head proudly. "The *señora* said for me to tell you that she will be back in a little while. She went across the street to the dressmaker. She did not want you to worry."

"Thanks," Ryan said over his shoulder as he took the steps two at a time.

* * *

Susan hurried in the door of the hotel. "Is the *señor* back yet?"

"*Sí*, he went up about ten minutes ago." He eyed the plump package she held in her arms. "I see you liked Maria's work."

Susan smiled and quickly mounted the stairs. When she reached their room, she hesitated a moment. She didn't know whether she should knock or just walk right in. She cracked the door open slightly and softly called Ryan's name.

Ryan smiled when he heard her timidly call his name. "Come on in, Susie. I'm taking a bath but I've got the screen up. Did you find a dress you liked?"

"Uh-huh." Susan laid her package on the bed and undressed. She sighed with pleasure as she stepped into the silk drawers and slid the matching camisole over her head. The soft silk felt like a caress on her skin after wearing her sturdy cotton undergarments with her breeches.

Carefully, she stepped into the simple soft blue cotton dress. The low, scooped neckline and short puffed sleeves were both edged with dainty white lace. The bodice, with its twelve tiny blue buttons, fit snugly about her slender waist before flaring into a full skirt. She hoped it made her look as delicate and feminine as it made her feel.

After buttoning her dress and knotting her stockings, she slid her feet into a pair of soft kid slippers. She was just putting the last ivory comb into her hair when Ryan stepped from behind the screen. She turned slowly toward him, anxious for his approval.

Ryan sucked his breath in as his eyes traveled from the top of her shiny auburn hair down to her feet clad in the dainty slippers and back to her face. He took the few steps separating them, his eyes never leaving her face.

Picking up a handful of her soft hair, he raised it to his nose before letting it slide slowly through his fingers. "You're absolutely beautiful." His voice was low and seductive, sending waves of excitement skittering down her spine. He felt her shiver as he folded her in his arms and kissed her hungrily.

She wrapped her arms around his waist and returned his kiss with equal ardor, pressing her body so close to his that she could feel his heart beating.

He broke the kiss and buried his face in her sweet-smelling hair to whisper against her ear. "If we do not get out of this room this instant, I will not be responsible for my actions."

Susan smiled up at him expectantly. "You promise?"

Ryan laughed and stepped away from her. "You little imp. Let's go eat. I'm starving." He took her hand and started toward the door.

Susan pulled him back. "Aren't you forgetting something?" she asked, looking down at his bare feet.

Ryan glanced downward and smirked. "Lady,

you make me forget a lot of things." He sat down on the end of the bed to pull on his socks and boots.

When he stood up, he found Susan admiring him. He was wearing a black shirt with a turquoise bola and snug-fitting black pants. He settled his new Stetson on his head.

"Susie, if you don't stop looking at me like that, we'll never get out of this room."

She laughed and quickly moved toward the door when Ryan made a grab for her.

As they descended the stairs, the desk clerk looked up at them and smiled broadly. His chocolate eyes twinkled mischievously. "*Señor* Sommerall, where is the other Ranger?"

"Oh, I decided I'd better leave him to guard the horses," Ryan answered in a serious tone.

The clerk nodded his head in approval. "Well, they will certainly be very well guarded. No one will get away with those horses with such a vicious dog as that to guard them."

Closing the hotel door behind them, Ryan tucked Susan's hand under his elbow and they started walking to the restaurant. "I think he's on to me," he said, smiling.

Susan chuckled. "Nah, you've got him convinced that Dog is the meanest critter in all of Texas."

When they left the restaurant, Ryan took Susan's hand, entwining his fingers with hers.

"It's cooled off some. Would you like to walk around for a while?"

Susan looked up at him and smiled. "Yes, I'd like that."

They strolled along the plank sidewalk in companionable silence, pausing occasionally to glance in a store window.

For the first time in days, Susan felt happy and at peace. Now that the incident with the outlaws was over and done with, she and Ryan could get on with the rest of their lives.

She glanced at Ryan and her heart swelled with pride. Walking beside him with their fingers entwined made her feel protected and loved. She couldn't remember a time in her life when she had been happier than at this very moment. She loved this handsome man more than she would have thought possible just a few months ago. Unconsciously, she squeezed his hand.

Feeling her gentle squeeze, Ryan raised her hand and kissed her fingertips. "What are you smiling about?" The smile she turned on him, coupled with the look in her eyes, made his pulse quicken.

"I was thinking about how happy I am," she answered honestly. "I can't think of a time when I've ever been happier."

Ryan stopped and pulled her to him. "And what has caused all this happiness?"

Susan looked him boldly in the eyes. "A tall, blue-eyed, handsome man."

Ryan's heart skipped a beat then took off in a wild race. His breath caught in his throat. He lowered his mouth and gently caressed her lips.

They were so lost in each other that the world around them seemed to have faded into obscurity. When he released her lips, they glanced guiltily around to see if anyone had seen them. Susan quickly stepped back from him; he cleared his throat self-consciously.

"I think we'd better go back to our room. I mean . . . that is if you're ready to."

"Yes." Susan smiled and slipped her hand back into his.

The friendly desk clerk started to speak when they entered the hotel, but one look at their faces told him that they were in a world where only they belonged. He sighed and smiled to himself wistfully. He was such a romantic and the handsome couple looked so in love that it made his eyes a little misty just thinking how happy they must be.

When they reached their room, Ryan closed the door behind them and pulled Susan into his arms, kissing her soundly. When he raised his head, he said, "I have a confession to make."

Susan cocked her head to one side and looked at him, perplexed.

"I really only meant to tease you when I asked for one room. I figured you'd protest."

"Wouldn't that have been a bit ridiculous? After all, I just spent a night in your arms on a blanket on the ground. Do you think less of me because I didn't act like a vestal virgin just because we're in a building now?"

"Hell, no!" he exclaimed. "I'm just glad I didn't have to spend half the night trying to figure out how to get you to let me in your room."

"Me, too. Now quit your complaining and kiss me."

"Yes, ma'am." Ryan chuckled and covered her lips with his in a breath-stealing kiss that made Susan tingle all the way to her toes.

Removing the combs from her hair, he ran his hands through the silken tresses.

"I like your hair down like this," he whispered. "I think I got distracted before I could tell you how lovely you look in your new dress. The color matches your eyes. Did I tell you that blue is my favorite color?"

"Uh-huh." She nodded. "That's why I chose this one." Susan smiled, reached up and removed Ryan's hat, ruffling his hair where the hat had marked it.

Standing with his arms locked behind her and their bodies touching from the waist down, she looked innocently up at him. "Aren't you supposed to remove your hat before a lady kisses you?"

Ryan swallowed hard. "Yes, ma'am." He felt himself growing hard. He took his hat from her and tossed it in the general direction of the dresser.

Susan slowly moved the bola down the string tie and unbuttoned the top button of his shirt. "Isn't your collar too tight?"

"It is now." Ryan's body temperature was rising rapidly. He tightened his hold on Susan, bringing her firmly against his hardness.

Standing on tiptoe, Susan pulled his head down to hers and, holding his head between her hands, she kissed him passionately.

Ryan groaned. He had intended to take it slow with Susan, but her actions told him she was as eager as he. Bending and catching her behind the knees, he picked her up and carried her to the bed, not breaking their kiss until he lay her upon the soft mattress.

He removed her slippers, pulled his boots off, and lay down beside her on the bed.

Turning on his side, supporting his head with one hand, he smoothed her hair across the pillow. "You are so beautiful," he whispered huskily. Slowly lowering his head, he caressed her lips tenderly. Gently nudging her lips apart with his tongue, he slipped inside to explore the inner velvet.

He raised his head to look at the beauty of her flushed features, her kiss-swollen lips, her eyes bright with emotion. The scooped neck of her dress barely exposed the tops of her breasts. He brushed his knuckles slowly across their softness before slipping the buttons open to reveal the creamy mounds hidden by the tight-fitting bodice.

His blue-gray eyes turned steel-gray as he watched the rhythmic rise and fall of her breasts. His heart raced erratically when the pink tip of her tongue flicked across her dry lips.

Her breath quickened at his touch, sending curls of desire flooding through her body. Slowly, Susan reached up and laid her hand softly against the side of his face. She could see the yearning in his eyes, and her body responded with a flood of hot moistness in answer to his undisguised desire for her. With gentle pressure, she urged his mouth down the few inches that separated her lips from his.

When Ryan broke their heated kiss and leaned his forehead against hers, they were both gasping for air. "Susie, my sweet, sweet Susie," he murmured.

Raising her slightly, he pulled the sleeves of her dress off her arms and lifted the silk camisole over her head, tossing it aside. Releasing the rest of the tiny buttons, he slowly slid the dress past her hips until she lay naked before him.

Ryan leaned back slightly to admire the treasure he'd uncovered. Reverently, he cupped one breast, then the other, rubbing his thumb across each nipple until it was swollen, rigid, and throbbing. He closed his hot, moist mouth around one rosy nipple, alternately suckling and flicking it with his rough tongue. Snuggling his face between her breasts, he gently rubbed his slightly whisker-stubbled cheeks across her tender nipples, loving the womanly scent that was uniquely Susan. He kissed the underside of each breast before moving down to place a kiss on her soft stomach. His hand closed over her mound.

Susan arched her body into Ryan's hand. He was lying almost full length on top of her, with one of his legs between hers. She could feel his hardness against her thigh. Her whole body was on fire and pulsating from the top of her head to the tip of her toes. She pulled at him, silently begging him to quench the fires burning within her.

Ryan moved back from her, understanding her urgent need for release. "Easy, little one," he whispered against her ear, his warm breath sending shock waves down her body. "We've got all night."

Susan's fingers trembled as she unbuttoned Ryan's shirt. She curled her fingers in the dark hair before gently running her nails down his chest, following the line of hair until she reached his belt. She wanted to feel him as he was feeling her. Sliding the belt open, she began slowly opening each button on his breeches.

When she released the second button and felt his hardness swell even more against its confines, she laid her hand against him, closing her eyes at the pleasant sensation. She was breathing so fast and shallow it was making her dizzy. Taking a couple of slow, deep breaths, she continued her exploration.

She glanced at Ryan as she released the next button. His head was thrown back and his face was contorted as if he were in great pain. He, too, was gasping for air. When she looked back to release the next button, she saw the reason for his pained expression. She released the rest of the buttons, and his manhood sprang forth from its confines stiff and proud. Timidly, she closed her hand around him. She heard Ryan suck in his breath and felt his body shudder.

Unable to restrain himself any longer, he shucked the rest of his clothing and settled himself between her legs. He cupped her face in his hands and gently suckled her neck before moving to her mouth. Her body was hot to his touch and he knew that she was ready for him. Without releasing her lips, he slowly slid into her.

Susan felt the exquisite pressure building rapidly as Ryan entered her. His hardness rocked her body with tremors that she knew would quickly lead to a welcomed explosion. When he ceased his movement, she frowned. The sensations started to ebb and she didn't want that. She squirmed, trying to get him to move within her again.

He pulled almost out of her and she clutched him to her. Agonizingly slowly, he moved in and pulled back again, setting the pace a little faster with each movement. Susan quickly caught the rhythm and moved against him.

Caught in the throes of passion, she tossed her head from side to side as her hips left the bed to meet Ryan's thrusts. "Yes, yes," she breathed as violent spasms began to rock her body. Her hips met his in an ever-faster tempo, matching him thrust for thrust as she cried out her pleasure.

Ryan was captured in Susan's release. His body stiffened as his seed shot deep into her womb. Still, she gripped him tightly, throbbing and pulsing.

Ryan momentarily collapsed on top of her as he waited for his racing heart to slow to its normal beat. Pulling Susan with him, he rolled to his side. Settling her head on his shoulder, he brushed her tangled hair back from her face and placed a kiss on her forehead.

Susan turned her face up so he could kiss her lips before she snuggled against his chest. She could feel his heart thudding under her hand as fast and strong as hers.

Raising up on one elbow, she let her eyes travel slowly from Ryan's feet all the way up his lean, well-muscled legs, past his slim hips, hard stomach, and narrow waist. She couldn't resist the urge to reach out and entangle his hair around her fingers, gently scratching his broad chest with the tips of her fingernails.

She felt his stomach muscles tighten when she toyed with the hairs curling around her fingers as her nails followed the line of dark hair down his stomach.

She smiled when she saw his not quite so limp member begin to stir.

Ryan grabbed her hand to still it. From the look in her eyes, he knew she'd discovered the power she held over him—and his body.

"You learn fast," he said, drawing her hand to his lips.

Susan blushed. She'd gotten carried away with her enchantment of exploring his body. She felt a strange sense of excitement knowing she had some control over that part of him which had given her so much pleasure.

"I had a good teacher," she whispered demurely. Her skin tingled as Ryan kissed each finger.

Ryan smiled. He wasn't surprised at her uninhibited passionate nature. Susan approached everything in life with zeal and enthusiasm.

He put one of her fingers in his mouth and sucked it, running his tongue over its sensitive pad. "That was just lesson number one," he murmured.

"Oh, my goodness. You mean there's . . . more?" Susan's whole body began to tingle. She found that hard to believe after what they'd just shared.

Ryan looked at her from beneath half-lowered eyelids, his voice husky as he assured her. "Oh, yes, there's more." He nibbled another finger. "Much, much more." He kissed the inside of her wrist before pulling her down on top of him. "We've only just begun."

Her body was already beginning to heat just from hearing him talk about the wondrous things yet to come. He pulled her up and positioned her where his mouth was right between her breasts. With his hands free, he could cup both breasts at the same time to suckle and lave her sensitive nipples. When he arched the bottom half of his body against her, she could feel his hardness as it almost, but not quite, entered her. As he continued to tease her with his mouth and his stiffness, she felt the familiar hot flames of desire licking at her core.

He was the master; she was his willing pupil.

This time their journey into the world of passion was long and leisurely.

Chapter Fifteen

Susan brushed at her ear and tugged the sheet over her head leaving only her face uncovered. Something soft tickled her cheek. Susan swatted at it. "Damn mosquito," she mumbled.

Masculine lips touched hers. "Oh, sleepy head, it's time to haul your body out of bed. We've got a lot of miles to cover today." Ryan tickled her chin with a lock of hair.

Susan slowly opened her eyes. Ryan was hunkered down on his haunches, eye level with her. Smiling, she reached out and pulled him back for another kiss.

"Good morning," she said, stretching.

"It's almost too late to be morning."

Susan noticed he had already shaved and dressed. "Why didn't you wake me sooner?"

Ryan smiled. "I figured you might need a

little extra sleep this morning."

Susan blushed at his subtle reference to the previous night. For them, the world outside their door ceased to exist. They had spent the night making love and whispering lovers' secrets, learning what pleasured and tantalized the other until the wee hours of the morning.

Giving her another quick kiss, he said, "I'll go get the horses ready while you dress. When I get back, we'll go eat breakfast then head for home."

"I'll be ready."

After Ryan left the room, Susan yawned and stretched lazily before leaving the soft bed. Quickly, she poured fresh water into the porcelain basin on the washstand. She splashed her face, then patted it dry with a towel hanging on the side of the stand. Completing her morning ablutions with haste, she dressed and was tying the end of her braid with a leather strip when Ryan returned. She'd already packed her saddlebags and needed only to add her brush and grab her hat.

Ryan picked up their saddlebags, tossing them over his shoulder. When their eyes met, he knew that she, too, would have liked to stay longer, but they knew they couldn't.

Leaving the town of San Saba behind them, Susan's thoughts turned to her father. She was eager to get home and make sure he was all right.

"How long do you think it will take us to get home?"

Ryan glanced at the dark clouds hovering over them. "If the weather holds and we push on, we should be able to get there about midnight."

"At least the clouds will break the heat a little," she said.

They traveled at a steady pace, stopping only to relieve themselves and get jerky and hardtack from the pack at noon.

By the middle of the afternoon the wind was growing increasingly stronger and unstable. Switching directions mercurially, it pelted them with particles of dust, leaves, and small twigs. The clouds were ominously dark, churning and seething in the sky above them, the smell of rain filling the air.

Ryan kept a watchful eye on the impending storm. The cloud bank rolling in from the southwest had taken on a greenish-black hue, a sure sign of hail and high winds. Sensing the danger, the horses' withers trembled and they flicked their ears in nervousness.

The storm was rapidly approaching when Ryan spotted a farmhouse about a half-mile down the road.

Ryan shouted so Susan could hear him above the rumble of thunder as lightning rent the air. "We'd better see if we can take shelter at that house up ahead until this storm passes. From the looks of it, we're in for a rough time."

Susan acknowledged his words with a nod of her head and nudged Spooky into a gallop.

*   *   *

An elderly farmer sat in a rocking chair on his porch, watching the storm clouds approach. With eyesight faded from age, he squinted at the three horses racing toward him, trying to make out who the riders were.

"Ma, we got company coming down the road," he shouted into the house.

"Who is it?" she asked, joining her husband on the porch.

He squinted harder. "Don't rightly know. Don't look like nobody from round here. Probably a family on their way somewheres and got caught in the storm."

The woman patted at her white hair pulled back in a neat little knot at the back of her head and smoothed her apron, making sure it was presentably tidy. Her lined face took on an excited glow. They didn't get much company so even strangers were welcomed.

"I'd better put some more taters in the stew, Pa. And whip up a batch of fresh corn bread." Not waiting for his reply, she hurried into the house.

The old man rested one hand on the bib of his overalls as he continued rocking slowly back and forth. "To be so little, that kid sure does ride good."

When Ryan and Susan reined up in the yard, they exchanged puzzled looks as the old man slapped his knee and burst out laughing.

"That's a dawg!" he exclaimed. "Ain't never seen a dawg ridin' a horse before. I thought these old eyes had surely gone bad," he explained.

Ryan chuckled. "I've had lots of folks get a laugh about that dog riding my pack horse. I'm Ryan Sommerall and this is Susan. Would you let me and the lady take shelter in your barn until the storm passes?"

The old man smiled, displaying an almost toothless grin. "Shucks, Ma will have my hide if'n you an' yore missus don't take supper with us. Put them horses in the barn and come sit a spell. We jest love fer someone ta come by. Gits kinda lonesome way out here."

"We appreciate the offer but we really need to be getting on as soon as the storm passes," Ryan said.

"Well, come on in ta the house anyhow. I'm a thinkin' we may have ta take to the root cellar. That's a mean-lookin' storm coming there."

Susan dismounted, handed Spooky's reins to Ryan, and followed the old man into the house.

The smell of baking filled the small house. The main room served as the kitchen and sitting room. Two doors, which Susan assumed to be bedrooms, opened off the main room.

The excited woman hurried to meet Susan, wiping her hands on her apron.

"Come in, come in," she urged. "I was just taking some fresh tea cakes from the oven. Would you like some? And maybe a glass of cool water?"

"Now calm down, Ma. They already said they'd take supper with us," he said.

Turning to Susan, he explained, "She gits so excited when company comes. Susan, this here is Mary Beth and most folks call me Tubbs."

"Tubbs?"

He flashed his toothless grin. "Well, I used ta be a bit on the heavy side but since I lost most of my teeth I can't eat as good as I used ta."

Susan jumped as a loud clap of thunder jarred the house followed by the sound of heavy rain and hail pounding the roof.

Ryan came through the door at the same instant, barely missing getting drenched. "Looks like we found your house just in time. That's some pretty damaging hail coming down."

The woman grabbed a towel and handed it to Ryan. "Pa, find the young man a shirt to wear till he dries out."

"That's all right, ma'am. I didn't get rained on much, but I don't want to track up your clean floor with my wet boots."

She waved a hand at him. "Oh, heavens. Don't you worry about that old floor. Believe me it's seen its share of muddy feet. Me and Pa raised us nine boys in this house. I declare sometimes I thought there was more mud on the floor than in the yard."

A gust of wind seized the screen door and whipped it open, banging it against the house. Ryan grabbed the door and latched the hook, then helped the older man shut the wooden door and put the bar in place.

"Yep, looks like we're in for a bad 'un. Might

as well sit a spell and have a cup of coffee," Tubbs said.

They had no more than settled themselves at the table when the sound of sizzling lightning followed by the splitting and crashing of a tree brought both men to their feet.

Tubbs looked out the window then turned back to his wife. He grinned sheepishly, pink gums showing. " 'member that old hackberry tree ya been pestering me ta cut down afore it blowed over on ta the house?"

Mary Beth raised a skeptical eyebrow at him. "Yes?"

"Well, ya can quit ya worrying now. It's gonna make some good firewood this winter." He turned to Ryan and chuckled. "Figured I'd git outta of cutting it down if'n I waited long enough."

Mary Beth shook her head in resignation. "Pa, you do beat all."

It had stopped hailing, and the lightning and thunder was growing dimmer in the distance. However, heavy rain continued to fall.

Ryan stepped out on the porch and studied the sky. When he entered the house, Susan looked at him expectantly.

"I know you're anxious to get home, but the storm is moving in the same direction we're going. I think, if the offer still stands, that we should spend the night here and head out first thing in the morning. Otherwise, I figure we're going to find ourselves riding in heavy rain all the way to Comanche."

Susan tried not to show her disappointment. "All right, if that's what you think is best."

Tubbs and Mary Beth were thrilled that the young couple would have to stay the night. Their kids were busy scratching out a living and taking care of their young families. Their neighbors were few and far between. No one seemed to have time for the old folks anymore, so most of their days were long and tedious. Now they'd get to visit a little longer.

The next morning Ryan and Susan were on the road before the sun peeked over the horizon. The cool air smelled fresh and clean from the previous day's rain which had been both a blessing and a curse. The farmers and ranchers needed the rain, but without the clouds to block the sun's heat, the humidity would be stifling by midmorning.

They began the morning excited. Only a few more hours and they'd be home. But as the miles between them and home narrowed, Ryan sensed that something was troubling Susan. She had grown quiet and introspective.

"You seem to be in deep thought. Is something bothering you?" Ryan asked.

"I was just thinking how suddenly a person's life can be irrevocably changed forever and through no fault of his own. I feel . . . different today than I did a week ago."

"Different? How do you mean 'different'?"

Susan shrugged her shoulders. "I'm not sure, really. Older, more mature maybe." She looked off into the distance. "More aware of the world and the perils awaiting the unsuspecting. Before the outlaws attacked us, if someone had suggested that I could point-blank shoot another human being, I would have been horrified at the very idea of such a thing. But I did—and without hesitation."

"Now don't go getting things out of perspective, Susie. You didn't *act* to kill a person, you *reacted* to protect your parents and yourself from an evil fiend. If you had not had the courage and ability to kill that man, he would have killed you. I wouldn't have made it in time to stop him. Don't forget, I only arrived in time to shoot the one who couldn't get on his horse."

"I guess so, but what about calculatingly tracking down and killing the other four outlaws? Was that also 'reacting'?" She shook her head negatively. "I don't think so. I was angry and wanted revenge."

Ryan was disturbed by Susan's troubled thoughts. They were approaching a small pond a hundred yards or so off the road. Ryan reined Pegasus toward it. Susan and Bluebell followed. This was something they needed to get out in the open and to talk about, to deal with and not let grow and fester. The fact that Susan trusted him enough to express her innermost fears made his heart swell with love for her.

"Let's water the horses and rest our backsides for a few minutes."

Ryan helped Susan dismount. Taking her hand in his, he said, "Walk with me and let's see if I can put to rest your fear of becoming a ferocious bounty hunter."

Susan stopped in her tracks, pulling her hand from Ryan's. "Don't make fun of me, Ryan. This is serious to me. In the past few days I have killed two men and helped, in some degree, to kill four others. And I don't feel any remorse or regret for my actions." Her eyes filled with unbidden tears.

Ryan pulled Susan to him, holding her tight. "I'm not making fun of you, Susie. I understand your confusion and apprehension. I'm only trying to help you put things in their proper perspective."

He tipped her head back so he could look into her eyes. "Susan, you are a strong, courageous woman. Few women would have had the courage, or ability, to do what you did. Those men were evil—worse than evil. They had to be stopped."

Susan wrapped her arms around Ryan's waist, resting her cheek against his broad chest. The rhythmic beating of his heart was comforting to her.

He kissed the top of her head. "You're basically the same sweet Susie you've always been. You'll still giggle over silly things with your friends. And cry when you find a wounded little bird or animal because you can't make it well. And cuss like a cowhand when you have to wade out in mud up to your knees to rescue a calf because you forgot to put your rope back on your saddle."

Again Ryan tipped her head back so he could see her face. He placed a gentle kiss on her lips. "Have you changed? Yes. You've become the self-assured and confident woman you were meant to be. The kind of woman a man hopes his wife will be. A woman who will stand with her man when the going gets rough. Strong when he needs help yet gentle and loving when he needs to be soothed."

When he kissed her, he was consumed with a feeling so intense it frightened him. He could no longer deny the words in his heart. "I love you, Susan Bradford."

Tears flooded her eyes again, but this time they were tears of happiness. She had recognized and had admitted to herself her love for Ryan months ago. Finally he had said the words that her heart had hoped and prayed for all these long months.

"I love you more, Ryan Sommerall." She stood on tiptoe, wrapping her arms around his neck, and kissed him with a passion that rocked them both with its intensity. "If you only knew how long I've waited to hear you say that."

"If you only knew how long I've wanted to tell you."

Susan looked at him in puzzlement. "Then why didn't you?"

Ryan felt the hairs on the back of his neck stand up and a shiver run down his spine. Why hadn't he curbed his hasty tongue before the words slipped out? He shrugged his shoulders and hoped he sounded convincing. "I don't know. I guess I was afraid to. I've never said that to a woman before."

She smiled shyly up at him. "I'm glad."

Ryan took a deep breath like a man who was about to step into water over his head. "Maybe . . .we shouldn't . . . What I mean is I think we need a little time to get used to the idea before we tell anyone else."

For just an instant Susan wondered if he regretted confessing his love, but she quickly dismissed the thought. After all, Ryan was a very private person. It was only natural that he'd be a little reluctant to share such a personal feeling with others so soon. Wasn't it?

"I understand. We won't tell anyone until you're ready. If that's what you want." She smiled, trying not to let her disappointment show.

Kissing her quickly on the forehead, Ryan took her hand and started walking back to the horses. "We'd better get moving if we want to get home by noon."

Susan felt absolutely exuberant. It was a beautiful day; they were almost home and Ryan loved her. How could it get any better than that? She would love to give Spooky her head and race with the wind. She wanted to let her happiness take flight and soar, but consideration for her horse won out.

Ryan chuckled at her barely bridled impatience. "I hate to burst your bubble, Susie.

However, has it occurred to you that your father is probably going to be less than happy, to say the least, that his daughter took off chasing outlaws?"

"Well, yes, that has crossed my mind. But, I left him a note telling him not to worry, that I was going with you," she said earnestly.

Ryan rolled his eyes skyward in disbelief at her naivete. "Oh, I'm sure that eased his mind greatly. I know if I were a father, it certainly would make me feel better knowing my impulsive daughter had taken off with a single man to face . . . whatever," he said caustically.

"I'll just tell him the truth. They'll understand."

Ryan groaned. "Susie, ah, that might not be such a good idea."

Susan's eyes grew round in disbelief. "You mean you think I should *lie* to my parents?"

"No. I'm not telling you to lie to your folks. But, if I may make a suggestion, I think it might be better if you just don't tell them . . . everything. Leave out the more dangerous things. Like when you charged the Indians, for example."

"I didn't charge the Indians. Spooky did. That wasn't my fault."

"Nevertheless, trust me on this. I think your father would be happier not knowing how much danger I let you get into."

"Okay. If you think that's best, I won't give them any more details than necessary. What are you going to tell them?"

"I'm going to do what any red-blooded American man would do. I'm going to blame it all on you."

"Coward."

Ryan laughed.

Chapter Sixteen

When they turned off the wagon road to the lane that wound its way through the scattered clumps of trees to her home, excitement as well as apprehension began to build in Susan.

As soon as they rounded the last bend and had a clear view of the house, she saw her mother walking to the clothesline with a basket of laundry. Relief flooded over her. She knew this meant her father was all right and probably at home. She nudged Spooky into a trot, wanting to dash to her mother but unwilling to ask any more of her weary horse.

Ryan followed her lead.

Molly saw them when they were still a couple hundred yards from her. She dropped the piece of wet clothing back into the basket and started running to meet them. Suddenly she stopped, turned around, and ran into the house. When Molly emerged again, Susan and Ryan were dismounting at the back porch.

"Is Papa here? Is he all right?" Susan asked as she ran to embrace her mother.

"Yes, dear. He's here and he's all right. Oh, Susan, I've never been so relieved and happy to see anyone in all my life. We've been worried sick about you. How could you go off and . . . Oh, never mind. Get on in here to your father before he gets out of bed and comes out here," Molly admonished as she ushered Susan through the door.

Susan looked over her shoulder to make sure Ryan was behind her as she hurried through the house to her father's bedside.

Ryan would rather have gone home instead of facing Seth at that moment, but he knew it would be just as difficult later. Besides, he could hardly desert Susan now.

He found his way through the house to Seth and Molly's bedroom by following the sound of their voices. He stepped into the room and stood shifting his hat from one hand to the other, waiting for the emotional reunion between Susan and her father to end.

"Pleased to see you're doing well," he muttered when he fell under the stare of Seth's accusing eyes.

"How in the hell could you do what you did?"

Seth's voice was low and slightly trembling with anger.

"Papa, please don't be angry with Ryan. He didn't—"

Susan's defense of Ryan was stopped by her father. "Damn it, answer me. What in the hell came over you to do such a thing? How could you possibly bring yourself to take my daughter into such danger?"

"Seth, I think you know I didn't voluntarily and of my own initiative take Susan with me. Or let her go with me, whichever way you want to put it."

"Then how the hell did she end up with you?"

Ryan turned to look at Molly. "Molly, how is your side where that man kicked you? Does it still hurt?"

Molly placed her hand to the side of her ribs. "It still hurts some, but it's getting better every day. I didn't know—"

"Kicked you?" Seth's voice rose with anger. "They kicked you, Molly? You didn't tell me that."

"I didn't know, Seth." Molly's voice expressed her bewilderment. "I thought I got hurt when I fell from the wagon."

"One of the bastards kicked her, Seth. Susan saw him do it."

"Yes, Papa, I did. It was the stinking little weasel who Ryan shot first. He kicked Mama because he thought she was dead and he wouldn't get to take her with him and have his fun with her."

293

Seth's face turned livid with rage. He turned his eyes to Ryan. "I hope you gut-shot the son of a bitch!"

"I think you're beginning to understand now why Susan felt she had to go with me. She also saw those men shoot you down as though they were casually eliminating a nuisance that was in their way. Remember, too, that she had to take a pistol away from the meanest, most vicious one of them all and kill him with it to prevent him from taking her with them."

Seth took a deep breath and exhaled in a long sigh. "I'm so relieved to get my daughter back unhurt that I'm having difficulty remaining angry with you, Ryan. I am deeply grateful to you for driving those bastards off before they could do Molly and Susan further harm and then going after them and killing them. I just wish I could have done it myself. But I still can't understand why you let Susan go with you."

Ryan shook his head. "I thought I just explained why. I reckon your problem is that you think Susan is exempt from feeling what you're feeling just because she's a woman. Well, she's not, Seth. And she knew she was capable of doing what she felt she had to do. I would have had to forcibly lock her up, or something, to keep her from going with me. And even then, she would have took out after me as soon as you turned her loose."

Ryan glanced at Susan then back at her father. "I just couldn't do that, Seth. I would have, mind you, if I'd thought she'd be in any real danger, but I felt sure I could protect her."

"That's right, Papa. We didn't hardly have any trouble with the outlaws at all. Ryan shot two of them from long range with his buffalo rifle. Then we easily ambushed the other two. I shot one at the same time Ryan shot the other."

Molly placed a hand on the bedpost to steady herself. "*You* shot one of the outlaws?"

"Yes, Mama. But I was in no danger," she hurriedly added. "They didn't even have a chance to shoot at us." She shrugged her shoulders nonchalantly. "The whole thing wouldn't have amounted to much at all if the Indians hadn't—" Susan clamped her hand over her mouth. "Oops."

"Indians!" Molly screeched.

Ryan groaned inwardly and looked up at the ceiling.

"You were attacked by Indians?" Seth asked incredulously.

Susan glanced apologetically at Ryan. "Well, kind of, but that wouldn't have amounted to much, though, if Spooky hadn't charged them."

Molly sat down on the bed. "Spooky charged the Indians with you on her back?"

"Well, of course I was on her back, Mother."

Seth rolled his head from side to side, raised his hands, and dropped them again.

"That didn't put me in any real danger, though. I shot one of the Indians and Ryan shot another. The Indians split and Spooky and

I went right on through. We would have been clear of them if Ryan had followed me."

Seth turned questioning eyes on Ryan.

"I couldn't follow her. There were more warriors coming in from behind us. I had to stop their pursuit."

"That's right, Papa. Ryan hauled Pegasus in and whirled him around and shot two of the Indians before they even knew what was happening. Then he stopped right there, surrounded by Indians, whirling Pegasus one way and then the another, fighting them all while I made my escape."

Seth seemed to relax with relief. "Then you were clear of it from then on?"

Susan hesitated a moment. "Well, no, not exactly. I couldn't very well run away and leave Ryan to fight alone."

"You mean you went back into it!" Seth thundered. "Damn it, Susan. The man was risking his life to save yours. Why didn't you keep going?"

"That's what I told her," Ryan murmured.

Susan raised her chin defiantly. "It wouldn't have made any difference if I had decided to keep going. I wasn't going to tell this because I didn't want Ryan to know. But, you see, Spooky decided to go back at the same time I did. I guess she didn't want to run off and leave Pegasus and Bluebell. So I was going back whether I liked it or not. But that doesn't mean I wouldn't have gone back to help Ryan anyway."

Ryan began to shake with silent laughter.

Seth was hyperventilating from frustration.

"It's all your fault, Seth," Molly accused. "I told you time and time again over the years that you shouldn't teach her the things you did and let her tag around all over the countryside with you. She's been running wilder here than she did back home." Molly twisted her hands in her apron in angry exasperation.

"Well, why have you let her do it? You know I've been too busy building fences and one thing and another to take much note of what she was doing. You're her mother. Mothers are supposed to keep their daughters in line."

Molly gave Seth a stern, reproachful look. "Now why did you say such a thing as that? You know all I ever get from her is 'don't worry about it.' She knows—"

"Stop it." Susan cupped her hands to her face. "I can't take any more of this."

"Oh, Susan." Molly rushed to her, raising her arms to embrace her. "I'm sorry. I—"

"And well you should be. Both of you." She included her father in her accusing glare. Susan brushed Molly's arms from her. Tears filled her eyes and ran down her cheeks. "You've both been talking like I've been on some kind of a childish lark. Well, I haven't! I fought and killed outlaws for you. Two of them. I fought and killed marauding Indians. I've been on the back of a horse ten to twelve hours a day, four straight days for you. Now you criticize and pick on me like I've been a naughty child. I've had enough of that. I won't hear any more." She turned to leave the room.

"Susan?"

Her father's soft voice stopped her. She turned to face him.

Seth patted the side of the bed and held out his arms to her.

Susan went to him and sat down beside him. Her eyes still brimmed with flowing tears.

Seth gathered her in his arms and pulled her to his chest. "You know your mother and I love you, baby. Our scolding you and snapping at each other was just a way of venting the anguish and frustration that's built in us over the past few days. That's a pretty long time to worry about our daughter being out with a Texas Ranger, chasing outlaws, you know."

"Yes, I know, Papa. But I had to do it. I just couldn't accept Ryan's going alone. I only did what you would have done if you hadn't been wounded. Don't you understand that? I just did what I had to do." Her eyes beseeched her father to understand.

"Yes. I think I understand your reasons. I guess what I'm having trouble understanding is that my little girl has grown into a young woman who is feeling more responsibility than I would like for her to. But we are very proud of you, Susan."

Susan sniffed and dried her eyes with a corner of the bed sheet. "Thank you, Papa."

Ryan cleared his throat. "Ah, I think I'd better

be going." Satisfied that the worst of Susan's scolding was over, he wanted to make his escape before any more questions could be asked.

Susan turned to Ryan. "Will you stay and eat lunch with us?"

Ryan shook his head. "I need to get on home, Susie. I'm sure Hazel has something fixed. I'll come back later this evening or send one of my men to feed your horses and do whatever needs to be done."

"Thanks, Ryan. Kyle and your men have been looking after things right along. Kyle hired two more men and he's had one of them spending every night around my barn."

An expression of puzzlement crossed Ryan's face. "Why did he hire two more men?"

"That's right. You wouldn't know about it, would you? They had to chase some Indians out of your pasture the other night. Kyle figured he'd better get some more help."

"Damn," Ryan exclaimed. "I knew the minute I heard about the Adobe Walls fracas that it would lead to a pack of trouble. Well, I'd better go."

Susan leaned down and pecked her father on the cheek. "I'll see Ryan out."

Seth held out his hand. "I'm obliged to you, Ryan."

Ryan clasped his hand. "Not at all. I had a personal stake in this, too, you know." He looked at Susan. "At least I'd like to think I have."

Susan smiled at him, a slight blush coloring her face.

Molly stepped to him and hugged him around his waist. "Thank you, Ryan. Thank you ever so much for watching after my impetuous daughter and bringing her home unharmed."

Ryan's face turned red with embarrassment. "Susan, will you please get me out of here before I get to feeling like some kind of a hero or something?"

Molly giggled.

Susan took Ryan's hand and walked with him to the back porch. As soon as they reached the privacy of the porch, she moved into his arms.

Ryan kissed her lightly on the lips. He stood with his arms locked loosely behind her waist, enjoying holding her. "I'll be back as soon as I can. I need to see what's happening with the Indian situation and if Heck's still in town."

Susan toyed absently with the buttons on his shirt. "Do you think the Indians are going on the rampage again?"

Ryan shook his head. "I don't know. Kyle's not one to get alarmed over nothing. If he felt the need for more men, then I fear there is the possibility of more raids. I'll know more after I talk to Kyle and the sheriff. In the meantime, promise me you won't take any chances. I don't want you riding off fishing or over in the pasture petting the horses. Nothing. Stay close to the house and keep your rifle with you at all times. Promise?"

Susan nodded. "I promise I'll be careful. But you sound like you already know there's going to be trouble."

Ryan shrugged. "I just have this gut feeling that there are going to be problems with the Indians. But you're not to worry. If I feel things are too dangerous, I'll move you and your family into town when I take Hazel. You'll be safe there until the Army can get the Indians back under control."

"I know. I'm just worried about you." She looked up at him, her eyes wide with fear. "I'm afraid for you. Ryan, I couldn't stand it if anything happened to you. I love you." She buried her head against his chest, hugging him tightly. She was afraid she was going to cry and didn't want him to see her tears.

He tipped her face up and kissed her. "Baby, nothing is going to happen to me. You're just tired. This past week has taken its toll on you. Get some rest, sweetheart, and everything will look better in the morning. I'll be back as soon as I can."

Susan tilted her head slightly, giving Ryan an impish grin. "You better come courting me properly, Mister Sommerall, or else you might find yourself on the wrong end of my father's shotgun yet," she teased.

Ryan laughed. "Yes, ma'am. In the meantime, will you please *try* to stay out of trouble? Between you and that crazy horse of yours, you're going to make an old man out of me before my time."

Susan laughed. Running her hand through the hair at his nape, she pulled his head down to hers. "I'll miss you," she said, before giving him a smoldering kiss that made his body harden with desire.

Ryan pulled her tightly against him, prolonging the kiss until they were both gasping for air when he finally released her. "I'll be back tomorrow or the next day for sure."

Susan stood in the yard watching Ryan as he cut across the pasture to his place. When he topped the last hill, he turned in his saddle and waved at her.

Susan smiled, pleased that he had known she would be watching for his wave. When she could no longer see him, she turned and went inside.

"Well, by George, you're back," Sheriff Ed Thomas greeted as Ryan stepped through his office door. "Don't see no bandages or nothing, either. I assume you got all them outlaws or you wouldn't be back yet."

"Yeah. I got them all, Ed. Didn't bring none in, though."

"I didn't figure you would. Hell, from what Heck told me about them, it would have been foolish of you to try. Where did you catch up to them?"

"I got my first shot at a creek that feeds the San Saba River. Got two of them there. Had to trail the other two a number of miles down the San Saba."

"Well, I'm glad you got them without getting hurt yourself. I sure hated I wasn't here to go with you, but I had to leave early to go to Lamkin and, of course, I didn't get back until nearly dark."

"I understand, Ed. Lord knows you got more than you can do and no deputies to help you. Is Heck still in town?"

"Yeah, he's still here. Probably will be for four or five more days. If he ain't at the hotel, I expect he's at Jack Wright's place playing billiards. He's been hanging out there some the past couple of days."

"I guess I'll check at Jack's place first. Care to come along?"

"Sure, but first, Ryan, there's something I've got to tell you. The day after you left to go after those outlaws, a fella showed up and asked a lot of questions about you and that man you killed in the gunfight here in Comanche."

Ryan stared at the sheriff, waiting for more details. "Who was he?" he prompted. "What's his name?"

"I don't know his name," Ed said, disgusted with himself. "Damn it, Ryan. The way the conversation went, I let him get away without getting his name or learning much of anything about him, for that matter."

"How in the hell could you do that, Ed? Sounds to me like he was more than just curious."

"Well, like I said, it's just the way the whole thing happened. He came into the office and

303

asked how to get to your place. I figured he was interested in buying some horses, so I gave him directions to your ranch. He thanked me and started to leave. But when I casually mentioned that you wouldn't be there, but Kyle could handle any horse trading he wanted to do, he didn't seem to have any further interest in going out to your place. He just started asking questions. Said he had read about the gunfight in the newspaper."

"Did he know the man I killed?"

"He thought maybe he did from the description I gave, but he didn't want to put a name to him since he wasn't absolutely positive. Didn't want the wrong name to go on a grave marker."

"I don't think I understand. If he thought he knew the man, couldn't he find out for sure through some relatives?"

"I asked him about that. He said if the man was who he figured he was, he didn't have any living relatives."

"Did he know me? Or did he indicate that he had ever known me?"

"Well, now that's the strangest part about the whole matter. I asked him if he knew you. He said he didn't know you, but he planned to get acquainted. I asked him what he meant by that. He said just to tell you that he would be back."

"Damn, Ed. That could be taken as a threat. Couldn't you have used that as a reason for a little more forceful interrogation?"

"I could and I did. To quote myself exactly, I said, 'Now look a here, fella. If you think you got some bone to pick with Ryan Sommerall, you better do it strictly in the open and above-board, and even so you're gonna run up against me, too.'"

"What did he have to say to that?"

"Said he didn't think you would want me to interfere in what was to be settled between you and him. Well, that got my dander up. I told him he would tell me what it was he wanted to see you about or I would hold him in jail till you got back." Ed paused to light the cigarette he'd finished rolling.

"Well, what did he say?" Ryan prompted.

Sheriff Thomas looked Ryan full in the eyes. "He said it was strictly a personal matter between you and him concerning the shooting of a Confederate Army officer on the battlefield at Chattanooga, Tennessee."

"Damn," Ryan muttered. He removed his hat and ran his fingers through his hair. "Damn!"

"Ryan, I don't understand this at all. I didn't think you had gone off to the war. I told this fella so. But he said you were there all right. Said you hadn't been officially sworn in to the Confederate Army, but you were there with the intent of doing so. Is that so, Ryan?"

Ryan paced the office from one wall to the other and stopped at the window to stare out into the street. "I was there, Ed. But that's about all I can tell you. Like the man said, it's a personal matter right now. And I would appreciate it if you wouldn't say anything about it to anyone else."

"Whatever you say. But, if I can be any help to you, all you got to do is ask. I'm sworn to enforce the law, but you know I don't have any reservations about using my authority to see that the interests of law-abiding citizens are best served, even if my actions don't exactly conform to the letter of the law."

Ryan nodded his head. "Thanks, Ed. I'll call on you if I need you. Is there anything else you have to tell me?"

"No. That's about it. I figured I had pried into his business and yours, too, as much as I could. He just walked out of my office, got on his horse, and rode away."

"Well, I guess that's the way it will have to stand for now. But if I should be gone when he comes back, do whatever—"

"You can count on it, Ryan," the sheriff interrupted. "I'll hog-tie him first and then lock him up until you get to talk to him."

"Good. Now let's go see if Heck is at Jack's place."

Heck was playing billiards with one of the saloon girls. The girl raised her hand in greeting when she saw Ryan and Ed enter the saloon.

"There's a couple of your fellow lawmen," she informed Heck.

Heck's face broke into a wide smile when he saw to whom the girl was referring.

"I've been hoping you'd get back before I had

to leave," he said as he crossed the room to meet Ryan and Ed. "Tell me you killed all them outlaws and I'll buy you a drink."

"I killed them all, Heck, and I'll have that drink if you'll let me do the buying."

"Shucks, no. Ain't no need of you spending your money. If I do the buying, it won't cost none of us anything. We get 'em free."

Ryan chuckled. "How do you figure that?"

"Well, it seems that somebody told this whole town that my money ain't no good. I ain't been able to spend a dime at the hotel, or the restaurant, or here in the saloon, the doctor's office, or nothing. They just write on a paper pad an' tell me it's taken care of."

Ryan smiled. "I reckon it's someone's way of saying thank you."

"I figured as much. I sure appreciate it, too. I didn't hardly have a dime when I first got here."

Ryan cleared his throat. "Ah, while we're on the subject of money, if you need some to get you back to Fort Smith, I'd be more than happy to lend you some."

"Thanks, Ryan, but I don't need it since Ed gave me the money he got from the sale of the outlaws' stuff. I got more money now than I'm used to having at any one time."

"Ed gave the money to you?"

"Yep. He sold them two outlaws' horses and saddles and guns and whatever else they had that was salable. He held out only enough to pay for their burying an' gave the rest to me."

"Hmmm," Ryan mused as he took a sip of whiskey.

"I know what you're thinking," Heck continued. "I questioned whether that was legal. Ed said it was legal here in Comanche County."

Ryan shot Ed a quizzical glance.

The sheriff shrugged his shoulders. "Like I told you awhile ago. I don't have any qualms about bending the law in whatever direction it seems to best serve the needs and well-being of law-abiding people."

Ryan smiled. "It's plain to see why you keep getting reelected, unopposed." He tossed back the remainder of his drink. "Let's play some billiards, Heck."

Ryan and Heck had just finished the tie-breaking game when Ben Walker, who owned the general store and doubled as the postmaster, came into the saloon.

"Hello, Ryan. Glad to see ya back. Got a letter for you over at the store. Looks like it might be important. It's got the Ranger seal on it."

Ryan frowned. The last thing he wanted right now was to hear about trouble from the Rangers. "Thanks for telling me, Ben. I was just about to leave. Is Mrs. Walker still at the store?"

"Yeah. Gladys can get it for you."

Heck drained the last of his drink and set the glass on the bar. "I'll walk over with you. I need to get some tobacco and you can tell me what happened with the outlaws on the way."

After entering the store, Ryan read his letter while Gladys Walker got Heck's tobacco. *Damn and double damn!*

"Looks like that's bad news from the way you're frowning."

Ryan glanced up at Heck. "It is. It's from Major John B. Jones. He's the commander of the Frontier Battalion of the Texas Rangers. He says they're having a bad time with the Indians and he needs all the good guns he can get. He's asked me to come help them because he needs my scouting and tracking skills as well as my gun."

Heck shook his head. "From the reports we've been hearing, it sounds pretty bad all right. Seems like the Indians have split up into small bands and are raising hell amongst the settlers. Especially up along the Clear Fork of the Brazos River and on up into the Double Mountain Forks."

"Yeah, I figured they'd catch the worst of it. Kyle said we'd had a few raids down this way by small bands but nothing serious yet. He figured they've mostly been after some good horses."

"What will you do now?"

Ryan grimaced. "I really don't have a choice. I'd rather fight them up there and try to keep them from moving here. I'll report to Major Jones as soon as I can get a couple of things taken care of." Ryan looked at Heck. "What are your plans?"

"Doc says I'll be healed well enough to ride

in another three or four days. Guess I'll head on back to Fort Smith."

Heck looked at Ryan long and hard, trying to find the words to express his feelings. "I hate the way it happened but I sure am glad I got to meet you, Ryan. If you ever get up Arkansas way, I'd consider it an honor if'n you'd stop by an' visit a spell." Heck stuck his hand out to Ryan.

Ryan clasped his friend's hand. "You know you'll always be welcome any time you come this way, Heck. No invitation needed."

"Thanks. You take care of yourself and that pretty little gal of yours. She seems to think mighty highly of you."

Ryan smiled. "Good luck, Heck. I'll tell Susan you said good-bye."

As Ryan watched Heck walk away, his thoughts turned to Susan. He stuffed the letter from Major Jones in his pocket as he walked to his horse.

As serious as the major's problem was, it couldn't hold a candle to the problem he had to face now.

The minute he had told Susan he loved her, he was wishing he could call the words back. He knew—had always known—that he and Susie couldn't have a future together. Why had he let his guard slip? Why had he been such a fool? Why couldn't he have kept his mouth shut?

Chapter Seventeen

"Four days!" Susan fumed as she hoisted her saddle on top of Spooky's back, tossing the stirrup up so she could tighten the cinch. "I haven't seen hide nor hair of that man in *four days*, and he thinks *that's* proper courting! Well, I've got news for him. Someone needs to teach him some proper courting manners."

Spooky flicked her ears forward and back, unconcerned, as Susan continued to fuss.

"Get that air out of there." Susan kneed Spooky in the stomach, forcing her to blow out the air she'd sucked in, and yanked the cinch tighter. "I'm in no mood for any shenanigans from you today."

Susan's ill temper was partially due to a bad case of cabin fever. She had promised Ryan that she'd stay close to the house and she had, but, she had also expected him to come calling in a day or two at the most. But this was the afternoon of the fourth day and still no Ryan.

She cut through the pasture to Ryan's place, letting herself through the gate that separated their two ranches. She momentarily wondered why there weren't any horses in his pasture. She decided that he must have moved them closer to his house in case the Indians returned and attempted to steal them again.

Riding across the land, inhaling the clean fresh air, eased her tension and anger, and she wondered if perhaps she was being too harsh on Ryan. After all, he probably had a great deal of work to catch up on since they'd returned from chasing the outlaws. A large ranch like his didn't just run itself.

She scolded herself for even thinking that Ryan wouldn't have come over if he could have. She debated whether she should turn around and go back home. But after only a few seconds of thinking about it, she decided she missed Ryan too much not to see him, even if only for a few minutes.

When she entered the yard, she saw Kyle leaving the barn and rode over to him.

"Well, howdy, Susan. Haven't seen you in a long time. How's your papa doing?"

Susan laughed. "Judging by the amount of grumbling he's doing, he must be doing real good. Mama's having a hard time making him follow the doctor's orders."

Kyle grinned. "Knowing Seth, I'll jest bet she is. If you're a lookin' for Ryan, he's over yonder." Kyle jerked his thumb toward the back of the stomp lot. "Might oughta warn ya, though, he ain't been in too good a mood lately. Maybe you can sweeten his disposition some."

Susan smiled and turned Spooky in Ryan's direction. "Thanks, Kyle. I'll see what I can do."

Ryan was digging a stone out of a mare's hoof with his pocketknife when he heard the horse approaching. He had seen Susan ride into the yard and stop to talk to Kyle a minute before heading in his direction.

Susan frowned. An uneasy feeling crept over her. She knew Ryan had heard someone riding up, yet he hadn't looked around to see who it was. Why?

"Ryan?"

Ryan continued checking the mare's hoof, trying to determine how bad the bruise was. "Thought I told you to stay close to home. What are you doing out wandering around?"

"Goodness, you are a grouch today." Susan dismounted and walked over to him. "Besides, I'm not 'out wandering around,'" she mimicked. "I came to see you. I missed you and wanted to see you. I didn't think—"

"That's just it. You don't ever think before you act, do you?"

"Ryan! What in the world is wrong with you? Kyle said you were in a bad mood, but this is ridiculous. Why should it make you mad just because I came to see you? You told me you'd be back to see me in a day or so. It's been four days and you haven't come by."

Ryan released the mare's hoof and straightened up. When he turned to face her, she could see the muscles in his jaw clenching and unclenching. His eyes were a chilling steel-gray.

"I've been busy."

"Busy? Too busy to come by, even for a few minutes, to see the woman you're supposed to be courting?"

Ryan stared at her for a long moment before letting out a slow, exasperated breath. "Susan, besides my duties as a Texas Ranger, I have a large ranch to run. I don't have time for courting."

Susan was sure she hadn't heard him right. "You don't have time for courting?" She shook her head in utter confusion. "Ryan, I don't understand. I love you and I thought you loved me and wanted to marry me."

"I never asked you to marry me."

"No, you didn't actually ask me to marry you, but we made love and . . . your actions . . . I thought . . ."

"Things have changed, Susan."

"Changed? How could things change in the space of four days, Ryan? Either you love me or you don't, it's that simple!" Susan didn't understand what was wrong with Ryan, but his attitude was beginning to make her angry.

Ryan shook his head. "No, Susan, it's *not* that simple. While we were gone, there was a man at the sheriff's office looking for me. Ed talked to him at great length and—"

"I don't care about some stranger who Sheriff Thomas talked to. How could that have anything to do with whether you court me?" she demanded angrily.

"Damn it, Susan. It has everything to do with it. Don't you understand?"

"No, Ryan, I don't understand—not at all. Maybe you'd better explain it to me. I seem to be a bit dense today!" she snapped.

"Why should I have been in a hurry to call on you when all I could do is tell you that there's no place in my life for you right now?" He was just as angry as she was, only the reasons were different.

Susan jerked her head back in shock at the harshness in his voice. If he had physically struck her, she wouldn't have been more stunned. She shook her head in denial.

Ryan exhaled a frustrated breath and raked his hand through his hair. "I don't know anything else to say."

Susan stared disbelievingly at Ryan. How could this be happening? This was the man she loved.

"Are you in some kind of trouble? Maybe . . . maybe I can help if you'll just tell me . . ."

The bewildered, hurt look on her face made Ryan's heart flip in his chest. He didn't want to hurt Susan, but for her own sake, he couldn't lead her on. He couldn't let her believe that they could have a happy future together when he wouldn't have given a plug nickel that he had *any* future at all. Now that they knew where he was, they would keep coming. And the next man who came looking for him might not give him any warning—only a bullet in his back.

Ryan's face was hard and unyielding, a muscle worked in his jaw. When he spoke, his voice showed no feeling, no emotion. It was an absolute monotone.

"Go home, Susan. There is no place for you in my life."

Susan felt like she had fallen into an abyss and couldn't stop her downward spiral. Her ears were ringing and she felt lightheaded. She opened her mouth to speak but couldn't make the words come out.

Ryan stared at her a moment, then turned his back on her, and walked away.

The pain in her heart was so great that Susan's mind was numb. She didn't remember mounting Spooky and making her way home. All she wanted was to reach the safety of her room before she fell completely apart.

Kyle heard the fast approaching horse and turned just in time to see the tears streaming down Susan's face and hear her anguished sobs. He called out to her, but she didn't appear to have heard him as she raced past him.

He looked back in the direction from which she'd come and saw Ryan leave the stomp lot and walk over to Pegasus.

Thinking that Ryan was going after Susan, Kyle hurried to him.

"What in the world did you do to that child?"

Ryan glared at Kyle. "Stay out of it, Kyle. It's none of your business."

Kyle stood open-mouthed, staring at Ryan as he mounted Pegasus, gouged him in the ribs, and headed in the opposite direction from Susan. Never had he known Ryan to be deliberately cruel to anyone or any thing.

Ryan raced across the pasture, heedless of the danger of his breakneck speed. He gave Pegasus his head, letting him run, trying desperately to escape the pain, but there was no escape. It clung to his heart with a tight-fisted grip that threatened to strangle the very life from his body.

"Whoa, boy, whoa." Ryan finally slowed Pegasus to a canter, then eased him to a trot until he cooled down.

He dismounted and ground-reined Pegasus. Guilt overwhelmed him as he realized the punishment the horse had endured because of his thoughtlessness.

He patted the stallion's neck, his voice choked with emotion as he sucked in deep, ragged breaths. "We've been through a lot of battles together, boy, but this is the hardest one yet, and you can't help me a bit."

Pegasus snorted, tossing his head as if he could feel his master's anguish.

The pain was so excruciating that he felt like someone had reached into his chest and ripped his heart from his body. He had hurt when his grandfather, and later his father, had died. But neither of those hurts could compare with the soul-wrenching anguish he felt now.

He was so angry, so frustrated, that he felt as if he would explode into a million pieces. He wanted to strike out at something—anything—everything.

The knowledge that, for a very precious, too brief moment in time, he had actually held a little bit of heaven in his arms, made the hurt more than he could endure. But because he did love and cherish her so dearly, he'd had no other choice but to set her free.

Raising his face to the sky, he released his rage in a gut-rending cry.

Ryan didn't go home that night.

When he returned early the next morning, he told Kyle and Hazel good-bye, mounted Pegasus, and rode away to join Major Jones and his Texas Ranger battalion.

Ryan could feel Susan's presence pulling at him with each mile that separated them. He'd known from the moment he'd made his decision to let her go that it would be the hardest thing he'd ever done in his life. But he couldn't have even begun to imagine the pain that had wrapped itself around his heart.

He reined Pegasus to a halt and pulled his Bull Durham tobacco sack and papers from his shirt pocket. His fingers trembled as he attempted to roll a cigarette. He managed to spill more tobacco than he rolled. He frowned at the sorry-looking object, thinking he'd rolled a better smoke than this on his very first try at the age of thirteen.

Ryan, would you like for me to do that for you?

He whirled in the saddle looking for Susan. He thought he'd heard her call his name, but it was only a trick of his imagination. He laughed self-consciously, remembering when she had said those words to him—just before she'd whacked him with a wet bandanna.

"Oh, Susie," he agonized out loud. "What have I done to us? I can't keep you and I can't let you go."

Ryan finished his skimpy, crooked cigarette and flipped the butt into the dirt. He knew what he had to do. He couldn't ride away from her like this. He had to talk with her, try to explain things if he could. He knew he'd hurt her badly and he hated himself for not being gentler with her. He hadn't meant to be so harsh and blunt but his own pain had gotten in the way.

He turned Pegasus around and headed back in the direction he'd come.

Susan stayed in her room the rest of the day and that night, pleading a bad headache. And after hours of crying and agonizing over why Ryan would have treated her the way he had, it wasn't a lie.

When the endlessly long, dark hours of night finally gave way to the first rays of light, she still had no answer for his actions.

"Susan?" Molly knocked on the door again. "Susan, Ryan is here and he'd like to talk to you."

"I don't want to talk to him."

Molly entered her daughter's room. She had heard Susan's muffled crying late into the night. It hadn't been hard for her to figure out that the two young people had quarreled. Ordinarily, she wouldn't have interfered but she felt sorry for Ryan. He looked as miserable as Susan did, and she knew how stubborn her daughter could be.

"I think you should at least hear what he has to say. It might help matters."

Susan stood with her back to the door, looking out the window. She stiffened her shoulders and continued staring out the window. "No. Tell Mister Sommerall I'm not interested in anything he has to say. He said quite enough yesterday."

"Give him a chance to explain, dear. Maybe—"

Susan angrily whirled from the window to face her mother. "Don't patronize me, Mother. I'm not a child. I do not want to talk to Ryan. I do not want to see Ryan. Just . . . tell him to go away."

Susan turned back to stare out the window but not before a tear began its descent down her cheek.

Molly sadly shrugged her shoulders and closed the door behind her.

"I'm sorry, Ryan, but Susan . . . Susan's not feeling well right now. Perhaps if you came back a little later."

Ryan wasn't surprised at Susan's refusal to see him. "I understand, Molly."

Molly could feel the pain she saw in the young man's eyes. "Could I give her a message, maybe?"

Ryan hesitated then shook his head. "No. No, there's no message. Good-bye, Molly." He tipped his hat and reined Pegasus around.

He had no one to blame but himself. He'd come back hoping somehow to make it up to Susan and to ease his own conscience, but it was probably just as well that she hadn't wanted to see him. He couldn't offer her anything more today than he could yesterday. Maybe it was best to leave things alone. It had been his intent to set Susan free; he just didn't know it was going to hurt so badly.

From where she stood at her window, she could see Ryan sitting tall in the saddle as he rode down the lane away from her house. She saw the big, black stallion toss his head and break into a trot.

Tears ran unheeded down her cheeks as she watched until man and horse disappeared from sight. For just a brief instant she felt a sudden impulse to run after them—a premonition almost. Instead, she closed her eyes, leaning her head against the glass pane, and freely gave into the tears that fell like drops of rain on the windowsill.

*   *   *

For two days Susan stayed in her room, sleeping little and eating even less. Over and over her mind replayed the times she and Ryan had spent together as she desperately sought to find something that would help her to understand why Ryan had rejected her.

She refused to believe that he did not love her. All of his actions said he did. Even when he was telling her there was no place for her in his life, he hadn't said it was because he didn't love her.

After wallowing in her misery for three days, and still not being able to find the answers for herself, she decided to confront Ryan. Anger was finally beginning to replace her grief. She didn't deserve the way he'd treated her and she wasn't going to stand for it.

She knew that she was taking a huge risk by putting her pride on the line. She might wind up humiliated and with her self-respect in tatters, but she deserved to know the truth.

Her heart told her that he loved her. If she was wrong, then he would have to tell her so face to face.

Hazel was in the garden gathering tomatoes when Susan rode into the yard. Kyle was sitting on the fence watching one of the younger cowhands breaking a horse. He waved to her but stayed where he was. She looked around for Ryan but didn't see him.

Hazel placed a large red tomato in her basket and dusted the dirt from her hands. "Good morning, Susan. How is your father doing?"

Susan dismounted and walked over to her. "He's doing fine. I, ah, came to see Ryan."

A look of surprise and then awkward discomfort crossed Hazel's features. "I'm sorry, Susan, but Ryan is gone."

"Gone?" Susan's smile faded as an uneasiness settled in the pit of her stomach. "Gone where?"

"He didn't tell you he was leaving, did he." It was a statement, not a question.

Susan shook her head, wrapping her arms around herself. "No. No, he didn't. When— when will he be back?"

Hazel could see the pain in the young woman's eyes. Kyle had told her of Susan's distress and of Ryan's foul temper the last time the two of them had been together. The next morning when Ryan abruptly left, she had almost asked him if he was going to stop by Susan's but then decided it was none of her business.

She shook her head sadly. She could tell that Susan was fighting to keep from crying. "I'm sorry but I don't know when he'll be back, Susan," she said sympathetically. Picking up her basket of vegetables, she walked to the young woman and placed her arm around her shoulders. "Why don't we go in the house? I made some fresh lemonade before I came out to the garden. We can have some and talk."

Susan's shoulders slumped in abject despondency. Ryan was gone and he hadn't even cared enough to tell her he was leaving or to say good-bye. Well, how much proof did she need that Ryan didn't love her? His actions had certainly made it clear enough.

Hazel guided the bewildered Susan into the kitchen, motioning for her to sit at the table. After pouring two glasses of lemonade, she set the pitcher on the table and took the chair across from her.

"I know that you and Ryan had a disagreement the day before he left, but I surely thought he'd come by and tell you he was leaving."

"He left the day after . . . I was here?"

"Yes."

"Oh, Hazel, he did come to see me that day. But"—Susan looked away, unable to meet Hazel's glance—"I refused to talk to him. I was so hurt and angry that I had Mother send him away." She was ashamed of herself for having to admit that she had acted so childishly.

"He didn't tell Mother that he came to say good-bye or that he was leaving." Susan looked at Hazel beseechingly. "Why?" She shook her head in disbelief, her voice trembling. "I don't understand why he'd . . ." She shrugged her shoulders despondently as she fought back the tears that sprang quickly to her eyes.

Hazel patted her hand. "I wish I had an answer for you, Susan, but I can't explain his actions, either. All I know is that it seemed to come over him all of a sudden. It started a day or so after he got back from killing those outlaws. He was happy one day and the next he was ill-tempered and depressed."

"Don't you have any idea what happened?" Susan asked.

Hazel shook her head. "No. This is the second time in recent months that it's happened. He got in a mood as black as this shortly after he met you."

"Shortly after we met?" Susan shook her head in puzzlement trying to remember what had happened between them that might explain his odd behavior.

"Oh, I didn't mean to imply that it was something you did. I think . . ." Hazel hesitated.

"Hazel, if you know something, please tell me."

"That's just it. I don't *know* anything. But I suspect something happened when he was just a boy. When he was about sixteen, he rode off to Tennessee to join the Confederate Army. But he was gone hardly any longer than it took to get there and back.

"I could tell by the way he acted that something was wrong. I know something happened, but I don't know what. I'm sure he told his grandfather and Kyle and his father when he returned from the war, but they never confided in me."

"That's strange. Why wouldn't they want you to know?"

Hazel laughed. "Oh, you know how men are. They think women can't keep a secret at all."

She grew serious as she remembered back to that time.

"I asked Kyle about it, but he told me there was no reason for me to be burdened with knowledge about something that I couldn't do anything about—or change. I know it's something they wanted to keep secret and I got the notion that they felt like it was something I might let slip out inadvertently."

Susan shivered. She thought back to the day they had all gone to town together. That was the day the man had challenged Ryan to a gunfight. She remembered overhearing Kyle ask, "Is that the sergeant?" And Ryan's answer, "He's been looking for me all this time. How many more will there be?"

When she had asked him about it, Ryan had told her it wasn't anything for her to worry about, just as Kyle had told Hazel. There had to be a connection. But what? What in the world could have happened ten years ago that would still haunt him today?

Hazel got up from the table and walked to the sink. "I wish I could shed some light on why Ryan's acting the way he is, but . . ." She shook her head and shrugged her shoulders in helplessness. "I don't know why."

Susan carried her glass to the counter. "I understand, Hazel. Well, no, I really don't understand, but I know you would help me if you could. Do you know where Ryan went?"

Hazel shook her head. "Not really. He said he was headed up to the Clear Fork of the Brazos

River to meet Major Jones and the Texas Rangers. He got a letter asking for his help with the Indians. But they could be anywhere by now."

"If . . . When Ryan comes home, will you let me know?"

"Of course I will. If I hear anything at all, I'll let you know."

Susan nodded her head and turned to leave.

"Susan, I've known that man since the day he was born. And, even though I can't explain what's happening, I just feel here"—she placed her hand across her heart—"that he's going to come to his senses and everything will work out."

Tears sprang to Susan's eyes, threatening to spill over. When she spoke, her voice was dull from the intense pain she felt. "I hope you're right, but I'm not sure anything will ever be right again. Sometimes . . . sometimes the hurt never heals."

Chapter Eighteen

Susan stood on the back porch and looked off toward Ryan's house as she had so many times since he'd been gone. More than a month had passed since he'd left, but they had heard nothing directly from him. She searched the weekly edition of the newspaper looking for any mention of him or the Frontier Battalion, the unit of the Texas Rangers he was with.

Each week she fearfully read the list of men killed in the fighting and said a grateful prayer when she saw Ryan's name was not listed. Yesterday's edition had said that about thirty Rangers from the Frontier Battalion had established a base camp on the Leon River, about forty miles upriver from Comanche. The paper stated their purpose was to clear out the Indians who had filtered through their patrols along the headwaters of the Brazos.

Although the article didn't give the names o the thirty Rangers, somehow she knew Ryar was one of them. Maybe it was intuition o wishful thinking or logic. After all, who could possibly know the area better than Ryan? What ever it was, Susan *knew* Ryan was there. The thought that, even though he was still in danger he was less than a day's ride from home wa somehow comforting to her.

She sighed, thinking how helpless and frus trated she felt. Yet she knew there was nothing she could do but wait. Wait and hope and pray She tried to stay busy every minute of the day hoping that hard work would keep her mind from dwelling on Ryan. But she quickly dis covered that her hands could perform her daily chores without her mind really being aware o her actions.

A gentle breeze caught the hem of her dress wrapping it around her legs. She lifted her face and inhaled the freshness. There was a hint o autumn in the air. It was the middle of Sep tember, yet she was surprised that she hadn' noticed the vibrant red, yellow, and orange hues that were beginning to adorn the trees *Well,* she thought, *at least the weather is turn ing cooler. Ryan will welcome a break from the blistering heat of summer.* She laughed at the irony. Even when she was trying *not* to think about Ryan, she was thinking about him.

When she turned to go inside, she saw a horse and rider coming down the lane to her house

She didn't recognize the man. She started to go into the house to get a gun but decided she was being overly cautious. She waited on the porch until he rode into the yard and stopped his horse.

He touched his hat brim. "Good morning, ma'am."

Susan nodded her head. "Good morning. Can I be of some help to you?"

The man glanced toward the barn. "I've got a notion that I turned off on the wrong lane. I'm looking for Ryan Sommerall's place. But this doesn't look much like a horse ranch."

"No." Susan smiled. "This is not Ryan's ranch. You don't have far to go, though." She pointed toward Ryan's house. "You can see his house and barns across the way there. The next lane up the road from ours leads to his house. You can go straight on across our pasture, if you like. There's a gate in the fence."

"Thank you kindly, ma'am." The man tipped his hat and started to rein his horse around.

"He's not home, however. In case you wanted to see him personally."

The man stopped. "He's not home?" He paused as though he was waiting for further explanation. "You mean he's not home at the moment, but he'll be back later in the day?"

"No, I'm afraid not. He's off fighting Indians."

The man's face took on a puzzled expression. "Do you mind explaining that a little bit further?"

"Oh, I'm sorry. I guess I thought everybody would know. You must not live around here."

"No, ma'am, I don't."

"Well, you see, Ryan is a volunteer Texas Ranger. He got a letter from Major Jones, the commander of the Frontier Battalion, asking him to come and help them fight the Indians. He left about a month ago."

"Damn." The man slapped the top of his saddle horn and looked away from Susan. "What does it take to get to see that man? First he's chasing outlaws, now he's fighting Indians. Doesn't he ever stay home?"

"I'm sorry, sir. You seem to—"

"Please forgive me, ma'am. I didn't mean to take my frustration out on you. It's just that this is the second time I've rode a long way to see him. And now he's gone again."

"There was a man at the sheriff's office looking for me." Susan began to feel a little nervous and apprehensive as she remembered Ryan's words. "You seem to want to see him very badly about something. You say you were here before?"

"Yes, ma'am. I was. About five or six weeks ago. I didn't get any further than the sheriff that time. The sheriff told me he was chasing outlaws. I don't suppose you have any idea when he'll be back?"

Susan shook her head. "No, of course not. That's about the same as trying to tell you when the Indian trouble will be over. If you wish to leave a message, I'll see that he gets it."

The man looked away thoughtfully then turned his eyes back to Susan. "I'm beginning to think that's the only way I'm ever going to get together with him. Will you please tell him that Ellis Thornhill would like to talk to him? I live in Weatherford. I'm a businessman there. Anybody there can tell him how to find me."

"It has everything to do with it." Suddenly those words that Ryan had said during their last angry confrontation registered in her mind.

"Okay, I'll tell him. It must be mighty important, though, to expect him to ride that far to talk to you. It's close to a hundred miles from here to Weatherford."

The man reflected on Susan's observation. "Yes," he agreed. "He would have to consider it important, wouldn't he? Don't let this alarm you personally, ma'am. Just tell him it concerns the shooting of a Confederate officer on the battlefield at Chattanooga, Tennessee."

"He's been looking for me all this time." Even now she could remember the pain that had been in his voice when he had spoken.

The man could not have shocked Susan more if he had dismounted and slapped her face. She stared coldly into his eyes as she backed slowly from him until her back was against the kitchen door.

"You must be mistaken. Ryan was not in the war. He couldn't have anything to do with what happened on that battlefield."

"That's what your sheriff thought. He had not officially joined the Confederate Army but

Ryan was there in Tennessee with the intent of doing so. Of course, he left mighty quick after the shooting."

"How many more will there be?" Again she remembered his anguish.

Susan stared coldly at him. "You know about the man Ryan killed in Comanche, don't you?" Her voice rose with emotion. "You want to kill Ryan, too, don't you?"

She had stepped toward him again until she reached the edge of the porch.

"Now, ma'am. I never said anything about—"

"I warn you, Mister. If you cause Ryan any trouble, if you harm him in any way at all, I'll kill you."

The man studied Susan intently. "I take it you're rather fond of this Ryan."

Susan stood her ground, her eyes locked with his. "You better believe me, Mister. I'll put a bounty on you. My father has money. I'll—I'll hire gunmen to hunt you down and kill you!" Her high-pitched voice rose in vehemence as hysteria threatened to overcome her.

The man backed his horse a couple of steps from her. "Just tell this man of yours that if he doesn't come to Weatherford, I'll be back here. In fact, I might look him up at the Ranger camp," he warned. He reined his horse around and trotted down the lane.

She stood a moment, staring after him. *He's going to kill Ryan!* Her terror-stricken mind locked on that single thought. She had to stop him. She dashed through the house to her room and grabbed her rifle. When she reached the porch again, the man was a hundred yards from her. She braced her rifle barrel against a porch post and took careful aim between his shoulder blades. Her finger curled around the trigger.

Don't shoot him! her tortured mind screamed at her a half second before she squeezed the trigger. *There are others. Ryan would want this one alive to get information that could lead him to others who might want to kill him.*

Taking a deep breath, she lowered her rifle and leaned against the post, trembling and feeling weak at how close she had come to killing the man. But she must do something. Ryan had to be told that this man was looking for him.

She would go to Kyle. She tried to convince herself that Kyle would find Ryan as she ran to her room and began to change into her breeches and shirt.

But would he? She began to doubt her reasoning. In the first place, Kyle would be hesitant to leave the ranch any less guarded than he had to. Furthermore, he probably wouldn't feel the urgency that she did. He would think that it could wait until Ryan returned.

She knew it couldn't wait, lest it be too late. Too late for Ryan, too late for her. This was what Ryan had been trying to tell her about the last time they were together and she had refused to listen.

She sat on her bed and pulled on her boots. Cupping her face in her hands, she began to feel the pain of having refused to talk to Ryan when he'd come to tell her he was leaving. Suddenly she felt the horrible anguish of having let Ryan down in the most selfish and childish manner.

Getting to her feet, she reached for her gun belt hanging on the bedpost. After buckling it around her waist, she checked the gun to be sure that each chamber was loaded. Her mind was made up as to what must be done. She must go to Ryan herself.

Picking up her rifle, she went to the barn and saddled Spooky. After filling a small canvas bag with oats, she hung it on the saddle horn and led Spooky to the back porch. Carrying her saddlebags and canteen into the kitchen, she filled the canteen with water and put a tin of beans, a few potatoes, half a loaf of bread and some dried apples into the saddlebags.

She was hoping that she wouldn't need any food at all. If she was lucky, she would probably find a ranch or farm family that would take her in for the night. She knew she would reach the Ranger camp by noon tomorrow. She hung her canteen on the saddle horn and fastened her saddlebags behind her saddle.

All she needed now was a bedroll just in case she did have to spend the night on the ground. She had left hers rolled up in the tack room when she had last used it and it was too musty-smelling to use now. She went to her room and took a wool blanket and rain poncho from a chest drawer and rolled the poncho around the blanket. She quickly wrote a note and left it on the kitchen table for her parents.

With the improvised bedroll secured behind her saddle, she was finally on her way. She considered going straight across country to where she thought the Ranger camp would be, but decided instead that she'd best take the road to the river. From there she could follow the river north until she found the camp which according to the newspaper was about thirty-five or forty miles upriver from the road.

She knew from past conversations with Ryan that it was about twelve miles to the river. She calculated that by sunset she would be about twenty miles upriver. She hoped she would come to a ranch or farmhouse to spend the night and that she would reach the Ranger camp early tomorrow. She settled down for a long ride.

When she reached the river, she was momentarily distressed to see that there was a heavy growth of large trees and underbrush on both sides. She went back up the road three or four hundred yards and then turned off where she would be traveling through only scrub mesquite and cedar. It was still rather thick, but there were no large trees or undergrowth to contend with. She would still be able to follow the course of the river easily.

After seven or eight miles she discovered that the mesquite on the other side of the river was much smaller and less dense and there was hardly any cedar at all. Using her field glasses, she could see that it continued that way for at least three or four miles ahead of her. It was probably the result of a fire in recent years. She decided to cross the river.

Once she was on the other side, she made good time for about seven miles. She rode easily through the sparse mesquite, trotting Spooky part of the time and walking her some.

Suddenly Spooky raised her head and pricked up her ears. Turning her head, she snorted a puff of air through her nostrils. Susan snapped alert and looked around her. She was quick to see what had attracted Spooky's attention.

About five hundred yards from her, six Indians had come over a slight rise that had hidden them from view until now. Two of them were behind her and continuing to ride to her rear at a gallop but at an angle toward the river. They were cutting her off from behind. Three of them were ahead of her also riding at an angle to the river, cutting her off from the front. A lone Indian was riding straight toward her.

Susan flapped her bridle reins and nudged her boot heels into Spooky's flanks.

"Run, Spooky!" she shouted.

The excited Spooky needed little urging. She instantly surged forward.

The Indians ahead of her had also put their horses to full speed. The two Indians behind her had started shooting at her with their rifles but they were out of range.

Susan leaned low across her saddle horn. "Run, Spooky," she urged again, pushing her hand forward against the side of Spooky's neck.

She knew the mare was giving all she had, but the angle between her and the Indians was closing rapidly.

"Spooky, you're gonna have to run," Susan pleaded, nudging her flanks again. "Damn it, I mean really run!"

The mare sensed the urgency in her mistress's voice. Her head stretched a little straighter with her neck. Her ears laid further back. Her belly sank lower to the ground as her legs coupled a little faster and with longer strides.

"Atta girl, Spooky," Susan praised. "You can do it. You can beat them."

Spooky was indeed beating them. The lead that the Indians had at the start and the angle at which they rode had given them at least a two-hundred-yard shorter distance to cover in order to intercept Susan. But Spooky had already robbed them of their advantage.

The Indians were no longer closing in; they were now riding parallel to Susan and about three hundred yards from her. They were flogging their horses, trying to stay abreast, but they were steadily losing ground.

Susan had her rifle out, snapping off a shot when she could turn her attention from the course Spooky was running. She hardly expected to hit them, but she might hold them at bay.

She rode at breakneck speed for fully a mile, and the Indians were being left further and further behind. Suddenly Susan was presented with a horrifying sight—a deep narrow gully. Susan realized in an instant that if she had to rein Spooky in and let her slide down the bank of the gully, the Indians would be upon her before Spooky could clamber up the other bank.

"Spooky, you've got to jump."

Susan had barely uttered her plea before Spooky raised her head and pricked up her ears. She began to break her speed. Susan saw that the gully was wider than she had first thought. Still, she nudged Spooky lightly.

"Please jump, Spooky. Please," she pleaded frantically.

Spooky further slowed her speed. Her nostrils flared even wider.

"Oh, my God, Spooky, don't chilly dip on me!" Susan's voice was shrill with fear. "Damn it, jump!"

Spooky measured her few remaining strides perfectly to have her legs gathered under her when she reached the edge of the gully. With a thrust of her powerful hindquarters, she cleared the gully. She stumbled momentarily when her hoofs hit the ground but quickly recovered and sprinted away.

Susan watched behind her as the Indian horses approached the gully. She was much relieved and gratified when she saw that they refused to make the jump. She was so far ahead of them by the time they had crossed the gully that she didn't think they would pursue her. Surely the Indians would realize that their ponies were far outclassed.

She held Spooky to a gallop, glancing over her shoulder every few seconds. The Indians were not following. Soon she could no longer see them at all. She slowed Spooky to a trot, cooling her down gradually.

As it began to grow late, Susan scanned the terrain with her field glasses searching for a farmhouse in which to spend the night. She knew she had little hope of finding one, however, because this land was not suitable for farming. This was cattle country and because the ranches would be large, she knew the ranch headquarters would be few and far between.

She traveled another four miles before she gave up finding a house. It was getting dark. She made her way to the river and let Spooky drink her fill. She then found a large pecan tree under which she would spend the night. She removed the saddle and bridle from Spooky and fed her the bag of oats before staking her in a patch of grass a short distance from where Susan would bed down.

Her encounter with the Indians had eliminated any thought of a fire. Her supper consisted of cold beans, dried apples, and a slice of light bread. By the time she'd finished eating, patches of stars had appeared in the sky.

She was thankful that there was no moon. The Indians would not be looking for trouble during a dark night. Still, she felt very much alone and frightened but she was also very tired. She rolled up in her blanket and, with her pistol on one side and her rifle on the other, she knew she'd done all she could so she would make it through the night. She closed her eyes, and with thoughts of seeing Ryan the next day, she fell asleep.

Susan awoke to the sounds of some noisy crows a short distance from her. She sat up abruptly. She knew their cawing could be signaling the approach of most anything, including the Indians.

She quickly unwrapped the blanket and grabbed her pistol. There was barely enough light to see clearly a short distance into the trees that surrounded her. She listened intently, but there was only the intermittent noise from the crows.

She decided her best bet was to get moving as quickly as possible. She only hoped that Spooky was the object of the crows' attention instead of the Indians. She was very much relieved when she left her campsite a mile behind her without incident.

She choked down what remained of her dried apples and light bread as she rode. The food wasn't very appetizing but at least it tended to ease her hunger pangs.

A little more than two hours and about ten miles later, she was surprised to come upon what was obviously a cattle drive trail. It was about a hundred yards wide. Not as wide as the Chisholm Trail, which she had seen where it crossed the Brazos River at Waco, but it was plain to see that it had been heavily used.

Thousands of cattle hooves as well as wind and water erosion had lowered the trail bed several inches below the normal ground level. There was hardly a blade of grass growing in the trail bed.

She was about halfway across the trail when suddenly she had company. A band of Comanches emerged from the cover of the mesquite trees. There were at least a dozen of them, and they were no more than two hundred yards up the trail from her.

Oh, my gosh, not again! was her only thought as she whirled Spooky toward the river and jabbed her boot heel into her ribs. There were several hoots and yells and a couple of rifle shots. The Indians were in hot pursuit. She was almost three hundred yards from the river. She could see that the river banks were cut back to make it easier to cross. The cattle had treaded the banks down, too, but not as much as Susan had perceived from further back.

Too late she realized that she had brought Spooky to the crossing at too fast a pace. Spooky managed to keep her feet under her as she plunged down the bank, but she was stumbling badly as she plunged into the three-foot deep water. Her gait had become more of a continuing stumble than a run, but she made it to the middle of the river before she finally went down.

Susan pitched over Spooky's head into the water. The current tumbled her over a couple of times, but she managed to hold her breath until her flailing hands grasped a small boulder underwater. She brought her feet under her and stood up. Spooky had scrambled to her feet and was splashing to the bank.

She turned toward the Indians. Several of them were already in the water and plunging toward her. They would be upon her in a matter of seconds.

She heard shots coming from behind her. Two of the Indians fell from their horses. The others pulled at their horses trying to stop them. A horse was splashing through the water behind her.

A great black stallion swept by her. Ryan's pistol was roaring. Another Indian fell. Pegasus collided with the Indian ponies with such force that he knocked three of them down.

Ryan holstered his empty pistol and pulled a loaded one from his waistband. Pegasus reared and pawed the air as though he was defying the Indian ponies to come near him. Ryan was leaning slightly out of the saddle and shooting past Pegasus's shoulder.

Several horses and riders had followed Ryan into the river to join the battle. Some of the Indians were still coming on, while others were trying to turn back.

Suddenly Susan was splashed so heavily with water that she covered her face with her hands to keep it from her eyes and nose. She was having difficulty keeping her feet under her as the water rocked against her body.

Ryan's arm circled her waist and lifted her from the river. He pulled her firmly to his side. A sense of safety swept over Susan, even though they were still in the midst of the battle.

Ryan sent Pegasus surging toward the river bank. Susan's extra weight seemed of no consequence to the powerful stallion. Spooky followed Pegasus as he sprang up the sloping river bank and carried Susan and Ryan rapidly away from the fighting men.

"Where in hell did you come from?" Ryan shouted at Susan.

Susan knew it was a rhetorical question and didn't bother to answer. She wrapped her arms around Ryan and buried her head against his warm neck. It felt so good to be in his arms again even if only for a few seconds.

Ryan stopped a couple hundred yards from the battle and lowered Susan to the ground. Spooky slid to a stop beside Susan.

"Stay here," Ryan ordered. "Run if you have to. I'll keep an eye on you." He reined Pegasus around and headed back to the battle scene.

Susan stood awestruck as she watched the fighting, cursing, yelling men. At least twenty more Indians had charged down the cattle trail behind the band who had pursued her. Some of them had continued down the bank into the riverbed. The Indians had been closely pursued by an equal number of Texas Rangers. The Indians were no match for the straight-shooting Texans. More than half of them had already been shot from their horses.

Those that remained were now effectively surrounded by the Rangers who were fighting the Indians in their favorite and most effective way—close quarters with six-shooters.

Ryan charged to the perimeter of the battle, then swerved off, and pursued a fleeing Comanche a short distance before shooting him from his horse. He reined Pegasus back toward the battle then suddenly changed his mind. He turned Pegasus toward Susan and galloped to her.

The shooting had ceased by the time he reached her.

"Is there something wrong at home?" Ryan asked anxiously as he reined in beside Susan and slipped from his saddle.

"No, nothing is wrong. Everyone is fine. I just had to tell you something."

Ryan took her in his arms and held her close against his body. He lowered his cheek to hers.

"I know there's some dire reason for your being here, but it's so good seeing you, to hold you and feel you, that I don't think I want to hear about it just yet."

Susan pressed close to him, wrapping her arms around his waist. "Now that I'm here with you it doesn't seem as urgent as it did when I left home to find you. But I had to tell you there's a man looking for you. I'm afraid he wants to kill you. He said he might look for you at the Ranger camp. I had to warn you."

"You talked to this man yourself?"

Susan sensed from Ryan's tone of voice that he was having difficulty comprehending what she was telling him.

"Yes. He was looking for your ranch but he turned off on our lane by mistake."

"Weren't your parents there?"

"No, they had gone to Comanche to get supplies."

"Can you describe this man?"

"Yes. I'd say he's about forty-five years old. He's not quite as tall as you and thin, almost skinny. He has dark brown hair, beginning to turn gray. He was well dressed and—"

"Hmmm, sounds like the same man Sheriff Thomas talked to," Ryan interrupted. "Damn, why can't he come when I'm home?"

"He got exasperated about that, too. He told me to tell you to come to Weatherford or he'd—"

Ryan stopped her again. "Did he tell you his name?"

"Yes. His name is Ellis Thornhill. He lives in Weatherford. He's a businessman there."

Ryan was rubbing his chin between his forefinger and thumb. It was apparent to Susan that he was in deep thought.

"Do you know him?"

"No." Ryan shook his head, puzzled. "I can't recall ever hearing his name." Ryan's expression turned somber. "Did he tell you anything else, Susan?"

Susan took a deep breath and exhaled it slowly as she spoke. "Yes, Ryan, he did. He

347

told me that you shot a Confederate officer on the battlefield at Chattanooga, Tennessee. Or at least he very much implied that you did."

"Damn," Ryan exclaimed as he took off his hat and ran his fingers through his hair. He slapped his hat against his leg. "Damn, is this going to hang over me for the rest of my life?"

Susan's anxiety was building rapidly. "Did you, Ryan? Did you kill someone there?"

Ryan gently grasped Susan's shoulders. "Yes, Susan." He looked away from her, thinking back to the day that had irrevocably changed his life. There was an expression of anguish in his eyes. "I killed a Confederate major at Chattanooga."

"But . . . how could that be? You weren't in the war."

"I was in the war, all right." He grimaced sardonically. "I was in the war about an hour."

He took Susan by the hand. "Come sit down in the shade with me. I guess the time has come when I have to tell you what happened."

Chapter Nineteen

Ryan guided Susan toward a large hackberry tree. He wanted to get her away from the ruckus of the aftermath of the fighting and he needed the privacy. Before they reached the shade of the tree, he heard a rider approaching from behind them.

"Does this lady need help, Ryan? Was she looking for us?"

"No, Clay. Well, she was looking for me, but it's just a personal matter. Lieutenant Brunson, this is Susan Bradford. My, ah, neighbor. Have you determined how many casualties we have?"

"Yeah, I have." He shook his head sadly. "We've got four dead and five wounded. Some of the boys are getting ready to take the wounded to the doctor at Stephenville."

"Oh, dear," Susan exclaimed with distress. "Am I the cause of those men getting killed and wounded?"

"No, ma'am," the lieutenant hastened to assure Susan. "No, not at all. In fact, your happening along when you did probably kept our casualties from being even higher."

"I don't understand."

"Well, you see, ma'am, you led them Indians right on into our trap—and on winded horses at that. Twenty of my men were pressing the Comanches toward the river crossing. Ryan and I and ten of my men were waiting in ambush for them here. There weren't more than three or four of them who escaped. But I'll let Ryan explain it to you. I've got things to see to."

"I'll help you as soon as I can, Clay. I need to talk to Susan."

The lieutenant lifted his hand in acknowledgment as he rode away. "Take your time. I think we've got things under control."

When they were settled under the tree, Ryan took tobacco and papers from his shirt pocket. This was among the hardest things he'd ever had to do. He feared what Susan's reaction would be when she learned the truth. Would she recoil from him in disgust? How would he be able to endure it if he lost her respect?

Susan took the tobacco from him. "I'll do that for you," she said softly. She realized that Ryan was fighting an inner battle. She waited patiently while he organized his thoughts.

Ryan took a deep breath and exhaled in a

long sigh. "Back in sixty-three, I decided I had to go off to the war. I had barely turned sixteen but I was a full-grown man. Had been for three or four years for that matter. Of course, my grandfather and Kyle and Hazel were against it. But I went anyway. It just didn't seem right that my father, at the age of thirty-seven, which I considered to be a rather advanced age, was in the war and I wasn't. At the time of the last letter we had from him, he was with General Bragg's troops in Tennessee. So I decided that's where I should go."

Susan handed him his cigarette.

"I headed north across Texas and on into Arkansas. I crossed the Mississippi River into Tennessee. I avoided the towns because I didn't want to take the chance of getting conscripted before I reached my father's outfit. The country folk who seemed to know anything about the whereabouts of General Bragg's troops kept directing me toward Chattanooga. They were right. About six o'clock one morning, I was confronted by two Confederate cavalrymen. It turned out they were scouting ahead of a cavalry platoon of about sixty men. They took me to a lieutenant. He asked me where I came from and what I was doing there. I told him I was from Texas and was looking for General Bragg to join up with him."

Ryan paused, looking off into the distance. His expression was whimsical as though he was reflecting back on something amusing. "That lieutenant said, 'So are we, boy. General

351

Bragg and his troops are engaged in combat with Union forces near Chattanooga. We'll be there in about three hours. What's your name?' I said Ryan. He cut me off before I could tell him my last name. He said, 'Consider yourself in the Confederate Army, Ryan. We'll sign you up officially later.' He turned to his troops and yelled real loud, 'Men, this is Ryan. He's come from Texas to join up with us. Somebody fix him up with a uniform.' Then he waved his platoon forward and we moved out.

"They had five or six pack horses. One of the men got a Confederate coat and cap from a pack. I put on the coat and threw the cap away. Well, there I was riding with a platoon of the Confederate cavalry. Little did I know that in less than three hours I would be charging the flanks of the Union Army."

Susan sat spellbound, not asking any questions. She knew Ryan was telling her all she needed to know as he relived that fateful day in his life.

"We could hear the explosion of the cannon-balls a good while before we got to the site of the battle. When we arrived, we were on the flanks of the battle lines. The lieutenant looked it over for a minute or two through his field glasses. Then he just simply led us on a charge right into the flanks of the Union lines. We charged in amongst the Union soldiers until we had emptied our rifles and pistols, then the lieutenant led us back to reload our guns.

"Some of the men had swords and continued

to fight as we retreated. As soon as we were reloaded, the lieutenant led us right back into the fight again. We made three charges. When we rode out after the third charge, there were fourteen of us left. Even though we had killed or wounded at least a hundred and fifty, maybe two hundred, Union soldiers, it goes without saying that we had not turned the tide of the battle.

"The lieutenant decided that another charge with only fourteen men wasn't going to help much. He guided us behind the Confederate lines and, since we had horses, he dropped us off one at a time along the battle lines to act as messengers for the battalion and company commanders.

"I just sat my horse for a couple of minutes or so, not knowing what to do. Just waiting for an officer to give me some orders. The cannon and rifle balls were coming in real heavy. Suddenly three men broke and ran. A major, who was mounted on a horse, shot one of them with his pistol and his first sergeant shot another one."

Susan gasped. "You mean they shot their own men?"

"Yep. Shot them in the back while the men were running. They were more nearly boys than men, though. The major aimed his pistol at the third man who was still running. I just raised my pistol and shot the major off his horse. He never moved after he hit the ground. The sergeant started yelling at his men to shoot me.

I turned to him and aimed my pistol at him. He was on the ground, trying to reload his rifle. I could see that he was wounded but I couldn't tell how bad.

"Some of the nearby soldiers were looking back and forth from the sergeant to me, but they didn't obey his orders to shoot me. He yelled at me that I was under arrest, that he would see me before a firing squad. I didn't shoot him. I guess I felt some compassion for him because he was already wounded. I told him to go to hell. I told him, if this is the kind of war you people are holding, you can *all* go to hell. I wasn't having anything more to do with it.

"Well, that's it." Ryan shrugged his shoulders. "I just rode away and went home. Had I remained there, I would have been shot by a firing squad in less than five minutes. We learned later that my father wasn't even with General Bragg's command at that time. He had been transferred to General Hood's command."

Ryan dropped his cigarette butt on the ground, grinding it out with his boot heel. He looked off into the distance and then back at Susan. A resigned, almost sad expression marred his features.

"I never really left it behind me, though. The threat of being arrested and tried for murder has been hanging over me for more than ten years now."

"But, Ryan, you didn't do anything wrong," Susan exclaimed. "That major and sergeant should have been charged with murder!"

Ryan shook his head slowly from side to side. "That's not the way it works in the military, Susie. Desertion under fire is an offense punishable by death. The major was acting within his authority."

"It still doesn't seem right," Susan protested. "Those boys were running away because they were scared and just couldn't take it anymore."

"That's the way it seemed to me, too," Ryan agreed. "That's why I shot the major to stop him from shooting the third man and almost shot the sergeant."

Susan was silent a few seconds as though she was reflecting on something. Her voice was low and tense when she spoke. "The man who tried to kill you in Comanche was the sergeant, wasn't he?"

"Yeah. That was the sergeant." Ryan looked off into the distance thoughtfully for a moment before turning his eyes back to Susan. "Now there's this man you came to warn me about. Actually, I already knew he was looking for me. Ed told me about him."

"Yes, I know that now. You tried to tell me about him." Her lower lip quivered. "That's why you told me there was no place for me in your life, isn't it?"

Ryan rose to his knees and pulled her to him. "Susie, please stop torturing yourself." He stroked her hair. "I didn't mean it."

His attempt to console her only released the river of tears and pent-up emotion that she had held back so long. Her body shook with violent sobbing.

"How could you say that to me?" The side of her clenched hand pounded his chest. "You know how much I love you."

Ryan rocked her gently. "Yes, Susie, I know you love me." His lips slightly brushed her cheek. "And I love you. I loved you then and I love you now. Please believe me."

"I know you love me," Susan wailed through her sobs. "That's why I'm so angry with you." Her hand pounded his chest again. "How could you do that to me? Nothing could cause me to say a thing like that to you."

"Susie, please, don't say any more." He sat down and lifted her sideways across his lap. "I think you know I didn't mean to say that to you." He cradled her with one arm and lightly brushed the tears from her cheeks with his fingertips. "I was trying to tell you that I couldn't ask you to marry me with this threat still hanging over me. Don't you understand? I knew that man was looking for me with the intent of trying to kill me or have me arrested, and I had to figure there would be others."

"Yes, I understand, Ryan. But it's different now. You told me what you did and what you're faced with. Surely you know that doesn't change my feelings for you. I love you with all my being. I love you now. I want you now, this moment. I'm willing to face with you whatever we have to face."

Ryan pressed her to him. "I know, Susie. I

know how you feel. I love you so deeply that I'm tempted to pretend that there are no men wanting to kill me. That it's just a figment of my imagination. But I can't do that, Susie. I love you too deeply. All I can do now is ask you to wait for me."

"You know I will." Susan's voice was soft and resigned. "I can't do anything but accept what you are willing to give."

Susan's words tore at his heart but Ryan restrained himself from expressing his emotion. "Maybe it won't be long, Susie." He stroked her hair. "I have a strong feeling that I can wring some information from this man in Weatherford that will bring this thing to an end."

Susan's body stiffened in his arms. "Oh, my gosh," she gasped. "I almost killed that man!"

Ryan held her from him and stared at her in speechless disbelief.

Susan's eyes were wide with renewed alarm as she mentally relived her experience. "I aimed my rifle at him when he was no more than a hundred yards away. But I didn't shoot," she hastened to assure Ryan.

Ryan's shoulders sagged in obvious relief. "Why did you even consider such a thing? Don't you know you could have been charged with murder?"

Susan's eyes were defiant as she met Ryan's exasperated expression. "Because I thought he meant to cause you bad trouble or even kill you. I would have shot him if I hadn't thought in the nick of time that you might want him alive."

"Well, I'm just thankful you came to your senses before you pulled the trigger." Ryan got to his feet. "I'll go speak to the lieutenant a minute and then we'll be heading home."

"Ah, Ryan. There's something I guess the Rangers ought to know about. There's six Indians about twelve or fifteen miles down the river somewhere. At least they were there yesterday."

"Six Indians? You saw them?"

"Of course I saw them. How else would I know they are there?" Susan reluctantly admitted. "They chased me awhile yesterday afternoon."

Ryan's breathing became heavy.

"Now don't get upset." Susan's voice had a patronizing tone. "It didn't amount to hardly anything at all. Spooky outran them easily." She turned and looked at Spooky with affection and admiration. "Spooky really left them behind when she jumped a gully that the Indian horses refused even to try to jump," she boasted proudly.

Ryan took off his hat and ran his fingers through his hair. "Is there anything *else* you think you should just throw in there?"

Susan turned back to Ryan. "No." She tossed her head nonchalantly to remove a lock of hair from her face. "That's all."

Ryan shook his head in dismay. "Susie, what am I going to do with you?"

Susan lowered her eyes. "I hope you'll just keep on loving me."

"You come with me, young lady," Ryan said, taking Susan by the hand. "I don't think I'll let you out of my sight until you're safe at home."

When the lieutenant saw Ryan and Susan approaching the river, he rode to meet them. "I don't think you ought to take the lady across there, Ryan."

"Yeah, I know what you mean. I just wanted to let you know that we're leaving. I have to take Susan home, but I'll be back in three days."

"Okay. I wish I could tell you to stay home, that we don't need you anymore. But you know that's not the case. If you and the other volunteers will just stick with us a few more days, I think we'll have things under control."

"I understand, Clay. I'll be back. Better keep your eyes peeled. Susan saw six Comanches yesterday about ten or fifteen miles downriver. 'Course there's no telling where they are by now."

"Yeah, that's a fact. I'll send a patrol out as soon as I can." The lieutenant touched his hat brim. "Pleased to have met you, Susan."

"I'm pleased to have met you, too, sir. And thank you for helping me."

"Just another day's work, ma'am." He nodded to Ryan before turning his horse to go back to the river. "Take care, Ryan, and we'll see you in a couple of days."

"I assume you left your parents a note. Did you tell them how you were going to go about finding me?" Ryan asked after they were mounted.

"Yes. I told them I would take the road to the river, then follow the river till I got to your camp."

"Good. We'll go back the same way. Keep a sharp lookout for your father or Kyle. Probably both."

"Oh, my gosh. I didn't even consider that. Do you really think they will come looking for me?"

"I'd be surprised if they didn't."

Susan frowned. She knew her father was going to be less than happy with her, to say the least, but she hadn't considered the notion that he'd come after her. She glanced sideways at Ryan. "You sure do get me in a lot of trouble, Ryan Sommerall."

Ryan laughed. "Sweetheart, you don't need any help from me. You have a propensity for getting into trouble all by yourself."

"Humph. I do not." Susan raised her chin stubbornly and nudged Spooky.

Ryan chuckled and followed Susan as she headed down the river.

"Ryan, the lieutenant seems to think it's very important that the volunteer Rangers continue to help the full-time Rangers. I didn't know there were so many of you."

"He wasn't referring to the volunteer Rangers like me. There's not many of us in the whole state. He was speaking of volunteers in general, like Billy Morgan, for instance."

"Billy Morgan? He's been helping the Rangers?"

"You didn't know that?"

"No, I didn't."

"He was there when I arrived. I rode with him in the same company for quite a while, up along the Clear Fork and Double Mountain Forks of the Brazos River. He was still there when I pulled back with the men I'm with now to drive out the Comanche in this area. We've tried to hold them north of the Clear Fork, but a few of them filtered through our patrols."

"How many volunteers are there?"

"I don't know exactly, but from what I've heard, there's at least eighty. I've met fifteen or twenty myself. They're mostly the sons of farmers and ranchers all along the frontier. The Rangers could not have brought the Indians under control to the extent that they have without them, and they can't afford to lose them now. That's why we can't decide individually to pull out now."

"I can understand that, but what are you going to do about this man in Weatherford?"

"He must have a compelling reason to find me, riding a hundred miles—twice—to do so. I'm getting the feeling that there's more to this Ellis Thornhill than meets the eye. He can wait. It might be best, for that matter, to let him stew for a few more days."

"Well, I hope you're right. I don't see how it

can be only a few more days, though. There must have been at least thirty Indians in that one band this morning."

"Thirty-two to be exact. But there's not any more bands that large around here. That was a case of four or five smaller bands getting together after the Rangers moved in here."

They had been traveling for about five hours when Ryan saw a flock of birds suddenly leave the trees ahead of them. He motioned for Susan to stop. He pulled out his field glasses and scanned the horizon ahead of them.

Susan had also seen the birds. "What is it? Do you see something? Is it Indians?"

Ryan put his glasses away. "No, it's not Indians, but from the look on your dad's face, you might rather confront some Indians instead of him. He doesn't look too happy, even from this distance. As I suspected, Kyle is with him."

Susan chewed her bottom lip. "Ryan, what should I do? I mean, they're going to want to know why I had to come find you. What should I tell them?"

Ryan drew a long, resigned breath. "I'll talk to your father."

As they rode to meet Seth and Kyle, Susan couldn't help worrying about what would happen between Ryan and the man in Weatherford. She was afraid. What if the man just gunned him down before Ryan had a chance to try to reason with him?

"When will you go to Weatherford?"

"I don't know for sure, Susie. I can't go until this thing with the Indians is settled."

"Will you come home first?"

Ryan shrugged his shoulders. "I don't know. Why?"

Susan looked away and swallowed, trying to hold back her tears. She refused to let Ryan see her cry. She tried to smile but her voice trembled in spite of her efforts. "Promise me you won't go to Weatherford to see that man until you come home first. Please?"

Ryan reined Pegasus up and leaned over to kiss Susan. This would be their last few minutes alone until he could come home. He figured they'd be in sight of Seth and Kyle when they rode around the gentle curve of the river just in front of them.

Susan wrapped her arms around Ryan and returned his kiss with equal hunger. She wished they could have had more time to spend together. Her fear for Ryan's safety was uppermost in her mind.

"Please come home first."

Ryan smoothed her hair from her face, brushing a lone tear from her cheek. "If it's that important to you, I promise I'll come home first."

As they rounded the bend, Susan saw her father and Kyle, and spurred Spooky ahead of Ryan. She wanted a word or two with her father before Ryan talked to him.

Kyle saw Susan riding toward them and decided he'd give father and daughter a few

minutes alone. He chuckled to himself. Someone was fixing to catch all billy hell and he
didn't want to be there when it happened.

"What are you grinning about?" Ryan asked
when Kyle reined in beside him.

"From the look on Susan's face when she
passed me, I'd say Seth's plan to give her a
good tongue-lashing is going to fall short of
its mark. How's it going with the Indians?"

"I think it's just about over. They have already
started forming up into a tribal band up on the
plains area in the panhandle. Colonel McKenzie
and the cavalry are keeping the pressure on
them, hoping to drive them back to the reser-
vation. I don't see how they can hold out much
longer. They know winter's coming on. I figure
another couple of weeks and things ought to be
quieting down."

Ryan glanced at Susan and her father then
back at Kyle before taking a long deep breath
and exhaling slowly. He knew Seth to be a fair
man but still he dreaded having to reveal what
had happened so many years ago.

Kyle read the uncertainty on his friend's face
and understood the reason for it. "Ya know he
ain't gonna hold it against ya, don't ya?"

Ryan nodded and reined his horse up beside
Seth and Susan.

Seth listened with concern as Ryan told about
what he had done in the war and his reasons for
doing it. He explained who the man was who
had insisted on shooting it out in the street
with him and about the man who was looking

for him now—the reason Susan had come to warn him.

Seth's anger at his daughter began to diminish as Ryan explained why Susan had felt so strongly about finding him.

Seth didn't know why people called it the Civil War; there was nothing "civil" about it. Even now, more than ten years later, its atrocities were still controlling the destiny of young men's lives. He could only hope and pray that Ryan's notion of talking to this Thornhill person would work out the way he expected. He feared, however, that Ryan could still be charged with murder.

He glanced at his daughter riding silently between him and Kyle as they headed toward home. How his heart ached for her. She might think she was a grown woman but she was still his little girl. He wanted to hide her away and protect her from the harsh and ofttimes cruel realities of the world. But that was not the way of things, as well he knew. Seth very much feared she would soon have to face the ultimate test of strength and character. And all he could do now was hope that he had done a good job as a father to make her strong and able to confront what lay ahead of her with courage.

Chapter Twenty

Susan sat with her arms wrapped around her legs, her chin resting on top of her knees.

She had come to the swimming hole thinking she might dabble a hook in the water to see if the fish were biting. But she decided that she didn't really feel like fishing. Even though it was a beautiful, warm October day, she felt too lethargic and melancholy to enjoy it.

Being here at their special place made her feel a little closer to Ryan.

Absent-mindedly, she tossed a small pebble into the water, watching the circles grow larger as the water rippled outward from the spot where it fell. When the water was smooth again, she picked up another pebble and tossed it in, watching the cycle repeat itself.

She wondered what Ryan was doing right at this moment. Was he engaged in battle with the Indians? Maybe fighting for his life at this very minute? The last paper had been filled with details of a battle up in the panhandle of Texas, at a place called Palo Duro Canyon.

There had been no mention of the Rangers Ryan was with. She wondered if the Frontier Battalion had gone up into the panhandle, too? She sighed despondently and picked up another rock.

"If you fill up the hole with rocks, there won't be any water left to swim or fish in."

Ryan!

Susan whirled, looking for him. Was her mind playing tricks on her?

Ryan walked out of the bushes and down the incline toward Susan.

"Oh, my gosh, Ryan!" Susan came to her feet and ran to meet him, tears spilling down her face. She threw herself into his arms, almost knocking him off his feet.

He folded his arms around her, holding her tight, and kissed her passionately. When he finally released her he feathered kisses along the side of her face and down her neck before returning to whisper against her mouth. "God, you feel good. It seems like years since I held you in my arms." His voice was husky and a little tremulous with the intensity of his emotions. "You don't know how badly I've missed you."

"Oh, Ryan, Ryan. I missed you so much. I can't believe you're finally here. Are you all right? You didn't get wounded, did you?"

She clasped his head in both of her hands then ran them over his cheeks, neck, and down his shoulders, across his chest and down his arms.

Her relief at finding him unhurt suddenly gave way to wrenching sobs. She buried her face against his chest, unable to stop her tears.

"Shhh, Susie, don't cry." Ryan held her to him. He understood how the long weeks of tension were finally taking their toll on her. "Shhh, baby, it's all right. Everything is going to be okay."

Ryan stooped down and picked her up in his arms. Cradling her against his chest, he walked down to where she'd been sitting when he first saw her. He sat down, holding her in his lap, and wrapped both arms around her, rocking her slowly back and forth.

When her tears were spent, Susan pulled her shirttail from her breeches and wiped her eyes and face. She was embarrassed that she'd fallen to pieces in front of him. Or more precisely, all over him.

"When did you get back?" She sniffed, trying to compose herself.

"How long have I been holding you?"

"You mean you came here, to the swimming hole, first?"

Ryan nodded his head.

Susan looked at him incredulously. "How . . . how did you know I'd be here?"

Ryan half ducked his head and gave her a

boyish grin. "Well, I wish I could say something romantic like I felt in my heart that you were here, but the truth is, I need a bath," he admitted, nodding to the clean clothes and bar of soap he'd managed to tuck under his arm just before she'd hurled herself into his arms. "I like my horse, and his strength and loyalty helped save my hide a number of times over the past weeks, but I don't particularly care to smell like him. Especially since I was on my way to my favorite girl's house to do some serious courting."

Susan whacked his shoulder. "*Favorite* girl! You better back up fast, Ryan Sommerall, or you're going to be in serious trouble with *this* girl," she warned teasingly.

Ryan laughed and pulled her head back against his chest. "Oh, Susie, I've missed you so much. There were days when I wondered if I'd ever be able to hold you like this again."

Susan wrapped her arms around Ryan and snuggled her face against his neck. "Is it over? Are you home for good?"

Ryan let out a long slow breath before answering. "I hope so. Colonel McKenzie's cavalry surprised several hundred Comanches and Kiowas who had gathered in Palo Duro Canyon. They apparently planned to spend the winter there. When the cavalry rode in, the Indians fled on foot into the rough terrain of the canyon, but McKenzie captured most of their horses."

Susan nodded her head. "There was something in the last issue of the paper about McKenzie accomplishing some sort of major victory, but it seemed to have more to do with capturing horses than anything else."

"Yeah. He captured about fifteen hundred horses and then killed them."

Susan jerked her head up and looked at Ryan. "Killed them! He killed *all* the horses?"

Ryan frowned and nodded his head. "He killed most of them. He selected about three hundred of the best and gave them to his Indian scouts and then killed the remaining eleven hundred and some odd."

"That's horrible. How could he? *Why* would he kill all those horses?"

"McKenzie's smart. He knows the Indians can't survive without horses. They can't hunt the buffalo or move about to find food. And they can't raid the white man's cattle." Ryan shrugged his shoulders. "They are virtually helpless without their horses and McKenzie knows that. The last report I heard said that some of the Indians had already started making their way back toward the reservations."

"Did he get the Indian who attacked those buffalo hunters at Adobe Walls?"

"Quanah Parker?" Ryan shook his head. "No. And McKenzie wanted him bad. From what his scouts could figure, Quanah Parker and his followers were supposedly on their way there but hadn't made it to the canyon when McKenzie hit the other Indians." Ryan shrugged his shoulders. "Who knows? If Quanah had been there, things might have turned out differently."

Susan settled her head against Ryan's chest. She was content to be held in his arms, listening to the strong rhythmic thudding of his heart beneath her ear. She wiggled, trying to get even closer.

Ryan silently groaned. "Ah, Susan . . ."

Susan muffled her giggle. She had felt his anatomy respond to her innocent movement, and it set her own heart beating at a faster rate.

She sniffed exaggeratedly. "You do smell like Pegasus." She looked at him with big, innocent-looking blue eyes. "Didn't you say something about coming here to bathe before doing some *serious* courting?" She began to unbutton his shirt.

Ryan's whole body started to tremble as her fingers lightly brushed against his heated skin each time she unfastened a button. He mutely nodded his head. He didn't dare try to speak. His voice was lodged somewhere between his stomach and his vocal cords.

"Well." She looked at him and batted her lashes. "Since your valet is not here, I'll be glad to help you, if you wish."

Ryan gulped. "Wish?"

Susan giggled and scooted off his lap, pushing Ryan back on the ground so she could reach the buttons on his breeches.

"You're such a pushover," she said, laughing as she moved down to pull off his boots and hers.

"Yes, ma'am." At this point, Ryan would agree to anything she said.

Susan stood up and slowly unbuttoned her shirt, dropping it to the ground. She undid the buttons on her breeches, letting them slide down her legs.

Ryan's eyes followed every movement of her fingers. When she kicked off her breeches and stood before him, wearing only her chemise and drawers, he sucked his breath in. Starting at her head, his eyes caressed her slender body all the way down to her pink toes and slowly moved back up her body.

Suddenly he found himself gasping for air. "You are even more gorgeous than I remembered," he whispered reverently. He saw her look at him—and frown. "What? What's wrong?"

"You're going to have to stand up so I can remove your clothes."

Ryan immediately stood up.

When Susan smiled at his eager compliance, her tantalizing look completely bewitched him. He stood mesmerized as she slowly smoothed her hands across his chest, letting the soft hairs curl around her fingers. Her eyes never left his as she leisurely pulled his shirt off, one sleeve at a time, letting it drift slowly to the ground behind him. She hooked her thumbs under his waistband and nudged his breeches past his hips.

He was so spellbound he forgot to breathe. He felt lightheaded, like he was floating somewhere just above the ground. His heart pounded erratically, sending his heated blood surging through his veins. Suddenly he began to pull air deep into his oxygen-starved lungs.

How foolish he had been to entertain even vaguely the notion that he should set her free. She had captured him in her spell without even being aware of doing it. He could never let her go, no matter how valid the reasons might be or how hard he might try. And he didn't want to try at all.

He took her hands in his, raised them to his lips, and kissed them. "Now it's my turn." His throaty voice skittered along her spine with promises of pleasures yet to come. He felt her shiver. "Cold?"

She shook her head, unable to voice the multitudinous feelings overwhelming her. Love, desire, relief that he was safe and standing beside her, all warred within her.

Ryan lifted her chemise over her head, letting it drop to the ground. He pulled her drawers down her slender legs and tossed them aside. Leaning over, he picked up the bar of soap and handed it to her. Then, picking her up in his arms, he walked the few remaining steps to the water. Hot, bare flesh touched equally hot, bare flesh.

When the water was at his waist, he released her, sliding her silky-smooth body slowly, sensuously down his hair-roughened torso. When her feet touched bottom, he caught her face in his hands and ran his fingers through her hair at the sides of her face. Pulling her head to him, he covered her mouth with his. Her lips parted as his tongue sought entrance. They were both breathing heavily when Ryan raised his head.

Susan slowly began to move the wet soap across his skin, watching as the tiny bubbles ran in rivulets down his muscular chest and arms. She felt the raw strength and power beneath her hands as she soaped his broad back. As she continued to wash him, she felt him tremble, but she knew he wasn't cold. On the contrary, his skin felt hot beneath her fingers.

Susan looked timidly up at him. "Are you in a hurry?" It had been so long since he had held her in his naked embrace, she suddenly felt shy.

"No," he lied, closing his arms around her. "Are you?"

Susan flushed. "Yes," she whispered.

Ryan's heart momentarily quit beating only to slam hard against his chest at her guileless honesty. That this beautiful woman he held in his arms wanted him as much as he wanted her was almost his undoing.

Ryan groaned, the sound coming from deep within his soul. He quickly ducked under the water to rinse the soap away, and then surfaced and took her in his arms.

He carried her to a grassy spot and knelt, gently lying her on the ground. He covered her with his body as his desire threatened to consume them both with its intensity and urgency.

Susan clutched him to her, locking her arms around him when he started to move away from her. His maleness was pressing hard against her stomach. She arched her body against it, wanting, needing, to feel him inside her.

Ryan positioned himself between her legs and slowly entered her, relishing the warmth as she closed around him, drawing him deeper within her. He threw back his head in agonized pleasure, fighting against himself to stem his release before she was ready. He pulled out and plunged into her, catching his breath as she arched her body to meet him.

He might have been able to hold back for a few more minutes, but Susan's urgent movements made that impossible. Repeatedly, he pulled back and plunged deep into her until he climaxed with such intensity that it stole his breath away. He collapsed against her, weak and gasping for air. Never in his entire life had lovemaking been as profoundly satisfying for him as what he'd just experienced. His only regret was that it had happened so quickly. He had been so engrossed in his own pleasure that he wasn't sure that Susan had reached her release.

"I'm sorry if I left you behind," he whispered apologetically, raising his head to look into her deep blue eyes.

Susan pulled his head down to hers and gently kissed his lips. "You didn't. I've thought and dreamed about our making love like this for too many weeks. Night after night, I lay in my bed aching to feel you inside me. Yearning for you to hold me and kiss me. Maybe it's wanton of me to think and feel these things, but I don't care. I love you, Ryan. With all my heart and soul, I love you."

Ryan looked at Susan's love-flushed features and smiled. "I don't think you're wanton because you have strong, honest feelings. I think you're beautiful and wonderful. And I want to spend the rest of my life with you, sharing and fulfilling those feelings. I love you, Susie. Will you marry me?"

Huge tears gathered in the corners of her eyes and spilled down her face into her hair. She was so overcome with emotion, all she could do was nod her head and whisper a tearful yes.

Ryan clutched her to him and buried his face against her neck. He, too, was overwhelmed with emotions. Love and relief. Intense love for the woman in his arms and immense relief that she hadn't let him throw their love away. Fear gripped his heart every time he thought about the things he'd said to her.

This time when he came into her it was slow and deliberate. Now that the edge was gone from their urgency, they were completely free to enjoy the sight, feel, and taste of each other.

Much later as Susan lay thoroughly sated beside Ryan with her head resting on his shoulder, she broached the subject they both had tried so hard not to think about.

"What are we going to do about the man in Weatherford?"

Ryan was toying with a strand of her hair. He let it fall and exhaled a long sigh. "I have to talk with him, Susie. I plan to spend a day or two here with you then go on up there and get it over with."

"I'm going with you."

"No, you're not. I want you here safe in case—in case there's trouble."

Susan raised up on one elbow and looked him straight in the eyes and said firmly, "I am going with you, Ryan. You need me. I talked to this man and I know what he looks like. I can help you find him."

Ryan sat up, hoping to reason with her. He didn't want them to have an argument over something neither one of them could control. "Susan, be reasonable. You know your father is not going to let you go with me."

Susan shook her head. "I've already thrashed this out with my father and my mother," she added, remembering the heated words between the three of them. "I convinced both of them that my place is with you now, Ryan. They understand and accept that. I can't stay here for three or four days, or more, wondering what's happening or has happened. I just simply must be with you."

Reaching up in a gesture of frustration and uncertainty, Ryan massaged the muscles at the back of his neck, then dropped his hand to his side. He knew when he was defeated. "All right. We'll leave at first light tomorrow."

Fear suddenly gripped Susan. "Ryan, we don't have to find the man in Weatherford. We can leave here today, tomorrow, before he comes looking for you again. We can go somewhere else. Someplace where no one will care what happened in the war," she urged.

Ryan pulled her to him. He'd seen the reactions play across her expressive face and correctly interpreted her fear for his safety. He nuzzled her head against his chest, resting his head on top of hers. He was so tempted to do as she asked but he knew he couldn't. At least, not yet.

"I can't do that, Susan. I have to talk to the man and try to reason with him if I can."

"What if the man won't *listen* to reason? What if he tries to kill you instead? Or maybe have you arrested and sent to prison?"

"I'll have to deal with that when I get to Weatherford. If I think he might try to get a warrant for my arrest, then I have no choice but to leave. Any law enforcement officer would be forced to try to arrest me if there was a warrant. I couldn't let them do that. But neither could I kill Sheriff Thomas or any other lawman."

Susan raised her head and looked at him in confusion. "What would you do?"

"Then I'd have to leave here and go somewhere else as you suggest. I've had plenty of time to think about it. In fact, nothing's been on my mind but this." He hesitated, searching for the right words to convey his love for her. "Susie, I know that I can't live without you in my life. If I do have to leave the country, I'm asking you to come with me." He held his breath, waiting for her answer.

Susan didn't hesitate an instant. "You just try to send me away from you again, Ryan Sommerall, and you'll know the real meaning behind the saying of 'the wrath of a woman scorned,'" she threatened sincerely.

Ryan pulled her to him. "What have I ever done to deserve you? I love you, Susie," he said, before covering her mouth with his.

The early-morning sky was streaked with purple as night reluctantly gave way to day. Susan glanced at Ryan as she rode silently beside him. She saw a muscle twitch in his jaw, evidence of his tenseness. The dark shadows under his eyes told her that he hadn't slept any better than she had.

Squelching a momentary pang of fear, she took a deep breath and squared her shoulders in determination. No matter what happened in the next few hours, she and Ryan would face it together. And one thing she knew for certain: tomorrow would determine the course of her life. Both of their lives. She prayed she wouldn't become a widow before she became a wife.

Ryan and Susan were still a few steps from the restaurant when a tall, lean man came out the door and turned toward them, picking his teeth.

They stopped abruptly and stood staring at the man.

"That's him," Susan whispered.

The man moved toward them, then realized he was the object of their keen attention. He stopped and returned Ryan's stare a moment before his eyes turned to Susan.

It was obvious that he recognized her immediately. He turned his attention back to Ryan and studied him intently for a few seconds before he spoke.

"You're Ryan Sommerall, aren't you?"

Ryan's failure to answer caused Susan to glance up at him. His expression of disbelief puzzled her.

"No. You're not seeing a ghost." The man's voice was low and calm. "I'm Major Ellis Thornhill, the man you shot on the battlefield at Chattanooga.

"You didn't die."

The cold tone of Ryan's voice sent a chill down Susan's spine.

"No. I didn't die."

"Move away from me, Susan."

Susan's pounding heart started to rise to her throat. *Oh, my God,* she thought. *It's happening again. Just like the day of the gunfight in Comanche.*

"Ryan, don't—"

"Get away from me, Susan." Ryan's voice was harsh and demanding.

Susan stepped sideways across the wooden sidewalk until she was in front of the restaurant.

"If you're thinking of shooting me again, you should be warned that I'm armed and prepared to defend myself." The major's right hand slowly swept his coat back and lodged it behind his pistol butt.

"You were armed then, too, Mister. The difference was you were using your gun to shoot scared, running boys in the back. Well, now we'll see how well you handle that gun when your victim is facing you and looking you in the eyes."

The major's eyes held steady with Ryan's, but there was no visible sign of anger or malice. His voice remained calm as he spoke. "This is not what I had in mind. It doesn't have to be this way."

"No, it doesn't. It's been a long time. I had begun to believe it was over and behind me and that others concerned felt the same. Of course, I didn't consider you since I thought you were dead. I was content to leave it alone, but evidently you were not. So be it. Now you'll die where you stand." Ryan leaned ever so slightly forward from the waist. "Whenever you're ready."

The major took a deep breath and let it out slowly. "Sommerall, you're taking this all wrong. I wasn't looking for a fight when I went to Comanche to talk to you and I'm not looking for a fight now. I just wanted to try to settle what's between us peaceably."

"You mean by 'peaceably,' that you expect
me to surrender to you and stand trial. Forget
it. I'll not stand trial for doing what was right.
I have suffered no remorse for killing you back
then, or thinking I had, and I'll not suffer any
for killing you again."

"Damn it, man! Do you think I would try
to take you personally if I wanted to see you
stand trial? The newspapers were quite explicit
about how fast you were in your fight with the
sergeant. I would have put United States marshals on you if I had wanted you arrested. It's
just a simple matter that after learning who it
was that shot me and where you were, I felt a
desire—a need—to talk to you. I would like to
explain why I did what I did at Chattanooga
and how I feel about things concerning you
and me now."

The major glanced about them. "Sommerall,
we're beginning to attract attention. Would you
please step into the restaurant and sit down at
a table with me?"

"Talk can't change anything now. I wouldn't
put any store by anything you had to say."

"Ryan, please." Susan's voice was just above
a whisper. "Talk to the man. It can't do any
harm to hear what he has to say." She sensed
that her plea had some persuasive effect on
him. "Please, Ryan, will you do it for my sake?"

Ryan's body relaxed slightly from his tense
stance. He glanced at Susan. The anguish in
her eyes tore at his heart, compelling him to

go against his better judgment. He nodded his head toward the restaurant door. "After you, Mister."

They entered the establishment, and the major led the way to a table in the corner against the back wall.

"Why didn't you tell me when you were at my house that you were the man Ryan had shot?" Susan posed her question as soon as she was seated.

"I decided that if he knew I was still alive, he would want to kill me. He did kill the sergeant, you know."

"He had no choice. The sergeant forced him."

"I know. The papers said the sergeant goaded him into the fight. But I learned long ago you can't believe everything you read. I had to figure that he might start shooting as soon as he saw me. I figured I had a better chance of talking to him if he thought I was someone who saw the shooting at Chattanooga. At least I would have the element of surprise. He would have to make sure it was really me he was seeing."

"That brings up a question or two that I've pondered. How did you determine from the newspaper reports and what you heard by word of mouth, that it was the sergeant who had been killed and that I killed him?" Ryan asked.

"Oh, several things convinced me. He spoke of seeing you before a firing squad. That suggested that he was, or had been, in the military.

Then there was the name Ryan. That's the only name anyone at Chattanooga knew you by, and they thought it was your surname. But I had no problem figuring out that Ryan was your given name."

"That's not much information to base such an important conclusion on."

"No, but that, along with the fact that he didn't come back, was convincing enough for me."

"Didn't come back?" Ryan looked at him suspiciously. "What does that mean?"

"I'm a businessman here. I own the hotel and livery and I operate a small freight line. The sergeant worked for me. I had sent him to pick up a freight wagon and team that a drunken driver had deserted in Hamilton. That's why the sergeant was in Comanche that day. He was passing through on his way to Hamilton. He didn't make it to Hamilton and he didn't come back."

"It was his own doing. He couldn't let the war end," Ryan said with empathy.

"No, he couldn't," the major agreed. "He was a bitter man. He couldn't accept the Confederacy losing the war."

There was an awkward silence. Finally Ryan spoke, "Well, you said you had something to explain. I'm listening."

The major took a deep breath and exhaled as though he was preparing himself for an unpleasant ordeal.

"Sommerall, it's easy to get young men to

rush off to war. They have fantasies and visions of glorifying themselves on the battlefield. Some of them do. But they don't like it too well when the cannonballs start exploding and the bullets start whistling by their ears and striking their buddies next to them. Most of them, in fact all of them in my opinion, would rather be someplace else."

"Can't say as I can hold that against them," Ryan stated.

"Neither can I. But they will stand their ground and fight, mind you, so long as everyone else stands with them. But therein lies the problem that a field commander is faced with. They will stand and fight *as a unit*, most of them, but before long a few of them can't take it anymore and decide to leave. You'll have one man break and run and then another and then two. If these few are permitted to—"

"I understand what you're leading up to," Ryan interrupted. "You're telling me that if those few are not stopped, even if you have to shoot them in the back to do so, then your whole unit will break and run."

"That's about the hellish sum of it."

"Well, Major, I don't agree with that. Men of courage understand and are tolerant of those few who can't stand before the gun. Or any other kind of threat. I don't believe your outfit would have broken if you and the sergeant hadn't shot those men."

"Then you've never seen an entire battalion break and run. Have you?"

"No, of course not. But I suspect that those who have did so because they were tired of being forced to try to defend a position when they were outgunned and facing overwhelming odds. Such as you were at Chattanooga," Ryan accused.

The major turned his face from them and looked out the large plate glass in front of the restaurant as though he was studying something in the street.

"We won the first battle at Chickamauga and sent the Union Army fleeing to Chattanooga. We were engaged in the second battle just outside Chattanooga when you arrived at the scene. The reinforced Union forces were counter-attacking. We were, as you said, facing overwhelming odds. I must admit that General Bragg was slow to order an organized retreat which is what he finally had to do."

He sat reflecting for a moment then shook his head as though to clear away an unpleasant vision. "We seem to have rambled."

"Yes, we have," Ryan agreed. "You were explaining how we could settle our personal differences peaceably."

"Seems to be a simple solution to me. I have no desire for vengeance. In fact, the more I learned about you, the stronger I felt about freeing you from this thing that I know has been hanging over you for the past ten years. It's been a heavy burden to me, too, Sommerall. I'd like to be free of it."

"Then why didn't you just leave it alone?"

"That wouldn't have settled anything, but neither will a gunfight. I'm not ready to die. Besides, if by some chance I did beat you, I'd still have your fiancee to face." He looked at Susan and smiled. "She threatened me with everything from killing me herself, to hiring gunmen to do it for her if I caused you any harm."

Ryan glanced proudly at Susan. A patronizing smile crossed his face. "That was no idle threat, Major. You were not more than a hundred yards from her house before you were under the sights of her rifle. She thought in the nick of time that I would want you alive in order to gain information as to who else might want to kill me. You are indeed a lucky man. You not only survived my bullet but hers, too."

The major studied Susan a few seconds. "Few men ever have the absolute love of a good woman, Sommerall. Why don't you accept it and spend the rest of your life trying to be worthy of it?"

"I have accepted it, Major, and I'm prepared to kill any man, including you, who tries to take it from me."

"Damn it, man! Haven't you heard a word I've said? It doesn't have to come to that. I'm asking that you and I simply declare that the war is over."

"I would like very much to do that. I have no desire for revenge, either. But how can it be over for me? I have no way of knowing there are not others who want to kill me on sight, just as the sergeant did."

The major smiled faintly. "There are no others, Sommerall. Never have been. No one else who saw you shoot me would hold a grudge against you." He chuckled derisively. "They would more nearly want to pin a medal on you."

"Maybe so. But it's still a matter of record for any die-hard Confederate to see."

"It's not a matter of record. Quite the opposite. I was unconscious for only about ten minutes or so. The lieutenant who led you in three charges against the Union flanks had some things to say about you. He told me you had distinguished yourself to the extent that, had you not shot me, I would be pinning a medal on your chest.

"Well, I just couldn't bring myself to charge you with shooting me to stop me from shooting my own men. Neither did I want it on my record that I had to shoot my own men in order to force them to hold the battle line. I ordered my adjutant that the record was to state that I was wounded by enemy fire."

Susan had silently prayed as she listened to the men talk that the incident that had haunted Ryan all these years was being resolved. She placed a trembling hand over his and said tremulously, "It's over, Ryan."

Ryan looked at her and read the pleading in her eyes. He got to his feet and extended his hand to the major. "The war is over."

The major rose to his feet and clasped Ryan's hand. "The war is over," he agreed. "If you'll come to the saloon with me, I'll buy you a drink."

"Thanks, but I'll have to decline. I don't care to leave Susan alone right now. There is one puzzlement, though, that I'd like you to clear up for me if you don't mind."

"Don't mind at all."

"You seem to have survived my bullet with no apparent ill effects. I sure thought I hit you dead on and killed you."

The major chuckled. "You hit me dead on, all right. Hit me right smack in the heart. I owe my good health to my build."

"You're joking, of course. I'd really like a straight answer."

"I'm giving you a straight answer. As you can see, I'm rather thin and raw-boned. I don't like the feel of a tight belt around my waist. I always wore my shoulder strap to help support my pistol and sword belt. You hit my shoulder strap. That leather strap took a lot of the penetration out of your pistol ball. It lodged between my ribs, but the doctor had no problem digging it out. I had some mighty sore ribs for a while, but that's about all."

"Well, I'll be damned," Ryan swore.

"I'm sure glad you were wearing that shoulder strap, Mister Thornhill," Susan said.

"Well, thank you kindly, ma'am." He turned to Ryan. "I'll be in Comanche in a few days to have a stone placed on the sergeant's grave. If you happen to be in town, maybe we can have that drink then."

"Maybe so. I'll take care of the grave marker for you if you wish."

"Thanks, but I'll do it myself. The sergeant was a good and loyal friend." He turned and started walking toward the door. "Thanks for coming and talking to me," he called back over his shoulder.

Ryan raised his hand in acknowledgment as he watched the major walk away. He still could not thoroughly believe that, after all these years, the past had finally been laid to rest. At long last, he was free of his albatross.

Susan didn't care that there were other people in the restaurant. She threw her arms around Ryan and with tears of happiness streaming down her face said, "Take me home, Ryan. We have a wedding to plan."

Chapter Twenty-One

Ryan breathed a sigh of relief when they turned onto the lane to Susan's house. "It's sure good to be at the end of this long hot ride. I can't hardly believe that it's still this hot in October."

"Yes, it is warm. So warm that I've been thinking. I guess I could wait one more day before I start making preparations for our wedding."

Ryan looked at her quizzically. "Why would you do that? What does the weather have to do with your planning our wedding? I want our wedding as soon as you can possibly arrange it."

"So do I, but what I was thinking about doesn't have anything to do with our wedding. It's just that this warm weather is not going to last much longer. We're liable to have a cold norther blow in most any day now. I was just thinking that if there was something you would like to do while it's still warm, something you can't do after it gets cold, why you ought to do it."

Ryan shook his head in puzzlement. "I can't imagine what you could be rambling on about. The only thing I've thought about doing while it's still warm is going skinny-dipping tomorrow morning at the . . ." He turned his head to look at Susan.

She was smiling demurely back at him.

Ryan's face broke into a grin. "Is that what you were thinking about doing?"

Susan giggled. "My goodness, you do catch on fast."

"Uh, could it be that you're suggesting we go together?"

Susan forced her face into a stern expression. "Of course not. We're not married yet. But then . . ." She reflected a moment. "I guess, if you were to arrive at the pool about ten-thirty tomorrow morning, which is the time I plan to be there, I couldn't forbid you to go swimming. After all, I did tell you that you could use my fishing hole whenever you wanted to."

"Yes, you did. You most surely did tell me that, and ten-thirty tomorrow morning is exactly when I plan to go skinny-dipping."

Susan giggled. "Now, isn't that a coincidence?"

* * *

Ryan was a bit surprised to find Spooky tied under the pecan tree. He was ten minutes early, but still Susan had beat him there. He tied his horse beside Susan's and made his way down the path to the edge of the creek.

He stood, mesmerized, gazing at the lovely nymph standing naked at the shallow end of the pool below him.

She turned slowly toward him and smiled knowingly. Her right hand reached out to him. Her forefinger opened and closed in the universally understood come-hither motion. She moved toward him in slow, short steps.

Ryan's heart pounded as he divested himself of his clothing and made his way to the water's edge to join her. His breathing was heavy and labored as she wrapped her arms around his neck and lifted her body until her face was even with his.

She wrapped her legs around his waist. His hands came to rest under her thighs. Fire surged through his veins, sending hot waves of desire throughout his body. Slowly and deliberately, she lowered herself onto him, drawing him deep within her, massaging the full length of him.

His breath was coming in ragged gasps. "I knew from the first moment I saw you here you were the enchantress of this beautiful place."

Susan smiled. "Yes, my love, and I shall beckon you here often."

SPECIAL BONUS CHAPTER!

Excerpting scenes from

The Magic

Robin Lee Hatcher

**Winner of the *Romantic Times*
Storyteller of the Year Award!**

**On Sale in April at your
local newsstand or bookstore.**

Prologue

London, 1696

The boy heard the sniffles and sobs coming
from other rooms in the dark, boarded-up
building. He'd been listening to the sounds
for about four days, and as he'd done more
than once during the endless hours, he wished
he could cry, too. Not so much for himself, but
for his father. He couldn't imagine the great sea
captain closed up in a place like this, shut away
from fresh winds and billowing sails.

But no matter how bad things became, no
matter how dark and hopeless things might
look, his father would never approve of his
twelve-year-old son giving in to tears, and so
the boy didn't cry. Some day, when both he and
his father were free, he would tell the story of

these days of captivity, and his father would slap him on the back and tell him how proud he was. Some day . . .

He felt something brush against his leg. He scrambled to his feet and kicked sharply.

Rats! How he hated the bloody creatures. They were always sneaking up on him in the dark, trying to bite him, slapping his bare feet with their skinny tails.

Well, they could bloody well find something else to chew on. He wasn't about to be their supper.

The sudden movement left him feeling light-headed. He'd had nothing to eat except some stale bread and brackish water since being brought to this place. Just thinking about food made his mouth water and his stomach growl.

A door creaked open behind him, spilling a stream of yellow lamplight across the straw-covered floor. He turned around, shielding his eyes against the unaccustomed brightness.

"Is that 'im, m'lord?" the one holding the lantern asked.

"Yes. That's him. See that he's taken aboard the *Seadog* tonight."

Rage blinded the boy as he recognized the hated voice. He lunged toward the doorway. "You bloody bastard! I'll kill you for what you did to my father."

A wicked blow to the side of his head knocked him back into the filthy straw.

"Behave yourself, boy, or you'll find yourself keeping your father company in Newgate." The man rubbed his hands together, as if wiping them clean. "I'm surprised he didn't teach you better manners. A boy should know how to speak to his betters."

The boy shook his head, trying to rid his ears of the dull ringing sound. He blinked as he braced himself on his elbows and glared up toward the black silhouette in the doorway. "You're not my better. You're a liar and a thief. When I get free, I'll prove my father's innocence and then you'll—"

Sharp laughter cut into his angry tirade. "You're a bigger fool than your father, boy. It would take a miracle to prove he's not a traitor." Again the low chuckle. "And it would take a magician to escape the place I'm sending you." The man backed out of the doorway, his laughter lingering in the stale air of the room.

"I'm not wrong!" the boy shouted as the door slammed shut. "I'll be back. I swear by my father's honor, I'll be back!"

Chapter One

Atlantic Ocean, April 1714

Cassandra Jamison leaned against the rail and turned her face into the fine, salty mist that flew up the ship's sides as the merchantman cut through the rolling Atlantic. She smiled, relishing the feel of the deck beneath her feet, the sun and spray on her face. Despite her trepidations over what awaited her at the end of the voyage, Cassandra couldn't help enjoying the journey itself. The first three weeks had flown by beneath mostly cloudless skies, with good winds and steady seas. Not once had she been seasick. In truth, she'd never felt better in her life.

"Ah, there's my sweet little sailor."

She turned as her uncle walked toward her

across the forecastle deck.

A tall, still handsome man in his early fifties, Farley Dunworthy, Baron Kettering, wore a full-bottomed wig over what Cassandra knew was a mostly bald scalp. His blue eyes—lighter than her own, more like her mother's—watched her with an affectionate gleam. He was fashionably attired in a long coat and waistcoat and wore scarlet silk stockings drawn over his knees and gartered below. Diamond rings adorned three of the fingers on his left hand, two on his right.

One would never guess that the family coffers have been in peril, she thought as she rose on tiptoe to kiss his cheek. But she didn't begrudge him his rich attire. Her uncle was an important man, a peer of the realm. The Baron Kettering couldn't be expected to appear as a pauper just because the family was experiencing some difficult times. And now, with the marriage settlement collected from Aldin Abernathy, those times would soon be behind them.

But she didn't want to think about Mr. Abernathy. The day was too beautiful to be spoiled.

"Good day, Uncle Far." She motioned toward the water. "Isn't it splendid? I should have insisted that you take me sailing long ago. I've never felt so wonderful in all my life. If only I'd known."

" 'Tis splendid, indeed, my dear. You know, before my brother Gregory died and I inherited his title, I used to captain the *Peacock* myself. I was rather successful in trade, I might add. I grew fond of sailing to foreign ports." He chuckled as he gazed affectionately at his niece. "I've never seen a girl as taken with the ocean as you are. If you'd been born a boy, I would have made you a captain of one of my ships when you were older."

"I'm one and twenty. Isn't that old enough? Perhaps you should teach me to captain a ship despite my being female."

Farley chuckled. " 'Tis not likely there's a man aboard who would follow your orders, Cassandra. They'd all be too busy trying to steal a kiss from you. You're far too pretty to think about doing a man's job." He turned his gaze out across the water. "No, 'tis better you marry well and provide some male heirs to inherit Tate Shipping when I'm gone. 'Tis bad enough there'll be no one to inherit my title."

Cassandra frowned. She'd been trying her best *not* to think of marriage or heirs. She would be forced to think of all that when they reached America. They were only a few weeks away from the Carolinas, where her betrothed, Aldin Abernathy, awaited her arrival in Charleston.

She saw Farley's eyes narrow and followed the direction of his gaze. At first, all she could see was the blue of the sky touching the green-black curve of the sea. She was about to ask what was wrong when he spoke.

"Do you see her?"

She squinted her eyes as he had done. "No."

"There." He pointed.

At first, she shook her head. And then she did think she saw something. It was a mere dot in the distance. "What is it?" she asked.

"Another ship. I thought I saw her yesterday, but I couldn't be sure. She's closer today. I think she may be following us."

"Is it an English ship?"

"I don't know. She's too far out to tell."

Cassandra peered harder, as if that would bring the ship into focus.

Farley turned away from the rail. "I think I'd best talk to the captain. Perhaps you should return to your cabin."

"But why?" She glanced at her uncle, surprised. " 'Tis so far away. What possible danger could it be to us?"

"I don't want to alarm you, my dear, but she could be a pirate vessel."

"A pirate vessel?" Cassandra looked back across the ocean, her pulse quickening slightly. "But surely they wouldn't bother a ship sailing under the English flag?"

"Pirates respect no flags, and they have no loyalties," Farley responded, his voice grave. He paused a moment longer, then walked toward the stern.

Despite her uncle's warning, Cassandra didn't return to her cabin. Instead, the wind blowing wisps of pale blond hair around her face, she made her way back to the quarterdeck, keeping her gaze all the while upon the small dot near the horizon.

Cassandra had never been a girl given to the

vapors. Perhaps it was because she'd seen her mother use the ploy too often through the years. Regina Dunworthy Jamison was famous for taking to her bed whenever life became too difficult. Cassandra had sworn never to do the same. She had little patience for such silly theatrics. She'd always thought it made much more sense to face one's fears head on.

Even so, she felt a strange tremor as she considered the possibility that her uncle's ship might be overtaken by pirates. Never once in her sheltered life had she imagined that she might come so close to danger as this. It was just a bit frightening—and exhilarating at the same time.

" 'Tis not who the master thinks it is, milady."

Cassandra gasped as she whirled toward the voice. The one-eyed sailor known as Mouse grinned, revealing the wide spot where several teeth should have been.

She tried to still her racing heart. "And how would you know who my uncle thinks it is?" she asked, surprise making her tone uncharacteristically haughty.

"I been wi' Master Dunworthy fer nigh on eighteen years. Ever since 'e took over Tate Shipping. I sailed under 'im in the early years when 'e captained the *Peacock*, before 'e become a lord 'n' all." His grin disappeared, and his voice lowered a notch. "I've come t' know 'ow yer uncle thinks. Better than ye, I reckon."

Cassandra frowned at the little man, uncertain how to respond. It wasn't that he was a stranger to her. She couldn't remember a time when he hadn't been coming and going from Kettering Hall, doing her uncle's bidding. She knew he was more than just a sailor, though why Uncle Far would turn the rough-looking, one-eyed man into a sort of secretary, she didn't know. Judging by his poor speech, she was certain he could neither read nor write. She couldn't begin to guess what possible help he could be to Tate Shipping.

Now, as he stood before her, watching her with a knowing glint in his lone eye, he made her feel . . . well, as if he could read her mind. She didn't like it. She didn't like it by half.

As the curtain of night fell over the Atlantic, Damian stood near the bow and stared toward the west. He heard the sucking of the wash around the hull, the whipping of great clouds of canvas overhead, the creaking of the blocks. Below, the bow wash piled high, then swept past in a blur of eddies and green waves that crashed together before shattering into a frothy wake. The *Magic* seemed as set upon her course as he was. It was almost as if the ship were a part of him. Perhaps she was.

He could still see the silhouette of the *Peacock* on the horizon, outlined by the last golden rays of day. How deceptively far away she looked.

But not far enough to save her.

Damian had given orders to his men just

an hour ago. They would proceed through the night under full sail. The *Magic* was one of the fastest three-masted square-riggers to traverse the seas, and her crew was a seasoned one. They knew how to coax extra speed out of her unfurled sails. They would have no trouble catching up with a merchant ship with a belly filled with cargo.

And what a cargo. Tea. Oriental silks. Spices. Porcelains. Such merchandise would bring a high price from the colonists in America. It would bring great wealth to the men who delivered such wares to the buyers.

And the loss of such a fortune in freight would bring great hardship to the one who lost it.

He smiled grimly. Aye, they would have no problem overtaking the *Peacock*. Damian planned to surprise her at dawn.

He turned, sensing a movement behind him. Oliver, his lieutenant, was crossing the deck with quick strides.

"Is everything ready?" Damian asked as the other man drew near.

"Aye. 'Tis ready." Oliver's brows drew together to form a single line of worry. "Sink me, but I ain't sure 'tis such a good plan, Damian. About the young lady, I mean."

"I didn't ask for your opinion."

"No, sir. That you didn't."

Damian glared at his lieutenant, waiting for him to continue. Oliver had never been one to keep his thoughts to himself. Damian knew better than to expect his friend to start now.

" 'Twould seem to me that the *Peacock*'s cargo should be enough. Dunworthy's never risked so much on one voyage. He's stripped his ship of all but fifteen of her cannon. She's manned by fewer than a hundred, and them not of much worth. And 'tis not *us* they'll be expecting. We ain't never yet had such an easy task set before us."

Damian raised an eyebrow. "And?"

"Ain't it enough that Dunworthy'll bear the loss? Must we take Miss Jamison, too?"

"Yes." There was a warning in the hard tone of Damian's voice.

"She's hardly more than a green girl. She's naught to do with Tate Shipping, and you can't hold her accountable for what Dunworthy's done." He paused, then added, "From what I've heard, she's an innocent lass."

Damian's jaw tensed, but in no other way did he reveal his surge of anger. "And which of his victims *wasn't* innocent? Wasn't Mouse innocent when Dunworthy cost him his eye? What about Professor? And what of you, Oliver? What of your innocence?" His harsh gaze flicked to the ragged scar that stretched the length of Oliver's face. "Do you remember what he did to you?" He turned toward the horizon once again. "She'll come to no harm. We'll be doing no more than her own uncle had planned for her. Most likely, she'll be better cared for by us than she would have been by the crew of the *Guinevere*. Once we've received the ransom, she

410

can be returned to her intended, none the worse for wear."

The lieutenant was silent for a long time before replying. "As you say, Captain." Oliver was only marginally successful at disguising his disapproval. Finally, when the ship's master remained silent, Oliver turned and walked away.

Damian listened as his lieutenant's departing footsteps faded into the sounds of the sea, all thoughts of Farley Dunworthy's niece fading with them. He refused to think of anything except the sweet taste of revenge. Already he was savoring the look of surprise on Farley's face when the pirate captain of the *Magic* boarded the merchant ship tomorrow at dawn.

Farley leaned back in his chair and lifted the glass of port to his lips. He sipped it slowly, enjoying the rich flavor as he rolled the liquid over his tongue before allowing it to trickle down his throat. As he did so, the tension began to ease from him.

The *Guinevere* was to have arrived two days before. He'd begun to fear that the disreputable captain of that questionable vessel had absconded with his funds. He'd worried that his plans were going awry. While Abernathy's marriage settlement had gone a long way toward clearing his debts, Farley needed a great deal more to completely overcome his recent losses.

His fingers tightened around the glass as he thought of the constant reports of pirates that had plagued Tate Shipping in the past three years. Time and again, his ships had returned to England, their holds empty, their captains telling tales of a swift vessel called the *Magic* that struck from out of nowhere and the buccaneer chieftain who bade them give his regards to Farley Dunworthy even as his men plundered the ships of everything of value.

Thank heaven Abernathy's proposal had arrived when it did. And thank heaven his niece was such a level-headed girl. When he'd explained to her how close to ruin they were and that her father and mother would end up penniless and homeless, she'd seen that there was little else for her to do but accept Abernathy's offer of marriage.

He sipped more port, then shook his head a bit sadly.

He would miss Cassandra. She was as close to a child of his own as he would ever know, and she'd always shown him great affection. True, he didn't think too highly of Abernathy. He suspected the man had a rather nasty temper and was given to overindulgence in strong drink. But he was rich and he wanted Cassandra enough to pay dearly for her. Those were his two most important qualities. The only ones that mattered to Farley.

He hadn't hesitated in accepting Abernathy's offer. As far as he was concerned, the end always justified the means.

*   *   *

Cassandra tossed restlessly in her bed, her dreams haunted by visions of weddings and pirate ships. One dream melted into another, neither of them making sense. She was grateful when she awakened abruptly.

She sat up, drawing her knees close to her chest as she wrapped her arms around her shins. She tried to forget her dreams but was unsuccessful. Mr. Abernathy seemed determined to invade her thoughts, whether waking or sleeping.

She didn't want to marry this virtual stranger, a man twenty years her senior whom she'd met only once, a man who lived across a vast ocean, away from her parents, her home, and everything she loved. But what else could she have done once Uncle Far explained things to her? She couldn't let her parents be thrown into debtors prison, could she? Was it so terrible a sacrifice? Perhaps she would learn to love Mr. Abernathy. Perhaps . . .

"But you don't love him, Cassandra." Her mother's voice drifted to her from the past.

"I'll learn to love him."

Regina's faded blue eyes reflected great pain. "You should love the man you marry. You should feel a grand passion for him."

"Your marriage was arranged, Mama, and it turned out well."

"Yes," her mother replied, her voice as soft as a sigh. "My marriage was arranged."

Remembering the wistful look that had

crossed Regina's face threatened to bring tears to Cassandra's eyes now, just as it had then.

A grand passion. It was what she'd always wanted, always dreamed of. It was why she'd turned down earlier offers of marriage. She'd been waiting to fall desperately in love. She'd wanted to marry according to her heart. She hadn't wanted to *learn* to love, to be merely content. She'd wanted more. Much more.

She swallowed the hot lump in her throat. It did no good to think of such things. She had her duty to her family to think about. Uncle Far wouldn't have asked this of her if there'd been any other way. Her parents and her uncle had always given her everything her heart desired. They had never failed her. She owed them too much to fail them now.

Slipping out of her bunk, she padded across the room on bare feet to the porthole and stared out into the night. Moonlight danced across the surface of an ink-black ocean, sparkling across the crests of the waves as they rolled toward the horizon.

Then she remembered her other dream, the one about the pirate ship. She recalled the vile captain of her dreams. He was fat and dirty, as all pirates were, no doubt. He wore a brace of pistols on his hips and had a bloody sword stuck through his belt. He swaggered and used foul language and threatened to use her in some unspeakable fashion.

She shivered, wondering if the ship her uncle had seen was truly a pirate ship. Then she scurried back to her bunk and snuggled beneath the blankets, seeking warmth and security and more pleasant dreams.

SPEND YOUR LEISURE MOMENTS WITH U

Hundreds of exciting titles to choose from—something for everyone's taste in fine books: breathtaking historical romance, chilling horror, spine-tingling suspense, taut medical thrillers, involving mysteries, action-packed men's adventure and wild Westerns.

SEND FOR A FREE CATALOGUE TODAY!

Leisure Books
Attn: Customer Service Department
276 5th Avenue, New York, NY 10001